Praise for Emma Miller and her novels

"There is warmth to the characters that will leave readers looking forward to seeing more."
—*RT Book Reviews* on *A Match for Addy*

"The characters...as well as the storyline, feel authentic."
—*RT Book Reviews* on *A Beau for Katie*

"A sweet tale."
—*RT Book Reviews* on *Anna's Gift*

Praise for Patricia Davids and her novels

"Davids' lovely story shows the beauty and comfort of the Amish world."
—*RT Book Reviews* on *Katie's Redemption*

"Davids' latest beautifully portrays the Amish belief that everything happens for a reason."
—*RT Book Reviews* on *The Christmas Quilt*

"Descriptive setting and characters."
—*RT Book Reviews* on *Plain Admirer*

D1374273

Emma Miller lives quietly in her old farmhouse in rural Delaware. Fortunate enough to be born into a family of strong faith, she grew up on a dairy farm surrounded by loving parents, siblings, grandparents, aunts, uncles and cousins. Emma was educated in local schools and once taught in an Amish schoolhouse. When she's not caring for her large family, reading and writing are her favorite pastimes.

After thirty-five years as a nurse, **Patricia Davids** hung up her stethoscope to become a full-time writer. She enjoys spending her free time visiting her grandchildren, doing some long-overdue yard work and traveling to research her story locations. She resides in Wichita, Kansas. Pat always enjoys hearing from her readers. You can visit her online at patriciadavids.com.

EMMA MILLER

A Beau for Katie

&

USA TODAY Bestselling Author

PATRICIA DAVIDS

An Amish Harvest

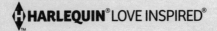
HARLEQUIN® LOVE INSPIRED®

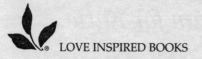

LOVE INSPIRED BOOKS

Recycling programs
for this product may
not exist in your area.

ISBN-13: 978-1-335-00875-6

A Beau for Katie and An Amish Harvest

Copyright © 2017 by Harlequin Books S.A.

The publisher acknowledges the copyright holders
of the individual works as follows:

A Beau for Katie
Copyright © 2016 by Emma Miller

An Amish Harvest
Copyright © 2015 by Patricia MacDonald

www.Harlequin.com

Printed in U.S.A.

CONTENTS

A BEAU FOR KATIE

Emma Miller

Whoso findeth a wife findeth a good thing,
and obtaineth favour of the Lord.
—*Proverbs* 18:22

Chapter One

Millside Amish Community,
Kent County, Delaware
July

Suddenly apprehensive, Katie Byler reined in her horse on the bridge, easing the buggy to a standstill. Next to the dam was the feed-and-grain mill, a business that had been there since colonial times and was one of the few water-powered mills left in Delaware. On the far side was the millpond, a large stretch of water surrounded for the most part by trees. Out in the middle of the pond, a pair of Canada geese bobbed, and overhead, iridescent dragonflies and some sort of birds swooped and fluttered. It was a beautiful sight with the morning light sparkling on the blue-green water, and on any other day, Katie would have taken delight in it. Today, however, she had serious concerns on her mind.

She may have let Sara Yoder talk her into something she'd regret.

Behind her, Sara, the county's only Amish matchmaker, stopped her mule and climbed down from her buggy. "What's wrong?" She came to stand beside Katie's cart. "Why did you stop?" Sara raised her voice to be heard above the rush of water under the bridge. "We're blocking traffic."

Katie made a show of looking in both directions, up and down the road. It was a private lane, and anyone using it would be coming to or leaving the mill. At the moment, the parking lot in front of the mill had only one car and it was parked, with no one inside. The lane behind her was empty. "*Ne*, I don't think so," she answered in Deitsch, the German dialect that the Amish used among themselves.

"Don't tell me you're having second thoughts." Sara folded her arms over her bosom and gave Katie *the look* from beneath her black bonnet, the look that had given Sara a reputation for taking no nonsense. "You said you would accept the job, and I gave Jehu my word that you would start this morning."

"I know I agreed to it, but now…" She met Sara's strong-minded attitude with her own. She liked the middle-aged woman, admired her really. Sara had gumption. She was an independent woman in a traditional society where most widows depended on fathers or sons to provide for them.

Katie narrowed her gaze on the matchmaker. Sara didn't have the pale Germanic skin of most Amish; she was half African American, with a coffee-colored complexion and dark, textured hair. Katie knew Sara's heritage because she'd asked her the first time they'd met. "How do I know that you're not trying to match me with Freeman Kemp?" she asked. "Because if you are, I'll tell you right off, it's a hopeless cause. He's one man I'd never consider for a husband."

Katie and Freeman had clashed when they were volunteering as helpers at a wedding the previous November. She'd been in charge of one of the work parties, and she'd made a suggestion about the way the men were loading chairs into the church wagon. Freeman had taken affront and had behaved immaturely, stalking off to sulk while the other men continued to work. It hadn't been an argument exactly, but it was clear that although her way was far more sensible, Freeman was offended by being told what to do by a woman. Katie couldn't have cared less. Growing up with older brothers, she'd learned early to speak up for herself, and if Freeman disliked her because of her refusal to be submissive, that was his problem.

Sara arched one dark brow and sighed. "Poor Freeman is laid up in bed with a broken femur. He hasn't asked me to find him a wife, and if he *did* discover he needed one this week, I doubt you're in any danger of him running you down and dragging you before the bishop." She shrugged. "It's because of his injury that he needs a housekeeper. You have no need for concern about your reputation, if that's your worry. Freeman's grandmother lives right next to him in the little house. She's in and out of Freeman's place all day long, and she'll provide the chaperoning the elders expect."

"That's not what worries me," Katie muttered. Sara was just like her: she never minced words. "I just don't want any misunderstandings. Freeman Kemp is one of those men all the single girls moon over. You know, him being so good-looking and so well-to-do." She nodded in the direction of the mill and surrounding property, the farmhouse and little *grossmama haus* where his grandmother lived. "I wouldn't want him to think that I'm one of them."

Sara laid a small brown hand on the dashboard of Katie's buggy. "If you're intimidated by Freeman, I'm sure I can get someone else to take the job. I wouldn't want to force you to do anything that made you feel uncomfortable."

"I'm not *intimidated* by him." Katie sat up a little straighter, tightened the reins in her hands and gazed ahead at the farmhouse. "Certainly not." She was probably making too much of a small incident. Freeman *had* made a remark about her bossiness to a friend of her brother's not long after the wedding incident, but he'd probably forgotten all about the unpleasantness by now.

"Good." Sara patted Katie's knee. "Then there's no reason to keep them waiting any longer. The sooner you start, the sooner you can put the house in order."

"Well, Uncle Jehu, if you hired a housekeeper without my say-so, you can just *un-hire* her." Freeman lay propped up on pillows in a daybed against the kitchen wall. "We need a strange woman rattling around here about as much as I need another broken leg."

"Now, boy, calm yourself," the older man said quietly in Deitsch. His arthritis-gnarled fingers moved, twisting a cord in a continuous game of cat's cradle, forming one shape after another. "It's only temporary. A younger pair of willing hands might bring some order to this mess we call a house."

Freeman glanced away. His uncle meant no insult. Calling him *boy* was a term of affection, but Freeman felt it was demeaning sometimes. He was thirty-five years old and he'd been running the family mill since he was twenty. Everyone in their Amish community accepted him as a grown man and head of this house, but because he'd never married, his uncle still thought of him as a stripling.

Uncle Jehu gestured with his chin in the general direction of the kitchen sink where Freeman's grandmother stood washing their breakfast dishes. "No insult meant to you, Ivy."

Freeman's paternal grandmother bobbed her head in agreement. "None taken. I said from the start when I came to live here I wouldn't be anyone's housekeeper. I've plenty of chores to keep me busy at my own place, not to mention waiting on customers at the mill. And what with my arthritis, I can't do it all." She eyed her grandson, sitting up in the bed, his leg cast from ankle to upper thigh, resting in a cradle of homemade quilts. "Jehu's right, Freeman. This house can stand a good cleaning. There are more cobwebs in this kitchen than the hayloft."

"You think I don't see them?" Freeman swallowed his rising impatience and forced himself not to raise his voice. "As soon as I get this cast off, I'll *redd* it all up. I did fine before I broke my leg, didn't I?" He still felt like a fool, breaking his leg the way he did. Anyone who'd been raised around farm animals should have known to take care and get a friend to lend a hand. He'd just been too sure of himself, and his own pride had gotten the better of him.

Ivy shook a soapy finger at him. "Stop fussing and make the best of it." She dipped a coffee cup in rinse water and stacked it in the drainer. "Maybe the Lord put this hurdle in your path to make you take stock of your own shortcomings. You've a good heart. You're always eager to help others, but you've never had the grace to accept help when you need it." She drew her mouth into a tight purse and nodded. "Jehu's already arranged the girl's hire for two weeks."

"And she's coming this morning," his uncle said as he twisted the string into a particularly intricate pattern. "So accept it gracefully and make her welcome."

A motor vehicle horn beeped from the parking lot.

"Another customer," Grossmama declared, quickly drying her hands on a dishtowel. "We're going to have another busy one at the mill. Didn't I say that buying those muslin bags with *Kemp's* printed on them and advertising would pay off? The Englishers drive from all over the state to get our stone-ground bread flour." Retrieving her black bonnet from the table, she put it on over her prayer *kapp*, and bustled out the door.

"With a housekeeper, we might get something to eat other than oatmeal," Uncle Jehu offered his nephew by way of consolation.

"I heard that!" his grandmother called back through the screen door. "Nothing wrong with oatmeal. I eat it every day, and I've never been sick a day in my life."

"Never sick a day in her life," his uncle repeated under his breath.

Freeman couldn't help chuckling. He was as tired of oatmeal as Uncle Jehu. There was nothing wrong with his grandmother's oatmeal. It was tasty and filling, but after eating it every morning since he was discharged from the hospital, he longed for pork sausage, bacon, over-easy eggs and home fries. And he was tired of her chicken noodle soup that they ate for dinner and supper most days, unless a neighbor was kind enough to drop by with a meal. "A few more days and I'll be up and about," he told his uncle. "I can take over the cooking, like I used to."

His uncle scoffed. "Unless you want to end up back in the hospital, you'll follow doctor's orders. A broken thighbone's a serious thing. In the meantime, the house is getting away from us, and so is the laundry." He shook his head. "It's a good thing I'm blind. Otherwise I would have been ashamed to go to church in a shirt that's been worn three Sundays and not been washed and ironed."

"No. Housekeeper," Freeman repeated firmly, emphasizing each syllable.

Jehu's terrier, Tip, leaped off the bed and ran barking to the door.

"Too late." Uncle Jehu broke into a self-satisfied grin. "Sounds like a buggy coming. Must be Sara Yoder and her girl now."

"You should send her back. We don't need her," Freeman protested, but only half-heartedly. He knew the battle was lost. He wouldn't hurt the poor girl's feelings by sending her away now that she was here. He would have to make the best of it.

"*Ne.* You heard Ivy. I already hired her." Jehu didn't sound a bit repentant; in fact, he seemed quite pleased with himself.

Freeman had a lot of respect for his mother's oldest brother, and more than that, he loved him. It was a pity when a man couldn't be master in his own house. Freeman was used to having his grandmother living in the *grossmama haus.* She'd been part of the household even before his parents died, and the two of them got along as easily as chicken and dumplings. But Uncle Jehu had only come to live with him the previous summer and didn't always seem to understand that Freeman liked to do things his own way. Caring for his uncle was his responsibility, and he was glad to do it, but he didn't want to have decisions made for him as if he were still a child.

"Fine," Freeman muttered, feeling frustrated that he couldn't even get up to greet Sara and the housekeeper properly. It was demeaning to be laid out in a bed like this. But after a complication the previous week, his surgeon had been adamant. Freeman needed to keep his leg elevated at all times for another three days. "Who is this housekeeper? Do I know her?"

"She's from Apple Valley church district, but the two of you have probably crossed paths somewhere."

"You can at least tell me her name if you're forcing me to have her in my house."

His uncle looked up, sightless brown eyes calm and peaceful. "Name's Katie. Katie Byler."

"Katie Byler!" Freeman repeated. "Absolutely not." He flinched as he spoke and pain shot up his leg. He groaned, reaching down to steady his casted leg. "Not Katie Byler, Uncle Jehu. Anyone but Katie Byler." He frowned. "She's the bossiest woman I ever met."

His uncle chuckled. "I thought you said your *mudder* was the bossiest woman you ever met. *Ya,* I distinctly remember you saying that." He rose, tucked his loop of string into his trousers' pocket and made his way to the door. He chuckled again. "And maybe my sister was. But I never saw that it did your father any harm."

"Please, Uncle Jehu," Freeman groaned. "Get someone else. *Anybody* else."

"Too late," his uncle proclaimed. He pushed open

the door and grinned. "Sara, Katie. Come on in. Freeman and I've been waiting for you."

Katie followed Sara into the Kemp house, pausing just inside the doorway to allow her vision to adjust to the interior after the bright July sunshine.

"Here's Katie," Sara announced, "just as I promised, Jehu. She'll lend a hand with the housework until he's back on his feet." She motioned Katie to approach the bed. "I think you two already know each other."

"Ya," Freeman admitted gruffly. "We do."

"We're so glad you could come to help out," his uncle said. "As you can see by this mess, you haven't come a day too early."

Katie removed her black bonnet, straightened her spine, and took in a deep breath. The girls were right about one thing; Freeman Kemp wasn't hard on the eyes. Even lying flat in a bed, one leg encased in an uncomfortable-looking cast, he was still a striking figure of a man. The indoor pallor and the pain lines at the corners of his mouth couldn't hide the clean lines of his masculine jaw, his white, even teeth, or his straight, well-formed nose and forehead. His wavy brown hair badly needed a haircut, and he had at least a week's growth of dark beard, but the sleeveless cotton undershirt revealed a tanned neck, and broad, muscular shoulders and arms.

Freeman's compelling gaze met hers. His eyes were brown, not the walnut shade of Sara's but a golden brown, almost amber, with darker swirls of color, and they were framed in lashes far too long for a man.

Had he caught her staring at him? Unnerved, she recovered her composure and concealed her embarrassment with a solicitous smile. "Good morning, Freeman," she uttered in a hushed tone.

Puzzlement flickered behind Sara's inquisitive eyes, and then her apple cheeks crinkled in a sign of amused understanding. She moved closer to the bed, blocking Katie's view of Freeman's face and his of hers and began to pepper him with questions about his impending recovery.

Rescued, Katie turned away to inspect the kitchen that would be her domain for the next two weeks. She'd never been inside the house before, just the mill, but from the outside, she'd thought it was beautiful. Now, standing in the spacious kitchen, she liked it even more. It was clear to her that this house had been home to many generations, and someone, probably a sensible woman, had carefully planned out the space. Modern gas appliances stood side by side with tidy built-in cabinets and a deep soapstone sink. There was a large farm table in the center of the room with benches on two sides, and Windsor chairs at either end. The kitchen had big windows that let in the light and a lovely old German open-shelved cupboard. The only thing that looked out of place was the bed containing the frowning Freeman Kemp.

"You must be in a lot of pain," Sara remarked, gently patting Freeman's cast.

"*Ne.* Nothing to speak of."

"He is," Jehu contradicted. "Just too stubborn to admit to it. He'll accept none of the pain pills the doctor prescribed."

Freeman's eyes narrowed. "They gave them to me at the hospital. I couldn't think straight."

Katie nodded. "You're wise to tough it out if you can.

Too many people start taking those things and then find that they can't do without them. Rest and proper food for an invalid will do you the most good."

Freeman glanced away, as if feeling uncomfortable at being the center of attention. "I'm not an invalid."

Katie sighed, wondering if a broken femur had been the man's only injury or if he'd taken a blow to the head. If lying on your back, leg encased in a cast propped on a quilt, didn't make you an invalid, she didn't know what did. But Freeman, as she recalled, had a stubborn nature. She'd certainly seen it at the King wedding.

For an eligible bachelor who owned a house, a mill and two hundred acres of prime land to remain single into his midthirties was almost unheard of among the Amish. Add to that Freeman's rugged good looks and good standing with his bishop and his church community. It made him the catch of the county, several counties for that matter. They could have him. She was a rational person, not a giggling teenager who could be swept off her feet by a pretty face. Freeman liked his own way too much to suit her. Working in his house for two whole weeks wasn't going to be easy, but he or his good looks certainly didn't intimidate her. She'd told Sara she'd take the job and she was a woman of her word.

"I agree. Rest is what he needs." Ivy Kemp came into the house, letting the terrier out the door as she entered. "But he's always been headstrong. Thinking he could tend to that injury to the bull's leg by himself was what got him into trouble in the first place. And not following doctor's orders to stay in bed was what sent him back to the hospital a second time."

"Could you not talk about me as though I'm not

here?" Freeman pushed himself up on his elbows. "Two weeks, not a day more, and I'll be on my feet again."

"More like four weeks, according to his doctors," Jehu corrected.

Katie noticed that the blind man had settled himself into a rocker not far from Freeman's bed, removed a string from his pants' pocket, and was absently twisting the string into shapes. She didn't know Jehu well but she'd seen how easily he'd moved around the kitchen and how he turned his face toward each speaker, following the conversation much as a sighted person might. She found him instantly likable.

"Do you know this game?" Jehu asked in Katie's general direction. "Cat's cradle?"

"She doesn't want to play your—"

"I do know it," Katie exclaimed, cutting Freeman off. "I played it all the time with my father when I was small. I love it."

"Do you know this one?" Jehu grinned, made several quick movements and then held up a new string pattern.

Katie grinned. "That's a cat's eye."

"Easy enough," the older man said, "but how about this one?"

"Uncle Jehu, she didn't come to play children's games." Freeman again. "She was hired to clean up this house."

Katie rolled up her sleeves. "So I was." She glanced Jehu's way. "Later on, I'll show you one you might not know, but right now I better get to work." She turned back in the direction of the kitchen appliances. "I can see I'm desperately needed. There's splatters of milk all over the floor near the stove, and I see ants on the countertop." She removed her black apron and took an everyday white one from the old satchel she'd brought with her.

"It sounds as if Katie has her day's work cut out for her." Sara clapped her hands together. "I'd best get on my way and leave her to it."

Ivy glanced out the window. "I see she's driven her own buggy."

"Ya," Katie confirmed. "We came in two vehicles."

"Katie lives in Apple Valley with her mother and brother," Sara volunteered. "Too far for her to drive back and forth every day. I have all those extra bedrooms since I added the new addition to my house. It seemed sensible that she should stay with me."

Especially since my brother just brought home a wife, Katie thought. Patsy deserved to have the undisputed run of her kitchen. Katie was quite fond of Patsy, who seemed a perfect wife for Isaac. But Katie didn't need to be told that an unmarried sister was definitely a burden on a young couple, so taking this job and living away for a while would give them time to settle into married life. Plus the money she earned by her labor would be put to good use.

"No need for you to run off so quick," Ivy told Sara. "Won't you take a cup of tea over at my place?"

Ivy Kemp was a neat little woman, plump rather than spare, tidy as a wren and just as cheerful. Again, Katie only knew her from intercommunity frolics and fund-raisers, but she seemed pleasant and welcoming.

"Tea?" Jehu got to his feet with more vigor than Katie would expect of a man near seventy. "Tea would hit the spot, Ivy. You don't happen to have any of those raisin bran muffins left over, do you?"

"As a matter of fact, I do." Ivy beamed, heading for

the door. "But I won't promise they taste as good as they did yesterday when they came out of the oven. You will stay for tea, won't you, Sara? I do love a chance to chat with someone from another church. I hear you made a good match for that new girl with that young man—what's his name…"

In less time than it took Katie to locate a broom, she and Sara had made their goodbyes, and the three older people had left to go next door to the *grossmama haus* for their tea and muffins. Ivy had invited Katie, too, but she'd declined. There was too much to do in Freeman's house and she wanted to get busy.

"I imagine you'll be wanting dinner at noon," she said to Freeman, careful not to look directly at his face and into those striking golden eyes. "Do the doctors have you on a special diet?"

"Oatmeal," he said testily. "I've been eating a lot of oatmeal."

Katie cut her eyes at him. "Odd thing for a sickbed."

"I'm not sick."

"*Ya*, you said that." She opened the refrigerator and grimaced. "I hope the milk and eggs are fresh."

"And why wouldn't they be?"

"If they are, they would be the only thing in that refrigerator that is. It looks as if a bowl of baked beans died in there. The butter is covered in toast crumbs and it looks like there's a hunk of dried up cheese in the back." She wrinkled her nose. "Pretty pitiful fare."

"Spare me your humor." Freeman shut his eyes. "Just cook something other than oatmeal or chicken noodle soup. Anything else. My grandmother has served me so much chicken soup it's a wonder I'm not clucking."

"I'll keep that in mind." She closed the refrigerator

door, thinking of the cut-up chicken that Sara had insisted they bring in a cooler. Chicken soup had been one of her options, since she'd known that Freeman was confined to bed and recovering from a bad accident. But she could just as well fry up the chicken with some dumplings. Providing, of course, that there weren't weevils in the flour bin. She'd have to take stock of the pantry and freezer, if Freeman even had a freezer or a flour bin. If they expected her to cook three decent meals a day, she'd have to have the groceries to do it.

She decided that cleaning the refrigerator took precedence over the sticky floor; she'd just sweep now and mop later. Once that was done, she decided she'd better do something about the state of the kitchen table. The tablecloth was stained and could definitely use a washing. Someone had washed dishes that morning and left them on the sideboard to dry, but dirty cups, bowls and silverware littered a side table next to Freeman's bed. A kitchen seemed an odd place for a sick man to have his bed, but she could understand that he might want to be in the center of the home rather than tucked away upstairs alone. And it could be that the bathroom was downstairs. She hadn't been hired for nursing, but, if she knew men, doubtless the sheets could stand laundering.

"That wasn't kind of you," she remarked as she cleared the table and stripped away the soiled tablecloth. "Chastising your uncle when he wanted to show me his string game. You should show more respect for your elders."

Freeman opened one eye. "He's blind, not slipping in his mind. Cat's cradle is for *kinner*. It was him I was thinking of. I wanted to save him embarrassment if you assumed—"

"I hope my mother taught me better than that," Katie interrupted. "I try not to form opinions of people at first glance or to judge them." He didn't answer, and she turned her back to him as she scrubbed the wooden tabletop clean enough to eat off. She would look for a fresh tablecloth, but if none were available, this would suffice until she could do the laundry.

"I don't mean to be rude," Freeman said. He exhaled loudly. "I didn't know you were coming—didn't know any housekeeper was coming. It was my uncle's idea."

"I see." Katie moved on to the refrigerator. The milk container seemed clean and the milk smelled good so she put that on the table with whatever else seemed salvageable. The rest went directly into a bucket to be disposed of. "It's been a good while since anyone did this," she observed.

"It's not something that I can manage with my leg in a cast."

"Six months, I'd guess, since this refrigerator has had a good scrub. You don't need a housekeeper, you need a half dozen of them if you expect me to get this kitchen in shape today."

"It's not *that* bad." He pushed up on his elbows. "Neither Uncle Jehu nor I have gotten sick from the food."

"By the grace of God." The butter went into the bucket, followed by a wilted bunch of beets and a sad tomato. "Do you have a garden?"

Freeman mumbled something about weeds, and she rolled her eyes. Sara's garden was overflowing with produce. She'd bring corn and the makings of a salad tomorrow. A drawer contained butter still in its store wrapping. The date was good, so that went to the table. "Is there anything you're not supposed to eat?" she asked.

"Oatmeal and chicken soup."

She smiled. He was funny; she'd give him that. "So you mentioned."

A few changes of water, a little elbow grease and the refrigerator was empty and clean. Katie started moving items from the table, thinking she'd run outside and get the chicken to let it sit in salted water.

"Butter goes on the middle shelf," Freeman instructed.

She glanced over her shoulder at him. "Not where it says *butter*?" She pointed to the designated bin in the door with the word printed across it.

He scowled. "We like it on the middle shelf."

"But it will stay fresher in the butter bin." She smiled sweetly, left the butter in the door and went back to the table for the milk.

A scratching at the screen door caught her attention and she went to see what was making the noise. When she opened the door, the small brown-and-white rat terrier that Ivy had let out darted in, sniffed her once and then made a beeline for Freeman's bed. "Cute dog."

"His name is Tip." The terrier bounced onto a stool and then leaped the rest of the way onto the bed. He curled under Freeman's hand and butted it with his head until Freeman scratched behind the dog's ears.

Katie watched him cuddle the little terrier. *Freeman couldn't be all bad if the dog liked him.*

She filled the kettle with water and put it on the gas range. She'd seen that there was ice. She'd make iced tea to go with dinner. And if there was going to be chicken and dumplings, she would need to find the proper size pot and give that a good scrub, as well. She planned the menu in her head. Besides the chicken dumplings, she'd have green beans and pickled beets, both canned and carried from Sara's pantry, possibly biscuits and something sweet to top it all off. She'd have to check that weed-choked garden to see if there was something ripe that she could use.

"What are you making for dinner?" Freeman asked.

Oatmeal, she wanted to say. But she resisted. It was going to be a long two weeks in Freeman Kemp's company. "I'm not sure yet," she answered sweetly. "It will be a surprise to us both."

"Wonderful," Freeman said dryly. "I can't wait."

Katie swallowed the mirth that rose in her throat. Her employer's nephew might not be the cheeriest companion but at least she wouldn't be bored. Sara had warned her that working in Freeman's house would be a challenge. And there was nothing she liked better.

Chapter Two

Freeman watched Jehu reach for another biscuit. It was evening and the air was noticeably cooler in the house than it had been in the heat of the afternoon. Being cooped up in the house was making Freeman stir-crazy as it was; the heat seemed to add to his irritability. Thinking back on the day, he hoped he hadn't been too ill-tempered with Katie. He didn't mean to be short with people; it was just his situation that made him crabby. That and the radiating pain in his leg.

Jehu and Ivy were seated at the kitchen table eating leftovers from the midday meal that Katie had cooked. He was lying in his bed, but Katie and Jehu had moved it closer to the table for the noon meal so that he could more easily be included in the conversations, and no one had bothered to push the bed back against the wall. Katie hadn't stayed to have supper with them, though he'd almost hoped she would. It was nice to have someone else to talk to besides his uncle and grandmother. Before Katie left to return to Sara Yoder's, where she was staying, she'd heated up the leftovers, carried them to the table and made him a tray.

"Good biscuits." Jehu felt around for the pint jar of strawberry jam Katie had brought them from her own pantry.

"I thought you must think they were," Ivy remarked. "Since that's your third."

Jehu smiled and nodded. "They are. Aren't they, Freeman?"

"Mmm," Freeman agreed. It was hard to talk with his mouth full. Nodding, he used the rest of his biscuit to sop up the chicken gravy remaining on his plate. He couldn't remember when anything had tasted so good as the meal Katie had served them this afternoon and he was now enjoying it all over again. The green beans were crisp and fresh, and the chicken and dumplings were exactly like those he remembered his mother making. His *grossmama* Ivy had always been dear to him, but no one had ever called her a great cook.

"She's done a marvel on this kitchen," his grandmother pronounced. "She's managed to find the kitchen table under the crumbs and I can walk on this floor without hearing the sand grit under my feet." She looked at Freeman. "We should have got her in here the week you got crushed by that cow."

"It was a bull," Freeman reminded her.

She lifted one shoulder in a *not convinced* gesture. "Not a full grown one."

"Nine hundred pounds, at least." Freeman reached for his coffee. It tasted better than what he usually made. Katie's work, again.

"Pleasant girl, don't you think?" his uncle remarked. For a man who couldn't see, Uncle Jehu had no trouble feeding himself. Somehow, he could eat and drink without getting crumbs in his beard or spots on his clothing. He'd always been a tidy person, almost dapper, if a Plain man could be called dapper. He liked his shirts clean and he wouldn't wear his socks more than once without them being washed. "That Katie Byler."

"Ya," Freeman agreed. The food was certainly a welcome relief from his grandmother's chicken soup, and the kitchen did look better clean, but there was such a thing as overdoing the praise. He wiggled, trying to get in a more comfortable position. He'd had an itch somewhere near the top of his knee, but it was under the heavy cast and he couldn't scratch it. Even when he wasn't in pain there was a dull ache, but he'd just about gotten used to that. It was the itch that was driving him crazy.

"A hard-working girl who can cook like that will make someone a fine wife," Jehu remarked.

"I was thinking the same thing." Ivy wiped her mouth with a cloth napkin; Katie had found a whole pile of them in one of the cupboards. "Girls like that get snapped up fast. And she's pleasant-looking. Don't you think so, Freeman?"

"What was that?" He'd heard what she said, but didn't really feel comfortable commenting on a woman's looks. Besides, he had a pretty good idea where this conversation was going. They had it all the time, and no matter how often he told Jehu and Ivy he wasn't looking for a wife, they continued looking for him.

"Pretty. I said Katie was pretty. Or hadn't you noticed?" She glanced at Uncle Jehu and chuckled. He gave a small sound of amusement as he spooned out the last of the dumplings from the bowl on the table onto his plate, without spilling a drop.

"I thought she might be, just by the sound of her

voice," Uncle Jehu said. "You can tell a lot about a person from their voice. Wonder if she's walking out with anybody?"

"Sara says not." His grandmother eyed the black-berry cobbler on the table. There was nearly half of the baking dish left, plenty for the three of them to enjoy.

Freeman's mouth watered thinking about it. Katie had made it with cinnamon and nutmeg and just the right amount of sugar. Too many women used more sugar than was needed in desserts and hid the taste of the fruit with sweetness.

"This coffee could use a little warming up." Freeman lifted his mug. "I don't want to put anyone to any trouble, but…"

"It won't kill you to drink it like it is," his *gross-mama* told him. "Too much hot coffee's not good for broken bones. Raises the heat in the body. Cool's best. Keeps your temperature steady."

Freeman swallowed the rest of his coffee. There was no use in asking Uncle Jehu to warm up his coffee. He'd just side with Ivy. He usually did, Freeman thought, feeling his grumpiness coming on again. The itch on his leg remained persistent, and he wondered if he could run something down inside the cast to scratch it without causing any harm.

"Freeman could do a lot worse," Uncle Jehu went on. "He's not getting any younger."

"Than Katie?" Ivy pursed her mouth. "You're right, Jehu. I don't know why I didn't think of that myself. She'd fit in well here. And it's long past time—"

"Don't talk about me as though I'm not here," Freeman interrupted. "And I'm not courting Katie Byler."

"And what's wrong with her?" Grossmama demanded, turning to him. "She seems a fine possibility to me."

"Absolutely not," Freeman protested, pushing his tray away. "And if this is something you've schemed up with Sara Yoder, you can forget it. Katie may make a great wife for someone else, but not for me."

Katie tossed a handful of weeds into a bucket. "Freeman wasn't as bad as I expected," she answered when Sara asked her how her day had gone. She, Sara and two of the young women who lived at Sara's had come into the vegetable garden after supper to catch up on the weeding. Ellie and Mari had started at the opposite end of the long rows of lima beans, while she and Sara had taken this end, giving the two of them an opportunity to talk privately.

Sara grinned. "I knew you could handle him."

Both she and Sara were barefooted and wearing a headscarf and their oldest dress. The warm soil felt good under Katie's feet. She loved the scents of rich earth and the cheery chorus of birdsong that seemed present in any well-tended garden.

"I think he'd be a good match for someone." Sara used her trowel to chop the sprigs of grass and work up the soil around the base of the lima bean plants. "What with the mill and the farm, he's well set up to provide for a family."

Katie rolled her eyes. "I don't know about that. Any woman who takes Freeman Kemp for a husband is asking for trouble. The man thinks he knows everything. Even when he doesn't. He tried to tell me how to scrub the floor. Can you imagine? And the man doesn't know where butter goes in the refrigerator. And when I tell him the truth of the matter, he gets all cross."

Sara added another handful of weeds to the bucket. They would go into the chicken yard and the scavenging hens would make quick work of them. Nothing ever went to waste on an Amish farm. "Men naturally think they know the best way to do things," she said. "But the wisest of them learn to think before they speak when it comes to women's chores."

"I guess no one ever told Freeman that." Katie tugged at a particularly stubborn pigweed. It came away with a spray of dirt, and she shook it off and added it to the pile. Sara's garden was as tidy as her house, row after row of green peppers, sweet corn, beets, squash and onions. Heavy posts set into the ground made a sturdy support for the wires that supported lima bean vines. Lima beans were one of Katie's favorite vegetables and they were the concern this evening. A summer garden that wasn't worked regularly soon became a tangle of weeds and a haven for bothersome insects.

"Does Freeman seem to be in a lot of pain? Ivy told me the break was a bad one. If he's irritable, that could be the reason," Sara suggested.

"Hard to judge how much pain a person is in." Katie pulled the weed bucket closer to them as they moved down the row. "I think he's more bored from having to stay in bed than anything else. I know it would drive me to distraction if I couldn't be up doing."

"Jehu is nice, though, isn't he?"

"He is. He was very welcoming. He told me not to pay any mind to Freeman's grumpiness. He's an amazing man, really. He knows his way all over that farm, doesn't need a bit of help. I think Freeman said he can see shadows. But you'd never know Jehu was blind the way he moves."

Sara tossed a weed in the bucket. "My cousin Hannah told me that he was a skilled leather worker for years. He still works for the harness shop down his way. Pieces he can stitch from memory."

"It's such a shame that he lost his sight," Katie said.

Sara paused in her weeding and gave Katie a thoughtful look. "It is, but God's will is not always for us to understand. All we can do is accept it and try to make the best of the blessings we have."

From the far end of the rows, Mari and Ellie began to sing "Amazing Grace." Ellie, a little person not more than four feet tall, had a sweet, clear soprano voice, while Mari's rich and powerful alto blended perfectly. Katie smiled, enjoying the sound of their voices in the fading light of the warm evening.

"I had a letter today from Uriah Lambright's aunt." Sara straightened up and rubbed the small of her back. "She says that the family is eager for you to come and visit. Have you given any more thought to considering him?"

"Evening," came a deep male voice.

The four women looked in the direction of the garden gate.

"Ah, James." Sara smiled at the Amish man in his midthirties who had just walked into the garden.

"Katie, do you know James?" Sara asked.

"We've met." She nodded to him. "Evening to you too, James."

James smiled at her and then turned his attention back to Sara. "Can I steal away some of your help?" he asked. "It's such a nice evening, I thought maybe Mari would like to take a ride with me."

Mari came toward them, blushing and brushing dirt from her skirt. Like Katie, Mari was barefoot with only a scarf for a head covering. "I wish you'd given me fair warning," she said, smiling up at James. "I'm not fit to be seen. Can you wait long enough for me to make myself decent and see where Zachary is?"

Zachary was Mari's son, a boy about nine years old. Mari and Zachary were staying with Sara while they made the transition from being English to becoming Amish again. Mari had been raised Amish, but had left the church as a teen and was now returning to the church.

James laughed and used two fingers to push his straw hat higher on his forehead. He was a tall, pleasant-looking man with a quick smile. "I'll wait, but you look fine to me. If you're going to change your clothes, you'd best be quick. Zachary's already in the buggy, and he's trying to convince me that we should go for ice cream."

Mari glanced at Sara who made shooing motions. "Go on, go on," Sara urged. "We can finish up here."

"You're sure?"

"Off with you before I change my mind and put James to work, too," Sara teased.

James swung the gate wide open and Mari hurried to join him. The two walked off, already deep in conversation.

Katie watched them for a minute. She wasn't jealous of Mari's happiness, but she *was* wistful. Katie wanted to marry and have children, but she was beginning to fear it would never happen. She had always assumed

God intended her for marriage and a family; it was what an Amish woman was born to. But what if He didn't wish for her to marry?

With a sigh, Katie returned to her work and she and Sara continued weeding until they met Ellie halfway down the row. "You're a fast worker," she told Ellie, observing her work. The soil behind Ellie was as neat and clean as a picture in a garden magazine.

"*Danke.* I try." Ellie's face creased in a genuine smile. "I think the beans at the far end will be ready for picking by tomorrow afternoon."

"If you can wait until after supper, I'd be glad to help you," Katie offered. She liked picking limas, and gardening with other women was always easier than doing it alone. "Willing hands make the work go faster," her mother always said.

"Great," Ellie replied. "It won't take long if we pick them together."

Ellie was the first little person that Katie had ever known, but someone who obviously didn't let her lack of height hinder her. Sara had explained privately that although Ellie had come to Seven Poplars to teach school, Sara had every hope of making a good marriage for her. Ellie was certainly pretty enough to have her choice of men to walk out with, with her blond hair, rosy cheeks, and sparkling blue eyes. Katie had liked her from the first, and she hoped that they might become good friends.

"All right," Sara said, looking across the garden. "I think we've got time to do another row. But there are a lot of full pods on this row. I think we better get to them. Who wants to pick while the other two keep weeding?"

"You pick," Katie told Sara. "I don't mind weeding. It's satisfying to see the results when I'm finished."

"Ya," Ellie said. "Good idea. I can weed, too."

"All right," Sara brushed the dirt off her hands. "It's a bumper crop this summer. Just the right amount of rain, thank the Lord."

"Let's get to it," Katie told Ellie. "Once it starts to get dark, the mosquitoes will come out, and we'll be fair game, bug spray or no bug spray."

Nodding agreement, Ellie and Katie began to pull weeds again while Sara sought out the plump lima bean pods amid the thick foliage. Conversation came easily to the three of them, and Katie found herself more at ease with Ellie with every passing minute. She was good company, making them double over with laughter at her tales of students. Katie hadn't attended the Seven Poplars schoolhouse, but she'd been there several times for fund-raising events, and Ellie was such a good storyteller that she could picture each event as Ellie related it. Her own school, further south in the county, had been larger, with two rooms rather than one, but otherwise almost identical. Both schools were first through eighth grade and taught by young Amish women.

Sara soon filled her apron with limas and had to return to the house for a basket for them and a second bucket to hold the weeds. When she returned, she brought a quart jar of lemonade to share. Katie and Ellie stopped work long enough to enjoy it before taking up their task again.

"I had a letter from one of my former clients in Wisconsin," Sara said when they'd reached midrow. "Dora Ann Hostetler."

"Do you know her, Ellie?" Katie asked, remembering that Sara had told her that Ellie had come from Wisconsin, too.

Ellie slapped at a hovering horsefly and shook her head. "*Ne*, but Wisconsin's a big state. A lot more Amish communities there than here."

"Anyway," Sara continued. "Dora Ann was a widow with three little girls. A plain woman, but steady, and with a good heart. I found just the man for her last year, a jolly widower with four young boys in need of a mother. She wrote to say that she and Marvin have a new baby boy. She also wanted me to know that her bishop will be visiting in Dover next month, and he'll be preaching here in Seven Poplars. She likes him and assures me that he preaches a fine sermon." She looked at Katie. "Will you be coming to church with us, or going home to your family's church?"

Katie paused in her weeding. "I think I'd like to come with you while I'm here," she said. Sara's mention of the letter from her friend reminded her of the one that Sara had received from Uriah's aunt. "You started to tell me earlier about the note from Uriah's family," she reminded.

"Yes, but..." Sara hesitated. "Would you rather discuss that in private?"

"*Ne*, I don't mind." Katie chuckled. "Actually, I'd like to hear Ellie's opinion."

Sara placed her basket, now nearly full of lima beans, on the ground. "Katie has an interested suitor," she explained to Ellie. "A young man who used to be a neighbor to her family here in Kent County."

"Uriah, his parents and brothers and sisters moved to Kentucky years ago," Katie said as she tamped down the weeds in the bucket to make room for more. "Uriah is the oldest."

"The family has a farm and a sawmill in Kentucky," Sara added. She continued searching for ripe beans. "Uriah's father made initial contact with me a few weeks ago about the possibility of making a match for his son with Katie."

Katie threw Ellie a wry look. "It was the *father* who asked about me, mind you, not Uriah."

Ellie sat back on her heels and glanced from Katie to Sara and back to Katie. "So you know Uriah from when you were younger?"

Katie nodded. "They left when we were twelve, maybe thirteen. He was in the same school year as I was. They come back every year or so to see family so I've seen him a few times over the last few years."

"Then you must have some idea of what you think of him," Ellie said. "Is he someone you can imagine yourself married to?"

Katie sighed. "That's the problem. I don't know. I mean, I know he's a good person and strong in his faith. He's shy; he's always been shy. I suppose that's why his father made the inquiry. And there's nothing *wrong* with him." She sighed again.

"Well, is he hardworking? Does he have any bad habits? Those are the kinds of questions I think you need to ask yourself." Ellie worked up the ground around the base of a plant. "But I guess the important thing is, do you like him?"

Katie thought for a minute. "I do like him," she said, then she wrinkled her nose. "I just never thought of him as a possible husband. He was just sort of always… there."

"So what you're saying is what?" Ellie asked. "Boring?"

"Ellie!" Sara's admonition was only half-serious. "What way is that to talk of a man you don't even know?"

"No... I wouldn't call Uriah boring," Katie answered. "He's serious, but not, you know, not deadly serious." She thought for a minute. "And he likes dogs. He always had a dog."

Ellie laughed merrily. "Now *there's* a recommendation for a husband. Or it would be if you were a dog." She shook her head. "It doesn't sound as if you're too excited about this offer. So there's got to be something about him that you don't like or you'd be more enthusiastic about the idea." She hesitated. "I know looks shouldn't matter to us, but...do you find him unattractive?"

"Ne," Katie insisted. "It's not like that. He isn't... ugly. He's... I don't know...average-looking, I suppose, and he has nice teeth."

Ellie giggled. "Nice teeth. There's a plus." She shook the dirt off a weed and tossed it playfully at Katie. "If I were you, I wouldn't be able to contain myself. Not boring, nice teeth, and too shy to come and check you out for himself. Yup. That's the man for you."

Katie and Ellie both laughed.

"Put that talk by," Sara chided, in earnest this time. "Uriah Lambright is a respectable candidate. I would have never brought him up to Katie if I didn't think so. His aunt tells me that he's building a house for his new bride, and that he's well thought of in his community. Not every worthy bachelor is forward around the opposite sex. And since Katie says that she has no objections to taking inquiries further, that's exactly what I'm doing."

"Could you do that?" Ellie asked Katie. "Marry someone that you weren't strongly attracted to? I know I couldn't. When I choose a husband, if I ever do, I want it to be someone I can love." She wrapped her arms around her tiny waist. "Someone I just couldn't live without."

"Some marriages do start with romance," Sara conceded, "but not all of them. I've arranged many matches between total strangers. There must be respect and liking, and then often, if both parties want the partnership to be successful, love follows."

"My mother says the same thing." Ellie got to her feet and brushed the dirt off the back of her dress. "She tells me that if I wait for romantic love, I may end up an old maid, caring for other people's babies and sitting at other women's tables."

"That's exactly what I'm afraid of," Katie agreed. "That's why I know I should take the Lambrights' offer seriously. I want romance. I want love. But what if that's not what God intends for me?" Without another weed in sight, she rose to her feet, too. "I'm not saying I'm ready to say *ya* to Uriah, but neither am I willing to just say no outright. What if he *is* the person God intends for me to wed? And so far, he's the only one who's shown any interest other than the occasional ride in a buggy home from a singing."

"I don't know." Ellie turned thoughtful. "I understand what you're saying, but I think I hear a *but* there." She looked up at Katie. "You're saying all the right things, but I think there has to be something about this Uriah that makes you cautious."

"I suppose it's that I'm not convinced that Uriah is interested in me," Katie admitted readily. "He hasn't written, and he hasn't come to see me. What if his family is more interested in this match than he is? I know that his parents and his grandmother always liked me, but I wouldn't be marrying them. What if Uriah's being pushed into this match?"

"That's always a possibility," Sara agreed. "And if that's the case, then I certainly wouldn't advise you to accept his offer of courtship. But you don't know the facts yet. Both you and Ellie are young, and the young tend to believe they have all the answers." She met Katie's gaze, waggling her finger at her. "I will tell you this. More than one young woman has broken her own heart waiting for the perfect man to appear from far off, while the one she should have chosen—" she pointed at Katie "—was standing right in front of her."

Chapter Three

There were no complaints from Freeman on the meal Katie cooked the following morning, and if not jovial, he was at least polite to her. Jehu had a third helping of bacon and toast, and Freeman did admit that her meal was an improvement over his grandmother's oatmeal.

Ivy hadn't come over to the big house yet; presumably, the older woman was enjoying a respite from the men and eating her preferred breakfast. Still, Katie missed Ivy's cheerful presence at the table. She liked Ivy's no-nonsense way of dealing with the men, especially Freeman, and she reminded Katie of her own *grossmama,* Mary Byler, who'd passed away several winters earlier.

Once everyone had eaten and the dishes were washed and put away, Jehu and the dog went to the mill and Katie turned to the laundry. "When is the last time those sheets of yours were washed?" she asked Freeman.

He scowled at her. "Not long."

"How long exactly?" she persisted.

"Probably when I came home from the hospital."

She sniffed in disapproval and pursed her lips. "It won't do, you know. Lying on dirty linens."

His dark eyes narrowed. They were still beautiful eyes, but the expression was peevish and resentful, like an adolescent who'd been told he couldn't go fishing with his friends but had to stay home and clean the chicken coop. "And how do you suggest that I change and wash these sheets?"

"Don't be surly," she scolded. "I'll do the washing, but you'll have to get out of bed so that I can strip it."

Freeman rapped on his cast with a fist. "Doctor says that the leg has to remain elevated."

Katie sighed with impatience. "We're both intelligent people. I think we can figure out a solution." The previous day, when she'd first come in, she'd noticed a wheelchair folded up and resting against the wall, the packing strap still wrapped around it. Clearly, Freeman had never used the chair. Resolutely prepared for resistance, she approached the bed. "Are you decent?"

"I should hope so. I try to do the right thing."

It took all of her willpower not to show her exasperation. He was wearing a light blue shirt, wrinkled but clean, rather than the sleeveless T-shirt he'd worn the day before. She'd wanted to know if he had trousers on under the sheet and blankets. And she had the feeling that he knew exactly what she'd been asking and chose to be difficult. "You know what I mean," she said briskly. "Are you wearing anything other than your skin below your waist?"

Two spots of color glowed through the dark stubble on his cheeks. *"Ya,"* he muttered. "Grossmama cut a leg off a pair of my pants so I could pull them on over the cast. The traveling nurse was coming to the

house when I first got home from the hospital so—"
He scowled at her, his blush becoming even more evident. "Why would you need to know what I have on under my sheet?"

Katie pursed her lips and regarded him with the same expression she used with her brothers when they were being impossible. "Because I need to change those sheets, and I can't get you out of the bed and into the wheelchair without your cooperation." She folded her arms resolutely. "You're certainly too heavy for me to carry, but if you're a miller, I'd guess that you have a lot of strength in your upper body. If I bring that wheelchair up beside the bed, can you use your arms to maneuver into it?"

"Didn't say yet that I want to get out of bed," he protested.

She could tell it wasn't much of an argument, more for show than anything else. "Of course you want to get up. You'd have to be thick-headed to want to stay there like a lump of coal." She tilted her head, softening her voice. "And, Freeman, you're anything but slow-witted if I'm any judge."

"I suppose I could manage to heave myself into the thing," he said grudgingly. "I hadn't decided if I was keeping it, though. Wheelchairs are expensive. I'll be back on my feet soon enough and—"

"It's going to be weeks before you're back on your feet," she interrupted. "Too long for you to lie in that bed." She stared down at him and he stared up at her and it occurred to her that they could possibly be there all day just waiting to see who would bend first.

He did.

"Fine," he finally muttered. "But, I warn you, there

aren't any more sheets in the house to fit this size bed. Am I supposed to sit in that contraption all day while you do the laundry and hang it out to dry?"

She tried not to show how amused she was. Stubborn, the man was as stubborn as a broody hen refusing to budge off a clutch of wooden eggs. She suspected he wanted to be out of that bed more than she wanted him to do it, but he wasn't going to make it easy for her. "You must have other sheets. In a linen closet?"

He nodded. "But I just told you. They won't fit. They're for larger beds than this."

"That's women's matters. No need for you to worry yourself over it." She gave him a sympathetic look. "I'm sure it will be painful…moving from the bed to the chair. If it really is too much, just say so."

Again, the scowl. "I'm not afraid of a little pain."

She went to the wheelchair, cut the plastic shipping strap with scissors and began to unfold it. "While you're out of bed, maybe you could find your razor. You're badly in need of a shave."

Being unmarried, Freeman should have been clean-shaven. Either he or someone had shaved him in the last week, but he had at least a five-day growth of reddish-brown beard. His hair was too long. Getting him shaven and onto clean sheets would be a small victory. And she'd found with her father and brothers that small steps worked best with men. You had to make them think ideas were their own. Otherwise, they tended to balk and turn mulish. She hesitated, and then suggested, "I could do it for you, if you like. My brother, Little Joe, broke two fingers on his right hand once and I—"

"I can shave myself. It's my leg that's broken, not my hand."

When she glanced back to the bed, Freeman was looking at the wheelchair with obvious apprehension. She understood his hesitation, but she truly did think his upper body was strong enough to move himself safely into the wheelchair. "If you did get in the chair, you could go out on the porch easy enough," she said with genuine kindness. "It's a beautiful day. You must be going mad as May butter staring at these kitchen walls."

"I am," he admitted.

Her irritation was fading fast. Freeman was a challenge. He might be prickly, but he was interesting. Being with him kept her on her toes and anything but bored. It must take a lot of energy for him to pretend to be so grumpy. And she suspected it wasn't his true nature. "What was that?" she teased.

His high brow furrowed. "I *said* I am. I'm tired of staring at this room. A house is no place for a man in midmorning."

"Which is our best reason for getting you out of that bed. An easy mind makes for quicker healing." She brought the wheelchair to the side of the bed. "Careful," she warned. "Let me help you."

"*Ne*. You steady the chair so it doesn't roll."

"It won't. I've put the brakes on."

"Stand aside, then, and let me do it by myself." Slowly, pale and with sweat breaking out on his forehead, Freeman managed the gap from the bed to the chair. Katie knew that it must have hurt him, but he didn't make a sound, and finished sitting upright with a look of pure satisfaction on his face.

"Wonderful," she said, squeezing her hands together. She raised the leg rest and carefully propped his cast on it. Then she released the brake and pushed him out of the kitchen and down the short hall to the bathroom. He told her where to find his razor and shaving cream. "You won't be able to see into the mirror," she said, handing him a washcloth and draping a towel around his neck. This mirror was small and fixed to the wall over the sink. "Is there another mirror I could bring in here?"

"I don't need your help. Just hand me my razor and soap and brush from over there," he said, pointing to a pretty old oak dresser that she suspected held towels and the like. "I've done this hundreds of times. I can manage without the mirror."

"If you'll tell me where to find scissors, I could trim the back of your hair. That's not something you can do yourself," she offered, putting his things on the edge of the sink.

"My hair is fine. Now go change those sheets you've been fussing about."

She made no argument but went and located a linen closet at the top of the stairs. As Freeman had said, it had sheets for double beds, but she could easily tuck the excess under the mattress. The important thing was that the sheets were clean. They would do for now. Next time, she would have freshly washed and line-dried linen to go on his bed, provided he didn't fire her first.

When she finished the task and returned to the bathroom, she found him still sitting at the sink, shaving cream on his face and a razor in his hand. There were uneven patches of beard on his cheeks and a trickle of blood down his chin. Wordlessly, he handed the razor to her, grimaced, and clenched his eyes shut. She ran hot water on the washcloth, twisted it until the excess water ran out, and pressed it over his face.

She'd said that shaving Freeman would be no different that shaving her brothers, but as she stood there looking at him, she realized it was. It was very different. She had to steady her hands as she removed the washcloth and began with more shaving cream. Her pulse quickened, and she felt a warm flush beneath her skin.

Shaving Freeman was more intimate than she'd supposed it would be and she was thankful that his dark eyes were closed. The act bordered on inappropriate behavior between an unmarried man and woman, but neither of them intended it to be anything other than what it was. She'd offered with the best of intentions and backing down now would be worse than going through with it, wouldn't it?

But what if her hands trembled and she cut him? How would she explain that?

She took a deep breath and plunged forward, silently praying, *Don't let my hand slip. Please, don't let him see how nervous I am.* The small curling hairs at the nape of her neck grew damp and her knees felt weak, but she kept sliding the razor down the smooth plane of his cheek. The blade was sharp, and Freeman held perfectly still. If he'd moved, even a fraction of an inch, she knew that the blade would break his skin, but he didn't, and she managed to finish without disgracing herself.

"All done." Heady with success, she handed him the wet washcloth. "See, it wasn't that bad, was it?"

"Thank you." He wiped his face and opened his eyes.

"I could still do something with your hair," she offered.

He wiped a last bit of shaving cream from his chin and tossed the washcloth in the sink. "Quit while you're ahead, woman."

She laughed. "You do look a lot better." And he did, more than better. Shaggy hair brushing his shirt collar or not, he had the kind of good looks that cautious mothers warned their daughters against. And with good reason, she thought, as she locked her shaking hands behind her back.

"I'm not a vain man."

She couldn't hide a mischievous grin. *"Ne?"* She thought that he wasn't telling the exact truth. In her mind, most men were as vain as any woman. They just hid it better. And Freeman had more reason than most to take pride in his looks.

"I'm a Plain man. I have more on my mind than my appearance."

"I can see that," she agreed. "But no one said that a clean and tidy man was an offense to the church."

He fixed her with those lingering brown eyes, eyes that were not as full of disapproval as they had been. "Do you have an answer for everything?" he asked. But she sensed that he was making an effort at humor rather than being sarcastic.

"I try." She nodded. "Now I'll leave you to finish washing up. Call when you need me to bring you back out to the kitchen."

"I think I can push myself," he grumbled.

Smiling, she left him to go throw the sheets in the wash.

She'd just started mixing a batch of cornbread when Freeman came rolling slowly down the hall. He looked pale, as if he'd run a long distance. She could tell he was in pain, but she didn't say anything about it. "Do you think you could peel potatoes for me?"

"I suppose I could," he said. "Isn't it too early to be starting the midday meal?"

"Too early for cooking. Not too early for starting the preparation. I've lots to do this morning, and you have to be organized to get meals on the table on time and still get the rest of your work done."

"Organization is a good thing," he agreed. "Not many people understand that. They waste hours that could go to good purpose."

"Mmm." She brought him a large stainless steel bowl, a paring knife, and the potatoes. "If you peel these, I'll cut them up and put them in salted water, ready to cook when it gets closer to mealtime."

"My mother was a good cook," he said.

"Mine, too. Better than me."

"She's still with you, isn't she?"

"*Ya*, thanks be to God. We lost my father a few years ago, but we were fortunate to have him as long as we did. *Dat* had five heart surgeries, starting when he was a baby. He was never strong, but he lived a full life, and he and my mother were happy together."

"It's important, having parents who cared for each other. Mine did, too. They died too soon. An accident." He shook his head, and she saw the gleam of moisture in his eyes. "I'd rather not talk about it."

Then why did he bring it up, she wondered. But she was glad that he had, felt that it was a positive step in their relationship. If she was going to work here, for the next two weeks, it would be better if they weren't always butting heads.

"Do you fish?" he asked.

"What?" She'd been thinking about what he'd said about his parents and hadn't been giving him her full attention. "Do I like fish? To eat?"

"*Ya*, to eat. But I meant to catch. I like fishing. It's what I usually do on summer evenings. We have big bass in the millpond, catfish, perch, as well as sunnies."

"I do like fishing," she said. "And crabbing. My *dat* used to take us to Leipsic. We'd crab off the bridge there. And fish, too, but we never caught many."

"It takes patience and know-how. Bass, especially, are clever. But very tasty. I use artificial lures for them."

Jehu strolled in, sniffing the air. "Making corn fritters?"

"Cornbread," Katie said.

"I love cornbread." He went to the table and sat down near Freeman. "Laundry going, I hear. You've been busy, Katie." He pulled his cat's cradle string out of his pocket. "Learned a new one this morning. From Shad, of all people. Shad is Freeman's apprentice. Good boy, hard worker."

"I wouldn't say apprentice," Freeman corrected. "Shad's got a long way to go before he can call himself a miller. Thinks too much of himself, that boy. Headstrong."

"Sounds likes somebody else I know," Jehu said. He turned his head in Freeman's direction. "Sounds like you got him up and out of that bed. And shaved, too, if I'm not mistaken. I smell your shaving cream." He turned toward the sink where Katie was grating a cabbage she'd brought from Sara's garden. "You're a good influence on him, Katie. Best thing in the world for him. Get out of bed, cleaned up, and stop feeling sorry for himself."

The screen door squeaked and Ivy joined them. The terrier ran across the kitchen and leaped up on the newly-made bed. "What are you up to, Katie? Don't tell me you're already starting dinner?" She smiled warmly. "Freeman, look at you. Up and shaved. I think I know who to give credit to for this."

Freeman grimaced, picking up another potato to peel. "Morning, Grossmama. I'm feeling better, thank you."

"I can see that for myself," she answered crisply. "And she's put you to work."

"I couldn't find a vegetable peeler," Katie said. "Just a paring knife."

"You won't, not in this house. I've got one if you need to borrow it. Help yourself." She picked up one of the potatoes Freeman had peeled. "Not bad," she said, "not good, but not bad. Be more careful. Waste not." She turned back to Katie. "I just made a fresh pot of tea, and I was hoping that you'd come to my house and have some with me."

"I don't know," Katie hemmed. "I've got a lot to do."

"It'll wait," Ivy told her, giving a wave. "Come on. We can get to know each other." She looked up at Katie. "You know you want to."

"You should go, Katie," Jehu encouraged. "I'll keep an eye on Trouble, here." He tipped his head in Freeman's direction.

Katie was torn. She *did* have a lot to do, but it seemed important to Ivy that they share a pot of tea. And God didn't put them on the earth just to sweep and wash, did He? In the end, people mattered more than chores. It was something her mother, though a hard worker, had instilled in her young. "Oh…why not?" she conceded.

"I'd like some tea," Freeman said. "But I like mine cold. The doctor said I should drink lots of fluids." He frowned. "Katie's busy. We didn't hire her to sit and drink tea. She has chores to do, and we were having a serious conversation about—"

"Fishing," his uncle supplied with a grin. "Which means that she's certainly earned a break. Go along with Ivy, Katie. Enjoy your tea. I'll make Grumpy his iced tea. Just as soon as he finishes peeling the potatoes."

Chapter Four

"Come along, dear. We'll have a cup of tea and get to know each other better." Ivy's invitation was as warm and welcoming as her smile as she led Katie down the walkway between the two houses.

The *grossmama haus* stood under the trees on the far side of the farmhouse where Freeman and Jehu lived. To reach Ivy's place, she and Katie had only to follow the brick path from Freeman's porch to a white picket fence. There, a blue gate opened to a small yard filled with a riot of blooming flowers and decorative shrubs. Katie counted at least a dozen different blooming perennials she could put names to and several she couldn't. There were climbing roses, hydrangea, hollyhocks and lilies, so many flowers that barely a patch of green lawn was visible.

Hummingbird feeders hung on either side of the front door, and the air was filled with the exciting sounds of the tiny, iridescent-feathered creatures, as well as the buzz of honeybees and the chattering voice of a wren. "How beautiful," Katie said. "Your flowers."

"They're God's gift to us and a constant joy to me,"

Ivy said. "They ask only for sunshine and rain and a little care against the weeds and they bloom their hearts out for us. I'm so pleased that you like my garden. Are you interested in flowers?" She pushed open the front door, ushering Katie into a combined kitchen and sitting room.

Everything inside was neat and orderly. The furnishings were simple: a sofa, an easy chair, a rocker and a round oak table and matching chairs. The appliances were small but new, and they fit perfectly into the small, cheerful cottage with its large windows and hardwood flooring. Colorful family trees, cross-stitch Bible verses and a calendar hung on the walls. A sewing basket sat by the rocker, and a copy of the Amish newspaper, *The Budget*, lay open on the sofa. In the center of the table rested a blue pottery teapot, a sugar bowl and pitcher, with two cups and saucers.

"I do love my tea, even on a warm day," Ivy said. "I hope you do, too. Coffee is invigorating, but tea calms the mind and spirit." She waved toward the table. "Please, sit down."

Katie took a seat at the table. "Your house is lovely."

"It's wonderful, isn't it? Freeman had it built for me just last year. It's the first new home I've ever lived in. I grew up in an old farmhouse near Lancaster, and then when I married Freeman's grandfather, I came here to the millhouse as a bride. I never had cause to complain, but I do love my *grossmama haus*. It's warm in winter, my stove doesn't smoke and the floors don't creak."

Ivy poured tea into one of the cups and handed it to her. Even Ivy's dishes showed her love of flowers. The cup and saucer were bright with green leaves and purple violets. "But I'm running on. It comes of living alone, I think. It's not easy, you know. I fear that when I do have company I never give them a chance to get a word in." Her speech was grandmotherly, but her eyes, alert and missing nothing, gave evidence of an intelligent and still vibrant woman. She smiled again, disarmingly. "So, tell me about your family, Katie. Do you have brothers and sisters?"

"Two brothers," she answered. "I'm the youngest. There's Isaac. He's the oldest and was named after my father. Isaac has the family farm, and then there's Robert, who lives across the road from us. Our family is small, but close. Isaac and Robert were always inseparable."

"Two brothers," Ivy echoed. "I always wanted brothers. I come from a small family myself. My mother had only two of us that lived past babyhood, my sister and me. My father longed so for sons, but it wasn't to be."

Katie stirred milk into her tea. "My father and mother were hoping for a girl. There hadn't been any girls born in my father's family for two generations."

"Funny isn't it, how patterns repeat in families? My husband was an only child and while we hoped for a large family, we were blessed with only the one child as well." She looked at the window and sighed. "I always imagined having a wealth of grandbabies to hug and fuss over, but there was only Freeman. With two sons married, I suppose your fortunate mother has grandchildren."

"Two so far, Robert's. Isaac just married. It's partially why I took this job. I really like Patsy, and I thought she should have time to settle into her home without a third woman in the house. Mother lives with us, as well. We lost my father a few years back."

"I heard about that, and I'm so sorry. Your brother Robert has children?"

"Twins. Boys. Just learning to walk. I adore them."

"So you're fond of children?"

"I am."

"I hope when you marry that you are blessed with more than a single child. It's hard not to indulge them. But Freeman's father was a precious child and a good man. He never gave us a night's worry. I know he's safe with the Lord, but losing him and Freeman's mother in that accident was a terrible loss. She was like a daughter to me."

"Freeman mentioned that they had died."

"A boating accident. They were fishing on the Susquehanna. She was from Lancaster County, and her uncle took them out. We don't know what happened. They may have struck a rock. They say the currents are dangerous. I was so distraught that the weight of it fell on Freeman's shoulders."

"I'm so sorry."

Ivy sighed. "Death is part of life. But a mother should never have to bury her child. I don't care what the bishop says. It goes against everything that is right and natural." She ran her fingertips absently along the edge of her saucer. "You must think my faith is weak, to talk so."

"Ne," Katie assured her. "I can't imagine how difficult it would be to lose both a husband and your only child."

Ivy swallowed, her eyes, so much like Freeman's, sparkled with tears unshed. "It was...very hard. They say it gets easier with time and prayer, but some days..." She broke off and looked out the window. A silence stretched between them, but it was one of shared loss rather than awkwardness. After a moment or two, she glanced at Katie and brightened. "How old are you?"

Katie thought it was an odd question. Why did Ivy care how old the housekeeper was? But she wasn't offended in any way. "Twenty-three," she answered. "Twenty-four soon."

"And have you been baptized into the church?"

"I have. Last summer."

"Good." Ivy nodded her approval. "I cannot imagine living through such loss without the knowledge that those I love are forever beyond pain and sickness and that I will someday see them again."

"That's true," Katie said. "I feel the same way about my father. I miss him terribly, but he suffered from his condition, and now he is at peace."

"*Ya.* I do believe that."

"And you aren't alone," Katie said. "You still have Freeman," she said. "And, as you say, he's a good man. He must be a great comfort to you."

"He is." Ivy sighed. "He always has been. Do you see what expense he went to building this house for me? I didn't need anything so fancy, but I love it. And I have two bedrooms, when one should have been plenty, so if you ever want to stay over, you're welcome to stay here with me."

"That's very kind of you," Katie said.

"I'm not saying that my Freeman is without his faults. I wouldn't want you to think that I'm as blind as Jehu. I'm afraid we did spoil him as a child. He's a good boy, and I love him dearly, but he *is* fond of having his own way. Like his father and grandfather before him, there's only one way to do something, and that's the Kemp way."

Katie smiled. "My brothers have accused me of always wanting things done the *Katie* way. They say I'm stubborn, but if my way is the best way, why should I change to please someone else? So long as the job gets done right and as quickly as needed?"

"Men do hate having women show them how to do something easier," Ivy said. "I'm afraid it's born in them. In some ways, I don't believe any of them ever grow up. They're like little boys in grownup clothing." She chuckled. "They never get past the age of wanting a woman to take care of them and clean up after them."

"Speaking of which, I'd best get back to my chores." Katie started to rise. "The tea was delicious, but if we're to have our midday meal on time, I should go."

"Please, don't go yet," Ivy said. "I promise, no more sad talk. I'm ashamed of myself that I invited you to come and chat and then went on about my losses. I'm a poor hostess."

"Ne," Katie insisted. "I don't mind. I'm glad that you felt you could share your heartache with me. My mother is a good person, and we're very close. I couldn't ask for a better parent, but she doesn't talk about such things... about missing my father. She was never one to talk about her feelings. She says that we should keep such thoughts private. What you said about it being hard to accept... I feel the same way." She reached out and squeezed Ivy's hand. "It eases my heart to know that I'm not the only one who wants to put her sorrows into words. But I better go." She gave a small sound of amusement as she stood. "As Freeman said, I'm not

being paid to sit and drink tea. I came to his house to work, and if his meal is late, you know he'll fuss."

"Let him fuss," Ivy insisted. "Sit down and have another cup of tea and tell me all about this offer of marriage you have from Kentucky that Sara was telling me about. If my grandson has something to say about what time his dinner goes on the table, he can say it to me because I'm keeping you here for my own pleasure. Besides..." She shrugged and mischief lit her eyes. "Sometimes, it's good for a man to wait on a woman."

"She's late, isn't she?" Freeman asked aloud, directing his question to no one in particular.

He was sure that it had been well before eight when Katie arrived the morning before. He'd slept well the previous night and had awakened at the first rooster crow. He'd gotten himself up and into the wheelchair and washed, shaved and dressed himself so that Katie would have no reason to criticize him. Now he was resting in the bed, waiting for her.

It seemed as if he'd been waiting for her to arrive for hours. He thought maybe they could sit on the porch this morning and shell the lima beans Jehu had brought in from the garden the night before. Freeman was looking forward to getting out of the house, if only just to the porch. He'd have a view of the mill from there and he could see the height of the water in the smaller overflow pond. Anything but staring at this kitchen all day, he thought.

He glanced at the mantel clock again and found only four minutes had passed since he last looked. "She was here earlier yesterday, I'm sure of it."

"Eight." Jehu held out a mug of coffee. "No reason

to think Katie won't be here on time this morning."
How he managed to pour coffee and carry it across the
room without spilling a drop when he was blind as a
scarecrow, Freeman couldn't imagine. "Drink this and
keep your trousers on. It will hold you until breakfast."

"If we ever get it," Freeman grumbled. "*Danke.* I
appreciate it." He took a sip of the coffee. As usual,
Jehu had forgotten to add milk, but Freeman wouldn't
mention it. He'd drink it black, one more indignity for a
man laid low by his own stupidity. All he had had to do
was wait until Shad arrived to help him with the bull.
But no, he had to do it himself. Couldn't wait. Couldn't
ask for help. He'd been so sure that he could manage
the half-wild animal, and the bull had made a sideways
jump and knocked him against the fence as easily as
if he was a ten-year-old child. He couldn't even blame
the animal. The beast hadn't intended to hurt him. He
was simply reacting out of panic. The other men, when
they'd caught up with him, had easily surrounded it and
driven it into a neighbor's pasture where they'd been
able to get a rope on it.

He couldn't have picked a worse time to get laid up.
Shad was just beginning to understand the milling process. He didn't know the first thing about controlling
the flow of water out of the millpond, and the financial
end of the business was beyond him. Everything was
done on the computer: all the billings, delivery sched-
ules, and bookkeeping. And the computer was in the
mill office, seventy-five yards away, but it might have
been seventy-five miles for all his ability to get there
and use it. There was no electricity in the house, no
telephone. They were in the office, strictly for business

and emergencies, and closely watched by the local deacon, who was suspicious of all such worldly electronics.

His grandmother could operate the old-fashioned, manual cash register. She could sell one-and five-pound sacks of wheat and rye flour to the customers, but she didn't have the faintest idea how to make a spreadsheet or send and receive email and she hadn't had much success motivating Shad to take initiative in the actual milling process.

What was happening to the family business while he was flat on his back weighed heavier on him than the pain of his leg, and Katie Byler disturbed him even further. Although...he had to admit she'd set the kitchen to rights, and he'd slept a lot better on clean sheets. He wasn't a slovenly man, and clean clothes and a shave made him feel more like himself. But he liked things done a certain way, and she didn't seem to understand that although he was temporarily incapacitated, he was still master of this house.

Not that he was an unreasonable man. He could see now that, considering the circumstances, having Katie come was a good idea. He'd set his mind to being more open to having this stranger in his house for a few days. There was no doubt that she had shaken his self-absorption and given him something to think about other than his own problems. She was an excellent cook, and she wasn't exactly hard to look at. To be truthful, Katie was more than average in appearance. The golden-blond locks that curled around an oval face, even features, and wide, thick-lashed blue eyes were enough to make any man look at her twice. A few golden freckles dusted her nose and cheekbones, but they didn't mar her fair German complexion; they only added to her beauty.

Freeman grimaced. He couldn't fault her looks. It was Katie's unnatural nature that made her less than what a proper woman should be. She was too quick to question a man's judgment, and too set in her own ways. No wonder she had to resort to a matchmaker to find a husband.

Not that he hadn't done the same, he grudgingly conceded. Several years earlier, he'd tired of his grandmother's murmuring about him being past time to wed. So, he'd consulted with a matchmaker to try and find a suitable wife. Not Sara Yoder, but a woman in Lancaster. Sara had not yet come to live in Seven Poplars, or he would have gone to her. It would have been easier face-to-face than doing everything by letter.

It turned out the matchmaker didn't have any more success than he'd had on his own. The three girls she'd suggested were all wrong. Different reasons, but all wrong for him. Of course, he'd found the right woman years ago, and she'd chosen another. It had been a bitter pill to swallow, but he'd had to accept it. He knew that his grandmother was eager for him to marry and give her great-grandchildren, but he wasn't going to just settle. If he couldn't find the right woman, one who made him feel eight feet tall, he'd remain a bachelor.

The mantel clock began to chime. "Eight o'clock. That does it," Freeman declared. "She's late. And what are we supposed to—"

"Good morning!" Katie called out as she came into the kitchen, eyes sparkling with energy, arms full, and cheeks pink with ruddy health. She set a covered basket on the table and whisked off the woven lid. She was wearing a dark green dress that fell a few inches below her knees, dark stockings and low, black sneakers. "Sara made blueberry pancakes this morning, and she had extra," Katie proclaimed. "I packed hot water bottles around them to keep them warm. And I've got real maple syrup and blueberry compote." She removed a white apron from her basket, shook it out, and tied it around her waist. "I'm going to just pop them in the oven for a few minutes and then they'll be ready."

After breakfast, Freeman sat in the bed, eyeing the porch. He wondered if maybe he could walk the couple of feet out the door and to a chair, with his uncle's assistance. It would just make him feel better. He'd only been using the wheelchair three days but he was already sick of it.

Katie wouldn't have it, though.

"Absolutely not," she declared. "You're still supposed to be keeping your leg elevated. You're going to be off your feet for at least six weeks—"

"That's an exaggeration. The doctor never said six weeks," Freeman protested. He'd probably be bankrupt by then. Shad would have done something stupid with the mill mechanism and the wheels would stop turning. Customers would start taking their business someplace else. He couldn't afford six weeks off from work.

"Was it six?" Uncle Jehu asked. "I thought it was seven weeks."

Freeman gritted his teeth, even though he knew from his uncle's voice that he was just teasing. You would think that a man's uncle would take his side once in a while instead of forever siding with either Grossmama or Katie. Men were supposed to stick together.

Ignoring the both of them, Katie sat down in the wheelchair and maneuvered it around the kitchen table. Then she leaned back, bringing the front end up. It was all Freeman could do not to warn her to be careful. He didn't want her taking a spill.

"This is kind of fun." She lifted one footrest and propped up her leg. "And this will keep your leg elevated just as the doctor ordered. I can put a pillow under, if need be."

"I suppose you're right," he said, begrudgingly. If he could get around by himself, he guessed he could deal with the wheelchair for a few days. Anything would be better than lying flat on his back in that bed another day. "I got up myself this morning."

"That's good," Katie said. She moved to a kitchen chair and began to remove her shoes and stockings.

"Why are you doing that?" He should have looked away, but he didn't. If she was bold enough to roll down her stockings in front of a man, she couldn't blame him if he watched.

"I mean to do some heavy cleaning. And bare feet wash easier than stockings." She tucked her stockings into her shoes and slid them under the chair and brought the wheelchair to the side of his bed. "Ready?"

He tried not to grumble as she held the chair so that he could get off the bed and into it. And he only gave a small groan as she lifted his bad leg onto the footrest.

"Your hair still needs trimming," she said, hands on her hips, regarding him critically. "Are you certain you don't want me to cut it for you?"

"I'll think about it."

She smiled. "Good. Want to go out on the porch? I saw some things out there that need doing. I thought I might start there this morning."

Freeman slowly made his way out onto the porch to where he could see the pond and the front of the mill.

She brought him a newspaper, a recent issue of *Farm Journal*, and a copy of *National Geographic* from her bag. "I don't know if you like to read," she said, almost shyly, "but I saw the old newspapers stacked up in that box beside the door, here on the porch, so I thought you must read them."

"I do like to read in the evening," he said, giving her a genuine smile. "When my chores for the day are finished. But where did you get these magazines? They aren't ours."

"My brother Robert takes the *Farm Journal* and he saves them for me. It's last month's, but there are some good articles."

"And the *National Geographic*?"

She colored a faint shade of pink. "Mine. I know it isn't accepted reading for most Amish, but there are good articles about African wildlife and killer whales and all sorts of topics that even the deacon couldn't object to."

"So you're a reader, too." He studied her closely. He wouldn't have thought her a reader. Most Amish weren't, but that held even truer for Amish women. "Maybe we have more in common than I thought. It was thoughtful of you to bring them; I appreciate it. I've seen issues of the *Geographic* before. I don't know why I haven't subscribed to it. They're interesting."

"I thought so. I know our *ordnung* teaches us to live apart from the world, but that doesn't mean we should be ignorant of it."

Maybe he'd been hasty in his judgment of Katie Byler, he thought. She wasn't a bad sort, once you got to know her better. He sighed and looked around at the yard and sparkling surface of the pond and took a deep breath of the fresh air. It felt good out here. Small fish were feeding near the surface, and he could just make out some of them jumping.

"You know, if you like to make fishing lures," Katie said. "Maybe we could bring some of your tools into the house. You could work on them at the kitchen table or even in bed. It would give you something to do…to help pass the time."

He nodded. "That might be a good idea. If you wouldn't mind, I can make a list of what I'd need. My workshop is over at the mill."

Katie had found a four-foot stepladder and unfolded it.

"What are you doing?" He'd seen the broom and thought she meant to sweep the porch, which could certainly use it. He had to admit that the porch was a little cluttered. There was a bucket with scraps for the chickens, a couple of fishing poles, a rake, a folding chair that he'd carried in to mend one rainy day, before he'd had the accident, and a few tools and cardboard boxes. "Why do you need a ladder?"

She used the broom handle to point at a bird's nest along the eaves.

There was a rip in the screen at the far end of the porch that let the swallows in. They'd made nests here in the spring when they were raising babies. Actually, they'd made four nests, two from the previous year. He winced. Had it been two winters ago that a tree branch had fallen and torn the screen? He should have cleaned away the old bird nests. The swallows wouldn't use the old nests next year. They'd build new ones.

"You need to get someone to fix that hole," she

pointed out. "You can't keep mosquitoes out without mending that screen."

"Haven't noticed they're bad. Besides, the barn swallows eat the mosquitoes."

"*Ne*, but I'll doubt you spend much time on the porch. And birds belong outside, not in. They make a mess." She looked around the space and sighed. "Not that you'd notice, I suppose." She climbed the ladder, revealing neat ankles and shapely bare feet before he realized he was staring and looked away.

"Are you calling me dirty?" he asked, not really offended. She had very high arches, and she seemed nimble. She certainly wasn't afraid of heights like Susan had been. He'd tried to get her to climb the steps to the top floor of the mill once, and she'd gone white-faced and clingy on him.

Katie used the broom to knock loose one of the swallow nests. "Now don't go all huffy on me, Freeman," she said between whacks. "I can't imagine how one man does all the work it must take to run this mill, even with the help of an apprentice."

"Hired man," he corrected. "I told Shad that I'd make him my apprentice if he showed promise. I'm still waiting."

"It must be a trial, trying to find good help."

He didn't bite on that one.

"What kind of a name is Shad?" she asked. "Sounds English. Is he English?"

"Shad Gingrich? *Ne*, his name is Shadrach. From the Bible. The fiery oven."

"Oh, that Shadrach. I didn't know there were any Gingrichs around here."

"There aren't. Shad's from Ohio. Uncle Jehu is a

friend of his grandfather. He boards at a farm down the road. His family wanted Shad to learn the trade and sent him here to me. He's a little young, though."

"How young?"

"Twenty-one."

"I thought you were twenty when you took over the mill here," she pointed out.

"But he's young for his age," Freeman said quickly. "Milling's serious. You can get hurt around the gears if you're not careful. And you can do a lot of damage to the equipment. It's expensive to repair and difficult to replace parts. There aren't many stone mills still in operation in this country. It's a dying art."

"All the more reason for you to have an apprentice, maybe more than one in case one doesn't work out."

"You're quick to give advice on a trade you know nothing of." He looked up at her. "What makes you think I can afford the price of a second hired man?"

"Apprentice. Take on one younger and he won't cost you as much, and he'll be more willing to take advice. And if you could afford to pay my wages, and I'll only be here temporarily, you can use that money to employ another apprentice." She climbed down, swept the fallen nest and the dirt around it into a dustpan before moving her ladder. "Wait," she said. "Is that Shad coming out of the mill?"

Freeman looked where she was pointing. "*Ya*, that's him carrying a fishing pole. Maybe planning on taking a little leisure on my time when he should be working. Shad!" he shouted. "Shad!"

Katie leaned the broom against the house. "You know, I think you'd heal faster if you weren't so out of sorts all the time. And maybe you'd be in a better mood if you could get out to the mill yourself and see what's going on."

"What? You think I can roll the wheelchair down these steps to the backyard?"

She gave him the same look a mother might give a trying child. "What you need is a ramp, and an apprentice who has time to go fishing has time to build a ramp." She started toward the screen door that led to the yard.

"Where are you going?"

"To tell Shad he needs to find the materials to build a ramp."

"You can't do that," he said.

She whipped around. "Can't do what?"

"Give my hired man orders."

"I can't?" She smirked. "Watch me."

He stared after her as she marched across the yard intent on having her own way. And then, he couldn't contain himself. He saw the humor in it and laughed.

Chapter Five

By noon the following day, Shad was well on his way to completing a wheelchair ramp from the house to the sidewalk, and Freeman supposed he should have been pleased. But Katie had invited him to join them for the midday meal and afterwards, when the family sat drinking iced tea on the porch, he'd had to watch Shad making calf eyes at Katie and praising her for her cooking. Every time Katie glanced in the boy's direction, Shad flushed to the roots of his hair. Finally, when Shad remarked for the second time on the amazing qualities of her blackberry pie, Freeman lost patience. "Time you were getting back to work, don't you think, Shadrach?"

"Oh, let the boy digest his dinner," Grossmama said. "He's been at it since early this morning."

Katie glanced up from the elaborate cat's cradle pattern Jehu was attempting and smiled at Shad. "And a good job he's making of it, too."

Shad clutched his straw hat and turned strawberry red up to his ears. It was clear to Freeman that he was smitten with Katie. Every time she opened her mouth, he stared at her as if he expected pearls of wisdom to tumble out.

"Should be finished by supper time," Shad boasted. "Or tomorrow morning at the latest. Solid as the Temple of Jerusalem."

"And we know what happened to that," Freeman quipped.

Katie chuckled, and for an instant, Freeman thought she was laughing *at* him rather than *with* him, but when he looked back at her, he saw that her attention was fixed on Uncle Jehu's string and the tangle he'd made of it.

"Maybe not quite right," Uncle Jehu said before adding his own laughter to Katie's. "I think I need a little practice on Grossmama's spinning wheel."

"A little," Katie agreed. "And Freeman's right. I should be getting back to work, too." She glanced at Freeman. "I brought Sara's hair scissors. After I get the dishes cleared away, I could cut your hair for you."

"Got stuff to do of my own." Grossmama looked at Uncle Jehu. "I could use your help, Jehu," she said.

"My help?" His uncle was trying to untangle his string.

"If you can spare the time."

"*Ya*, time's something I've got plenty of," Uncle Jehu said.

The four of them quickly scattered: Shad to resume his hammering, Freeman's grandmother and uncle to do whatever it was she needed doing, and Katie to clean up the kitchen. Freeman sat there on the porch for a few more minutes.

He had to admit that minus the birds' nests and the boxes and all the rest of the clutter, the porch looked a lot better. The floor could do with a fresh coat of paint, and he still had to fix that torn screen, but Katie had scrubbed and swept and scrubbed some more. From somewhere, she'd found a large crockery butter-churn, gray with a blue wheat design, one that hadn't been used in several generations, and planted tarragon, rosemary and lavender in it. The lip of the churn had a big chip out of it, and there was a hairline crack down one side, but it looked handsome standing by the door, and the herbs made the porch smell fine.

He couldn't get to the mill until Shad finished the ramp, but Katie had promised they'd get him there by the next afternoon. It would take a big load off his mind just to make certain everything was all right with the mechanism and the grain stores. He wanted to check on his cats, too. Shad said he was feeding and watering them but he worried that their water wasn't being changed regularly.

People made a habit of dropping unwanted cats and kittens at farms or along rural roads. And he'd always had a soft spot for strays, so much so that his neighbors had brought him any they found. He wasn't sure how many cats he owned now, but he took his responsibility seriously. He provided good veterinary care and nutritious food for them. In return, the cats kept his grain stores free of rodents. He'd explained to Shad how much to feed the cats and to be certain they had fresh water every day, but Shad didn't like them. So how did he know the boy was actually caring for the cats as he should? And if he was feeding them, he certainly wasn't giving them attention, petting them or calling them by name. Some were tamer than others, but Freeman knew every cat as an individual and he was concerned for their welfare.

Shad's hammering made it difficult to think, so Freeman gave up his comfortable spot on the porch and rolled the wheelchair into the kitchen. Katie was at the sink, soap bubbles up to her elbows, scrubbing away at a large pot. "Nearly done there?" he asked.

"Almost." She turned to smile at him. "Last one."

"You can cut my hair if you're set on it. You've run on about it so much that I suppose I'll have to let you trim it up to get you to stop harping on it."

She laughed. "I suppose I have been annoying." She turned the pot upside down on the drain rack and dried her hands on a towel. "I see you shaved yourself this morning."

He rubbed at his chin. He thought he'd done a passable job. He'd gotten the job done with a nick or two. He didn't think it looked half bad. But he could see by the amused expression in her eyes that she had a different opinion.

"I'll need the razor to shave the back of your neck, so I may as well trim up those rough spots on your chin," she offered.

"Doesn't matter much one way or the other."

"It might, if you have company on Sunday. It's visiting Sunday, and it might be nice if we... I mean, if you...invited someone over. You need contact with friends, especially other men."

"That's true," he admitted. "I have a lot of fondness for my grandmother and Uncle Jehu, but it would be good to hear what someone else has to say. Nothing against you, you understand, but you're a woman."

She shrugged. "I am that." She gave him a half

smile. "So, it's settled. Your uncle said that he'd be glad to invite whomever you want. And I'll be happy to make some food for your guests and run it over on Saturday. It's always nice to have something to offer them."

"That's decent of you." Today, she was wearing a gray-blue dress. He liked the blue with her yellow hair. It suited her.

"I'll be glad to do it." She went to her basket and found the scissors. "I'd rather not do this in the kitchen," she said. "I've just swept the floor, and it's hard to get up all the little bits of hair."

"Sounds like you've done this before. Cut a man's hair."

She nodded. "I always cut my *dat*'s, and my brothers'. My mother isn't so good at cutting hair." She smiled. "It always ends up crooked."

"How about yours? Do your haircuts end up crooked?"

"Not yet." Her eyes lit with mischief and she opened and closed the scissors rapidly. "But there's always a first time."

He groaned. "Great." He glanced around. "So if not here, where? The back porch?"

"Too noisy with all that hammering," she said. "How about the front porch? It's not screened in, and with that little breeze, most of the stray hair will just blow away." She picked up the scissors, a comb and a towel that lay folded on the counter and walked purposefully toward the hallway that also led to the living room and the front entrance hall.

"What about me?" he called after her. "Aren't you going to push me out there?"

She stopped, turned, and gave him an amused look.

"*Ne.* I am not. Like you told me yesterday, your leg is broken, not your arms. You can manage."

This time when he laughed, she laughed with him.

"You should have seen him, Ellie," Katie said as she removed a still-warm egg from one of the row of hens' nests along the back wall of Sara's chicken house. "He talks about not liking to be dependent on others, then he's asking for this and that. He wants iced tea with extra ice, coffee with more milk than coffee, dumplings with extra broth." She shook her head. "It never ends."

Ellie slid her hand under a clucking hen and pulled out two eggs. "He likes the attention, I suppose."

Katie deposited her egg gently in the straw-filled basket. Sara's chicken house was so new that you could still smell the new lumber and the large casement windows were still relatively clean. The floor was ankle-deep with sawdust, and the laying boxes and roosts were painted a lovely shade of gray-blue. Katie had always been fond of chickens; they were such useful birds. She had never seen a henhouse as nice as this one, and she secretly vowed that when she had her own home, she'd have one built that was just as well-designed.

"Is he handsome?"

Katie inspected another nest. There were three eggs here, two large and one small, probably laid by one of the young pullets. "I suppose. But it's a man's character and not his looks that are important."

"So you aren't interested in him?" Ellie asked.

"Of course not. Whatever gave you that idea? I told you, the man is too set in his ways. I only agreed to help out there as a favor."

Ellie was quiet for a minute, then she said, "I was just thinking. Sara is clever. Do you think she might have placed you in Freeman's household because she thought the two of you might make a match?"

Katie made a face. "Sara wouldn't do that, would she?" She thought for a moment and then shook her head. "Doesn't matter. Freeman doesn't think that way about me. I'm not even sure that we could be friends. It seems like everything I say, he has something to say back."

"*Ach*, a shame." Ellie removed two more eggs from the last nest. "Sixteen. That's two more than yesterday. Sara will have eggs to sell soon. Johanna, down the road, has regular egg customers. English. She said she could take any extra we have and sell them for Sara."

Katie took the basket. "Did Sara tell you that I had a letter from Uriah today?"

"From your Kentucky Uriah, personally? Not from his father?"

"*Ya.*"

Ellie pushed open the chicken house door and held it for Katie. "See, you spoke too soon. He *is* interested."

"I don't know." Katie sighed and pulled a letter from her apron pocket. She set the egg basket on the grass. "Listen to what he says and then tell me whether you think he's interested."

Ellie folded her arms and waited expectantly.

"It starts with *Kathryn*. Not *Dear Kathryn*, just *Kathryn*."

"Go on."

"*You are of an age and mind to marry,*" Katie read. Ellie rolled her eyes. "Romantic."

Katie nodded. "He continues... *I am the same. Sara says that you have been baptized into the Old Order Amish Church and are in good standing with your community. Likewise. I am building a house and need a wife. If you are of a mind, I will send money for a train ticket. Best you come to Kentucky. This is the busy season for my crops and lumber mill. If you are agreeable, write and say when you are coming. I am hard-working, respectable, and not the best with words. We are not strangers because we grew up next door. I remember you were kind. My bishop tells me marriages built on faith and respect are solid ones. If you come we can see if we are a good match. If you decide not, I will pay your way back home without ill will. Your friend, Uriah.*"

Ellie nibbled at her lower lip. "Gets right to details, doesn't he?"

Katie stifled a giggle.

"But you think he's a good person?"

Katie nodded. "He was a gentle boy. Never complaining. Sweet."

Ellie pointed at the letter in Katie's hand. "I'm not sure his sweetness comes across there."

"*Ne*, it wouldn't. In school, he would never speak up, but he got good grades in math and he always included the younger children in games."

"Kind, then." Ellie considered. "So he could be a disaster...or a treasure. Hard to tell."

"Exactly." Katie picked up the basket of eggs and started toward the house. "Which is why I'm trying to decide if I should accept his offer and go to Kentucky and find out."

* * *

The mantel clock chimed nine times and Freeman paused and looked at his grandmother. "It's getting late," he said. "Should I end here?"

"Ne," she answered. "Don't stop yet. You're just getting to the exciting part."

"Go on," his uncle urged.

Freeman shifted the large German Bible on his lap and continued reading from *Exodus*, the story of Moses leading the Israelites out of slavery in Egypt. He kept on until he finished the passage and then closed the holy book. "How's my High German?" he asked.

His grandmother nodded. "Better, much better."

"You would make a good preacher," Uncle Jehu said. "You're content to let God's message speak for itself, and aren't tempted to add your own words."

"Don't wish that on me," Freeman said. Being chosen as preacher for a community was a great responsibility that lasted a lifetime. It wasn't one he would ask for. If it came, he would accept, but he'd never felt that he was called to serve the Lord that way. "There are many better shepherds among my neighbors."

His grandmother took the heavy Bible and carried it back into the front room. Freeman cherished the book. It had been passed down to him from his great-grandfather on his father's side, and it was a possession that he valued greatly. "Thank you," he called after his grandmother. "I should be the one doing that."

"And you will," Uncle Jehu said. He rose and went to the sink and came back with a glass of water. "In case you get thirsty in the night."

His grandmother returned. "I see Katie's been busy

in there, as well. That girl's a whirlwind for cleaning." She came to the bed and kissed him on the cheek. "You look so much better, Freeman. I've been worried, not so much over the broken bone in your leg, I knew that would heal, but I've been concerned about you. But I can see that your spirits have risen. You're more your old self."

"Ya," Freeman agreed. "I do feel stronger."

She gazed down at him. "Do you think that has anything to do with Katie? It seems to me that she's brought energy to this house. And to you."

"I don't know about all that," he replied, "but she's got enough energy for two women."

His grandmother smiled. "I'll bid you a good night. Sleep well."

Jehu rose. "I'll walk you to your door, Ivy."

"Walk me to my door?" She uttered a sound of amusement. "It's not fifty feet from the house. Why would I need you to do that?"

"You never know. It's a full moon tonight, and I heard some of the neighbors saying that their livestock seemed uneasy the last few nights. Raymond said something had lifted one of his Muscovy ducks. Nothing left in the yard but feathers. He thought we might have a coyote prowling around. If so, a full moon night's the worst for predators. No sense in taking any chances."

"Jehu, it's barely full dark. And what you'd do about it if a coyote did come up in the yard, I'm not sure."

His uncle held open the kitchen door for all. "All the same, Ivy, I'll rest easier knowing you're safe inside." She shrugged and gave in good-naturedly, and the two left together. As the door closed behind them,

Freeman could hear his uncle talking about wanting to go to Dover in the morning.

Freeman lay back against his pillows. It had been a good day, he realized, an excellent day. Truthfully, he hadn't had such a good day in a long time. Was it possible that his grandmother had hit on something when she'd linked Katie to the improvement in his health and spirits?

Was that possible?

Chapter Six

Katie reined in her horse close to the back door of Freeman's house and called a greeting to Ivy and Jehu on the porch. It was Saturday afternoon, and she'd brought the groceries that they'd asked her to pick up for them at Bylers' Country Store as well as the fried chicken and potato salad that she'd prepared for them for Sunday. Both Sara and Ellie had insisted on sending something as well: coleslaw and a sweet potato pie from Sara, and Ellie's pickled eggs and an applesauce cake. Since no cooking would be done on the Sabbath, everything could be eaten cold.

"There was no need for you to go to the trouble," Jehu insisted as she began to carry the dishes into the kitchen. "But I'm glad you did. My mouth is watering already."

"And I do appreciate you saving me a trip to the store." Ivy followed them inside. "Did we give you enough money?"

"More than enough," Katie assured them. "I have change for you both." She glanced around the kitchen.

Both Freeman and the wheelchair were nowhere in sight. "I see Freeman managed to get himself outside."

"Ya," Ivy replied with a beaming countenance. "Eli and Charley stopped by to see him. Nothing would do but that they all go out to the horseshoe pit. They usually play horseshoes one evening every week in decent weather."

"Pretty warm out there," Uncle Jehu commented. "Might be they're thirsty by now. Would it be too much trouble for you to take them some cool water?" He waved toward the mill. "The horseshoe pit is on the far side of the mill, near the little pond. Just follow the path. You can't miss them."

"Of course I wouldn't mind," Katie answered. "But I don't want to intrude on Freeman and his friends."

"Nonsense." Ivy peeked into one of the paper grocery bags she'd carried in from Katie's buggy. "This is the best week Freeman has had since his injury. You've perked up his spirits more than the doctor's medicine. I know he'd be happy to see you. And I'm sure they'd appreciate the water."

"Throwing horseshoes is hot work," Uncle Jehu added as he removed three pint-size canning jars from the cabinet. "And a drink delivered by a pretty face is always welcome."

"And what makes you think I have a pretty face?" Katie teased, putting things into the refrigerator. "I might have a nose like a sweet potato and whiskers on my chin."

"Ivy told me," he answered. "But it wouldn't matter if you did have a big nose and *no* chin. Beauty comes from inside, and your words and actions show me more than I could ever see when I had my sight."

Katie swallowed, touched by Jehu's opinion of her. "Then," she managed, "you must know that you have a pretty face, too."

"Pretty hairy," Ivy said, and they all chuckled.

"Well, I can do better than water for the men folk," Katie said. "I brought blackberry iced tea. I'll take some of this cake, too."

Once the groceries and food were put away, Katie packed slices of cake, napkins, a quart of the blackberry tea and the jars to be used for glasses in her wicker basket and carried it down the hill. She followed the man-made water-course around the mill to a picnic area. Freeman was sitting in his wheelchair in the shade of a tree, his broken leg elevated by the leg rest. He was laughing and shouting suggestions to the two men throwing horseshoes.

Freeman's two friends stood at the farthest peg, and Katie recognized the taller man from the chair shop in Seven Poplars. Eli was a skilled craftsman and the manager and partial owner of the Amish-run business. Eli saw her, waved and made a throw that clanked as it hit the peg. The other man, shorter and blond-haired, groaned and made a show of throwing his straw hat down beside the peg and pretending that he was going to stomp on it.

She put her basket down on one of the picnic tables near where Freeman sat. "Anyone thirsty?" she called. "I brought some blackberry tea and cake."

"Katie." Freeman's smiled widened as his friends walked toward them. "This is Katie Byler, the girl I told you was helping out while I'm laid up," he explained. "Katie, this is Eli and Charley. He's a Byler, too. Are you two cousins by any chance?"

"Ne," Katie replied. "Not that I know of."

"Lots of Bylers," Charley agreed. "Glad to know you, Katie, even if we aren't cousins." He beat the sand off his hat on his trouser leg and replaced it on his head. "And I'd like some of that tea. Eli's been feeding me dust this afternoon."

Eli, a nice-looking dark-haired man about Freeman's age, walked up behind Charley to join them. "How's that chair working out for you?" he asked Katie. "Her brother broke a kitchen chair and she ordered a new one from the shop," he said. "Oak, wasn't it?" he asked Katie.

"It was." She poured the first jar of tea and handed it to Charley. "And so far my brothers haven't got the best of it."

Charley looked from Freeman to Katie. "Been some job, hasn't it?" he teased. "Cleaning a path through Freeman's kitchen?"

Seeing that Freeman was smiling, she smiled, too. "It wasn't that bad."

"This is fine tea, Katie." Charley took a gulp. "I appreciate it."

"You're welcome," she answered, handing Eli and then Freeman jars of the blackberry tea. "But don't let me interfere in your game. I was just on my way home."

"Ne, don't go yet," Freeman protested, good-naturedly. "Stay a while. I need you to help me keep an eye on Charley. He cheats if you don't watch him close." He motioned toward a tree stump beside his wheelchair. "Sit here with me."

"I'm not a cheat!" Charley retorted, then grinned. "And if I did nudge my horseshoe an inch closer to the peg, it would be because I learned the trick from

Freeman when we were kids." He drained his glass in four gulps. *"Goot!"* he pronounced. "Really taste those blackberries. I'll have to tell my Miriam to make some." He wiped his mouth with the back of his hand and set the jar on the picnic table. "I thank you for the drink, but I want you to know that Freeman is only making fun. I really don't *need* to cheat to beat him at horseshoes."

Freeman groaned. "Listen to you. How long has it been since you beat me? Months. Tell her, Eli."

Eli offered a slow smile that lit his eyes. "Let's finish this game and I'll give you my opinion on who's a good player and who's not." He downed his drink and walked back to the horseshoe pit. "Winner plays Freeman," he called.

"I wish," Freeman replied. "I'd be doing well to balance on one foot without trying to toss a shoe in the right direction."

"Maybe he could throw from the wheelchair," Katie suggested.

Freeman frowned. "I doubt that's possible."

"Of course you could do it," Katie encouraged. "You could try, at least. You never know. You might be a better horseshoe thrower sitting down than standing."

"Easy for you to say." Freeman glanced at her sideways. "But I'd be the one looking like a fool."

"She's right," Charley said. "Good idea, Katie. We'll even spot him half the distance. What more could he ask for?"

"Who's saying that you'll be playing Freeman?" Eli called. "The last time I counted, I was ahead."

"Just warming up," Charley answered.

Katie laughed as the men resumed their game. When

she glanced back at Freeman, she found him studying her. Self-conscious, she turned away and saw a boy in his early teens accompanied by a much smaller child, walking down from the mill. The boys were carrying cane fishing poles and the older one had a tin can, presumably bait, she thought. "Looks like you have some fishermen," she said, gesturing toward the newcomers.

"The King boys." Freeman waved, and the young people waved back. "I let the neighbor kids fish down here. It's safer than the big pond because the banks aren't as steep and the water is much shallower here. Good for little kids. Lots of sunfish and a few nice-sized catfish." He raised an eyebrow. "The water's too warm and not deep enough for the big bass."

"You seem to know a lot about fishing."

"Not as much as I'd like to." He offered a hint of a smile. "The bass still outsmart me most of the time. Grossmama says it's good for my character. She thinks I show a lack of humility as it is."

Katie laughed.

He cocked his head. "That mean you agree with her?"

She shrugged.

"Still," she said, "it's kind of you to give the children a place to fish." Charley yelped with pleasure, and she glanced back toward the horseshoe players to see that he'd made a ringer. "I like your friends."

"I've known them for years. They're good men."

And I think you are, too, Katie mused as she watched Freeman finish a slice of the cake and toss the crumbs to a mother mallard and her ducklings that paddled over to beg for scraps. The baby ducklings were adorable, small bobbing balls of feathers with black eyes.

They couldn't have been much more than a week or two old. "It's nice here," she observed with a contented sigh. "Peaceful."

Charley groaned as Eli won the round.

"In spite of Charley?" Freeman teased.

"Ya," she answered. "In spite of Charley." She turned her attention to the little boy on the edge of the pond who was concentrating on his fishing line with the cork bobber. The child was as cute as the ducklings. He wore dark trousers, a straw hat and a green shirt identical to his older brother. Both boys were barefoot and had the same light brown hair, blue eyes and freckled snub noses. "They look so much alike, they must be brothers," she said, indicating the youthful fishermen.

"They are," Freeman said.

Katie's gaze lingered on the smallest boy. She could imagine having a son like that of her own some day. Seeing him reminded her that having children, having a family of her own, was her main reason for considering Uriah's offer.

"Freeman!" Eli called. "You're up. Roll yourself over here and prepare for a whipping."

"Go on," Katie urged. "Try it, at least. You can't do any worse than Charley."

"Thanks a lot," Charley said. But his easy grin told her that he'd taken no offense at her teasing.

"Maybe Katie would like to show us how the game is played." Freeman threw her a challenging look.

"You think I couldn't?" she flung back playfully.

"Come on, Katie," Charley dared. "Start him off. Throw just one set for Freeman."

Freeman glanced at Charley. "Don't encourage her."

Katie put down the jars she'd been gathering and

walked over to the peg. She reached down and picked up a horseshoe. "Are you certain you want me to throw this? I might show the three of you up."

Eli stepped back to give her room. "We'll take the risk. Go ahead. Throw."

"For who?" she asked. "You or Freeman?"

"By all means, start off for me," Freeman called. "Start me off with a ringer."

Katie turned the heavy horseshoe in her hand, gauging the weight.

"Come one, Katie. You can do it!" Freeman encouraged.

Here goes nothing, she thought. She sighted the far peg, took a long stride and let the horseshoe fly out of her grasp exactly the way her father had taught her. And then, unconsciously, she shut her eyes. She gritted her teeth, prepared for the men's laughter, but instead, what she heard was the solid metal clunk of her horseshoe striking the peg.

"Ringer!" Charley yelled.

"Good throw," Eli pronounced.

"Look at that!" Charley yelped with excitement. "A ringer. First try."

Opening her eyes, she turned to Freeman and threw him a triumphant look. His face showed his obvious surprise...and something else she couldn't quite put her finger on. "I played with my brothers," she explained, suddenly feeling embarrassed, with no idea why. She walked toward him. "Every Saturday. And they never spotted me any distance. Not since I was eleven years old."

Freeman didn't say anything, only nodded, but he kept watching her. Studying her.

Katie gathered up the empty jars the men had drunk from, feeling flushed and slightly uncomfortable. Why did Freeman keep looking at her?

"Thank you for the tea and the cake," Eli said. "I appreciate it."

"We all appreciate it," Charley added. "And, Katie, you can play doubles with me anytime."

As Katie turned to walk away, Freeman spoke loud enough for only her to hear him. "I never expected that. Not in a hundred years, Katie." His voice was surprisingly gentle and filled with... What was that? *Admiration?*

Katie mumbled something about seeing him Monday and walked briskly up the hill, carrying her basket. Halfway to her buggy, her heart was still beating too fast. What was wrong with her? she wondered. And then it occurred to her why she was feeling this way...happy and scared at the same time. Hot and cold. Bold and shy.

She stopped in midstride, taking her basket in her arms and clutching it tightly. She had to be mistaken. It couldn't be true.

She couldn't possibly *like* Freeman.

Chapter Seven

Freeman stretched his good leg and shifted his weight to find a more comfortable position in the wheelchair. They'd finished the noon meal more than an hour earlier, and the porch with its faint breeze off the millpond was a cool retreat from the midsummer sun. Katie had returned to her task of pulling weeds in the flowerbed by the steps after clearing away the dinner dishes, and he'd been just sitting here watching her. He was surprisingly in a good mood. It was nice, after the quiet weekend, having Katie back at the house again with all her chatter and giving orders, so nice that he couldn't think of much to complain about.

"Finding any flowers in there?" he called to her. "Or just weeds?"

"Plenty of flowers." Katie tossed another handful of chickweed into the wheelbarrow.

"Grossmama said she had perennials in there, but I couldn't see them," Freeman said. "I was meaning to try and clean them up for her, but I had so much to do at the mill, I just didn't get to it."

"I can see that," Katie replied. She'd come prepared

for outdoor work today. Her apron was a sturdy one, her blue dress faded from much use and many washings, and her pinned-up hair covered with a denim-blue scarf instead of her usual *kapp.* The blue of her dress made her eyes seem even bluer. He wondered how it was that he hadn't noticed how large her eyes were and how they didn't seem to miss a thing.

"So Ivy asked you to do some weeding for her?" Katie said.

"A while back." He shrugged. "But I've been really busy. Did you have a good visiting Sunday?" he asked in an attempt to steer the conversation away from his failings in the yard maintenance department. His Sunday had been somewhat of a disappointment. They were supposed to have company, as Katie had suggested, but that fell through. An illness in the family. So there'd been no one here to talk to but his grandmother and Uncle Jehu, and they'd spent so much time together recently that they'd already heard all of each others' stories and opinions. He'd enjoyed seeing Eli and Charley on Saturday, and the next day had been a bit of a letdown after the fun he'd had with them. And, he had to admit, with Katie. Seeing her in a social capacity had been surprising, but in a good way. His buddies would be talking for a long time about the ringer that Katie had made.

"It was nice," Katie said. "Sara had a bunch of company. Rebecca and her husband came by with their family, and brought home-made peach ice cream. And there were…other people."

Freeman smiled. "Sounds as if I missed something good."

"You did. Sara and Ellie made lemon pound cake on

Saturday, and it was nice to have the peach ice cream to serve with the cake to guests."

The cake and ice cream sounded like something he would have enjoyed. Why hadn't she thought to bring him a slice of cake? He was especially fond of lemon pound cake, so much so that he could almost taste it. "Must be pretty lively living at Sara's," Freeman observed. "Always somebody coming by."

"I like it. It's not home, of course, but Sara makes me feel as if it is."

"You said *other people*. Who else came to visit?" he asked.

She hesitated. "There was LeRoy, a cousin of someone. Guengerich, I think Sara said his last name was. Up visiting relatives from western Virginia. She said that he wanted to meet me."

"One of Sara's clients?" Freeman frowned. He didn't know any Geungerichs from Virginia, but he could picture the man in his imagination—tall, rangy, hat brim a little too wide, and beady eyes too close together. Freeman seemed to recall that someone had told him that those members of ultra-conservative churches in the mountains wore only a single suspender on their trousers. Two suspenders were deemed too fancy. He wondered if this LeRoy fit the image. "Is he in the market for a wife?"

Katie glanced up at him and shrugged. She had stopped weeding. "Doesn't matter if he is or isn't. We didn't hit it off. He asked me to go for a walk with him, but we didn't have much to talk about. Mostly he went on about the mildew in his garden. I don't think I responded the way he wanted me to. He lost interest pretty quickly after I told him he should make a spray from baking soda and dish soap and treat it with that."

"What makes you think he wasn't interested in you?" Freeman straightened up, liking the tale better now that it was clear that this Virginia stranger hadn't taken Katie's fancy.

"Because when he left Sara's after the ice cream and cake, he went home to take supper with Jane Stutzman."

"Jane? I know her. Pretty girl."

"*Ya*, she is. I'm sure LeRoy thought so."

"But if he wasn't to your liking, what difference does it make who he had supper with?"

She stood up and brushed the dirt off her skirt. "It doesn't. I'm not really seeking a match, anyway. I'm already spoken for—sort of. I'm seriously considering the suit of an old neighbor of mine. Uriah. And he's already said that he is willing to marry me."

"Old, huh?" Freeman frowned. "How old? Old enough to be your father? Your grandfather?"

Katie laughed. "*Ne*. Nothing like that. Uriah's my age. I just meant that we grew up next door to each other. Did you think I was planning on marrying a graybeard?"

He considered. "It happens. Lots of girls marry older men, especially girls who have a hard time in the marriage market."

Her eyebrows went up and he could tell her dander was ruffled. "You think I'm having a *hard time*?"

He shrugged. "No offense, but Sara, well, we all know that she specializes in hard-to-place cases."

"And?"

Freeman couldn't tell by the expression on Katie's face now whether she was annoyed or intrigued by the way this conversation was going. "You *are* living with the matchmaker."

"So you think that means I'm one of Sara's hard-to-place matches?"

"I didn't say that." He rolled the wheelchair closer to the open screen door. "It's just that Sara has a reputation for being the best at what she does. I'm surprised that she'd introduce you to this LeRoy and then he'd run off to Jane Stutzman's and leave you standing there. Doesn't sound like the type of man Sara should be trying to fix you up with. The whole idea of a matchmaker is to find someone suitable for you. Obviously LeRoy wasn't someone who would be suitable."

Katie folded her arms and got a stubborn look on her face. There was a little bit of dirt on her chin, and he thought about mentioning it to her, but it seemed as though she was already on edge, so he didn't. "So you have something against matchmakers? Or is it Sara you doubt?"

"I like Sara well enough."

"So it's the whole matchmaker thing?"

Freeman shrugged.

"Funny you should think that."

"And why is that?"

She fixed him with a stare that could have burned through steel. "It just strikes me as odd, you having so many opinions on me finding a husband when you're older than I am and have no wife. Surely the church elders have mentioned it to you. Most men your age have a family already."

"I'll marry when the time is right," he answered brusquely. "I have a lot of responsibility with the mill and—"

"Sound like excuses to me." She came up the steps to the porch and he had to roll back to make way for her. "With men," she went on, "it should be easy. You are the ones who do the asking. Women have to wait for someone to notice them."

"And go to matchmakers, apparently."

"Some do," she agreed. "I think it's better to consider someone like Sara who's made dozens of matches—maybe even hundreds. And not one of her couples has ever failed. Can you believe that? Every marriage arrangement she made has been a success. Look what she did for Addy and Gideon Esch. Have you been to the new butcher shop?"

Freeman nodded.

"Everyone thought that Addy would stay home with her mother until her hair turned gray, but Sara found her a husband. And they're happy. Sara says that they'll be welcoming a little dishwasher or sausage maker into their family by winter."

"Theirs does seem like a good match," he agreed. "And from what I hear, Gideon's parents were in despair of his finding a wife. So, it seems that Sara—"

"Knew what she was doing when she brought them together," Katie finished, cutting him off. "Like I said. She's good at what she does." Her expression changed, becoming suddenly vulnerable. "But it doesn't seem to be working for me. Not unless you count Uriah, and his family contacted Sara, not him. It was my brother Isaac who suggested we let Sara handle the negotiations."

He gave a doubtful grunt. "Negotiations? Sounds like Uriah is buying a sheep. How long has it been since the two of you have seen each other? Exchanged words?"

"A year. Maybe a little longer. But it's not as though he's a stranger," she added quickly. "And we know the family well. They're good people, well thought of by their church community."

He rolled back to make room for her. "You've never met anyone here in Kent County you wanted to marry? None of the boys you grew up with? Walked out with?" he added.

"*Ne.* I've ridden home from singings with boys a couple of times, but no one has ever wanted to walk out with me. Sometimes, I wonder if there's something wrong with me. I see younger girls courting, marrying. Even having their first child. And I'm still living with my mother and brother. And now his wife." Her eyes grew large and wistful as she sat down on the edge of a chair. "So I have a lot of faith in Sara and her wisdom, maybe not so much in myself when it comes to finding the right man."

He lowered his cast to the floor, leaned forward, and lowered his voice. "Are you asking my opinion?"

She looked up suddenly. "Your opinion? On what?"

"You know. Your...trouble. Dating."

She drew herself up, the apples of her cheeks growing rosy. "Certainly not. I'm just explaining to you why Sara—"

"Well, since you asked," he said, interrupting. "My guess is that you're a little too outspoken for a woman. Too quick to give your opinion on things."

"What do you mean by that?" She rose and began to pace the length of the porch. "Do you think I should be like Jane? Say, '*Ya*, LeRoy,' and never have a thought of my own?"

"I didn't say that. I *said*, that in my estimation, you

have too many opinions. You never hold back from giving them, asked for or not."

"Why shouldn't I speak my mind?" she demanded, spinning around to come toward him. "You do. You've got opinions on how scrapple should be cooked, how much milk goes in coffee even when it's not yours," she sputtered. "Men give opinions all the time."

"But you're not a man. You're a young woman. Hasn't someone ever told you that you should show more...more..." He hesitated, searching for the right word.

She stopped in front of him and waved away his argument with a quick gesture. "Maybe it's in my nature, or maybe because I grew up in a household with brothers, but I've never wasted time with mealy-mouth pretense. I'm a sensible woman with just as good a mind as you or any other man. If I think something, I say it."

"That might do among the Englishers, but the bishops tell us that a woman's place is—"

"I know what the Bible says." She dropped her hands to her hips. "If I had a husband, I would show him the respect due—"

"But you have no husband." He shrugged. "Maybe your headstrong attitude is the reason. You have a face and form to attract any man with eyes in his head, but your manner—"

"You approve of my face, then?" She cocked her head to one side.

"I'm sorry." He felt his face grow warm. "I shouldn't have said that."

She studied him, seeming to consider if he was being truthful. "You think I'm pretty? Is that what you're giving your opinion on now? My looks?"

"Katie Byler. You are the most outrageous…" For seconds, it seemed to him that his enjoyable afternoon was fast sliding into chaos. And then he shook his head and chuckled. "You're never boring. I'll say that for you."

Katie didn't take that as the compliment he meant it to be. She pointed at him. "Back to what you were saying. So, you approve of my being pretty so long as I mind my tongue and don't speak my mind?"

"I didn't say that. You asked me why you weren't attracting more suitors and I—"

"I did *not* ask you that," she exclaimed. "You took it upon yourself to give your view on a matter that I consider none of your affair." She headed back down the porch steps. "I think it's time we ended this conversation before one of us says something that we can't take back." She pointed toward the kitchen. "There are leftovers in the refrigerator. I'm going back to Sara's, where I won't offend anyone with my outrageous behavior."

"But it's early," he said, immediately contrite. He didn't want her to go. The best part of his day was when she was here…even when she was giving her opinions. "You never leave this early. I was hoping that I could have a little more iced tea before—"

"You know where it is," she said, charging down the sidewalk, barefoot. "You're capable of fetching your own tea."

"Wait. If you're bound on going, I'll have Shad hitch up your buggy and—"

She raised her hand. "No need. I can do it myself. A handy skill if I'm going to be left an old maid." With that, she turned her back on him, and hurried off, her back stiff, her movements quick and sharp.

Freeman stared after her, not certain what had gone wrong. All he'd done was give her his honest opinion.

Now she was angry with him.

Thunder rumbled in the distance as Katie hurried to Sara's clothesline. When she'd left Freeman's house, barefoot and without her basket, the sun had been shining. By the time she turned the horse into Sara's lane half an hour later, dark clouds were scudding overhead and the sky in the west was fast darkening.

Katie jerked a bath towel from the line so hard that two clothespins catapulted into the air. Mumbling under her breath, she shook out the towel, folded it quickly and tossed it into a laundry basket in the grass. Try as she might, she couldn't get Freeman's advice out of her head. She was annoyed... and his know-it-all attitude had ruined what had been a lovely day for her.

And to think... Saturday she'd actually thought she might be falling for him. She felt as if steam might come out of her ears.

What made Freeman Kemp think that he had the right to criticize her? she fumed. And not only her. He'd insinuated that Sara didn't know what she was doing. Not to mention the unkind things he'd hinted at about Uriah, a man he'd never met. What had ever caused her to have such a high opinion of Freeman, she didn't know. No wonder he was well on his way to being an old bachelor. She yanked a dishtowel off the clothesline, sending another pin flying.

"Whoa. What has the laundry done to you today?"

Sara began to gather the fallen clothespins. "A bad day?"

"Ach." Katie shook her head. "I'm sorry. I didn't mean to…" She sighed and let her thought go unexpressed.

Sara dropped the clothespins into their bag and reached for the top corner of a sheet. "I don't know who got on your bad side but I wouldn't want to be that person."

Together, Katie and Sara removed and folded the sheet neatly.

"Forgive me." Katie exhaled. "I'm just in a sour mood."

Sara moved along the clothesline with efficiency. "What went wrong at Freeman's?"

Katie felt the steam rising again. "That man."

"What?" Sara asked. "You came home Saturday all smiles and talk of him. I thought you liked him."

"I did." Then Katie quickly corrected herself. "I mean, I *do* like him—as an employer. But…"

Sara's dark eyes twinkled as she reached for a white pillowcase snapping in the wind. "But…he said something to set you off."

"Yes. No. He's just…" She searched for the right words, ones that might not sound judgmental. "So sure of himself."

"About?"

"You name it."

"Anything in particular?" Sara pressed.

Katie leaned over the clothesline. "He took it upon himself to give me advice about finding a husband."

"Oh, my." Sara's bonnet strings fluttered in the breeze.

"It's none of his affair," Katie said.

"I'd heard that Freeman was outspoken," Sara replied. She tucked several clothespins in her mouth and began to snatch washcloths off the line.

The first drops of rain spattered on Katie's cheeks. "Oh, no!" she cried, and she hurried to get the clothes down before rain drenched them. Grabbing the last towels, Katie added them to the laundry basket, picked it up and ran for the open carriage shed with Sara two steps behind.

Laughing, they ducked into the shelter seconds before the first wave of rain hit the roof of the outbuilding. "That was a close one," Sara said.

Katie nodded. It was a three-bay shed containing Sara's buggy and small pony cart, her own buggy, and racks for holding the harnesses and cleaning supplies. The space smelled of leather and the peeled cedar crossbeams that formed the structure of the roof. Katie had always been fond of carriage sheds. For Amish children, they were a favorite spot to play in all seasons, cool and shady in summer and out of the wind and weather in winter.

"I'm sorry for being so contrary," Katie said after a moment.

"*Ne.* I have always believed in heeding your feelings. Keep them bottled up inside and eventually they explode."

"But I didn't need to take my temper out on the wash," Katie allowed.

Sara shrugged. "Why not? You can't hurt a towel's feelings. And clothespins are made of wood. What can they expect but to end up as kindling?" She sat on a wagon seat that her hired help, Hiram, used when he cleaned and oiled the harness. She motioned for Katie to sit beside her.

Lightning struck a dead tree across the pasture and Katie blinked at the flash and loud crack. Rain sheeted down the roof and formed a curtain at the front of the shed. "I think we got the wash in just in time," she mused.

"You think?" Sara laughed. She pulled her legs up and wrapped her arms around them as a child might do. She was barefoot, her skin tanned to a honey-brown, her small, sturdy feet high-arched. "You're not afraid of storms, are you?"

Katie shook her head.

"Me, neither." Sara stared out the open doorway. "In fact, I've always liked them. Of course, I don't care to be outside when there's lightning nearby. I'm not so foolish. But this is nice, hearing the rain on the roof, and knowing how much the garden and the farmers' crops will love the water."

"It is a good sound," Katie agreed. With the arrival of the storm, her anxiety had passed. Freeman's words no longer had as much power to affect her as they had. Maybe because now that she'd calmed down a little, she knew in her heart of hearts that he hadn't meant to be unkind to her. It was just his way. Maybe a little bit like her own way, sometimes.

"Rain always eases the heat." Katie glanced sideways at Sara, thinking how wise and calm the older woman seemed. Without realizing that she was going to share what had happened with Sara, she found herself repeating the conversation between her and Freeman that had upset her so.

"It sounds as though he meant well," Sara offered. Mischief gleamed in her expression. "But men rarely understand very much about women and the way they will accept well-meaning, if poorly expressed, advice."

"He's a fine one to tell me how to find a husband when he's obviously had no luck finding a wife," Katie declared.

"But do you think he was trying to be unpleasant in saying those things?" Sara asked.

"*Ne*, but—"

"Then he said them either as a friend or as an interested party."

Katie looked at Sara and blinked. "What do you mean, *interested party*?"

Sara shrugged. "Maybe that's not right. It's probably that he is genuinely concerned. You've been a big help to him and his family. I'm sure that he means well."

Katie didn't say anything.

"And maybe…" Sara fixed her with a compelling gaze. "There's some merit in what the man said."

Katie was taken aback. "You're not taking Freeman's side?"

Sara laced her fingers together. "Personally, I like outspoken women. I've often been accused of speaking my mind, as well. But I'm not in the market for a husband. It might be that once you stop smarting from the supposed insult, you'll give some thought about the good sense of what he said."

"So I should simper and stare at the ground and say, '*Ya*, Freeman. Whatever you think, Freeman'?"

"Only if you want him to take you for a very silly girl," Sara told her, laughing. She stood. "The rain is letting up. You can bring the clothes in with you when you come." She smiled at her. "Just think about it, Katie. And ask yourself why a man like Freeman would take such an interest in a female friend's affairs." Sara removed her apron and pulled it over her head and dashed out of the shed, walking swiftly toward the house.

Katie followed a few steps until she stood at the edge of the shed. Drops of water were still sliding off the roof and they splashed cool and clean across her face. What had Sara meant by that, she wondered. Could it be that Freeman was right and she was wrong? Or was it more than that? Why did Freeman care about her finding a husband?

Chapter Eight

Katie squeezed the sponge, letting the excess soapy water fall back into the pail before turning again to the dirty windowsill, which she attacked with glee. She couldn't guess when Freeman's parlor woodwork had last been scrubbed, and it gave her a fierce satisfaction to clean away every trace of dust and cobwebs so that the room would be fit to host church Sundays once he'd fully recovered from his accident. It was a lovely front room, or it would be when she finished with it.

There were two windows on the front and a fireplace and another window on the west wall. The fireplace had been closed up and a cast-iron stove added for heating, but the original mantel still remained, as well as the original hardwood floor. The dwelling had been built in the early nineteenth century as a simple farmhouse and it retained much of the original plastered walls and handcrafted wainscoting. Once the windows were washed, the room would be clean and bright and perfect for prayer and contemplating the glory of God.

Thunderstorms had passed in the night, leaving the morning cool and refreshing; it would be a nice day to work outside. If she got all the woodwork in here scrubbed before it was time to begin the noon meal, she might have time to start painting the porch outside this afternoon. Ivy had assured her that there was unopened white paint in the cellar that had been purchased for the front and back porch. As with weeding the flowerbeds, Freeman had had good intentions, but hadn't gotten to the actual painting.

The thought of him made her smile.

Freeman had been unusually pleasant at breakfast, praising the crispiness of her scrapple and taking a second helping of her *pfannkuchen* served with Sara's homemade blueberry syrup. She'd half expected him to be cross after their exchange the previous afternoon and her leaving early in a huff, but he made no mention of it, and she was content to let ruffled feathers lie.

She eyed the smudgy windowpanes that were six over six. They would be next, both inside and out. She'd seen ammonia under the kitchen sink, and used copies of the *Budget* would do to shine the glass to a fare-thee-well. She'd scrub this room from top to bottom and bring in flowers from Ivy's garden so that the spacious chamber would glow with welcome. It was a fine old house that Freeman had inherited from his parents, and if he ever found a bride to please him, she'd not have cause to complain that a careless housekeeper had left it untidy.

She dipped her sponge again into the soapy water and, hearing a sound behind her, turned to see Freeman in the doorway. He was in his wheelchair, attempting to maneuver his outstretched leg through the opening.

"I can't find the scissors. The large ones with the black handles," he said. "Do you know where they are?"

"In the big drawer below the window, just to the left of the sink," she answered as she squeezed the excess water from the sponge. "Where they belong, and where you should be sure to put them when you're done with them."

His eyebrows went up. "You think I need to be told to put away my own scissors?"

She nodded. "If you put them back in the same place every time, you'll always know where to find them. Can't find them if one day they're left here, the next there." She gestured with the sponge.

He gave her a rueful look. "They are *my* scissors. I think I'm free to put them where I like."

She shrugged. "*Ya*, but of no use to you if you can't find them."

"I'll have you know that I organize all my tools and know exactly where they are."

She beamed at him. "An excellent practice." She hesitated. "Can you think of somewhere you'd rather keep the kitchen scissors than the kitchen drawer? On the porch, maybe?"

"*Ne*. They'd soon rust out there. The big drawer is fine."

"Good. We agree." She shook the damp sponge at him to emphasize her instruction. "All I'm saying is, remember to put them back. I found them under your hospital bed yesterday, and last week they were on the porch." She turned back to the windowsill and began to scrub it again. It was time that they moved the bed out of the kitchen. If he could get himself in and out of the wheelchair, there was no reason his bed couldn't go in the empty downstairs bedroom. The kitchen would be easier to maintain without his bed taking up a large portion of it.

There was no sound indicating the departure of the wheelchair. Katie glanced over her shoulder. "Something else you need?"

Freeman straightened his shoulders and an odd, almost embarrassed expression flickered over his handsome face. "Katie?"

"Ya?" She lowered her sponge and gave him her full attention.

He took a deep breath. "I hope...that is... I..." His forehead creased and he stopped and then started again. "I wanted to ask you. Did I hurt your feelings yesterday, saying what I did about you being outspoken?"

"Ne. What would make you think that?" She didn't meet his gaze, but she could feel her cheeks flush.

"You seemed...well...you left in a rush. Early. And you left your shoes."

Now she felt a little silly. "I did finish early. I needed to get home ahead of the storm," she said quickly, which was true, after a fashion, and not exactly a fabrication. She decided to ignore the subject of her shoes. "And a good thing that I did. Lightning struck a tree—"

"On the road when you were driving back to Sara's?" He rolled the wheelchair a little farther into the room.

She shook her head, feeling foolish that she'd made something of nothing in an effort to cover her own discomfort. *"Ne.* After I got home. It was just a dead tree in the neighbor's field."

"Lightning can be dangerous. I knew it to strike a man's horse once, while he was driving. The animal was never the same. Never safe to trust in harness again."

She dropped her sponge in the bucket and took a few steps toward Freeman. "I was in no danger," she admitted. "And my horse was already safe in Sara's barn."

"Good." He struck the armrest of the chair with the flat of his hand to emphasize his words. "I'd feel responsible if you came to harm on the way home from the mill."

She smiled, touched by his genuine concern for her welfare. "It would hardly be your fault," she said lightly. "You have no control over the weather."

"I guess not, but I'd feel responsible just the same."

"But I'm clearly not hurt."

He chuckled. "Or the horse."

She smiled again and nodded agreement. "Or the horse, thanks be to God."

"Amen to that."

He smiled back at her, and before she could think better of it, she asked, "What kind of things? Specifically."

"I'm sorry?" he answered.

She wondered if it was mistake, going down this path, but it was too late. And maybe she really did care what he thought. "Yesterday. When you said I was too outspoken. What did you mean? What sort of things do I say that make me outspoken?"

Freeman pressed his lips together in a thin line and tugged at the lobe of one ear. "Are you sure you want to hear this? It's just my opinion."

She nodded. "*Ya*, I want to know." She shrugged. "Being myself doesn't seem to be working. Maybe a man's perspective could be..." Not just any man's, she thought. Freeman's perspective, because increasingly, what he thought mattered to her. "Maybe you could tell me," she suggested. "Point out what I say or do that's offensive, when I do it."

He ran a hand through his hair. He wasn't wearing a hat, and it struck her how nice his hair looked now that she'd cut it and he'd washed it. There were little highlights of auburn that shimmered when he moved his head. His hair had felt soft and smelled good. She could remember the smooth texture as it had slipped through her fingers. Cutting Freeman's hair had been nothing like cutting her brothers' hair and she wondered if it had been immodest of her to initiate such an intimate task.

"I didn't say you were offensive."

She just stood there looking at him.

"I don't want to hurt your feelings," he said huskily.

She crossed her arms, waiting.

He exhaled, knowing he wasn't going to get out of this. "It's not always *what* you say," he told her slowly. "So much as *the way* you say it."

She swallowed, her mouth dry. "I don't understand. Give me an example."

He hesitated. "It's…well…like you just did. About the scissors."

She stiffened, feeling suddenly self-conscious. "You were offended because I asked you to put them back when you were finished with them? If you already knew to do it, you wouldn't have had to come to me asking where they were."

"And there's that, too. That's what I mean." He pointed at her. "I'll tell you what raises a man's hackles. It's not about right or wrong. It's your tone. It comes out sounding as if you're giving orders to a child."

"But that wasn't my intention." Now she was upset

that he had taken her words all wrong. "Truly, all I was doing was stating the truth. I certainly don't consider you a child. It's just that in my experience, men... most men never remember to put household items back where they belong. They simply leave them lying where they've last used them."

"But I don't do that," he defended. "At least I don't think I do."

"Someone did," she reminded him. "Twice the scissors were left out this week."

He looked down, exhaled and looked up at her again. "Point taken. But when you brought up the scissors, you didn't politely ask me to put them back where I'd found them. You *told* me where I should put them when I was done. And you were quick to point out the previous error of my ways."

Katie thought for a moment and then grimaced. "When you put it like that, I can see what you mean. It didn't come out as I intended. I was joking." She met his gaze. "Sort of."

"Then you should have made it clear that you were teasing. A smile would have helped. A softer tone, maybe." He exhaled as if considering his next words. "Katie, the truth is that...you can be intimidating."

"Me?" She touched her collarbone, in genuine surprise. "Intimidating? To a man?"

"*Particularly* to a man."

"Okay." She gritted her teeth. "Maybe I am a little overbearing at times. I'll give you that. But if you knew my brothers and how they—"

"Sorry, Katie. No excuse. I'm not your brother, and neither is any young man you might want to walk out with. And I...or *he* would rather not be chastised by a pretty girl he's interested in. The minute a man hears a woman talking like that, he begins to imagine what it will sound like in twenty years. Truth be told, it scares us."

What registered first was that he'd referred to her as a pretty girl again, and the second was that when she'd told Sara what had happened, Sara had said nearly the same thing.

She felt herself smiling again. She couldn't help it. *Freeman thought she was pretty.* She met his gaze again and realized he was waiting for her to say something. "So...you think it something so simple that's keeping me from finding a beau?" she ventured, her voice sounding low and husky. *He thought she was pretty.* "I never supposed that speaking directly was such an affront to men."

He settled back in his chair and folded his arms over his freshly ironed blue shirt. It was short-sleeved and looked ever so much better since she'd mended the tear on the left shoulder seam and sewn the loose button back on. In her mind he looked more like a successful mill owner and not so much like the hired hand.

And he thought she was pretty.

"Some men are more easily offended than others," he explained. "And some are drawn to mealy-mouthed women who have no opinions. I think you can find a happy medium between being yourself, Katie, and being a shrew."

She arched one eyebrow. "A shrew?"

He made a comical grimace. "Very near. Sometimes."

"I never meant that." She nibbled on her lower lip. Did she really come off sounding like a *shrew*? "I need to work on this, don't I?"

"Afraid so." He held her gaze for a moment and then lifted his shoulder and let it fall. "If you want, I could give you some pointers. If I hear you say something that's...could be said differently, I'll tell you."

She considered his offer. She *did* want to marry; she wanted children and a home of her own. And for an instant she imagined herself mistress of not just any house but *this* one. After all, he did think she was pretty. And even though they had a rough start, they did seem to get along well, now that they knew each other a little better. "So you'll tell me if I step over the line?"

He nodded. "As gently as I can."

He smiled at her and she smiled back. And they both just kept smiling at each other. It should have been an awkward moment, but it wasn't. She liked the feeling it gave her, him looking at her that way.

Finally, she glanced back at her bucket. "I suppose I should finish up this window."

"Ya," he agreed. "There's a stack of paperwork waiting for me over at the mill. Computer stuff. Billing. Tax records. My head is clearer now that the pain has eased off my leg. I was thinking I could do a little work. I've fallen behind since the accident."

Katie tucked a wisp of hair behind her ear. "Couldn't it wait until afternoon? I could take you then."

"I don't need you to take me." Freeman started to roll himself backward, out of the room. "I'll be fine on my own."

She followed. "You can't roll yourself up that concrete ramp. It's too steep."

He stopped where he was and looked up at her, clearly amused. "There you go again."

She stopped where she was. "What?"

"You're being bossy. Telling me what I can and can't do. And you've got that tone."

"What tone?"

He eyed her.

She gave a harrumph. "Well, you won't be all that concerned with *my tone* if you try to manage that slope by yourself, roll down that ramp, crash and break your head. Maybe an arm or two. Or maybe the other leg." She pointed. "Then you'll have a matched pair."

"I hadn't thought about how steep the ramp is." He looked up at her, the corner of his mouth turning up in a sheepish smile. "So, maybe I do need a little help."

"I think you do, Freeman," she said, taking on a sickeningly sweet tone. "We wouldn't want you to be injured, now would we?" She came up to his wheelchair and patted him patronizingly on the hand as she might have done an invalid person. She went on with the same sing-song voice. "So, I think the *best* thing would be for you to wheel yourself to the foot of the ramp and shout for your hired man to come out and push you up."

She met his gaze and smiled a simpering smile to match the simpering voice.

Freeman took one look at her, burst into laughter and rolled himself out of the parlor. She could still hear him laughing as he went down the hall and she chuckled to herself. She wasn't sure what had just passed between them, but she was certain something had changed. Something for the good, she was quite sure.

Freeman sat on his porch and watched a very short-statured woman climb his steps, carrying a large wicker picnic basket. While he had never met Ellie, he knew this had to be her when he saw her pull into the mill parking lot in a little pony cart. She was the only female little person in the county.

"Hi, I'm Ellie, Katie's friend." She smiled at him. She was so small that they were almost eye-to-eye with him in the wheelchair and her standing. "I live with Sara Yoder and she wanted me to run these canned spiced peaches over. And a fresh-baked blueberry coffee cake."

"Nice to meet you, Ellie." Freeman smiled at her and then called over his shoulder, "Katie, your friend Ellie is here."

"Ellie!" Katie pushed open the kitchen screen door, drying her hands on her apron. She was wearing a scarf, rather than her prayer *kapp,* and wisps of blond hair stuck out here and there, framing her face. He liked her in the scarf; it softened her face. "What a nice surprise."

"I was telling Freeman, this cake just came out of the oven. Sara and I have been baking most of the day," Ellie explained, "and I thought it would be a nice break to get out of the house and drive over here."

"Come sit for a few minutes," Freeman said, indicating the chair to his left.

The little woman, dressed in a bright green dress and starched white *kapp* settled the basket into his lap. "I hope you like blueberries. Because there's blueberry cake and blueberry jam."

"Love them," he assured her. He opened the basket to find the cake, two quarts of peaches and several pints of jam. "This is a real treat," he said. "I know we'll enjoy everything. Tell Sara how much we appreciate her thinking of us."

It was kind of Sara to send the goodies, but secretly, he was a little disappointed. He hadn't been expecting company, and he'd been hoping that he could persuade Katie to take him back over to the mill. He'd finished most of the backed up billing and computer work yesterday when Shad had helped him up the ramp, but he wanted to show her the interior of the mill. It was already Friday afternoon. Somehow the week had gone by in a flash, and there would be two long days before she returned on Monday.

"Did Sara have a good crop of blueberries?" Uncle Jehu asked.

Freeman introduced his uncle. He and Jehu had been sitting there on the porch, enjoying glasses of lemonade and passing the time while Katie cleaned up after the midday meal. Shad had left work early to go to a dentist appointment, and Grossmama was waiting on a customer at the mill. Friday afternoon was usually a busy one, with locals and tourists stopping to buy stone-ground flour, and homemade jams and jellies from the small shop.

"She did," Katie said as she lifted the basket out of his lap. "Sara has a lot of blueberries. We've picked and frozen more blueberries than I've ever seen in my life, and we've eaten our share of them."

"I don't think I've eaten my share," Uncle Jehu said. "And I don't think I ever will."

"Well, I don't want to keep you from your chores, Katie." Ellie turned to her. "I'll just be on my way."

"You don't have to rush off," Freeman insisted, remembering his manners. "Please. Stay a while and sit with us. Katie?" He looked up at her. "Do we have more of that lemonade left?"

"We do," she said. "*Ya*, Ellie. No need to go so soon." She laughed, giving a wave. "Enjoy your summer while you can. Soon enough the *kinder* will be back in school and you'll not have a moment to sit and visit."

Freeman waved the little teacher to one of the chairs at the old table Katie had brought from the shed. He'd thought it far past its prime, but with a good scrubbing and a pretty blue tablecloth, it made the porch look downright inviting. Katie had added mismatched wooden chairs as well and it had become the perfect spot for their evening meals.

Freeman watched Ellie climb up into one of the chairs at the table. She was so short that her feet dangled just like a child's might. She didn't seem to notice. In spite of her size, Ellie was an attractive young woman with a ready smile, bright blue eyes, and blond hair. Katie had spoken of her often, and he knew the two were fast becoming good friends. Any other time, he would have been glad of Ellie's company, but selfishly, with Shad leaving early, he'd been hoping to have some time alone with Katie. He wanted to explain the workings of the mill, and he thought that she'd be interested in its history.

"I'll just cut this cake and we can all have some," Katie offered. "Unless you've had your fill of blueberries," she said to Ellie.

Ellie laughed. "Can't say that I have. Sara has a way with cake."

"I think I'll take a slice over to Ivy," Uncle Jehu said. "And some of that lemonade. No need for her to sit over there alone and miss out on the cake."

"Much traffic on the roads today?" Freeman asked Ellie.

"Not bad," Ellie replied, admiring the fresh cut flowers in a Mason jar in the middle of the table. "These are so pretty. I love black-eyed Susans." She returned her attention to Freeman. "But I took the back way. And the pony's car-wise."

Katie whisked away the cake and Jehu followed her into the house. Jehu was soon on his way to the mill with cake and lemonade, and Katie brought a tray of refreshments to the table on the porch. Soon the three of them were enjoying the snack. Two more cars pulled into the mill and an English woman got out of the vehicle and took a photograph of Ellie's pony and the cart with her cell phone.

"I wonder if the bishop would object?" Katie asked Freeman.

Ellie laughed, and the two of them began relating a story involving Sara and a tourist at Bylers' Store.

"And then," Ellie explained. "Before the woman knew what had happened, Sara had the woman's camera and was taking a picture of her and her husband. She gave the camera back and hurried away, leaving the Englishers gape-mouthed and without a photo of the quaint little Amish lady."

"At least Sara thought it was funny," Katie said with a giggle. "You don't want to get on her bad side."

"Does she have a temper?" Freeman asked. And at that, both girls laughed even harder. He found himself having a good time, a much better time than he'd expected. He liked watching Katie so at ease and enjoying herself. She looked especially pretty in her tidy scarf and dark green dress. She seemed so happy, and seeing her smile and enjoy herself made him content as well.

Ellie finished her cake and lemonade and the two women carried the empty plates and glasses into the kitchen. Freeman could hear them giggling together like schoolgirls. It was good to hear laughter in the house. For too long, he and his grandmother and uncle had been too serious.

"What's so funny?" he asked when Katie and Ellie came back onto the porch.

Katie looked at her friend and they both giggled again. "Girl stuff," she assured him.

Ellie walked to the steps and then turned to Freeman. "Thank you for the lemonade," she said. "I hope your leg is better soon."

"Thank you." He nodded. "Come again. Any time. You don't even have to bring cake." He flashed a grin. "But you can."

"I'll walk you out to the cart." Katie looped her arm through Ellie's.

Freeman watched them go, talking. Then Ellie climbed up into the cart, picked up the reins and drove out of the yard. Katie stood watching her friend until she pulled onto the road and then returned to the porch.

"What did I miss?" he asked her.

"Wouldn't you like to know?" She giggled. "What do you think of my friend Ellie?"

"I like her," he answered. *But I think I like you better.*

Chapter Nine

"So you're not going to tell me what was so funny?" Freeman asked Katie as she came up the porch steps.

Katie shook her head. "If we'd wanted you to hear, we would have told you." She cut her eyes at him and teasingly said, "Women's business and not for your ears."

He uttered a disgruntled sigh that she could tell was more for show than genuine disagreement. "Fine hired help you are. Much too saucy." He rested his hands on the rims of his wheelchair. "You should show more respect for the man who pays your wages."

"Should I?" Her blue eyes twinkled. "I suppose you could point out to me a more respectful way of telling you to mind your own beeswax."

He considered that for a moment. "I doubt it."

"So…" She rolled her eyes, enjoying the verbal play between them that she was pretty sure was flirtation. "I suppose I'm being too forward again."

Freeman shook his head. "*Ne*, Katie. In this instance, I'd say you were just right." His smile became a sheepish grin, and she thought again how very attractive he was. Particularly when he smiled. "I had no right to pry about what was said between you and your friend."

"Even when you pay my wages?" she teased. She could feel the telltale heat of a blush washing over her throat and cheeks, but she was having too much fun to back down now. Instead, she fixed him with a penetrating gaze.

And it was Freeman who surrendered. "You have me there." He chuckled. "I'm afraid whatever respect I demanded as your employer is long lost."

"Not lost at all," she assured him, her mood changing to one of all seriousness. "I do respect you, Freeman. Even more for being a man of uncommon good sense."

"Then we're friends?"

She nodded, giving her attention to the folds of her skirt and smoothing it. "Friends." And maybe, she thought, maybe they were just friends. But maybe Ellie was right that it was something more.

Katie definitely wanted it to be more; she was beginning to realize that. But this was unfamiliar ground for her. Unconsciously, she caught a handful of the material in her skirt and gripped it. She'd never had a beau, never understood what her girlfriends meant when they said they were all giddy or had butterflies in their stomach every time they saw the object of their affection. But she certainly didn't feel like herself in Freeman's presence. Was she right that day they'd played horseshoes? Was she falling in love with him?

A mockingbird's trill song sounded loud and clear from the tree by the porch, and the sweetness of it pierced and enhanced her deep musing.

Ellie definitely thought Freeman was interested in

her beyond her cooking and housekeeping skills. "Freeman likes you," Ellie had whispered when they'd gone into the kitchen together. "It's as plain as the freckles on your nose."

But if Ellie was right, what did she do about it? Did she do anything? Where did their relationship go from here? And how? What came next? For once in her life, Katie was at a loss.

Freeman gestured toward the entrance to the mill on the far side of the yard, where Ivy and Jehu were standing close together and talking animatedly. "Have you noticed that those two have gotten very friendly lately? More so, I think, since you've come to help out. You've cheered us all up."

She glanced at them and smiled. "More than *friendly*, I think." Her heartbeat slowed to near normal as their conversation turned less personal. "Have you noticed how she watches him when he does his leather work at the kitchen table?" she asked. "And how he perks up whenever she comes into the house? They like each other, all right."

"Of course they do," Freeman said. "Why wouldn't they? We're family. My grandmother is a good woman, and Uncle Jehu, well, he's Uncle Jehu. Who wouldn't like him?"

"I don't mean *like* each other," she explained patiently. "Not as you *like* your friends Charley and Eli, but more than that. The way a man likes a woman and a woman likes a man." She glanced at them. "I think they are both lonely, and it wouldn't take much to convince them that they're good for each other."

"You mean as a couple?" A frown creased his forehead. "But he's younger than she is."

"Not so much that it would be indecent." Katie shrugged. "So your grandmother isn't a young woman. It's no matter. She's still vital and full of life." She considered Freeman for a moment. "Do you have a problem with the idea of the two of them as a couple? Is there some reason you wouldn't want them to court?"

Freeman thought for a minute and then said, "Not really. There are no blood ties between them."

She smiled at him. "So how do we get them together? How do we make them realize how perfect they are for each other?"

Freeman put up his hands, palms out. "We don't. We stay out of their business. It's never wise to interfere."

She brushed away his argument with a wave of her hand. "Nonsense. Ivy probably feels like she can't make the first move, even if she wants to. And your uncle is shy. We have to find a way to get them together, to help them see that marriage would be in the best interest of them both."

"Marriage?" He looked at her as if she'd just said the most absurd thing. "You want me to try and convince my grandmother and my uncle to marry each other?"

She chuckled at his typically male reluctance to grasp what she'd been trying to tell him. "Who else are we talking about? Of course, to each other."

He shook his head slowly, though she could tell he was thinking about the idea. "It sounds like trouble to me," he said.

She folded her arms. "But you agree with me that they're perfect for each other."

"I didn't say that."

"Freeman." She sighed and let her arms fall to her sides. "You know I'm right. Admit it. How many men do you know who would think to carry cake and lemonade to a woman? And doesn't Ivy always laugh at Uncle Jehu's jokes, no matter how many times she's heard them?"

"That's a good point," he agreed. "She does laugh at his jokes." He looked up at her. "So you think that the two of us should endeavor to bring them together?"

"I do," she said. "They deserve to be happy."

Freeman looked doubtful. "And you know what would make them happy?"

"It's a natural thing; God meant us to walk on this earth two by two. She's widowed and he's alone, too. They need someone and they like each other. Why shouldn't they marry?"

He sat there for a moment and then looked up at her. "I guess we've come to the conclusion that there's no reason why they shouldn't. What I'm unconvinced of is that we should have a hand in trying to unite them. I've always believed in minding my own affairs and letting others mind theirs."

"Even when it would bring about something good and positive?"

"Your opinion," he reminded her.

She frowned. "If you're so set against them finding happiness together, then you should certainly stay out of it." She was quiet for a moment and then went on. "I know they aren't my relatives, although I've come to care for them both in the past several weeks. But..." She drew in a deep breath and forged ahead. "I won't be here after today, so I suppose you're right. It's foolish of me to talk about us trying to support a courtship between them."

"What do you mean you won't be here?" He scowled.

Then it dawned on him what she meant. "Wait. You've been here two weeks already? I don't think that's right."

"*Ya*, it's been two weeks," she told him.

"Well, I…" He stopped and started again. "I may have agreed to two weeks, but that was only supposed to be a trial. Sara must have told you the job would likely be longer than just the two weeks. You can't leave us now, Katie. I'm not ready to run this household yet. I'm not back on my feet yet. Who would do the washing? And cooking? I don't think Grossmama's oatmeal would be good for my recovery."

She averted her gaze, pressing her lips together in amusement. Obviously, Freeman didn't want her to leave. She wondered if she should tell him that talk of oatmeal might not be the best way to convince her. But the truth was, she didn't want to leave either. "I suppose I could stay on another week," she offered, looking back to him. "If you're certain you can't manage without me."

"Another two weeks, at least, and not a day less."

"I don't know—" she hemmed, mostly because she didn't know that she should give in too quickly to his demands. He was just becoming bearable to live with. She didn't want to put any ideas in his head that he could tell her what to do.

"No buts, Katie," Freeman insisted, though not unkindly. "If it's a matter of how much we're paying you, then we can renegotiate."

She shook her head, aghast that he should think that she was greedy. "It was never the money, Freeman. What you pay is more than fair."

He nodded. "Good. Then there will be no more talk

of you leaving us yet. I'll expect you back promptly on Monday morning."

Katie tried to hide her delight. He wanted her to stay as much as she wanted to be there. "*Ya*, Freeman, if you think that's best," she murmured before looking up at him through her lashes. "But there's one stipulation. If I do come back for another two weeks, you'll let me move that bed out of the kitchen. It…it's too…" She grimaced. "It takes up too much room and it gathers dust. You'll get far better rest in one of the downstairs bedrooms."

"Agreed." He nodded. "So you'll stay on at least another two weeks. It's settled."

She lowered her gaze to her bare feet. If he saw her eyes, he'd know how pleased she was. She wanted to shout with joy—rush down to the millpond and leap in, fully dressed. She was staying on here with Freeman, Jehu and Ivy.

"And maybe there's one more condition," she ventured.

"Oh? Another?" His voice showed amusement. "What more could you ask of me?"

"That you'll consider what I said about your grandmother and your uncle. That you'll think about helping me find ways to make them see how much they need each other."

He stroked his chin. He was clean-shaven, but he'd missed a spot on the left and a small clump of reddish whiskers had sprung up. She found the mishap as endearing as his argument for keeping her on in order to avoid his grandmother's oatmeal.

"I'll think about it," Freeman allowed. "But I'm making no promises."

"That's all I ask," she said. "Because, if you do think about it, I know you'll come to the conclusion that I'm right."

"Woman, have you ever considered that you usually think you're in the right?"

She smiled sweetly. "It's because I am. And you know it."

The following morning dawned rainy and wet, but it didn't stop Freeman from repeatedly wheeling himself to the screen door to look out into the yard. Uncle Jehu was at the sink washing the breakfast dishes, and Ivy had gone to the mill to tend the store.

"Your coffee's getting cold, boy," his uncle warned. "What are you doing by the door? Katie doesn't come again until Monday."

"I'm not looking for Katie," Freeman answered, trying to ignore the fact that his uncle called him a boy. He knew it was said out of affection, but it still rubbed like a rough spot under a harness. Maybe Katie was right. Maybe it would be better for them all if Uncle Jehu married his grandmother and he moved into her house and out of this one. Maybe they were too much in each other's shoes for comfort.

"So who are you expecting?" Uncle Jehu persisted.

Freeman tried to find patience. His uncle's curiosity was normal enough. But it made it hard when a man could find no privacy with a delicate matter in his own house. Did he always have to discuss everything with his uncle and his grandmother?

"Too wet for horseshoes," Jehu said when Freeman didn't answer right away. "Not Eli or Charley. The way that wind smells, it will rain all day and into the night." He found a clean hand towel to dry the bowls and spoons on the sideboard.

"You're right. No horseshoes today," Freeman agreed.

Uncle Jehu dropped the clean spoons into the knife and fork drawer. "Make for damp traveling to church tomorrow. Not too far. At Big Peachy's. Not too far to walk for Ivy and me, but if it's still wet, we'll take the buggy." He turned his head as he would if he were sighted. "Unless you've a mind to come to worship with us. Then we'd take the buggy regardless of the weather."

Freeman shook his head. "I'd not thought to go. It would be too much to ask for someone to come for me on the Sabbath. Help me in and out of a buggy. Too much," he repeated.

"It must be a trial to you, missing service and the company of the community." Uncle Jehu carefully hung the towel on a hook near the sink. "Not to mention Big Peachy's wife's raisin-nut bread." He grinned. "I'll smuggle you home a few slices if there are any left after the second sitting."

Freeman nodded. He'd missed several Sabbaths since the accident and it did trouble him. All his life church Sundays had been a solid part of his life, and he found it difficult to stay at home while his grandmother and uncle went to worship and to hear the word of God as revealed to the preachers and the bishop.

"So who are you expecting this morning?" Uncle Jehu persisted. "Some of the church elders come to bring you spiritual comfort?"

Freeman gritted his teeth. He should have just told his uncle, but he hadn't been sure he was ready to speak his intentions aloud. Not that he could go on much longer that way. If he didn't speak his intentions, how would he ever know what chance he had? "Sara Yoder," he answered under his breath.

"What's that?" Jehu touched his ear.

Freeman knew very well his uncle had heard him. "I'm expecting Sara Yoder."

"The matchmaker?"

"Yes," Freeman agreed reluctantly. "The matchmaker. I sent word by way of Shad last night. I'm expecting her this morning."

"And you had Shad take this message? Not Katie, even with her staying at Sara's house?" Freeman's uncle's mouth twitched into a smile. "Why would that be?"

Freeman sighed with resignation. He should have known there would be no way to do this privately. Not with him still laid up. "Because I didn't want Katie to know anything about it. I have business with Sara."

"Ach." The older man nodded as he settled into a chair at the table, where he'd already arranged some of his leather working tools and a partially finished pony bridle. "Well, it's about time."

Freeman didn't respond.

Jehu picked up a leather punch and rolled the head between his fingers, feeling for the correct prong. "You know, you couldn't do better than Katie. You should have taken a wife years ago."

"I didn't say I wanted to speak to Sara about Katie."

This time it was Jehu who didn't respond.

"Okay… I want to talk to her about Katie," Freeman conceded.

Jehu searched for the right piece of leather. "Couldn't you just ask the girl to walk out with you yourself?"

"It's not that simple, Uncle. Picking a woman to live with for the rest of your life is serious business. I don't want to make a mistake I'll live to regret."

His uncle scoffed. "You're talking about *her*, now. Not Katie. The one who left you at the altar."

"She didn't leave me at the altar," Freeman answered testily. *But it was close enough.* "I made a mistake once. How do I know that I'm not doing the same thing again? I want to talk to the matchmaker because…she knows about these things."

His uncle frowned. "That was ten years ago. Susan's happily married with three children. It's time you let her go."

"I'm trying. It's not so easy." He considered how much more to say, and then went on. "I'm afraid I don't know my own mind. How do I know that I'm not grasping at straws, trying to convince myself that I could be happy with Katie because I'm lonely and need a wife and she's a good cook?"

"*Are* you just interested in Katie just for her cooking skills?"

"Of course not," Freeman said. "She's kind and clever and she understands me. She understands my ways. And she makes me laugh. I like that she makes me laugh," he said as much to himself as to his uncle. "And there's something about her that…" He didn't finish the sentence, because he didn't know how to explain the way she made him feel. It was as if when she was there with him, everything seemed right in the world and when she wasn't there, it was if something was missing, not from the mill, but his heart.

"Sounds like you've about made up your mind about Katie." Jehu nodded. "Or you wouldn't have wanted to meet with Sara about her."

"You know how I am," he explained. "I need all the facts. I don't want to make a fool of myself. Sara's introduced Katie to prospective suitors, and there's some sort of arrangement with a farmer in Kentucky. I just want to know what's what. Not that I've made up my mind or anything."

"There's no betrothal or they would have said so. I know Sara. She wouldn't have sent the girl if she'd been spoken for."

Freeman wheeled his chair around to face his uncle. "Are you saying Sara Yoder set this up? Set *me* up? That that's why she sent Katie here to begin with?"

"Who's to say what goes on in a woman's mind? I asked Sara to make a recommendation for a housekeeper and I might have mentioned that I was concerned about the fact that you were still single. But I don't know why she sent Katie." His uncle laid down the bridle with a shrug. "What I do know is that you better snatch Katie up fast before it's too late." He chuckled. "Then you'll not have to eat your grandmother's oatmeal for breakfast every day for the rest of your life." He got to his feet. "I think I'll take myself along to the mill. See if Ivy's in a better mood than you are."

"Good idea," Freeman said. "She enjoys your company."

"Does she?" Uncle Jehu asked, turning to his nephew. "She tell you that?"

"*Ne.* But I know her."

Jehu seemed to think on that as he placed his tools and the bridle back in a small leather chest. "Sounds like a horse and buggy just turned into the yard," he remarked. "That will be your matchmaker."

"And…"

"And?" Jehu asked, standing there.

"You said you were just leaving," Freeman reminded him.

"So I was. Good luck with Sara." Chuckling to himself, Jehu left the house.

Sara soon came up the porch steps in her cloak and black church bonnet, both splotched with dark spots of water. "Fit weather out there for ducks," she said, walking into the house as Freeman held the screen door open for her.

"I appreciate you coming over, Sara. I'm still not quite up to traveling." Freeman fought his nervousness as she hung her bonnet and cape over the back of a chair before he ushered her to the table. "Would you like coffee?" he asked.

For ten minutes they exchanged neighborly talk about crops and coming school fund-raisers and a visiting bishop from the Midwest who'd preached recently in Seven Poplars. And then, when all the polite greetings and inquiries after the families' health and the likelihood of abundant crops had been given and received, and he was feeling a little calmer, he turned to the important matter of Katie's availability.

Better now than never, Freeman thought. "I imagine you know why I asked you here."

"I can guess. Katie," she said simply.

"Katie," he repeated, his nervousness coming back to him in one great flood. "Sara, I don't know how this works," he admitted. "I've not brought up my—" he cleared his throat "—interest in Katie to her. She told me that there's a man in Kentucky who wants to marry her. But she said nothing about a firm commitment."

Sara tented her hands on the table. "Katie's a fine young woman. She'd make you a proper wife."

"So you think we're well-suited to each other?" he asked, unable to hide his excitement.

Sara looked at him with those dark eyes of hers. "I just said that, didn't I?"

"I've not made up my mind, of course," he hedged. "I wouldn't want to have you think otherwise. I'm just trying to find out the lay of the land, as it were. Do you know how she feels about me? I wouldn't want to approach her if there was no chance she…" He felt heat rise on the back of his neck. "If she wouldn't be interested in me."

Sara smiled. "So there *is* an attraction on your part? I can't say I'm surprised." She looked around the kitchen. "She seems to have done a fine job in here. I saw Jehu on the way in and he speaks highly of her."

Freeman's eyes narrowed. He had suspected Sara might have had an ulterior motive when she chose Katie to be his housemaid. Now he was afraid they'd all been in on it: Sara, Jehu…maybe even his grandmother. But that wasn't a good reason to change his mind; he had enough sense to know that. "She said something about you communicating with the man in Kentucky. I'm not hiring you as a matchmaker," he said. "If I do decide to pay court to her, it wouldn't be fair or right for you to expect a fee from me as well."

Sara laughed. "I can't say for sure if Katie would accept an offer from you to court her, but I *can* tell you that your pocketbook is safe. Whatever arrangement I may or may not have made with Katie's family, or a man's family in Kentucky, you and I have no such arrangement."

He pushed his wheelchair a little from the table, his nervousness rising again. "Are you saying there's a betrothal agreement with this man in Kentucky?"

"There is a firm offer for a betrothal, in writing," Sara replied. "Katie is in the process of deciding whether or not she will go visit him and his family and see what's what."

He dared a glance at Sara's pretty, round face. "So what you're saying is that if I wanted to ask her to consider walking out with me, it's not too late?"

"That's something that you'll have to ask her. You know our Katie." Sara shrugged, but her dark eyes sparkled with amusement. "She's a woman who knows her own mind."

Chapter Ten

"I've always liked the way the mill smells," Freeman said to Katie as he took in the cavernous interior of the mill with a sweeping gesture. "Molasses, grain and water."

"Me, too," she agreed. She pushed his wheelchair closer to the now motionless grindstones. She'd worn a new lavender-colored dress today, with a white apron over it, and the simple lines of the plain but neatly-sewn garments gave her a wholesome look that was accented by her crisp white *kapp*. He couldn't keep from looking up at her. He'd missed her all weekend. Missed her more than he was comfortable with.

Their voices echoed slightly, taking him back ten years to another beautiful woman who'd stood beside him in this room, bringing bittersweet memories of someone he'd rather forget. Susan had been equally pretty, but in a much more delicate way, dark where Katie was fair, soft-spoken and modest rather than brash. And the contrast didn't end there. Being alone with him in the vast mill, with massive oak beams, shadowy corners and fluttering pigeons in the rafters had unnerved Susan. She'd been uncomfortable here, even a little frightened, but Katie gave no such impression. Instead, she appeared to be enjoying the experience as much as he was. Encouraged by her eagerness, Freeman pushed thoughts of Susan to the furthest recesses of his mind.

The huge millstones were motionless, the mechanism silent, but in his mind Freeman could almost hear the familiar churn of the waterwheel, the whoosh of tumbling grain down the chute, and the grinding rumble of the granite stones. Along the walls, baskets of corn waited to be ground into meal. A fine dusting of wheat flour coated the wide pine floorboards and every visible surface. There was too much dust to suit Freeman and he frowned. "Shad should have swept this up this morning. Wheat dust is highly explosive under the right conditions. The boy may not have the brains to make a miller."

"No one's complained about the quality of your flour while you've been laid up," Katie observed. "Shad's young yet, and as you say, there's a lot to learn. Maybe you're too hard on him."

He opened his mouth to reply, then closed it, mostly because he didn't want to argue with her, and maybe because he knew she was at least half-right.

Katie wandered over to run a palm over the furrowed surface of a millstone that rested against one wall and stared up nearly three stories at the hand-hewn oak rafters barely visible in the semi-darkness. This section of the structure soared from where they stood to the hand-cut cedar shingled roof. Two-thirds of the first floor supported a second story containing the granary.

He pointed to a metal chute that ran from the grain

bins to the wooden hopper above the millstones. "If I pull this lever, grain comes down the hopper into this mechanism called the shoe."

Katie returned to stand beside his wheelchair as he pointed out the control that would open the gate on the sluice box, sending a flow of water over the wheel and bringing the mill to life. Freeman knew that he was running on, perhaps boring her with the details of turning corn, wheat and rye to flour and animal feed. He kept sneaking glances at her, half expecting to see her eyes glaze over as he prattled on about the proper distances you had to keep the rotating millstone above the fixed one for different processes. But, to his surprise, Katie listened intently to what he was saying.

"Shad has been grinding horse feed this morning, a special order for a customer who keeps a stable of harness horses west of Dover."

Katie nodded. "I've seen his truck hauling away the bags of feed."

"*Ya*, English. A good customer."

He was surely prattling now. What was wrong with him? His uncle's advice to seriously consider Katie only added to his own conclusion that she was the right woman. And his talk with Sara Yoder had gone well. Now was the time to speak up, to ask Katie if he was someone she would consider courting. Courting wouldn't commit him to marrying her. Either of them could change their mind. So where was his nerve? Why was he going on about milling rather than speaking up about what was really on his mind?

The night before, he'd hardly slept for mulling the question over and over in his head. Was he making the right decision? Should he ask her to walk out with him?

Maybe it would be a mistake. If he asked to court her and she turned him down flat, it would be impossible for her to go on working here. It would be too uncomfortable for them both. That would mean that she would go away, and he might not see her again.

But if he asked and she agreed, how could he be sure that he wasn't making another huge mistake like he had with Susan? Englisher couples might divorce after marriage if they were unhappy, but the Amish did not. They would be bound to each other for better or worse for the rest of their lives. There were issues with Katie's forceful personality that worried him. He didn't want to repeat his parents' mistakes in their marriage. His mother had ruled the house, making all the decisions while his father did whatever she told him. Was that what he wanted?

The loud flapping of wings and a hoarse caw broke through his thoughts and he turned to see what was causing the disturbance. Katie's reaction was even quicker than his. She hurried to a corner of the room near a dirty window. "Shoo, kitty," she cried, clapping her hands.

A tiger-striped barn cat streaked away, ears flattened and crooked tail giving away the animal's identity. It was Mustard, a half-grown stray that Freeman had rescued from a watery grave when some heartless person had thrown him out of a car window into the millpond. The weighted bag had landed in shallow water, and Freeman, fishing along the wooded bank, had heard the pitiful cries of the drowning cat and adopted him.

But Katie had no eyes for the cat. Her attention was fixed on a black, feathered object crouching against the dusky wall. "It's a crow," she pronounced. "I think he's injured. Poor thing."

Black eyes gleamed as the bird hopped back, nearly losing its balance. "Don't get too close," Freeman cautioned. "The state officials say that there's bird flu around. Crows are one of the types of birds that are most often affected."

"Ne." She crouched down to get a better look at the crow. "He isn't sick. I think he has a broken leg. See how he doesn't put any weight on it? And the good leg is tangled in a length of corn string."

One of the bird's wings drooped and his feathers were ruffled. "He must have had a fight with the cat and come out second-best." Freeman wondered why the crow had come into the mill. Pigeons made their home here and they came and went through openings in the eaves. And sometimes owls nested in the granary, attracted by the mice that the cats missed, but he'd never seen a crow in here.

"Look how it's watching us," Katie said. "He's frightened, but brave."

He rolled his chair a little closer to see. "I think the string is knotted around his foot. Poor thing. Crows are said to be among the most intelligent of birds." He looked at Katie. "It could be that I could put a splint on his hurt leg. But don't think I can catch it. It may fly if I come any closer."

Katie stood up and looked at him. "You would try to heal it? A crow?"

He nodded, only slightly embarrassed at his show of tenderness. "I've always had an unnatural softness for creatures," he admitted. "Abandoned cats, mostly, but a few dogs, the donkey past his prime that you see grazing in the pasture, a blind ox. Once I even brought home a skunk that had been hit by a car. But my *mam* put a stop to that. Out went the skunk, and me with it. She made me bathe in tomato juice and shaved my hair as bald as an onion. Still I stank for months." He shrugged. "The bishops say animals have no souls, but they feel hunger and pain as we do. Surely a merciful God would expect us to do what we can to lesson their suffering if we can."

"I agree," she said untying her apron.

"Don't—" he began, but before he could finish, she'd thrown the apron over the crow and gathered the struggling bird up in it.

"Shh, shh," she soothed, cradling the bundle against her.

The crow gave a hissing croak and quieted. "Let me see that leg," Freeman said. She came closer so that he could examine the crow's legs. One leg was bent unnaturally and when he felt it, it seemed as though he could feel the bone move as if it was broken. The good leg had a corn string knotted tightly around it, cutting into the flesh. Freeman removed his penknife from his pocket and carefully sliced away the strands. The skin was broken but the injury to this leg didn't seem severe. "That's better," he said. "It had to be painful."

Katie crooned to the bird as she might a sick child. "Be still," she murmured. "It will be better. I promise."

"Don't make promises you can't keep," Freeman warned. He was touched by the kindness in her eyes and the fearless way she held the crow. "And be careful. He has a sharp beak."

"What makes you think it's a male?" she asked. "I don't think you can tell just by looking at him."

"Male or female, it makes no matter. And I have to call him something. Let's take *him* to the house and see what we can do for the break."

"If you think that's best, Freeman," she murmured, smiling up at him with shining eyes. She passed the bird to him, and he held it gently, so close he could feel the frightened beating of the creature's heart. But the crow had stopped fighting against the encompassing apron.

"It's afraid," he said. "Fetch one of those empty baskets, the one with the lid." She did as he instructed and they placed the bird in it and fastened the lid.

"You hold the basket," Katie said as she took hold of the wheelchair handles to push him back to the house. "You don't want to drop him and break the other leg."

Freeman glanced back over his shoulder at her and felt something shift within his chest. He exhaled slowly, certain of his mind now, certain that he was already half in love with this kind young woman. He'd made a bad choice when he'd courted Susan, but Katie was nothing like Susan. He couldn't imagine Susan getting anywhere near an injured crow. So maybe he and Susan had been too different. Maybe losing her to another man was God's way of leading him to a happy marriage. To Katie.

"Wait," he said when they reached the bottom of the ramp. "Stop pushing."

"What's wrong?" Katie slowed the chair to a halt.

"I have something I need to talk to you about." He felt short of breath. "Don't laugh," he said.

She walked around his chair to face him. "I won't," she promised. She waited.

Freeman wasn't sure what to say. He only knew that he had to say something and this was the time to say it.

"What is it, Freeman?" she asked when still he hesitated. She waited and then said, "You know you can talk to me about anything. Friends talk to each other."

"That…that's just it, Katie. I was hoping… I wanted to ask…" He looked down at his cast and then up at her again. "I was hoping you see me as more than just a friend."

The crow scratched at the bottom of the basket and croaked feebly. Katie took the basket from him and placed it on the ground. When she stood upright again, she looked him squarely in the eyes. "What are you trying to say?"

"Well…we get along, don't we?" His heart raced. If only he wasn't stuck in this chair. Surely, he'd have more courage to speak his mind if he could stand on his own two feet.

She nodded, her expression showing that she was clearly puzzled.

"So I was wondering if you… I mean…if we could see if…"

Katie waited, surprising him with her patience while he attempted to untangle his tongue.

"I was wondering if you would consider letting me court you," he said in a rush, his voice louder and more forceful than he'd intended.

Her eyes widened. "Are you serious?" Then she clapped both hands over her mouth. "You mean it?" she asked, her words muffled.

He couldn't tell if she was for or against, for sure. "J-just to see," he stammered. "A trial walking out. So we'd know if we're…" He exhaled heavily. Susan was the only other woman he had ever walked out with. When he had asked her, it had come so easily. He didn't know why he was finding this so hard.

She lowered her hands. "So we're not talking about officially courting but a...*trial* courting?" She was grinning ear to ear. "To see if we actually *want* to court?" she asked.

He nodded. "Exactly," he said, relieved she understood what he was making such a mess of saying.

"Freeman!" she cried and flung herself at him, neatly missing his cast and wrapping her arms around his neck and kissing him full on the mouth. "*Ya*! Of course I would. I could. I didn't think you—" She broke off and kissed him again, this time a tender and sweet caress. "Oh, Freeman," she whispered. "I'd love for you to court me."

"Katie." She smelled as sweet and fresh as she looked. He loved the feel of her pressed against him and the taste of her lips. "Katie," he repeated, unable to say anything else.

This time, it was she who became shy, suddenly pulling back. "That was inappropriate, wasn't it?"

He clamped the brake on the wheelchair and pushed himself up, awkwardly standing on one foot. "Maybe," he allowed breathily. "But I liked it just fine."

"So..." She backed away from him, her face radiant. "We've agreed? A *trial* courtship? You and me?"

He nodded. "Agreed." He reached out a hand to her, hoping that she would kiss him again. Instead, she snatched up the basket with the crow and fled the mill.

"Katie," he called after her. And then he was laughing too and savoring the sound of her name on his lips.

* * *

"He seems very nice, your miller," Patsy remarked as she formed ground beef into patties. She was chubby and tow-haired, with thick glasses, a pointed chin, and a kind disposition. Katie thought she was the perfect wife for her brother Isaac. "A pity about his broken leg," Patsy continued. "But by the grace of God he wasn't killed by that bull."

Patsy, Katie and a group of friends were gathered in the kitchen of Katie's childhood home, preparing for a barbecue. Some of those who'd come were married women, some walking out with prospective husbands, and others, like Ellie, hoping to find someone special. It had been Katie's brother Isaac's idea to host a birthday celebration for his wife Patsy. They'd invited two dozen guests, including Katie and Freeman, Ellie, Nona, who was one of Patsy's sisters, and Thomas Stutzman.

Since all of the guests were in their twenties and thirties, Katie's mother had gone visiting for the day to allow the young people to enjoy themselves without an older member of the community dampening their fun. Isaac had promised volleyball, men against the women, as well as an archery contest, and fast hymn singing. They would stuff themselves with picnic food, splash in the farm pond and drink homemade ginger ale until dark, when Isaac had promised that they would have a bonfire, complete with hot dogs and marshmallows to roast.

"If Freeman has a fault, it's that he has his own way of doing things," Katie observed as she cut a pan of still-warm brownies into squares. "He's so nice, though. I still can't believe we're walking out together. It's so new that it doesn't seem real. At first, when I went there to help with the housework, I thought Freeman was difficult, but after you get to know him, he's really sweet."

Ellie paused from slicing a watermelon into wedges, smiling mischievously. "Now she says *difficult*. I won't tell you what she called him that first day when she got home. But I knew she must like him. All she could talk about was Freeman this and Freeman that."

Katie chuckled. "*Ya*, I did say he was grumpy."

Patsy's older sister Meta, married three years and about to give birth to her second child, was as plump and cheerful as the birthday girl. "The same with her." She pointed a mayonnaise-covered spoon in Patsy's direction and motioned with it to emphasize her words. "Our *mam* said that if Isaac didn't ask to marry her soon, she would drive over herself and fix it up with his mother because Patsy was so *narrish* over him that she couldn't toast bread without burning it."

"I never called Isaac grumpy," Patsy protested. "He doesn't have a grumpy bone in his body." She looked at Katie for support. "Does he?"

Katie shook her head. "*Ne*. As brothers go, I've been blessed."

Almost as if he'd known they were talking about him, Isaac appeared outside the kitchen window. "That food almost ready?" he asked. "I'd like to get the hamburgers on the grill. I'm starved."

"You're always starved," Katie teased.

"*Ya*. Fortunately, my new wife is a *goot* cook." Patsy blushed with pleasure as he winked at her. "I'm waiting for those baked beans of yours," he said.

"We'll be ready in two shakes of a lamb's tail," Katie told him. "Hold off for a few more minutes, and there will be enough to fill even you."

"But maybe not Thomas," he teased.

"Ya," Patsy said. "Even Thomas." And the women all laughed.

Katie had been delighted when Freeman had eventually agreed to accept Isaac's invitation. He'd been stuck at home for weeks, and he needed an outing. With Shad and Uncle Jehu's help, she'd gotten Freeman into the buggy at the mill. He'd been able to drive the horse, something that pleased him immensely. And when they'd arrived at her home, Isaac and Thomas had been all too willing to assist him in getting out and into his wheelchair. The doctor had promised that Freeman would soon be on crutches, and he was eagerly looking forward to it. Freeman was outside with the men now; she could hear snatches of his laughter through the open windows.

"He has a fine business," Meta said. "Your Freeman? The mill?"

Katie nodded. She supposed he was considered a good catch, but she hadn't thought at all about what he had. It was who he was that was important. That, and the way she felt when they were together. All the way here, they'd laughed and talked, with Freeman showing her a fun side of his personality that she was just coming to appreciate.

"So, I suppose you're calling it off with that man in Kentucky," Jane asked. She and Thomas, Ellie's friend, had the same last name but weren't related.

"Of course," Katie replied. "It wouldn't be fair to Uriah not to tell him that I was going with someone."

Jane giggled. "Two men wanting to court you at the same time—that must be something."

"I wish Victor hadn't brought that stranger," Ellie

commented, glancing out the window as she handed a plate of watermelon wedges to Jane.

"Who?" Katie asked, looking out the window, too. "His cousin Jakob? The blacksmith from Indiana?"

"Yes, Jakob. Just because he's little like me, everyone will think we're meant for each other."

"What's wrong with him?" Jane asked. "He seems pleasant enough, and Victor says he's the best farrier he's ever seen. Just because he isn't as tall as—"

"Ellie," Meta admonished, "I've never heard you talk bad about anyone. How can you find fault with him for being…small when—"

"When I am?" Ellie sighed with exasperation. "You have no idea what it's like. How my parents searched far and wide for a short husband for me. One was an Old Order Mennonite boot maker from Ontario."

"Something wrong with boot makers?" Patsy asked. "At least you'd always have good shoes with soles on them."

Ellie rolled her eyes. "He was in his fifties and had eleven children. A good man, I'm sure, but not for me. I'm not marrying someone just because he's little like me." She rested her small hands on her hips. "I was born Amish and I stay Amish. I don't care if God's love leads others to a different path, but that's not for me. I could never wed a man, dwarf or giant, who didn't share my own path."

"No one's asking you to marry Jakob," Jane said. "Just to welcome him to our community. We can use another blacksmith and farrier now that Thomas has made it plain it's not for him."

"You needn't worry about that," Katie said, coming to her friend's defense. "I've never known Ellie to be unkind to anyone, and certainly not unwelcoming to a newcomer."

"Ne," Ellie said, shaking her head. "I deserved that. I said what I shouldn't. Naturally, I won't be rude to Jakob. Just don't expect me to ride home with him."

Meta laughed. "We won't, not when Thomas is around. The way he looks at you, I'm thinking he'll be popping the question soon."

Ellie shook her head. "I don't know why everyone keeps saying that. Thomas and I are just friends."

"Well, *friends*, if we don't get out there with this food, the men will all be at the door wanting to know where it is," Katie reminded them.

The afternoon and evening were as much fun as she'd hoped. Because he was confined to the wheel-chair, Freeman couldn't participate in the games, but Isaac and the others made certain he wasn't left out. They asked him to officiate at the volleyball match and archery contests. Later, when everyone gathered around the fire to make s'mores, Katie sat beside him and let him hold her hand in the semi-darkness.

"I'm glad we came," he said.

"Me, too," Katie agreed. Today had been one of the best days of her life. Her skirt was still damp from where she'd waded in the pond, and she'd come in third behind Thomas and Isaac at archery. Best of all, Free-man had cheered loudly for her. Now, here in the semi-darkness with the navy-blue sky arching overhead, the bright scattering of stars, and the warmth of Freeman's touch, she was almost giddy with happiness.

"I wish we were riding home together," he whispered to her. "I wish I could take you back to Sara's myself."

She didn't answer. She wished it, too, but it was

late, and she knew that he was tired and probably in pain from being up all day. Thomas had invited her to ride back to Sara's with the two of them, and Ellie had insisted.

"I like your brother and sister-in-law," Freeman said, still holding her hand tightly.

She smiled, glad that they had hit it off. "You did so well traveling today that you'll be ready for church next week," she said. "It's time."

"Ya," he agreed. "It is time, but there's only one way I could possibly go."

"Oh?" She met his warm gaze.

"Ya." He grinned, bringing his nose very close to hers. "You have to come with me."

Chapter Eleven

Katie met his gaze in the darkness, the firelight flickering light and dark against his features. "You want me to come to church with you?" she asked, her throat tight with emotion. "Then, everyone would know that we…"

"That we're together?" His warm chuckle was a comforting hug that brought tears to her eyes. "That we're courting? We are, aren't we? I thought that was settled." He squeezed her hand again and then released it.

She struggled to find words to convey her desire to go with him, but not to rush what might be an enormous commitment. "I *would* like to come to worship with you, but this is so new. I thought…" She didn't finish her sentence. What did she think? She thought they'd agreed they would merely consider a formal courtship. But she also thought that she'd never been happier in her life than she was right now. With Freeman.

"Not having second thoughts, are you?" he asked. His tone was teasing, but he genuinely wanted to know what she was thinking.

She shook her head, shifting in the lawn chair. "*Ne,*

Freeman. This feels right. I've been praying, and... I think this is what was supposed to happen. I've been so happy since I've come to work for you at the mill house, and I love your family. And..." She almost said "And I love you," but kept the words to herself, not quite ready to speak them.

"Good, because we're a package. If you marry me, you accept Grossmama and Uncle Jehu. And he will continue living with us as long as he wants."

She placed a marshmallow on a green willow switch and held it over the coals of the fire. Everyone else was gathered around the fire, too, talking and laughing, but she felt like it was just the two of them. "I understand, and I'm fine with it. I always imagined myself living with extended family. I think it's the way we should all live. But you know, he and Ivy could come to their own arrangement. If they decide to marry, I'm sure Ivy will want Jehu to move into her house."

He looked amused. "They aren't even courting. How can you have them married already?"

She laughed. "Of course they're courting. Men." She shook her head again. "You see everything and understand nothing about a woman's heart." Her marshmallow flamed up and she withdrew the stick and blew on it. "Oh," she exclaimed. "It's burned."

"Just the way I like it," Freeman steered the stick toward him and leaned over to take a bite.

"Careful," she cautioned. "It's hot. You'll—"

"Ah!" he said, touching his lip. "It's hot." A dribble of marshmallow fell onto his chin.

"I warned you," she teased. "But you never listen to reason."

He dabbed at the melted marshmallow and rubbed

his sticky finger on the tip of her nose. "Now everyone will wonder what we've been up to."

He laughed, and she laughed with him.

"How will I get this off?" she asked, rubbing at the sticky, warm marshmallow on her face.

"Fortunately for you, I come prepared." He removed a clean handkerchief from his trouser pocket and gave it to her.

She moistened the corner of his handkerchief with a little of the water in her glass and wiped away the marshmallow on her nose. "Now you," she said. Obediently, he allowed her to clean his chin.

"Satisfied?" he asked, leaning closer to her than he probably should have.

"Hey, Ellie," Thomas called loudly from beside them. "I dare you to go into the pond again."

"What? Wading in the dark?" Ellie's laughter rang out.

"If you go, I'll go," Thomas dared.

Amid a flurry of giggles and excited calls, Thomas and Ellie and then the rest of the party left the bonfire and moved toward the pond, leaving Katie and Freeman alone.

"You can go if you want," Freeman offered.

"*Ne*, I like it fine where I am," Katie said. She placed another marshmallow on the end of her willow bough. "I'll try not to burn this one," she promised.

"Actually, I'm glad they left us alone," he said. "There's something I've been wanting to tell you."

"Something bad or good?"

"Nothing that changes anything between us. At least, I hope not," he replied. "It's just…something I need to tell you. Something you need to know and I wanted you to know from me, before you hear it from anyone else."

A ripple of apprehension slid down her spine, and she pulled the marshmallow back out of the heat before it had even started to blister. "Okay."

"Ten years ago, I thought I was in love with someone," he said quietly. "We were planning to marry."

Katie sat quietly for a moment. Freeman was older than she was; she wasn't silly enough to think he had never taken a girl home from a singing or escorted someone to a picnic or a fund-raiser, but it wasn't as easy to hear from him as she had thought it would be. "What was her name?" she asked quietly.

"Susan."

"And you and Susan courted?"

"We did, for the better part of a year. Then she broke it off and chose someone else." He shrugged. "End of story."

"And you've never courted anyone since?"

"I took a few girls home from singings, but nothing serious. No."

"So that's why you've remained single so long." Katie's mouth felt dry and she picked up her glass to take a sip of water. "You must have cared for her very much."

"I did. She married him, moved to Ohio, and they have three children. As far as I know, they've been happy together."

"But she hurt you," Katie said softly.

He took his time responding. "She did. And maybe I used my hurt to avoid moving on, starting the family that everyone expected, but whatever it is, it doesn't matter anymore. But I wouldn't have felt right not telling you."

She nodded. "I'm so glad you did." *Ten years.* Sad, she thought, that Freeman had mourned his lost love so long. She hesitated, trying to push down the curiosity that a woman would naturally feel for an old rival. She reached for another marshmallow from the bag in the grass. "Is it okay if I ask you…what she was like?"

"Of course." He chuckled. "She was nothing like you, Katie, if that's what you're asking. Nothing at all. Petite, soft-spoken, gentle and biddable. As far from you as December is from July."

She thrust her marshmallow back into the fire. "Well, if we ever meet, I'll kiss her on both cheeks and thank her."

"For what?"

She giggled, staring into the fire. "For being foolish enough to walk away from the finest catch in Kent County."

"I have a feeling that next time we come, you'll be walking on your own," Katie said cheerfully as she pushed Freeman's wheelchair out the automatic doors of the large medical complex. The visit had gone smoothly and much quicker than she'd expected. Not only did Freeman have a new, smaller and lighter cast, but he had permission to start walking.

An English child holding an adult's hand stopped and pointed at them, and the embarrassed mother tugged the little girl's hand. "Mama, look at the cowboy. He has a boo-boo."

"Sorry," the red-faced woman said. And then to her daughter, "Didn't I tell you not to talk to strangers?"

"But I wasn't," the child protested. "I just said—"

Katie glanced down at Freeman and pressed her lips

together to keep from giggling out loud. He grinned back at her. "A cowboy?" she whispered.

He shrugged. "I've been called worse."

Chuckling, Katie pushed him down the sidewalk to a bench where the driver would pick them up. The clock in the doctor's office had told her that they'd have to wait fifteen minutes, but she didn't mind. The bench was in the shade, and she was content to be with Freeman.

Making sure he was in the shade, too, she sat down beside him. "I gave Isaac money and asked him to buy tickets for us for the Millers' spaghetti supper Friday night. The Ray Millers. They live out on Route 8. It's a benefit for the Troyer baby who's up at the DuPont Children's Hospital. Isaac and Patsy are going to the benefit, and they said they'd be happy to come by and pick us both up and take us home afterwards."

Freeman's brow furrowed. "A benefit supper? I don't mind the donation, but I'm not sure I'm ready to go out in public. Not to something like that." He turned to her. "I wish you'd asked me about it first."

"Nonsense," she said, brushing off his protests. "It will do you good; maybe you can try your crutches. And it will certainly help the Troyers."

Freeman frowned. "I would have liked the chance to make up my own mind if I wanted to go before you committed us to having your brother go out of his way to take us."

"Fine." She folded her hands on her lap and watched a minivan go by. "If you don't feel up to it, I'll go by myself. I go to things like this by myself all the time."

"That's not the point, Katie. A man likes to be asked. Susan never—"

"Susan?" She turned to him. "Your old girlfriend's involved in whether or not we go out to a benefit supper?" She gave an exasperated sigh. "I don't know what to say. I thought you'd welcome the opportunity to go out and be with people."

He ran his hand over the new cast. "Maybe I would have, but now I feel as if I'm being told what I should and shouldn't do."

"I'm sorry, Freeman." She raised her hands and let them fall. "You're right. I should have asked you first. I'll tell Isaac that we've changed our minds and—"

"*Ne.* I'll go, but next time—ask me."

"I will," she agreed, somewhat chastened. She didn't know why he'd taken it wrong, but she'd have to tread more carefully, she supposed. She smiled at him, ready to move away from any unpleasantness. Not that she was concerned. This was the way two people got to know each other. "I'm so pleased that your recovery is coming along so well. In no time at all, you'll be dressing those millstones single-handedly."

"I sure hope so, because I've had enough of this thing." He tapped the wheelchair. "That looks like our driver coming now." He indicated a blue van that had just turned into the parking lot. "We can stop at the medical supplies place and pick up my new crutches, and then I have a surprise for you."

"A surprise?" She smiled at him. "What is it?"

He smiled at her. "I'm taking you to Rita's for a gelato."

"A what?"

"A gelato. It's kind of an ice cream and Icee all in one," he explained. "Have you ever had it before?"

"Never, but I love ice cream."

"Wait until you taste this. You'll be wanting me to take you every day for another."

Freeman frowned with concentration as he took another half dozen steps and stopped to lean more heavily on his crutches. He was breathing hard, and he still felt a little unsteady. "This isn't as easy as it looks," he said to Katie.

"It doesn't look easy." She stood beside him. "Maybe you've walked enough for one day."

"*Ne.* I need to build up my strength." He couldn't believe how weak he'd gotten in such a short time. His lips tightened into a thin line as he walked through the parlor and out onto the open front porch. Sweat beaded on his forehead, but he was pleased with himself. By the next week he'd be back in the mill putting in a few hours each day. He might not be ready for lifting, but there was nothing wrong with his mind. He could direct Shad, answer the telephone and wait on customers. His only regret was that more time in the mill would mean less time in the house. He'd loved the time with Katie every day, but he needed to get back to work.

Freeman took another step. Then another.

"Don't wear yourself out," Katie said as she followed him out onto the porch.

"I won't." The benefit spaghetti supper that had almost caused their first argument was that night. The thought that she hadn't consulted him before making arrangements for them to go with Isaac and Patsy still rubbed him the wrong way, but he'd given in, and that was the end of it. It wasn't worth getting upset about a second time. It was just something they were going to have to work on.

He lowered himself gingerly onto a high-backed wooden bench, and rested the crutches against his cast. Then he patted the space beside him and she took a seat. She was all in russet today, russet dress and scarf, and russet apron. He smiled at her. "I was thinking that maybe we could get a swing for out here. Maybe some chairs and a little table. Peachy has some solid outdoor furniture at a decent price. Unless you'd rather have new furniture in one room in the house. Maybe a new couch and chair in the parlor?"

She gave him a mischievous smile and curled her legs, tucking her bare feet under her. "I'm not sure that is a question you should be asking me. That's more for a husband and wife to decide, don't you think?"

"Once we're married, we *will* be husband and wife," he answered. "My furniture in the parlor belonged to my parents—you might rather pick something out yourself."

Katie rested two slender fingers against her lips. They were perfectly shaped lips to his way of thinking. Her lips had a natural peach tint that added to her attractive features. Katie was a looker. That was for sure.

"Freeman, aren't you getting ahead of yourself? When did we start officially courting?"

He liked the way her blond hair curled in little ringlets around her sweet face, but best of all, he liked her eyes, never dull, always sparkling, lively and full of swirling depths. With eyes like Katie's, a man would always be guessing what she was up to. He'd never be bored.

He chuckled. "When did we start courting? I thought we talked about this the other night at your brother's. Obviously we're courting. We started courting about five minutes after I got the nerve to ask you that day in the mill."

"But at the mill that day you said it was a *trial* courting." He could tell that she was trying not to smile, but she couldn't help herself.

"I know what I said, but…" He stopped and started again. "But whatever I said that day, I'm saying now that we're courting, Katie Byler. And I intend to marry." He nodded, giving finality to his statement,

"Okay, then. We're courting. Officially now." She laughed and reached for his hand. Turning it over, she ran a finger over the calluses on his palm. "You have good hands," she murmured. "Hands tell a lot about a man."

"Do they now?" He didn't pull his hand away. He liked this playfulness in Katie. He liked sitting like this together. It made him happy to think that soon they could do it every day if they chose. They both were hard workers, but a man and his wife should take time for each other, to his way of thinking. Katie was easy to be with. She knew when to talk and when to sit quiet. It was one thing that he and Susan had always bumped heads on. While she never made assumptions and never disagreed with anything he said, she always had to be chattering away about this or that and sometimes he just wanted a little quiet. There were times when silence brought a couple closer than words.

She curled his hand into a gentle fist and released it. "Ivy's taking the buggy and going to Byler's to buy groceries to take over to the Marvin Kings. You heard they have his sister and her five children staying with them. They're the ones whose house burned last month."

He nodded, gazing out into the yard. Since Katie

had come into his life, he had to admit the place looked better. The flowerbeds were weeded, the lawn was cut and she'd even painted the rails on the porch. "Jehu said the church districts are planning a house raising for them at the end of the month. The husband works construction, and he's been away. He burned his hands trying to save things from the house, and he missed a few weeks of work."

"The King place is small," she said, "and they have the daughter with cerebral palsy, as well as four other little ones. I'm sure they can use the extra groceries."

"We'll get them back on their feet again, both families. Our elders have taken up a collection for propane appliances for the new house. And the Seven Poplars community is providing the plumbing and bathroom fixtures for two full baths and the kitchen. Your Sara is donating a freezer and two sides of beef."

"I didn't know," Katie said. "Sara does a lot of good and never says a word about it."

"I wouldn't have known if my grandmother hadn't overheard Preacher Dan mention it to our bishop last church Sunday." He thought about his grandmother driving to Byler's Store and then on to the Kings' by herself. "Maybe Uncle Jehu should go with her," he suggested. "Just to keep her company." He nodded. "He's been sitting on the back porch since our noon meal, cat-cradling."

Katie shook her head. "Not cat-cradling, I don't think. He's learning to knit. I told him if he likes playing with yarn so much, to get Ivy to teach him to knit. Then he could make mittens for the school kids and scarves for the elderly. He liked the idea and Ivy was tickled to give him some instruction. I think it worries him that he can't contribute more."

"Ya," Freeman agreed. "A difficult thing for a man to lose his eyesight. God's ways are sometimes hard to understand."

"And harder to accept with grace," Katie agreed. "Yet, we must. None of us can know His plan. We must rejoice in the blessings and endure the losses. But your uncle is a wise man. He has much to give to the community, especially to the younger people. He's a fine example of what a man should be."

"Exactly why he should go with Grossmama rather than let her go alone," Freeman said. He thought for a moment. "She hasn't left yet for the Kings' yet, has she?"

Katie shook her head. "I don't think so. Why?"

"I was just thinking, maybe she'd like some company," he said, quickly warming to the idea. "And Uncle Jehu might want to go."

Just then Ivy appeared around the corner of the house. "There you are. I heard your voices. I'm leaving now. I'll be back before dark, but I don't know just when. Don't worry about me." She gave a wave. "I'm perfectly capable of driving a horse."

"I know you are, but be careful," Katie warned. "The traffic is busier on Fridays, especially Route 8."

"Don't worry," Ivy said. "I always take the back roads." She tightened the strings on her black bonnet that she wore over her prayer *kapp.* "Yoder Road is quiet. Not many cars."

Katie rose and walked to the porch railing. "Freeman thinks you should ask Jehu if he wants to come with you. Jehu and Marvin King go way back. It would be company for you, don't you think?"

Ivy's smile faded and suddenly she looked nervous. "Take Jehu? I don't imagine he'd want to go."

"You won't know unless you ask him," Freeman suggested. He could tell by his grandmother's expression that she wasn't opposed to the idea. In fact, he suspected, she liked it.

"I'll give it a try," Ivy said with a shrug. She waved goodbye and disappeared around the end of the house again.

Freeman picked up his crutches and got shakily to his feet. "Think I'll take a stroll through the garden."

Determined, he made his way back through the house and down the ramp at the back porch. Uncle Jehu was no longer on the porch, although a pile of yarn and a tangle of something that might have been a scarf lay on the floor beside his chair. Katie followed Freeman down the walk and into the garden.

Going was a lot harder on the dirt, and they didn't stay long, just long enough to prove his point—that he could do it. As they exited the garden gate they heard the jingle of harness and the family buggy rattled past the house. Ivy was driving and his uncle was sitting beside her.

"Home later," Ivy called, happily.

"Don't hold supper!" Uncle Jehu hollered in their general direction. "We're getting subs at Byler's. Ivy and me."

"See," Katie said as she waved goodbye to them. Then she turned to Freeman. "You were right."

"You mean I had a good idea for a change?"

"Now, what's our next step?" Katie asked.

"Our next step?" He stopped to catch his breath.

She smiled the prettiest smile, his Katie. "To get them married, of course."

Chapter Twelve

"You don't think that we're doing the wrong thing, interfering in Uncle Jehu and Grossmama's personal lives?" Freeman asked as he made his way gingerly up the ramp to his back porch.

Katie laughed. "Now's a fine time to wonder, isn't it? I think the deed is done." She stepped around him and held open the door, all the while bestowing on him an endearing smile that made him feel as happy inside as though he'd swallowed a glass of sunshine.

"I'm glad you're fully on board with the idea," she went on, her eyes twinkling. "I wouldn't be surprised if you aren't enjoying our success more than I am. You're good at this. Maybe you could give Sara a few pointers in the matchmaking game."

"It was your idea." He placed the first crutch on the porch floor and took time to get his balance before putting his full weight on it. "I've known that my uncle is lonely, but I wasn't thinking about Grossmama. She's always been so independent—I didn't think she would want to marry again at her age."

"Maybe her age is exactly why she'd want to. Who

wants to grow old alone if there's a special person who can fill the empty space in your home?"

"And heart?" he suggested. He settled into his chair and sighed with relief as he took the weight off his good leg. He felt a little light-headed from the exercise, but he'd never admit it to Katie. He wanted her to see him as strong, able to protect her, not someone that needed to be cared for like a child.

"And heart," she agreed, taking the chair next to his and pulling it a little closer.

"I agree that it would be easier for me to have them settled, now that it looks like I'll be bringing a wife home this fall." He glanced at her. "If we call banns in September or October, we can marry in November after the crops are in. If you're agreeable."

"So soon?" she asked, wide-eyed. "I didn't think…" She looked down at her hands and then back up at him. "I assumed we would wait at least until spring."

"And why would we do that?" he asked her, realizing just how eager he was to marry her, now that his mind was made up. "We're of an age to know our own minds, aren't we? I know I'm past the time I should have married. And clearly, we're well suited." He met her gaze, resisting the urge to take her hand. They had both agreed they would be cautious with physical affection; there would be plenty of time for that after the wedding. "I don't want to rush you, but I don't see the need to drag out our courting any longer." He waited for her reaction, and when she just looked at him with doe eyes, he asked. "You do feel the same way, don't you, Katie?"

She lowered her head shyly. "*Ya*, I suppose, but you surprised me. It's all been so fast between us." Her cheeks took on a rosy hue and she nibbled on her lower lip. "I wouldn't want to make a mistake."

"You're the answer to my prayers. You could never be a mistake," he assured her. "And…" He waited until she raised her head and met his gaze straight on again. "I think it's time you broke the news to Kentucky Uriah. I feel like you've put it off long enough. It's not fair for him to think one thing when the truth is another." He tugged at the hem of her apron playfully. "I don't like thinking I've got competition."

"No competition. I already wrote to him." She clasped her hands together in her lap. "I told him that I was walking out with someone here."

"Did you tell him you were betrothed?"

"I didn't because I'm not," she said.

He couldn't tell if she was teasing him or not. "I'm doing that now," he said firmly. "And it's not a *trial* betrothal. Can we set a wedding date for early November? That's the traditional month of marriage, when most of our guests will be free to attend. And I'd want a big wedding and that would give us time to choose our cooks and helpers and get out all the invitations. We can hold the service here, if you like. I want as many people as possible to share our happiness."

"Are you sure you don't want to wait a little longer before we decide?" she asked.

"I see no reason to wait. I won't change my mind. I want you for my wife."

"And I want you for my husband," she replied.

"So it's settled. I'll look at the calendar and speak to my bishop." He reached out and squeezed her hand, happier than he thought he'd ever been in his life. "And then you'll be mine."

* * *

On the following church Sunday, Katie accompanied Freeman, Ivy and Jehu to services at the Detweiler home. Once they arrived, Freeman and Uncle Jehu joined the group of men standing in the barnyard, while the women went into the house to wait until it was time to be seated. There Katie found herself eagerly welcomed into the crowded kitchen as Ivy introduced her to Viola, her hostess, and those women, girls and children of the worship community that she hadn't met before.

Each Amish church district made up their own larger family, worshiping and sharing the daily patterns of their lives, supporting those who needed help and taking pleasure in each other's company. When an Amish woman married, she would naturally attend her husband's church and live by the rules set by the community and the elders, so it was important that whomever Freeman married fit in, heart and mind. Many of these people, young and old, male and female, would be an intimate part of her life for years to come. Naturally, Katie couldn't help wondering if they would like her and if she would feel at home among them.

Shortly after their arrival, the older male members of the community and male guests filed in and took their places on benches on one side of the room, followed by the older women and honored women visitors who sat on the opposite side. Next came the unmarried women and the teenagers. Men and women always sat separately but young children and infants were passed between the groups at their leisure. When all were seated, an older man, the *vorsinger* or song leader, began the first hymn in a slow falsetto. Everyone joined in, and the elders took their seats near the front of the large living room. The hymn was a long one with many verses, and at the closing, the congregation knelt for the opening prayer and then rose in unison for the Bible reading.

The second hymn was always the *Loblied*. Gradually, Katie felt at ease as the voices rose in the much-loved song. She'd grown up in another district, with different preachers and another bishop, but this service was familiar and comforting. She liked red-haired Preacher Dan, who Freeman and Ivy had spoken of so highly, and she enjoyed his sermon on faithfulness. From her seat between two unmarried girls, she could see Freeman sitting several rows ahead of her on the far side. He'd been given a place by the aisle so that he could stretch out his leg and his crutches were under the bench. He couldn't see her without turning his head, and it pleased her to watch him without him being aware of it.

Morning service lasted nearly three hours, including the singing of hymns, Preacher Dan's sermon, a shorter sermon by the bishop, and the deacon's announcements of coming events and a planned day of fasting and silent prayer in sympathy for those caught up in foreign wars and displacement. Generations earlier, the Amish had been driven out of their homelands in Switzerland and Germany, many having suffered death and torture because of their religious beliefs. The bishop reminded them all that they must not forget that people today also suffered cruelly because of their faith in God. They might not be Amish, but it was the duty of the community to offer what help they could by remembering and praying for the victims.

The bishop's words touched Katie, and she went

from the service to the communal dinner in a more serious state of mind than she had come in that morning. She'd rarely heard an Amish preacher or bishop urge his congregation to contemplate the plight of Englishers and consider their suffering. It was a good thing, she thought, a possible way to help, because she had a great belief in the power of prayer and in God's mercy. And it also brought back to each of them what sacrifices their own Amish forebearers had made so that they could find peace and a new home here in the United States of America.

After the closing hymn, everyone went outside where long tables had been set up for the traditional shared meal. Freeman was waiting for her near the corner of the house. "Are you doing okay?" he asked quietly, his expression anxious.

She nodded. "Of course, Freeman. I like your community."

"And is Grossmama looking after you? She promised me that she would."

"She is," Katie assured him. "Everyone is kind, and I like your Preacher Dan."

"Good. Good. Come, I want you to meet him and our bishop." Already nimble on his crutches, he led her over to where a group of the elders had gathered and introduced them. They exchanged a few pleasantries before Ivy came to ask her to assist in serving the food.

"Dinner," the bishop announced. He patted his ample stomach. "I like the sound of that." He smiled at her. "We are pleased to have you with us, and pleased that our friend Freeman has finally found someone he wants to spend his life with."

Katie flashed a shy smile at Freeman and then hurried away after Ivy, who explained to her that there had been a bit of a mishap in the kitchen involving two ornery little boys and a tray of sandwiches. The interior of the kitchen was a barely controlled chaos with crying babies and toddlers, giggling teenage girls whispering to each other, and Viola giving instructions. Katie saw the remains of the sandwiches scattered on the floor, found a broom and dustpan and quickly set about clearing the mess. The meat, cheese, lettuce and rolls on the table were being reassembled by an elderly white-haired woman in black and one of the girls, but what had fallen was obviously beyond saving, except as bounty for the chickens. Viola pointed the way to the poultry yard and Katie carried away the scraps.

Returning from the chicken house, she washed her hands and joined the other young women in transporting the meal to the first sitting, which consisted of the men and guests. The women and children would eat afterwards, partaking of the same food but with much less formality than was expected of those at first table. With the men fed, the women would be free to visit and eat at their leisure. And whatever cleanup chores were required, Ivy assured her that they wouldn't be expected to do it. Dish detail was regularly assigned to the teenage boys—quite a sensible arrangement, Katie thought.

Even with the loss of a great deal of the contents of the sandwich tray in the kitchen accident, there was more than enough food to feed everyone. As the men took their places at long tables under the trees in the yard, Viola put a pitcher of ice water into Katie's hands. "Emily's setting the glasses. Pour those who want water, then come back for the iced tea, then lemonade, then root beer."

"I have a better idea." Katie started uprighting glasses on a tray. "It will go quicker if we fill glasses here. Then we can each carry a tray with an assortment and ask everyone what they'd like to drink. It'll go faster that way."

"Well... I suppose...we could try it that way," Viola said, seeming flustered.

"Katie." Freeman called to her and motioned her over to where he was sitting.

"I'll be right back," she told Viola. Then to the other girls assigned drinks, she said, "Put the glasses on the trays and start pouring." She made her way to Freeman and bent her head to hear what he wanted to tell her.

"Must you be so..." He exhaled and started again, speaking under his breath. "Just do what Viola asked. No need to rearrange the process."

She straightened up, making a face at him. "But my way is so much easier. We'll be done in no time and people will have what they want to drink faster."

"Katie, you're new here. Best not to make a fuss," he whispered.

She took a breath before she responded. "So what you're saying is that I should do it less efficiently so as not to make waves?"

He glanced at the men at the table, then back at her. "Please, Katie. Don't be difficult. You don't always have to be in charge."

"*Ne*, I suppose not." She could feel her cheeks burning. "I suppose Susan would not have done such a thing," she murmured. "I'm sure she knew her place."

"*Ya,*" he said, obviously exasperated with her. "You're right there. Susan never made a fuss in public."

"I'm sure she didn't." Katie walked away, embarrassed, wanting desperately to have the last word, but too in control to make a complete fool of herself in front of Freeman's friends.

Once the drinks were poured and served, some in the manner Viola had instructed and some the way Katie had suggested, Katie returned to the kitchen. At the sink, she filled a dishpan of water and began to wash whatever she could find in the kitchen. Strictly speaking, washing dishes was work and work was not performed on the Sabbath, but most Amish women were too practical to fret over small sins and they cleaned up whatever came to hand when it was needed. Viola came in and began arranging casseroles on the counter, and Katie turned to her, dried her hands on a towel, and smiled. "It's so kind of you to have me in your home," she said.

"*Ya.* You are welcome here." Viola was brisk but not unfriendly.

"I hope I didn't speak out of turn. About the drinks. I didn't mean to cause a problem. I just get in a habit of doing things a certain way and…" She met her hostess's appraising look. "My mother tells me that I'm too forward. I ask your pardon if I offended you."

"For what?" Viola's lips curved up in a smile. "You were trying to help. And I've been called forward myself. I think we'll get on well enough, Katie Byler." She patted Katie's hand. "It's pleased I am that our Freeman has finally stopped moping over that Susan and looked around for a sensible young woman. I only hope that the two of you don't knock heads. You and Freeman, I mean. He's full of himself, but then most men are before they have a wife and children."

Katie chuckled.

"Now, if you wouldn't mind, there's another bucket of scraps for the chickens in the corner. I don't want fruit flies; you know what eager houseguests they can be." Viola, a thin bird of a woman with a snub nose and metal-rim glasses, pointed at a bucket on the floor. "Go out through the side door. It's quicker."

Katie picked up the bucket of garbage and went in the direction Viola sent her, down a hallway, through a utility room and side porch. She completed her task and was just hooking the door on the chicken house when Freeman came up the path, moving easily on his crutches.

"Katie. I was looking for you."

"So you found me." She realized her tone of voice was less than kind. She looked up at him, balanced on his crutches. He was getting stronger fast; soon he'd be able to put weight on the casted leg and would only need one crutch. She took a deep breath. "Freeman. Before you say anything, let me apologize." She set the bucket down. "I should never have said anything sarcastic about Susan. And you were right—I *was* too forward. I should have done what Viola asked, and I told her so. I'm sorry." She didn't want to argue with Freeman. She loved him. What was wrong with her that she spoke before thinking?

He shook his head. "I came to say that *I'm* sorry. I'm a dunce." He grimaced. "I should have kept my mouth shut and let you pass out drinks anyway you please. It was just that I wanted to make a good impression on my church family. And you did… I mean you have. There was no reason for me to worry; I should have known that. Viola likes you. She told me so. And several people came to me, just to say how happy they were with our betrothal announcement." He shrugged. "I suppose this is what comes of me not marrying younger. The older a man gets, the more convinced he is that he knows more than he does."

"A woman, too." She smiled up and him and he smiled back. She looked up to see his uncle approaching. "Uncle Jehu."

The older man came down the path at a steady pace, keeping to the center of the walkway with confidence. How did he do it? Katie wondered. Ivy had explained that Jehu could see light and dark shadows, but he certainly couldn't see the objects around him. "You never cease to amaze me," she said. "Are you part bat, that you can find your way without seeing?"

Jehu laughed merrily. "*Ne*, not that I've noticed. I just have a good memory."

"Uncle Jehu built this chicken house and the shed beside it," Freeman explained. "This used to be his farm."

"Ach," Katie said. "I didn't know."

"And how would you?" Jehu asked her. He looked to his nephew. "There was something I wanted to talk to you about, if you have a minute. I was going to wait until tonight, but this seems as good a time as any."

Katie reached for the bucket. "I'll leave you two alone."

The older man shook his head. "No need. You've a sensible head on your shoulders, and I trust your judgment. I'd like your opinion, too, Katie." He took a deep breath and straightened his shoulders. "What would you say, Freeman, if I told you that I'd want your permission to walk out with Ivy?" He leaned in. "Am I a fool to think of marrying at my age?"

"Well, it's about time," Freeman replied enthusiastically. "Katie and I have been trying—"

Katie gave Freeman a hard tug on his arm, so hard, she was afraid she'd knocked him off balance and he was going to take a tumble. But it was enough to silence him. "Jehu! I think it's a wonderful idea," she said with enthusiasm. Freeman opened his mouth to speak again and she brought a finger to her lips, in an exaggerated motion. "I know how highly Ivy thinks of you."

"I hope so," Jehu said. "We've known one another for more than forty years, and I've always admired her. She knows my faults, and I've suffered her filling oat porridge for breakfast whether I wanted it or not." He looked up at Freeman. "I felt it right to ask for your blessing before I asked her if she'd be willing to court. Do I have it?"

Freeman grinned and nodded. "With all my heart, Uncle. You two are both dear to me, and I believe that marriage is something that would make you both happy."

"I think so, too," Uncle Jehu said. "I had a good marriage to a good woman, and I miss that companionship. It's not good for a man to be alone. Or a woman." He turned his head and smiled at Katie. "It seems you've come to the same conclusion."

"I knew it all along. It just took me a while to find the right girl," Freeman told him.

Uncle Jehu ran his fingers through his beard and tugged at the strands thoughtfully. "Well, the way I see it, there's no time like the present." He gave a wave. "No need to worry about us riding home with you in the buggy, following afternoon service. Ivy likes to walk home on Sundays when she can, and it's not far. It might do me a world of good to walk with her."

"Whatever you think best," Freeman agreed.

"I don't know about that." Uncle Jehu shook his head. "What I think best at the moment is for me to go back to the table and have a second piece of peach pie." He rubbed his midsection and chuckled. "But, common sense tells me I've eaten enough for one meal and need to leave enough for someone else." He gave a nod. "It heartens me that you two approve. I'd not want to cause trouble under our roof or any other. But one thing I promise you, if your grandmother will have me, I'll do my best to care for her the way she deserves."

"I know you will," Freeman assured him as he walked away.

When they were alone again, she poked him in the side. "You weren't supposed to tell him it was our idea to see them together," she chided.

He pulled away from her, apparently ticklish. "I figured pretty quick that I said something wrong. You almost knocked me over."

She laughed with him. "Oh, I did not. A big strong man like you?" She dropped her hands to her hips. "It's best if he believes it was his idea to court your grandmother. Not that we'd come up with it and were trying to—"

"Manage their lives?" Freeman asked. He chuckled. "But we are, aren't we?"

"Maybe a little," she said, stepping in front of him to face him. "But with the best intentions."

"Thank goodness you stopped me," he told her. "I wouldn't want Uncle Jehu to think that I was trying to force him out of my house."

"He doesn't. He wouldn't. He knows what a good person you are."

Freeman leaned on his crutches and drew the tip of his index finger down her chin. "You think I am, Katie?"

Emotion constricted her throat. "I know you are," she murmured, looking into his warm eyes. "The best."

"Goot." He grinned at her. "Remember that when you're tempted to crack my knuckles with a spoon."

Chapter Thirteen

From the mill's loading dock, Freeman waved as Preacher Dan drove out of the parking lot with six bags of chicken feed and two of hog chow in the back of his wagon just as the truck from R & W Stables was pulling into the lot. Freeman glanced at Shad. "Can you manage this order?"

Shad nodded. He removed his straw hat and used a handkerchief to wipe the sweat off his forehead. *"Ya."* A wide smile split his narrow face. "Bagged and waiting for'm. Same as last month and the one before."

"I'll leave you to it, then," Freeman pronounced. Loading the horse feed and mineral blocks was routine, but a task he wasn't quite ready for yet. He was off his crutches now. His doctor wanted him to put weight on the leg, but he needed the assistance of a cane, which wasn't exactly conducive to loading hundred-pound bags of feed.

Freeman eyed Shad. The young man might be a bit undersized for a miller, but he was strong for his size and he could move fast when he put his mind to it. Maybe he would prove his worth, as Katie and Uncle

Jehu seemed to think. Shad's effort had improved by leaps and bounds in the last few weeks. Back at the start of summer, Freeman wouldn't have given him much of a chance of lasting until autumn, let alone keeping his job long enough to serve his apprenticeship. If it hadn't been for the accident, Freeman knew he probably would have sent Shad home to his mother and looked for a steadier employee. Katie's stubborn insistence that what Shad needed was more encouragement and more responsibility, rather than less, might have been what made the difference.

Freeman hated to admit it, but as an employer, he had a lot to learn. Maybe more than that, there was a great deal of wisdom he had to gain. Truth was, he had Katie to thank for saving his relationship with Shad. He would have lost a valuable asset because he hadn't been willing to try patience and trust. Katie was quite the woman, wise beyond her years. Hard to believe that he'd only really known her for a little more than eight weeks. Having her in his life had changed it so much for the better.

Using his cane, Freeman made his way down the ramp and toward the house. A fat mallard hen trailed after him, and following her, beak to bobbing tails were nine fluffy ducklings. "Go on back to the pond, *Mommi*," he said, waving his arm. "You're going to get your babies flattened in this parking lot." The duck paid no attention, so he dug in his pants pocket and came up with a handful of shelled corn. Using the food as bait, he led the ducks out of the lot, across the drive and down to the water's edge. He scattered the rest of the corn and then, while they were picking at the bright yellow kernels, he made his getaway.

Mingled peals of laughter from the yard drew his attention and he looked up to see his grandmother and uncle sitting side by side in a swing under the maple trees. Balls of multi-colored wool were scattered all around their feet, and Grossmama was waving a length of knitting and giggling like a girl.

"What's so funny?" Freeman called.

"She's taunting a blind man," his uncle replied. "Just because my knitting is a little uneven."

"Uneven?" Grossmama doubled over with glee. "Freeman's tame crow could knit better with his beak tied behind him than this man. I wouldn't put this poor excuse for a baby blanket in a dog's bed."

"You see how she mistreats me," Uncle Jehu protested, pulling the little terrier into his lap and scratching behind the dog's ears.

His grandmother stood up and started picking up the stray balls of wool. "Pay no attention to him," she said. "There's none so blind as he who will not see."

Freeman looked from one to the other; they were obviously enjoying themselves. More importantly, each other. The two had been inseparable lately, so he supposed their courtship was going smoothly. Probably Katie could take credit for that blessing, as well. He couldn't remember when he'd seen Uncle Jehu smile more, and his grandmother now sang in the mornings when she worked in her flower garden. Maybe Uncle Jehu and Grossmama would have decided to court if Katie hadn't joined them, but there was no telling. They'd always been a family, but he had no doubts that Katie Byler had brought joy into this house and drawn them all closer.

Now that his leg had almost mended, Katie no longer came daily to help with the housework. Due to their ages and circumstances, Uncle Jehu and Grossmama might get around the rules. But it wasn't seemly that he and Katie, about to call their banns, should spend every day in each other's company. Nor did it seem right that she should be his housekeeper. It was the right decision but that didn't keep Freeman from missing her presence or from feeling that without her some of the light had gone out of his home.

Katie did come to visit his grandmother several times a week, and she was quick to lend him a hand where it was needed. Sometimes, she could be persuaded to walk down by the millpond with him, and several times he'd taken her out in the rowboat. They'd made the excuse that they were fishing, when really, it was a way to be alone together without crossing any unwritten rules of behavior for courting couples. They were in full view of anyone passing by, yet no one could approach them, and no one could overhear their conversation.

Once she stopped working for them, Katie hadn't returned to her brother's home, but had remained at Sara's. With the wedding so close, Katie had decided it would be better to leave his brother and new wife to themselves. Katie and Freeman continued to worship together on church Sundays and visit her family on the alternate Sabbaths. Twice, they had driven out in the evening to spend time with other young couples, but as much as he enjoyed the company of his friends, he found that he liked being alone with Katie best.

Freeman had never thought that he would talk to anyone the way he talked to her. She was a good listener, and she never held back when she had an opinion, but she was sensible. If he could defend his position and it was better than hers, she would come around without the least bit of resentment. Standing there seeing how Uncle Jehu and Grossmama were having such a good time together reminded him how much he and Katie found to laugh about. He'd often wondered if he'd ever find a woman that would fill the empty part in his life, and now, thanks be to the Lord God, he had. Katie Byler was the answer to his prayers.

They'd set a wedding date for the second Thursday in November, and they'd already picked their couples to attend them. The wedding couldn't come soon enough to suit him. Despite his earlier concerns about her strong personality and his determination that he be the master of his own house, Katie was his choice for a wife. He felt at odds without her beside him, and he expected his life to go smoother once the formalities were over and they could settle into married life.

As Freeman walked toward his grandmother and uncle, he realized she must have been talking to him and he hadn't heard a word she said.

"Told you. You may as well talk to your knitting needles," Uncle Jehu said. "The boy's not heard a word you've said."

"Ya," Freeman said. "Sorry. I was…"

His uncle laughed. "Woolgathering. Mind's on Katie, you can count on it."

"I'm sorry, Grossmama," Freeman said. "I'm listening now. What was it you said?"

"I said," she repeated merrily, "that Jehu and I were considering a day in October."

He blinked. "For?"

"We're doing no such thing," Uncle Jehu told her.

Playfully, he flung a ball of wool in Ivy's direction. "We'll marry—*if* we marry—in December. We'll not be stealing the thunder from all you young rascals." He looked back at Freeman. "First we get you and Katie settled and then we'll see."

Freeman stared at her. "Married? The two of you have decided—"

"Sweet huckleberry buckle," his grandmother exclaimed, coming to her feet. "You can't think that we mean to waste the remainder of our days courting. Of course we're considering setting a wedding date."

Freeman caught her to him and hugged her. "Congratulations. I think that's wonderful. Katie will be thrilled."

"Well, you're not to tell her yet, because we'll want to do that ourselves, once we speak to the bishop," Grossmama said. She kissed his cheek. "But you're a good boy. If I had a dozen grandsons, you'd still be my favorite."

"You know I'd do anything for you," Freeman said, releasing her and stepping back. "I'd be lost without you."

"The best thing you can do for her now," Uncle Jehu said, "is to marry that pretty girl of yours come November and give us a bevy of grandbabies to bounce on our knees."

"I'll marry Katie," Freeman promised. "As to the grandchildren, that's up to the Lord. You know we'll welcome as many as he chooses to send us."

"Amen to that," his grandmother whispered. "It's been far too long since we've had a new babe in this house." She beamed at Freeman. "But you cost me many a night's sleep. You were so set in your ways that I thought you'd end up an old bachelor with a house full of cats."

"Are you calling me hard to please?" Freeman asked.

"Truer words never spoken," Uncle Jehu chimed in. "Until sweet Katie came to us, we were both afraid that we'd be in our graves long before you ever found a woman you'd want to take to wife."

"I think that's it for this batch," Katie said as she turned off the heat under the pressure cooker. "We'll let it cool down and then put the last six quarts in." She and Ivy were in Freeman's kitchen, where they'd been canning tomatoes all morning. Two dozen pints and an equal number of quart jars stood on the windowsill. So far, every jar had been sealed. They looked wonderful and would taste even better when the temperature dropped and the cold winds of winter whipped around the farmhouse. Katie had always loved canning. It was hard work, usually in a sweltering kitchen in the first days of September, but the rewards were so great. It wasn't like sweeping the floor, where the results lasted only a few hours. There was nothing like pantry shelves filled with jars of fruit and vegetables to make a woman pleased with her efforts.

Ivy carefully ladled hot skinned tomatoes into waiting Mason jars. "It's so good of you to come and help me with this," she said. "And good of Sara to spare you."

"I'm glad to do it," Katie replied. "Canning is one job I never minded. And you've had such a bumper crop of tomatoes this year. It would be a shame to let any go to waste." She wiped down the jar rims with a clean dishtowel, added lids and screwed the rims into place. Then, using hot mitts, she lifted the filled jars and moved them to the counter beside the gas range.

Ivy finished filling the last jar and went to the sink to wash her hands. "Iced tea?" she asked.

Katie nodded. *"Danki."* Ivy made good tea, flavoring it with fresh mint leaves from her garden and using raw sugar instead of the white refined sugar that most people used. "I had a nice letter from Uriah yesterday," she said. "He said more in it than he ever has before. He seems like a good man. I hope he finds someone who will make him happy."

Ivy filled two glasses with ice and poured cold tea over top. "I know he must be sorry that you've chosen to wed someone else."

"He sounds as if he is." Katie glanced at her and smiled. "He says that if things don't work out, if I decide that I don't want to marry Freeman, he's still willing." She shrugged, amused that she'd gone years hoping for a husband and now she had more than one man willing to wed her.

Ivy chuckled. "Maybe you should think again. This Uriah might have more sense than my grandson. Look at him." She pointed out the window. "Practically running across the yard, barely using his cane. I keep telling him not to get ahead of himself. Not to push himself too hard. Nobody can tell him anything. He always knows best." She shook her head. "He won't always be easy to live with, Katie. I warn you. I love him, but I know him all too well. God never made a more hardheaded man."

They heard the slam of the porch screen door. Ivy glanced up. "Don't bring that crow in here, Freeman. We're canning. We can't have feathers flying around while we're putting up food." She turned back to Katie. "You tell him, Katie. He won't listen to me. I don't want that crow in the house. Nasty bird."

Katie went to the kitchen door. Freeman did have the crow. It was riding on his shoulder. There was no cord on its leg. Apparently the crow sat there of its own volition. "Your grandmother wants you to leave the crow—" she began.

"I heard her," Freeman answered. "This crow's a lot cleaner than that dog of Uncle Jehu's, but she doesn't have to worry. I'm not bringing him in." He walked over to a hanging wooden bar that he'd suspended from the rafters in one corner of the porch and gently transferred the bird from his shoulder to the perch.

The bird settled, Freeman followed Katie into the kitchen. "That all you've got done?" he asked looking at the rows of cooling jars. "I know there's another half bushel basket of tomatoes outside. You think you'll get them all done today?"

Katie looked at Ivy and rolled her eyes. "Maybe we will and maybe we won't," she said. "Mind your own beeswax. If we don't finish today, I'll come back tomorrow."

Freeman wandered over to the stove, paying her no mind. "These finished?" he asked, indicating the pressure canner.

"Ya," his grandmother replied. "Just waiting for the steam to die down."

Freeman set his cane against the counter and reached up to remove the weight from the top of the canner. "You've got to remove this to release the pressure," he explained, as if he thought neither of them had ever canned tomatoes before.

"Careful," Katie warned. "You'll burn your—"

"Ouch!" A hiss of steam came from the canner and Freeman jumped back, rubbing his thumb and forefinger together.

"You okay?" Katie asked, suppressing the urge to giggle. It wasn't nice to laugh at his pain, but how could he be so silly as to not know you didn't just remove the weight?

"Fine." He licked his injured finger.

"You need a cold cloth for that?"

"Nope," he told her.

"Then wash up and sit down at the table. We've got hot vegetable soup and ham sandwiches for nooning."

"Sandwiches?" he asked pitifully. "I hope you've made a stack of them. I'm starving."

"Canning days you're fortunate to get sandwiches," Ivy said. "When I was growing up, we made do with stewed tomatoes on bread when my mother was doing up vegetables." She looked around. "Where's Jehu? He's not usually late to table."

"In the garden," Freeman said. The tip of his finger was red and he went to the sink and ran cold water on it. "He said he wanted to pick the last ears of corn for you. No more fresh corn until next summer now."

Katie handed him a towel to dry his hand.

"I don't see salt," Freeman said, looking at the counter. "You didn't forget to put salt in the jars, did you? My mother always put a half a teaspoon of salt in every jar. To help seal it, I think."

Katie grimaced. "Salt makes the tomatoes salty, and we don't need to add salt when we don't have to. Especially not for your grandmother or Uncle Jehu. Too much salt can cause high blood pressure. Strokes.

We don't need salt to make the jars seal. That's an old wives' tale."

Freeman looked skeptical. "You always used salt, didn't you, Grossmama? I'm sure you're supposed to."

"Maybe I did and maybe I didn't," she said, taking a plate of sandwiches Katie had made earlier from the refrigerator. "But we decided not to do it this year."

"All the same, what does the canning book say?"

"Freeman, will you let it go?" Katie said. She wanted to swat him with a damp towel. "We know what we're doing. We don't need your advice on canning. This is women's business, not men's."

"I'm just trying to help," he protested.

"I know," she answered, trying not to let her annoyance with him show. "I know you are, but—"

"You have to admit, I've been right in the past. You asked me for advice, and I—"

"Might have needed it before," she said. "But not now. I've already caught a husband, haven't I? So I must not be doing everything wrong."

"Whoa. Whoa." He shook his head. "Sorry. All I wanted to do was make a suggestion, but if you don't want it, that's fine."

The screen door banged again and Katie heard footsteps on the porch for a second time. "Uncle Jehu?"

"Got some corn," he replied. "I've husked it outside. Thought it might go good for lunch with the soup and sandwiches."

"Bring it in," Ivy ordered. "I'll put a pot of water on." She looked at Katie. "It won't take long to steam the corn."

"How long?" Freeman asked.

"Maybe five or ten minutes to heat the water. Another five to steam the corn," Katie said. "We can sit down and start on the sandwiches. The soup's almost heated."

"*Ne*, that's fine." He smiled at her. "I'd like you to see something. It will just take five minutes. If you wouldn't mind coming out to the mill while the corn cooks."

Katie looked back at Ivy.

"Go on, child. I can manage six ears of corn."

"We'll be right back," Freeman assured his grand-mother.

Katie removed her soiled apron and hung it over a chair, then followed him out of the house and across to the mill. "What are we going to see?" she asked, tickled to have a few minutes alone with him. She'd been sad when he insisted she couldn't work as his housekeeper anymore; she missed him on the days she didn't get to see him. But when they did see each other, Freeman was good at making sure they were always able to steal a few minutes alone.

"It's a surprise," he said. He'd left his cane in the kitchen, so he linked his arm through hers. If anyone saw them, she knew he could make the argument she was assisting, but she knew better. He liked this inno-cent physical contact as much as she did.

"It's for you. For us." He led her across the yard and into the back section of the mill, an area that she'd never seen before. "I've got a workshop back here," he explained. "And there's something here for you." He opened a back door and motioned to her. "See what you think of this."

She paused, letting her eyes adjust to the dimmer light inside the building. Standing in the center of a large room was a dark oak dresser and a bed with a tall carved headboard and turned foot posts. "Oh," she breathed as she approached the bed and ran a hand over the nearest post. Carved into the headboard and posts were tulips and a pattern of vines. The craftsmanship was lovely, the tulips stained red and the vines green. "You made this for me?" she asked. Tears clouded her vision. "Freeman… I don't know what to say." It was so sweet of him. The intricate flower pattern wasn't really her taste, but she would have glued her mouth shut before she would have ever admitted it. If Freeman thought this was beautiful, then she would learn to love it as she loved him.

"*Ne*. I didn't make them." Freeman shook his head. He walked to the tall dresser and pointed out the same tulip-and-vine pattern on the front of the drawers. "A Mennonite fellow down in Greenwood makes these. I just remembered they were here. Susan and I saw them at the state fair and I had him make them for—"

"You had the set made for Susan?" she interrupted, feeling as if she were the pressure cooker on the stove. She was suddenly so angry that she thought steam might come out of her ears.

Freeman didn't seem to notice. He looked so pleased with himself. "*Ya*. I never gave them to her, of course. It was supposed to be a wedding gift. She saw it and liked it and I ordered it. But by the time the cabinet-maker finished them, Susan and I had already parted ways. It's been sitting here all these years. I pulled the canvas off and polished them up. What do you think?" He leaned against the doorframe. "Pretty, aren't they?"

She turned to him, planting her hands on her hips. She didn't know if she wanted to holler at him or cry.

She felt as if suddenly the ground beneath her was shifting. How could she have been so mistaken? How had she not seen this before? "You think I want to sleep in a bed you bought for another woman?" she demanded.

Freeman stared at her in obvious confusion. "Why not? It's brand-new. Nobody ever slept in it. I thought you'd like it."

"But you bought it for her." Her voice didn't sound like her own. "For Susan."

He frowned. "What difference does it make who I bought it for? It's an expensive bedroom set. I thought that you—"

"You thought wrong!"

He drew himself up. "No need to get huffy with me. Most women would—"

"You bought it for Susan," she interrupted. "I'd sleep on the floor before I'd sleep in her bed. In what she picked out."

"That's the dumbest thing I've ever heard, Katie."

Katie backed away. At first she was angry. Now she was hurt. So hurt. She could feel tears burning her eyes. "Am I always to be second place to her, Freeman? To Susan? Is it me you love and want to marry? Or is it still Susan? Are you still in love with her?"

He scowled as if that were the most ridiculous thing a person had ever said to him. "*Ne!* Of course not."

"But you *wish* I was more like her." She walked past him, out into the humid day. Away from the pretty bed and dresser that weren't really hers. That would never be hers. "Tell the truth, Freeman. You do wish I was Susan, don't you?"

"Sometimes, maybe I do," he blurted. "At least she

wasn't a shrew. Susan would have had the good manners never to throw a gift back into a man's face."

"But I'm *not* Susan. I'm going to say what I think. You know that about me. And I'm never going to be the biddable wife you want."

"You're being hysterical." He waved his hand. "Blowing this all out of proportion."

"Am I?" She shook her head. "I don't think so. This just shows how little you know me. How little you understand about who I am."

"Katie, don't make more of this than it is. If you don't like the bedroom set, fine." He threw up his hand. "We can sell it."

"There's no need." She wanted to turn and walk away. Run. But she held her ground, looking up at him. His face was flushed and she could tell he was angry, too. "Keep it and give it to the next girl you court."

"Katie. Listen to reason."

"I am," she flung, tears running down her face. "And reason tells me that I can't marry you. Find someone else," she cried. "Someone who will say 'yes, Freeman, of course Freeman,' like Susan. Because I can't do that. I won't."

His eyes narrowed. She could see his shoulders tense and feel the anger emanating from him. "If that's the way you feel," he said, "then so be it. Better to end it now before any more harm is done."

"You're right," she answered hotly. "Before anyone's heart is broken."

Chapter Fourteen

Katie knocked on the partially open door of Sara's sewing room. She'd been awake most of the night, and had alternated her hours between pacing the floor and praying on her knees. The prayer might have helped; the walking hadn't. And now that she'd come to a decision, she felt that she had to confide in Sara before doing anything else.

"Yes?"

Katie pushed open the door and stood in the doorway.

The dark-eyed matchmaker looked up from the treadle Singer sewing machine and smiled. "I was wondering where you got to this morning." Sara gathered the olive-green skirt she'd been stitching and held it up. "What do you think of this fabric? I'm making a new dress for one of Wayne Lapp's girls. It's a lovely blend. It should wash well and come off the line without a lot of wrinkles."

"It's lovely," Katie said. The Lapps had a houseful of children and a limited income. Sara was a master seamstress, and a new dress would be welcome and could be handed down to smaller sisters when the recipient had outgrown it.

"Well, don't just stand there. Come in." Sara waved her in.

This was one of Katie's favorite rooms in the house—Sara's sewing room. A battered old pine table held cut and pinned lengths of cloth that, once stitched together, looked like a black Sunday dress for someone. Katie tried to compose herself as she took in the pleasant room. Nearly square, it was painted a restful pale blue with two large windows, a colorful rag rug, and two rocking chairs placed side by side to catch the light. One wall boasted an oversized maple cabinet rescued from a twentieth-century millinery shop and open drawers revealed an assortment of various sizes of thread, needles, scissors and paper patterns. A small walnut table with turned legs stood between the windows and held a cheerful bouquet of yellow zinnias and blue cornflowers. Sara loved fresh flowers and she placed them throughout her home. It was a practice that Katie wanted to emulate when and if she ever had her own house.

Sara studied Katie's face. "Why do I get the idea that something has gone very wrong for you?"

Katie was afraid she was going to burst into tears. She still couldn't believe what had seemed so good between her and Freeman had turned out so badly, so quickly. "I need to talk to you." She swallowed, trying to regain her composure.

Sara nodded. "Of course. When you didn't take supper with us last night, and then didn't come down to breakfast, I guessed that you were upset." She rose from her chair at the sewing machine and motioned toward the rockers. "Will you sit?"

Katie rubbed her hands nervously on her apron. "*Ne.* What I have to say won't take long." She looked at Sara with what she knew were puffy and probably red and swollen eyes. She'd cried last night, but she was done weeping, and she hoped she could carry on without making a fool of herself. "I've broken off my betrothal to Freeman," she said quietly. "It's over between us."

"Oh, Katie." Sara brought fingertips to her lips in a sigh. "Why? Did you argue?"

"We did."

"That happens with every couple." Sara looked down and then back up at Katie. "Are you sure this isn't something that can be smoothed over? A lovers' quarrel?"

Katie shook her head. "*Ne.* I wish it was, but this can't be fixed."

Again, Sara hesitated. "I'm so sorry. I was so sure that the two of you were a solid match." Her eyes filled with compassion. "I believed that you were right for each other, that you were in love."

"I was in love with him," Katie assured her. "Maybe I always will be, but loving someone doesn't mean that you'd be a good wife for him." She caught the hem of her apron, balling it in her fist. "I can't marry Freeman, because he still cares for the woman that he almost married ten years ago. She's been a shadow between us from the beginning. I should have seen it sooner. And… I can never measure up to her memory. I realized yesterday that I couldn't marry him, knowing he loves her."

Sara exhaled loudly, sounding impatient now. "You two. You're like a pair of goats knocking heads. I knew you were both strong-willed, but sometimes that works best in a marriage. One balances out the other. You and

Freeman are alike in so many ways. Is it possible that you misinterpreted his—"

"*Ne.*" Katie shook her head. "There's no mistake. He brings her up all the time. He compares us. All the time. I can't live that way. Not for the rest of my life."

They were both quiet for a minute.

"The decision is yours," Sara said softly. "But I have to advise you not to be hasty."

"I've made up my mind, Sara. I know I'm doing the right thing." As she said the words, she felt less sure of them, but she refused to second-guess herself.

"I hope you are." Sara's eyes crinkled at the corners. "Because Freeman seems such a sensible man. I find it hard to believe he'd still be mooning over a woman after ten years."

"Well, it's true." Katie put her hands together and intertwined her fingers. "I can't marry him knowing that he'd rather I was someone else. I won't try to compete with a ghost."

"A ghost?" Sara lifted a brow questioningly. "Is she dead?"

Katie shook her head. "Not dead. Married with a family of her own. But he remembers her as all the things I'm not. *Sweet Susan. Meek Susan.* A woman who knew when to give way to a man's will. Biddable, that's what he called her. And that's what I'm not."

Sara approached and took both of Katie's hands in hers. "Please reconsider. It's easy to make decisions in anger."

"He took me out to the mill to show me a *surprise.* He's kept the bedroom set he bought for her. He thought it would be our wedding bed. Can you imagine? Susan's bed? I couldn't sleep a night in it." A tear trickled down

Katie's cheek and she dashed it away with the back of her hand. "He doesn't need someone like me, Sara. He needs someone who will say yes to every notion he has. We'd never be happy together." She sniffed.

Sara plucked a handkerchief from her pocket and handed it to her. "Blow your nose. Dry your eyes. This isn't the first argument that an engaged couple has had. As I said—"

"I value your advice, Sara," Katie said firmly, "but I can't go through with this knowing what I know. It wouldn't be fair to either of us."

"I can understand why you're so upset, but you have to remember, men often don't have a clue as to how women think. And if we women are honest about it, we're not always so good about telling our men what's going on in our hearts or our heads." Sara sighed. "I've been matching couples for a long time, and yours was one I felt certain would be successful."

"I'm sorry to disappoint you, then."

"Oh, Katie, you haven't disappointed me." Eyes misty, Sara held out her arms and hugged Katie tightly when she moved into them. "I know you're hurt," Sara murmured. "I can see it in your eyes. All I'm saying is that I wish you would give it a few days before making up your mind that you can't find your way past this. Let me talk to him."

"*Ne.* I've made my mind up." Katie shook her head emphatically. "I spent the night wrestling with this, and my decision is final. I won't marry Freeman. And I won't sit around moping over it. I want to go to Kentucky to visit Uriah and his family. I think that marrying him would be best."

Sara frowned. Doubt flickered in her eyes. "Again,

I have to counsel you against impulsiveness. If you and Freeman love each other, misunderstandings can be straightened out."

"Ne." Katie shook her head firmly. "I won't change my mind. If you'd been there, Sara, you'd understand." She folded her arms over her chest. "I think Freeman was relieved. He wouldn't have backed out of our engagement because he's not that kind of man, but I think he realized I was right. We're not suited." She let her hands fall to her sides. "So if Uriah still wants me, and if he doesn't have two heads or something terrible, then I'll marry him."

"I can't help thinking that you're making a mistake," Sara said. "At the least, you should wait a decent time before considering Uriah's offer."

"Aren't you the one who told me that marriages are made in heaven?" Katie raised her chin stubbornly. She knew Sara was going to try to talk her out of this, but she'd already decided she wouldn't be swayed. "If Uriah and I have respect for each other, if we marry to make a new family, we can learn to love each other. It's better that way. No foolish delusions of love between us, but the opportunity to form a strong union, one where we can raise our children in the faith."

Sara looked troubled. "As your friend, I recommend you wait a few days, or better still a few weeks. This may look differently in time."

"If I wait, I'll lose my nerve," Katie insisted. "I should have accepted Uriah's offer months ago. I'm going to walk over to the chair shop this minute and call Uriah's father's harness shop. His sister has invited me to come and stay with her. And I'm going."

"Decisions made in haste are often repented in leisure," Sara told her. "Once Freeman has a chance to think about the mistake he's made, then maybe the two of you can see your way through this."

"I told you, Sara. I'm through with Freeman." She walked to the door, eager to be out and on her way. The sooner she made the phone call, the sooner she'd be headed for her new life. "I'm going to Kentucky as quickly as I can make the arrangements. I know what I'm doing, and I know what will make me happy in the long run. Falling in love with Freeman was a mistake. And the best thing I can do is to move on with my life and forget him."

Freeman dumped a scoop of horse feed into the donkey's outdoor feed bin in the corral and watched as the aging animal ambled over. Business was slow at the mill this morning, and he could find nothing to occupy his mind. His leg ached. The doctor said that it was healing fast, but that he had to expect a little discomfort in the process. Freeman leaned over the rail and stroked the back of the gray donkey that had a darker gray mark across his shoulders. The animal wiggled his ears and munched at the grain.

"Look at you," Freeman said. "Not a care in the world." The donkey just kept eating. The crow Freeman and Katie had rescued hopped across the grass and came to rest a few yards from where Freeman stood. It opened its mouth and let out a raucous caw. Freeman dug in his trouser pocket and found a crumpled biscuit from breakfast. He tossed a piece to the crow and the bird gobbled it and croaked again, wanting more. Freeman threw the rest of the bread, picked up the grain scoop and walked back toward the house, using his cane for support on the uneven ground. He'd put the grain scoop away on his next trip to the barn.

It was a fair day, not too hot, and slightly overcast, with a light breeze. Autumn was coming, his favorite time of year. Ordinarily, Freeman would have rejoiced in the break from the late summer heat, but today nothing pleased him. The crow made a few hops as if to follow him and then flew up to the top of a fence post and perched there, beady black eyes staring at him.

"That's it," Freeman said. "Nothing more. You'll be so fat you won't be able to fly." The bird had made an amazing recovery once the broken leg was splinted.

"Stray animals, it's all I'll have," Freeman muttered under his breath. "Cats, crows and useless donkeys." It was probably for the best that he and Katie had parted ways when they had. He wasn't cut out for marriage. He was meant for the bachelor life. No matter how hard he tried to make it work with a woman, it ended badly. Shouldn't a man know when it was time to give up on a bad idea?

Over the last twenty-four hours Freeman had gone over and over his and Katie's parting argument, and he couldn't see where he'd put a foot wrong. He'd honestly expected her to be pleased with the bedroom suite. It was brand-new and it wasn't as if Susan had ever slept in the bed. It made no sense. What kind of man did she think he was? If he still had feelings for Susan, he certainly wouldn't have entered into a courtship with Katie. It hurt him that she thought he was that man. And the fact that she didn't know him better than that made him wonder if he really knew her. He exhaled, too worn-out to keep going over it all in his head. Maybe this was all for the best. Maybe it was good to learn her character now rather than later when it was too late to back out of a bad marriage.

"Freeman!"

His grandmother and Uncle Jehu were just coming out of the garden, each carrying a bushel basket of lima beans. Freeman crossed the distance to where they stood near the gate, passed her the metal scoop, and took the heavy basket. Even though he was still using the cane to walk, he was finding he could carry quite a bit of weight. "I'll carry these back to the house for you," he offered.

"You can help us shell them, too," his uncle said. "No sense wasting your day lazing around feeling sorry for yourself."

"That what you think I'm doing?" Freeman asked. It was a barb that hit too close to home. He couldn't stop thinking about Katie and wondering how their happiness could have ended so quickly. She'd been wrong to take offense about the bedroom suite, and she'd been mistaken when she accused him of still being in love with Susan. How did things get so confused between them? His worries about Katie had never been that he wanted her to be someone else. Rather, he'd been afraid that he wasn't strong enough for such a woman. A man should be the head of his house. He didn't want to end up like his parents, with the wife's word being what counted. After knowing Katie, he could see that someone like Susan would have been all wrong for him. Susan was too meek, too unwilling to give an opinion or an idea.

"It's plain that you argued," Uncle Jehu said. "You may as well tell us what you argued over."

"I don't see that that'll be of any use to anyone."

"Come on. You may as well tell us," Grossmama said. "You know I'll have it out of you before the day is over."

Unwillingly, feeling like a boy who'd done something wrong and been caught in his mischief, he explained about the bed. And, as he expected, which was why he hadn't told them what happened in the first place, he got no sympathy.

"Ridiculous," his uncle declared. "What ever possessed you to think that Susan's bedroom suite would please Katie?"

"I agree," his grandmother said. "You were completely in the wrong."

"Wait a minute. You weren't there," he defended. "You didn't hear what she said to me."

"Nonsense," Grossmama replied. "She's as bad as you are. Such impulsive behavior out of two grown people who love each other." She shook her head. "You're unhappy without her, and if you don't come to your senses, you'll be unhappy for the rest of your life."

Freeman clenched his teeth together. He would never be disrespectful to his grandmother, but she was wrong to interfere in his affairs. She didn't understand why he couldn't allow Katie to have her way.

"Listen to her," Uncle Jehu said. "You're making a big mistake. Ivy's telling you the honest truth. You'll never meet another woman like Katie, and you're a fool if you let her go."

"You two don't understand," Freeman protested. "I'm not my father. I can't be ruled by a woman the way he was ruled by my mother."

"Ah, so is that what the trouble is? You think your mother made your father unhappy and you don't want to see yourself in the same fix?" Grossmama asked. She headed for the house and Freeman had no choice but to follow. "He loved her," she went on. "He let her do and say what she wanted until it was something he cared about. And then it was his will that won out. Your father was a good man, Freeman, but he wasn't a forceful man. He was my son, my only child. No one knows him as I did. He used to say that your mother saved him a lot of worry by making small decisions. It left him free to make the big ones. It was the way their marriage worked. No one can judge whether what they did was always the best, but it was their choice to make. And if you've rejected Katie because of something you believe made your father less than he was, you're dead wrong."

"You're a man grown," Uncle Jehu insisted, walking on the other side of Freeman so that he was caught between the two of them. "Not a foolish boy. And men and women work out their differences. You don't turn your back on each other." He stopped and set his basket of pole limas on the ground and pointed a finger in Freeman's direction. "If you love her, you should be man enough to do what it takes to settle this nonsense. Of course, if it was just a marriage of convenience—"

"You know that it wasn't," Freeman said softly.

"Then admit that you were wrong," his grandmother said. "If you'd told me you meant to give her Susan's furniture, I could have told you that it was a crazy scheme. I'd have told you Katie wouldn't go for it, and I have to say, I wouldn't either." She gestured. "Sell the set or give it to Jehu and me for a wedding gift. We'll be needing a marriage bed, and I always liked those tulips. Cheerful, they are."

"She's right," Uncle Jehu chimed in. "A woman wants to pick out her own furniture. I've got a fine bed that suited me and my wife for a lot of years, but I wouldn't think to bring a new wife to it." He shook his head, making a clicking sound between his teeth. "For a smart boy, Freeman, you sometimes set me to wondering if your brains are made of wood."

"I think it's too late. Katie and I both said things that shouldn't have been said," Freeman explained. "I don't know if we can take back those angry words."

"Of course you can. The Bible tells us to forgive," his uncle said as he took Ivy's hand in his. "And not just others, but ourselves. We're human and we make mistakes, but a smart man doesn't let a mistake bring him to his knees. Pride and hurt feelings don't mean much compared to a future without the woman who makes up your other half."

Freeman looked from one to the other and then down at the grass at his feet. He tapped at a weed with his cane. "You think I made a mistake in letting her go?"

"What do *you* think?"

He stared at the ground. "I think... I think I love her and—" his voice cracked "—I think I'll never be happy without her." He looked up at his grandmother. "You really think I made a mistake in letting her go?"

"Are you slow-witted, grandson?" Grossmama demanded. "Haven't we just said that?" She pursed her lips. "Now, what are you going to do to make it right?"

The distance from the mill to Sara Yoder's house wasn't far, but it seemed to Freeman to take forever for the horse to cover the miles. Now that he looked at his argument with Katie from another direction and had time to think it over, he couldn't see how they'd let the problem divide them. He didn't know how *he* had let their misunderstanding go so far. He'd been angry that she accused him of still loving Susan and he hadn't been willing to listen to her side. Katie might have been equally to blame, but that didn't matter. He'd let two whole days and nights pass without reaching out to her. That had been his second mistake, and the sickness in his belly proved that nothing would be right until they mended this disagreement.

He shook the reins over the horse's rump. "Get up!" he cried, relieved he could drive again. The animal picked up speed. The wheels of the buggy clattered on the hardtop road, and the farmland on either side of the road sped by.

He was moving so fast that when he turned the horse into Sara's drive, the buggy went up on two wheels before righting itself and bouncing into place. Freeman's pulse quickened. He wasn't sure what he'd say to Katie when he came face to face with her, but he'd think of something. They belonged together, and if he had to light a match to Susan's bed to prove to Katie that he put her first, then that was what he'd do.

When he reined the horse up short near Sara's back door, he saw the matchmaker sweeping the porch. "Sara!" he called. "Is Katie here? I have to talk to her."

Sara leaned her broom against a post and came down the steps.

"It's nothing we can't settle," he went on. "Just a misunderstanding with two hotheads facing toe-to-toe." He looked around, hoping that Katie had heard the horse and buggy drive into the yard, hoping that she would come out of the house.

Sara looked up at him. "Freeman," she said gently. "Katie's gone."

He felt a sudden heaviness in the pit of his stomach and went lightheaded. "Gone where?"

Sara's voice was thick with emotion. "I'm so sorry. I tried to talk her out of it, but you know how she gets. Freeman, she's gone to Kentucky."

"Just like that?" He looked away; his eyes were burning.

"I tried to convince her not to make any decisions while she was so upset. I told her she was being impulsive."

"I did something stupid. Katie misunderstood, and we ended up arguing. It was all my fault. But I came to make things right, to ask her to forgive me." He looked down at Sara, standing beside his buggy. "She can't be gone."

"Do you love her?"

"With all my heart."

Sara considered him for a moment, then reached up and rested her hand on his forearm. "Then you have to go after her, Freeman. You have to stop her before it's too late." Her round face was taut with concern. "Because I think she means to marry Uriah as soon as the wedding can be arranged."

Chapter Fifteen

"Can you go any faster?" Freeman demanded of the van driver. They were approaching the bridge over the Delaware and Chesapeake Canal on Route 1, headed toward the Amtrak Station in Wilmington. "We have to get there before the train leaves." Before Katie leaves for Kentucky, he thought anxiously.

"We have to get to the train station in one piece and without me getting a speeding ticket," Jerry Kaplan answered. Heavy raindrops beat against the windshield and the wipers kept up a steady rhythm.

Freeman leaned forward, gripping the armrest. Jerry, a retired state trooper, was the fifth driver he'd called. The first four drivers who usually transported the Kent County Amish and whom he'd called were either busy or couldn't be persuaded to drive as far as Wilmington. Freeman had never hired Jerry before but Roman at the chair shop in Seven Poplars, where he'd made the phone calls, had recommended him. Jerry was a long-distance driver who also took passengers to the train station or to the Philadelphia or Baltimore airports in his big SUV.

"A lot of other motor vehicles are passing us," Freeman said. "They can't all be speeding, can they?" The front passenger's seat was pushed back so that his healing leg wasn't cramped, but Freeman couldn't appreciate the comfort. All he could think of was getting to Katie before it was too late—finding her and convincing her to give him a second chance.

"Most are," Jerry replied. He was a big man, balding, soft-spoken, and still physically fit, despite his seventy-one years. "And most of those who do pass us, we'll see again when we hit heavier traffic up ahead. We would have stood a better chance of catching up with your lady friend if we'd left an hour earlier." He glanced over at Freeman. "If you remember, I told you there were no guarantees."

"I know," he agreed. "You were honest with me. And I appreciate you taking the time to drive me. It's just that it's so important I reach her before the train pulls out."

Jerry Kaplan seemed a decent man and was a good driver. He was certainly an honest one. Freeman had offered the retired policeman twice his normal fare to drive him to Wilmington and three times it if they got there in time to stop Katie from leaving. Jerry had refused the additional fee and declared that his usual charge was fair for them both.

Ordinarily, Freeman would have enjoyed talking with the Englisher. But he had no words or thoughts to spare for anyone but Katie. How could he have been such a thick-headed fool? Why had he been so quick to defend himself and so slow to see her side of the disagreement? Katie was the best thing that had ever hap-

pened to him and he might lose her forever because of
his own stubborn desire to always have things his way.

He tapped his good foot impatiently as traffic ahead
of them slowed to a near stop. Who was he to criticize
Katie for willfulness? He was worse than she was because he'd experienced heartbreak before. He should
have realized how special his and Katie's relationship
was and fought to protect it.

Freeman felt a sick hollowness inside. All he wanted
was the opportunity to speak to Katie before she got
on that train to Kentucky. He was certain he could get
her to reconsider.

If only Jerry could get him there on time.

When Sara told him that Katie had left for the train
station, he'd felt as if he'd taken a blow to his midsection, and he still felt sick. He'd gone directly from Sara's
house to the Seven Poplars chair shop to use the phone
and call for a driver and check the train schedule. He'd
left his horse with one of the young men there and asked
him to get the animal home to the mill and tell his family where he'd gone.

For once, Freeman wished that the elders in his
church approved of cell phones for their members' personal use. Englishers carried their phones everywhere.
If both he and Katie had a cell phone, he wouldn't have
to chase her down. They could've settled this misunderstanding with one call. But maybe talking to her
by phone wouldn't have been enough. And maybe if
he *did* get to her before her train pulled out, she'd still
reject him.

And then what? He had no backup plan. The only
thing he knew was that he loved Katie. He wanted her

for his wife. And if he lost her, he'd never find happiness with another woman.

Freeman glanced at the clock on the dashboard. Seven minutes since he'd last checked the time. How far had they gone? And how much farther was the train station? "Please, God," he whispered under his breath. "I'll be a better man. I've learned my lesson. Let me get there before it's too late."

Jerry braked and pulled to the curb half a block from the train station. "It will be faster if you get out here. I'll park in the garage and find you inside," he said. "Good luck. I hope you find your lady friend."

Freeman was unbuckled and halfway out of the door before the SUV came to a complete stop. With the help of his cane he took the sidewalk toward the front entrance of the station. People carrying suitcases crowded the way, and a few glanced at him with curiosity. He didn't pay any attention. He barely avoided tripping over a baby stroller loaded with packages and ducked around a woman stopped on a motorized scooter to reach the main doors.

Inside, he passed through a throng of passengers and those who'd come to see them off or pick them up. He looked around for a screen that showed arriving and departing trains. The station was a noisy place with dozens of people milling about: college students, military men and women on leave, families with small, excited children. There was even a blind man with his seeing-eye dog near the entrance doors handing out some sort of pamphlet.

Freeman pulled a piece of paper with the information

on the train to Kentucky from his pocket and checked the overhead screen. Almost at once he saw that the train had arrived on time…and it was leaving on time. By the big clock on the wall, he had a minute. Maybe less. Heart pounding, he glanced toward the line waiting by the elevators and then walked as quickly as he could manage to the stairs leading to the track level. "Wait for me," he muttered. "Wait for me, Katie." His heart felt as though it was in his throat. Passersby bumped into him, but he paid no heed as he took one step after the next, using the handrail to steady himself.

As he reached the top of the stairs and the open platform, he heard the sound of the wheels on the track. The train was moving out of the station, slowly gathering speed. *"Ne!"* Frantically, he looked along the nearly empty platform. No one sitting on the benches, no familiar Amish dress, no young women at all.

One car after another rolled past. Inside, passengers stared out the windows or settled luggage overhead or under their seat. Freeman scanned the faces. There were no prayer *kapps*. No Katie looking back at him.

He stood there stunned, unmoving, unable to accept his loss as the train pulled away. *"Ach*, Katie," he rasped. He leaned against the wall. "What have we done to each other?" Her merry face rose in his mind's eye. He could almost hear the peal of her laughter, see the way she tilted her head when she giggled.

A uniformed Amtrak employee pushed a broom down the platform, cleaning up dust and litter. He leaned down to pick up a candy bar wrapper. "Can I help you, sir?" he asked.

Freeman shook his head. He glanced around. The

two of them appeared to be the only ones left on the platform.

"Are you waiting for the next train?" the young man asked.

Freeman shook his head, but he registered what the young man had said. *The next train.* This wouldn't be the only train. And missing Katie here didn't mean he couldn't catch up with her farther down the line. He'd find the ticket office and buy a ticket on the next train going south. Better yet, he'd have Jerry drive him on to the Philadelphia airport. If he took a plane, he could get to Louisville ahead of Katie.

He started for the stairs.

"There's an elevator there, sir," the boy called after him.

Freeman hesitated. He could manage the stairs again, but the elevator might be faster. He turned back and his heart skipped a beat. Sitting on a black suitcase just beyond the elevator, half-hidden, was a figure in a black dress and bonnet. The woman's face was buried in her hands.

It took a moment for it to register what he was seeing. Whom he was seeing.

"Katie?" he called. Goosebumps rose on his arms. "Katie!" he bellowed.

She looked up, saw him and leaped to her feet. Then she just stood there and stared at him. "Freeman?"

One moment they were both standing on the train platform looking at each other, and the next she was in his arms and he was covering her tear-stained face with kisses. "Oh, Katie, darling," he murmured in Deitsch. "You're here. I found you. I thought I'd lost you. I thought—"

"I couldn't go." Her words came in a rush. "I realized that if I couldn't have you, I wouldn't marry Uriah. It wouldn't be fair to him. I wouldn't marry at all. I couldn't. Loving you, I couldn't, Freeman. I could never love anyone but you. I'm so sorry."

He pulled Katie hard against him and held her, oblivious to the amused gaze of the young Amtrak employee. "Forgive me," he said. "I was wrong. I'm such a fool to quarrel with you over—"

"*Ne*, it was me," Katie insisted, looking up at him, teary-eyed. "I'm the one who—"

"Shh." He kissed her tenderly on the lips. "Hush, darling, hush," he said. "Just tell me that you'll give me another chance. Give *us* another chance. Marry me, Katie, and I promise I'll never mention Susan again."

"*Ya*, Freeman, I will marry you," she whispered. "And talk about her as much as you want." She gave a little laugh, clinging to him as the sound of an approaching train shook the platform under their feet. "We'll talk about her every day as long as I can be your wife."

"She was right, you know," Freeman said, holding her tightly. "She and I were never meant to be together. I was meant to be *your* husband and none other. Can you forgive a hardheaded—"

"Miller?" Katie finished for him. "The sweetest man…"

The grinding wheels of the approaching train drowned her words, but Freeman stood there, not willing to let her out of his arms, paying no heed to the shriek of brakes and the hiss of the opening doors.

"I love you, Katie Byler," he murmured into her ear. "I always will."

"And I love you," she answered.

"Kiss her again!" the Amtrak employee with the broom urged.

Freeman did just that to the laughter and applause of the arriving passengers.

Epilogue

Katie laughed as bells on the horse's harness jingled and red and blue lights flashed on Thomas's buggy as he drove over the dam and turned into Freeman's lane. Freeman squeezed her hand in the darkness and her pulse quickened. She was so full of happiness that she thought it must be bubbling out of her and overflowing, filling the buggy and spilling out into the yard.

She wanted to pinch herself to make certain that she wasn't dreaming, that this was her wedding day, and that Freeman, sitting beside her in the buggy, was her husband for now and forever, so long as they both lived. The day had been glorious, everything that every Amish bride hoped for: friends, loved ones, good food, fellowship, God's word and the blessings of church and community. She had so much to be thankful for.

She glanced out at the falling snow. Propane lights shone from the house windows, softened by the swirl of white. This was a gentle snow, billowing flakes spinning through the cold November night to frost everything in a glory of pristine icing.

"We're here!" Thomas proclaimed as he jumped

down out of the driver's seat and stomped around to the back of the buggy to open the rear door.

"How deep is it?" Freeman asked.

"Three or four inches." Thomas gazed out into the snow-blanketed barnyard. "But the weatherman forecasted another three before morning."

"Sara says five more inches at least," Ellie chimed in from the front seat where she'd ridden beside Thomas. "I think she's right. It smells like more snow to me."

"It can snow all it likes," Katie said. Ivy and Uncle Jehu were both staying with friends for the next couple of days, and Katie welcomed the thought of being snowed in with Freeman. How wonderful it would be to have a few days shut away from the world together.

Katie looked out the window. The mill loomed big and black in the distance. Not a single star or hint of moonlight pierced the darkness. The only sound was the crunch of snow under Thomas's boots, the creak of the horse's harness and the snort of the horse.

Freeman climbed out and reached to steady her as she prepared to get down. "Careful," he said to her. "The step is slippery." And then to Thomas, he said, "Thanks for getting us here safely."

"Easy enough," his friend replied. "No traffic on the road tonight. A few inches of snow is nothing to a good horse and buggy. By morning, Amish farmers will be pulling Englishers' cars and trucks out of ditches. Those who don't have the sense to wait for the snowplows."

Ellie leaned over the seat back to speak to Thomas. "Still, the sooner we're back to Sara's, the better. You've still got to drive home after you drop me off."

"Got the basket with the food and wedding cake?" Thomas asked.

"Ya," Ellie answered. "Right there." She pointed to a spot on the floor behind the bench seat. "Plenty to keep Katie from cooking for a few days."

"No need to get your shoes wet," Freeman said, looking up at Katie. "Put your arm around my neck."

Katie did and he swept her into his strong arms.

"Careful of your leg!" she warned.

"My leg is fine," he assured her as he carried her to the back porch and set her gently on the step. "Thanks," he said to Thomas. He pushed open the porch door and Katie walked in ahead of him.

"Blessings!" Thomas handed Freeman the basket and headed for the buggy.

"Be happy!" Ellie cried, waving.

Katie smiled and waved back, thinking how fortunate she was to have made such a good friend as Ellie.

"Let's get you inside." Freeman turned the kitchen doorknob and then stepped back to let her cross the threshold ahead of him. "I guess if we were Englishers, I'd be carrying you all the way in."

She laughed. The warm kitchen, so familiar and yet so strange, enveloped her. This is our home, she thought as she walked in, mine and Freeman's. *Our woodstove, our gleaming wooden table with the bouquet of holly leaves and berries, our calendar on the wall.* With trembling fingers, she untied her bonnet strings and slipped off the formal black head covering and her heavy black cape.

Freeman took them from her and hung them on hooks beside his own coat and black wool hat.

"Welcome home, wife," he said huskily. He set the basket of wedding food in the center of the table.

She swallowed, her own words caught in her throat.

"Happy?" he asked.

She nodded, for once at a loss for words. She was just so filled with joy right now; there weren't words for it.

Freeman took her hand in his warm one and held it. "It's been a long journey getting to this point," he said. "I nearly overturned the apple cart, but I'll try to do better in the future."

"It was no more your fault than mine," she managed, gazing up at his handsome face. "My willfulness. Always wanting to do things my way. I've a lot to learn about marriage."

"Don't we both?" He chuckled. "But we have time and the grace of God to try and get it right." He leaned down and kissed her, a slow, gentle kiss, his lips fitting perfectly to hers, sending sweet sensations of joy radiating through her heart and body. "I love you, Katie Kemp," he said.

"And I love you, Freeman Kemp." She laughed, liking the sound of her new name, and he laughed with her.

"I've a gift for you, darling. Would you like to see it?"

She looked up at him quizzically; it wasn't their tradition for a man and woman to give each other a gift on their wedding day.

"Yes or no?" he teased.

"Of course!"

Taking Katie's hand, he led her through the kitchen and up the staircase. She'd never been further than the linen closet on the second floor of the farmhouse.

She knew this was where the bedroom was that they would share as man and wife, but she had never thought it proper that she go there before they were married.

A propane lamp on a Victorian marble-top table lit the wide upstairs hallway. Wide floorboards of yellow pine stretched the length of the passage. Someone had left an arrangement of pine and holly on the deep windowsill. Katie inhaled the crisp scent of fresh-cut greens.

"Close your eyes," Freeman said as they reached a closed door.

"Should I trust you?" she teased, but did as he asked.

A door hinge squeaked. "Sorry, I'll have to fix that," he said. "All right, you can open your eyes."

It took a moment for Katie to realize what she was looking at and slowly a smile spread across her face. "Did you buy this?" She took in the beautiful pine bed with bluebirds and sheaves of wheat carved into the head and footboard. A tall wardrobe and dresser completed the set.

"Ne," he answered softly. "I made it. The bed. The other pieces were my great grandmother's. I always liked them and I thought you might."

"I do."

"I made the bed just for you, Katie. For no other woman but you." He sounded almost bashful.

She sighed. "I love it, Freeman. I do." She looked up at him through teary eyes. "I'll try to be the best wife to you. I promise."

"And I promise never to expect you to be anyone but yourself."

She smiled at him as she began to remove, one by one, the hairpins that held her starched white prayer *kapp* in place. "And I'll promise to *try* not to be too bossy," she whispered. And then she was in his arms and nothing mattered but the new life that they were beginning together, a life blessed by God and shining with hope.

* * * * *

AN AMISH HARVEST

Patricia Davids

This book is lovingly dedicated to my grandson Josh.
Of all the things in life that make it worth living,
your smile is at the top of my list.
May God bless and keep you always.
Grandma Pat

Saying, What wilt thou that I shall do unto thee? And he said, Lord, that I may receive my sight. And Jesus said unto him, Receive thy sight: thy faith hath saved thee.

—*Luke* 18:41–42

Chapter One

"Don't do this to me now!"

Samuel Bowman yanked his chisel away from the half-finished table leg rotating on the lathe in front of him as it spun to an untimely stop. Laying his tool aside with care that belied his frustration, he brushed away the loose ribbons of wood shavings to make sure he hadn't marred the piece. It was the last leg for a special table. An intricate piece, it had to be finished this morning if he was going to have the set completed on time.

"What's wrong, *brudder*?" Timothy, Samuel's second brother, paused on his way past. He held a cardboard box full of hand-carved wooden toys. Also a skilled woodworker, Timothy's designs were simpler and more modern than Samuel's.

"The lathe quit." A breakdown was the last thing Samuel needed. He murmured a prayer and held his breath as he flipped the machine's switch off and then back on. Nothing.

Timothy grimaced in sympathy. "Let me get these to the gift shop, and I'll take a look at it. Mother has a lady who wants to see a few more of my samples. Can't keep the *Englisch* customers waiting. Is that the table for the Cincinnati dealer?"

"*Ja*, and it has to be finished today. I need the lathe working."

"Don't worry. It will all get done on time. I'll look at it when I get back." Timothy went out the woodworking shop's front door.

It was all well and good that Timothy thought the table would get done. He didn't have to do it. There was more than Samuel's reputation for prompt work hanging in the balance. His father had invested the last of the family's savings in this venture to expand their shop and add the showroom area now packed with Samuel's finished works. The family badly needed the money a contract for future sales to the high-end furniture store would generate.

Amish-made furniture was always in demand and Samuel was one of the most skilled carvers in the area. It was his God-given gift, and he put it to good use. Up until now, he'd only sold his work locally from the family's gift shop. But their Amish community of Bowmans Crossing was off the beaten path. Few tourists ventured into the area. Samuel knew he needed to reach a bigger market if the family operation was going to expand. With five sons and only enough farmland to support one family, the woodworking business needed to grow, and quickly, or his brothers would have to look elsewhere for work.

Samuel checked over every inch of the machine and couldn't find anything wrong with it. He glanced across the shop and spied the second of his four younger brothers stacking fresh lumber by the back door. "Luke, did you put gas in the generator this morning?"

"I told Noah to do it."

"And did he?"

Luke shrugged. "How should I know?"

Samuel shook his head in disgust. "Why do I have to do everything myself?"

Luke tossed the last board onto the stack and slowly dusted his hands together. "Want me to go check?"

"Never mind, I don't have all day." Luke's lackadaisical offer rubbed Samuel the wrong way. Again. He loved all his brothers, but none of them had the drive that was needed to make the family business a success. Luke and Timothy would rather go out with friends than work late in the shop. Noah had his head in the clouds over a new horse. Joshua had up and married at girl from Hope Springs leaving them short a farmhand. Samuel had no time for such foolishness.

Luke hooked his thumbs in his suspenders. "When is Father going to replace that ancient piece of junk? We need one of those new diesel generators to power this place. The bishop has already said we could use it in our business."

"Our engine may be ancient, but it will last one more year and then maybe we can afford a better one. Provided you stay out of trouble. You know why father doesn't have the money to buy a new one."

Luke took a step forward, his face set in hard lines. "Because of me, is that what you're saying? He didn't have to pay for a lawyer. I had a public defender."

"That would have been okay if you hadn't pulled Joshua into trouble with you."

Luke flushed a dull red. "No matter how many times I say I'm sorry, it will never be enough for you, will it?" He turned away and stormed out of the building.

Samuel regretted his jab at Luke, but his brother's attitude irked him. It always had. He knew Luke was trying to make up for his poor choices in the past when he'd rebelled against his strict Amish upbringing and left home for the big city. He'd fallen in with bad company and ended up using and selling drugs. When their brother Joshua went to try and talk sense into him, they were both arrested and jailed. It had been a difficult time for the entire family.

Even so, it was wrong of Samuel to throw Luke's failures in his face. What was forgiven should not be mentioned again. He would find Luke and apologize later. Now he needed to get the table leg turned. He could only put out one fire at a time.

He grabbed the tool chest from the bench beside the back door in case a lack of gasoline wasn't the issue. If the generator required more than a simple fix, he wouldn't be able to finish on time, and this opportunity would pass him by.

The engine was housed in a small shed at the back of the woodworking shop. The pungent smell of exhaust filled the small room. As Samuel suspected, the fuel gauge needle sat on empty. He should have filled it himself instead of depending on someone else.

The red gas can was sitting on the floor beside the generator. He picked it up. The light weight and faint slosh revealed it was less than half-full. It would take precious time to go get more. He decided against it. Half a can would be enough to finish the job.

He opened the generator's gas cap and began pouring in the fuel. Strong fumes hit him in the face. Maybe he should've waited until the old machine cooled down a little more.

It was his last thought before a blinding flash sent him flying backward into oblivion.

"Did you hear what happened at the Bowman place?"

"I haven't. Something serious?" Rebecca Miller glanced from the cake she was slicing to her mother, Ina Fisher. Ina was putting away the goods she had picked up at the local market on her way to Rebecca's house. *Mamm* was always eager to share what news she gathered along the way when she came to visit. The Bowman family lived several miles away across the river. Rebecca seldom saw them except at church functions.

"Well, I stopped at the Bowman gift shop after I left the market this morning. I wanted some of Anna's gooseberry preserves. You know how much I like them."

"I do." Her mother's plump figure was proof that she enjoyed her sweets.

"Anyway, Verna Yoder was at the counter."

"I didn't know she worked there." Verna was her mother's dear friend and one of the biggest gossips in the county. The woman somehow knew everything about everybody. She and Rebecca's mother were birds of a feather.

"Verna doesn't actually work there. She was helping Anna for a few minutes. She told me everything. A few days ago, Samuel was putting gas in their generator for the wood shop and it exploded. His face and hands were badly burned. They aren't sure if he'll see again."

"Oh, no." Rebecca pressed a hand to her heart and uttered a silent prayer for the young man from her Amish community and for his family.

"As if that wasn't enough, the building caught fire

and a large part of their work was destroyed. They have seen many trials and tribulations in that family."

"Will he be badly scarred?" Rebecca asked, thinking of Samuel's rare smiles. He wasn't known for his sense of humor. That would be Noah, the youngest, who was the family clown. Samuel was always a serious fellow, one who seemed to study others rather than try to entertain them. She always thought his dark brown eyes looked more deeply into things than most other men.

To be blinded. How terrible for him.

"Verna only said that his face and hands are heavily bandaged. Time will tell if he is scarred. It is all in God's hands. I know his family is grateful his life was spared."

"As am I. I will pray for his healing." Rebecca didn't know Samuel well. He hadn't been among her husband's close friends, but he had made her husband's coffin in his wood shop.

She could still smell the pungent odor of the red cedar panels he chose instead of the simple white pine that was used for most Amish coffins. Walter had always loved the smell of cedar. She didn't know how Samuel knew that, but she had been grateful for the special touch even though her mother reported that some people in the church thought it was too fancy for an Amish casket.

"Verna has no idea how the family will manage. Anna is about to tear her hair out trying to run the gift shop and take care of Samuel, too. Apparently, he's a cranky patient. Harvest is coming on, and her men will soon be in the fields and won't be able to give her the help she needs. Of course, Verna heard that she sent Gemma Yoder away in tears when she tried to help."

"I wonder why?"

"That Gemma has had her sights set on Samuel for ages, but I can't see her being much help in the sick-room. The girl cries at the drop of a hat."

"What is the church doing to help?" Rebecca knew their community would rally around the Bowman family.

"A group of men have volunteered to repair the build-ing, but Isaac won't let them start until everyone is fin-ished with their harvest or the weather puts a stop to the field work. I'm sure the church will take up a collec-tion to help cover his medical expenses next Sunday."

Rebecca's finances were meager, but she would give what she could. "What else can we do to help?"

"Why don't we each fix a meal and take it over. That would lighten Anna's burden."

"That's a fine idea. I'll make up a casserole and bake another carrot cake for dessert." She finished slicing the one in front of her and slid two pieces onto the white plates she had waiting. She carried them to the table where her mother joined her. Her mother stopped in to visit every Tuesday afternoon, and Rebecca always made something special to share with her.

Her mother smiled and took a seat. She forked a bite into her mouth and sighed. "I like your carrot cake al-most as much as I like Anna's gooseberry preserves. It's too bad the Lord gave Anna all sons and left her without daughters to help in the house. And such trou-blesome boys, too. I remember how humiliated she was when Luke and Joshua were arrested on drug charges. My heart ached for her. I don't know how she bore it."

"Joshua was wrongly accused."

Mother pointed a finger at Rebecca. "But Luke

wasn't. An Amish fellow selling drugs, what is the world coming to?" She clasped her hand to her chest and shook her head making the ribbons of her white *kapp* jiggle.

Rebecca chose to ignore her mother's dramatic flair. "Luke repented and has remained a solid member of the church. We should not speak harshly of him."

Her mother's lower lip turned down in a pout. She stabbed her fork into her cake. "I wasn't speaking harshly. I was merely stating a fact."

"Joshua married a lovely girl last month. Surely his wife is helping Anna."

"They are still away on their wedding trip. Anna has two sisters near Arthur, Illinois. The newlyweds are staying with them and visiting cousins in the area. Anna wrote and told them not to cut their visit short. Verna thinks it was a foolish thing to say. I agree."

Rebecca thought back to her own wedding trip. She cherished every moment of the time she and Walter spent getting to know each other's families. Her marriage might have been short, but it had been sweet. Tears pricked the back of her eyes, but she blinked them away. He was only out of her sight for a little while. Someday, they would be together again in Heaven. Until then, she would live her life as God willed.

"I saw John at the market. He asked about you." The tone of her mother's voice changed ever so slightly.

Rebecca braced herself for the coming conversation. "How is my brother-in-law?"

"Lonely."

A twinge of pity pushed Rebecca's defenses lower. "He told you that?"

"He didn't have to say it. It was easy to see. His

wife has been gone for three years. He has to be lonely. You're lonely, too. You try to hide it from me, but I'm not blind. I don't know why you won't consider marrying John. Everyone in his family is for it."

Rebecca concentrated on her cake. "It's barely been two years since Walter died. I know everyone thinks it's a good idea, but I'm not ready." Would she ever be?

Her mother reached across the table and covered Rebecca's hand with her own. "Walter loved you. He loved his brother. He would want to see you both happy."

How could she be happy with someone other than her beloved? He was the yardstick by which she measured every man. None could come close to the sweet kindness in his voice, the tender touch of his hand, the sparkle that sprang to his eyes each time he caught sight of her. No one could replace him, but her mother was right about one thing. The loneliness was sometimes hard to bear.

"Walter would want to see you holding a babe of your own. Don't let your sadness rob you of that joy. You aren't getting any younger."

"I'm only twenty-five. I've got time." Rebecca's dreams of a family had died with Walter. She mourned that loss almost as much as she mourned her husband. If only they had been blessed with a child, then she would have been able to keep a part of Walter close to her heart and she wouldn't be so alone.

Her mother sat back and picked up her fork again. "Time has a way of slipping by us unnoticed, Rebecca. Don't throw this chance away. Give John some encouragement. You could have children of your own, companionship, security. I don't want you to be alone all your life."

Was her mother right? Should she consider remarrying, if not for love, for the blessings a family would bring?

Rebecca studied the cake in front of her. She did want children. She liked John, but was that enough? Could she grow to love him in time? Not as she had loved Walter, of course, but enough to be content in her later years?

"I'll think about it." That would satisfy her mother and allow Rebecca to change the painful subject.

"*Goot.* I've invited him and his folks for supper on Sunday after church services. I'm sure the two of you can find a few minutes alone. Are you still working for the Stutzman family?"

Rebecca shook her head as much at her mother's blatant attempt to manipulate her as to answer her question. "*Nee*, Mrs. Stutzman's mother arrived to help with the children and the new baby. I'm unemployed again."

She wasn't a trained nurse, but her experience caring for her husband during his long illness had taught her a great deal. She put that knowledge to use helping others in the community such as new mothers or those with infirm elderly family members who required extra attention. Sometimes an English family would hire her, too. It wasn't steady work, but she found it rewarding. It kept the loneliness at bay and kept her from being a burden on her mother or the church community. She knew they would provide for her, but she hated accepting help when she was able to work.

"So you will be home now."

Rebecca nodded. "Until I find another job."

"*Goot*, you are free to visit with John whenever he wants. I'll let him know."

Rebecca closed her eyes. "*Mamm*, don't pester the man."

"He's always happy to hear from me. You wouldn't need to work at all if you married again. John makes a nice living as a farrier. His first wife never complained."

Rebecca cast her mother a beseeching glance. "I'm sure a horseshoer in an Amish community earns a decent wage. Can we drop the subject now?"

Her mother shrugged. "I don't know why you are so touchy about it. You're going to let a good man slip out of your grasp if you aren't careful. I'm simply trying to steer you in the right direction."

Rebecca was saved from replying by the arrival of a horse and buggy that pulled up to the gate outside. The interruption was welcome. "I wonder who that is?"

"I'm sure I don't know who it could be."

Her mother's feigned innocence caused Rebecca to look at her sharply. "Did you invite John over today?"

"It's no sin to be friendly."

Rebecca cringed inside, braced for an awkward afternoon and then opened the door. But it wasn't her brother-in-law. Isaac Bowman stood hat in hand on her small front porch.

He nodded to her. "*Goot* day, Rebecca. I hope I haven't come at a bad time."

She stepped back. "Not at all. Won't you come in, Isaac? My mother and I were just enjoying some cake and coffee. Would you care to join us?"

"I'd rather say what I've come to say and not waste time."

Rebecca stepped out onto the porch with him. "As you please. I've only just heard about Samuel. I'm very sorry."

"*Danki.* That is why I've come. I want to offer you a job. My wife needs a live-in helper until Samuel recovers. She is having trouble managing the store and the house with him abed. Noah normally works in the store in the afternoons but I'll need all my sons in the fields when we start harvesting."

"Can't you close the store for a time? I'm sure your customers will understand. Or hire someone to work in it for your wife."

"I could, but I'd rather not. You will think I'm cruel, but my wife needs to get away from Samuel. Away from thinking she must do everything for him. I know you took care of Emil Troyer before he passed away. The old man was blind, so you have had some experience with a sightless person. Please say you will help us, at least through the corn harvest. Anna won't listen to me, but she knows you have experience with sick folks. She might listen to you. If you can't help, maybe you could suggest someone else."

Rebecca glanced over her shoulder. Her mother was scowling and shaking her head. If only her mother hadn't latched on to the idea of pushing John and her together. Rebecca didn't want to spend the next days and weeks thinking of excuses to avoid him. A new job was exactly what she needed. She graced Isaac with a heartfelt smile. "I can start today if you don't mind waiting while I gather a few things."

His expression flashed from shocked to pleased. "I don't mind at all. *Danki*, Rebecca. You are an answer to my prayers."

Samuel waited impatiently for his brother to adjust the pillows behind him. As usual, Luke was moving with the speed of cold molasses. With his eyes covered by thick dressings, Samuel had to depend on his hearing to tell him what was going on around him. Maybe forever.

If he didn't regain his sight, his days as a master carver were over. He wouldn't be of any use in the fields. He wouldn't be much use to anyone.

He refused to let his thoughts go down that road. He prayed for healing, but it was hard to seek favor from God when he had no idea why God had visited this burden on him. He heard Luke shaking the pillows and then finally felt him slide them into place.

"There. How's that?"

Samuel leaned back. It wasn't any better, but he didn't say that. It wasn't Luke's fault that he was still in pain and that his eyes felt as if they were filled with dry sand. After six days, Samuel was sick and tired of being in bed and no amount of pillow fluffing would change that, but he didn't feel like stumbling around in front of people looking hideous, either. Only his mouth had been left free of bandages. He chose to stay in bed to avoid having others see him like this, but he didn't have to like it.

He licked his swollen and cracked lips, thankful that he could speak. The doctor thought he must have thrown up his hands and that protected his lower face to a small degree. "It's fine. Is there water handy?"

"Sure."

Something poked his tender lip. He jerked away.

"Sorry," Luke said. "Here is your water."

Samuel opened his mouth and closed it around the drinking straw when he felt it on his tongue. He took a few long swallows and turned his head aside. He was helpless as a baby and growing weaker by the day. His legs and his back ached from being in bed, but he didn't want to blunder around the room and risk hurting his hands in another fall. One was enough.

Luke put the glass on the bedside table. "Is there anything else I can do for you? Do you want me to fluff the pillows under your hands?"

Before Samuel could answer, Luke pulled the support from beneath his right arm. Intense pain shot from Samuel's his fingertips to his elbow. He sucked in a harsh breath through clenched teeth.

"Sorry. I'm so sorry." Luke gently placed Samuel's bandaged hand back on the pillow. "Did that hurt?"

Samuel panted and willed the agony to subside. The pain was never gone, but it could die down to a manageable level if he was still. "I don't need anything else."

"Are you sure?" Luke asked.

"I'm sure," Samuel snapped. He just wanted to be left alone. He wanted to see. He wanted to be whole. He wanted the pain to stop.

He caught the sound of hoofbeats outside his open bedroom window and the crunch of buggy tires on the gravel. His father must be home. A few minutes later, he heard the outside door open and his mother's voice. She must have closed the store early.

"*Mamm* is back." The relief in Luke's voice was almost comical except Samuel was far from laughing. He heard his brother's footsteps retreat across the room. At least he was safe from Luke's help for a little while. Their mother was a much better caretaker. She could be smothering at times, but her heart was in the right place. Like a child afraid of the dark, he found her voice soothing and her hands comforting.

An itch formed in the middle of Samuel's back. With both hands swaddled in thick bandages, he couldn't reach to scratch it. He tried rubbing against the pillow, but it didn't help. "Luke, wait."

His brother's footsteps were already fading as he raced downstairs. Samuel tried to ignore the pricking sensation, but it only grew worse. "Luke! *Mamm!* Can someone come here?"

It seemed like an eternity, but he finally heard his mother's voice from the foot of the stairs. "I'm here, Samuel, and I've brought someone to see you."

He groaned as he heard the stairs creak. The last thing he wanted was company. "I'm not up to having visitors."

"Then it's a pity I've come all this way." The woman's voice was low, musical and faintly amused. He had no idea who she was.

Chapter Two

Samuel cringed. He hated people seeing him this way. Was this another gawker like the last girl who had come to help? All Gemma Yoder could do was sob at the sight of his bandages and burned peeling skin. She'd been worse than no help at all. Thankfully, his mother had quickly sent her packing.

"It's Rebecca Miller," his mother said. He could tell she wasn't pleased.

He heard them move closer. He knew the name even if he didn't know the woman well. "Walter Miller's widow?"

"*Ja*. Walter was my husband." The tone of her voice changed slightly. Samuel sensed the loss beneath her words. Why would she visit him? They barely knew each other. She wasn't one of his mother's friends. It was common for Amish neighbors to help each other, but she didn't live close by.

"Thank you for coming, but as I said, I'm not up to company."

"I can see that. Why are you still in bed?"

"He's in bed because he was badly burned. I'm sure

my husband told you that," his mother chided. "Samuel, your father has hired Rebecca to help us for the next few weeks."

No wonder she was upset. He had overheard her telling his father that she didn't need or want someone to help with his care after the last woman left. His father rarely went against his wife's wishes. Why this time? Samuel rubbed his back against the pillow still trying to ease that itch. "I'm glad you will have help in the store."

He caught a whiff of a fresh scent that reminded him of spring flowers. Amish women didn't wear perfume, so perhaps it was the shampoo she used. His sense of smell had become more acute since the accident. Whatever it was, he liked the delicate fragrance, but he didn't like visitors.

"Lean forward." When she spoke, she was close beside him.

"Why?"

"Because I said so."

That was bossy. He did as she said and was immediately rewarded by her fingers scratching the exact spot that had been driving him crazy. How did she know?

"I'm not familiar with what it takes to run a store, but I do know how to care for sick people. You should be up and out of bed unless you want to end up with pneumonia on top of everything else. Anna, you know this. Why are you letting him be so lazy?"

Her mild scolding annoyed him. "I'm not steady on my feet. Mother knows that."

"Ah, the explosion addled your brain," Rebecca said as if discovering something important.

"My brain is fine. It's my eyes and my hands that were injured. I can't catch myself if I start to fall."

"Rebecca, Samuel needs constant care. He will be up when he's ready." He felt his mother smooth the covers over his feet and tuck them in.

"He won't ever be ready if you coddle him, Anna."

"She isn't coddling me," he snapped. He couldn't see. He couldn't use his hands. He needed help with everything. Couldn't she see that for herself?

"Then you should move downstairs so your mother doesn't have to run up here every time you call. You aren't trying to make things more difficult for her, are you?"

"He's not making things difficult for me," his mother said quickly. "I don't know why my husband thinks I need help. I'm managing fine."

"Hello? Is anyone about? Anna, is the store open?" a woman's voice called from downstairs.

"*Ja*, we are open. Just a moment," his mother answered.

"Go on, Anna. I can manage here. Samuel, do you need your mother to do anything for you before she leaves?" Rebecca's voice was so sweet he could almost hear the honey dripping from her tongue."

"*Nee*, I don't need anything at the moment," he said through clenched teeth. If she was trying to be annoying, she was doing a fine job.

"Excellent. You see, Anna, Samuel and I will rub along well together. Don't keep your customer waiting. I'll sit with him until you come back. He and I need to get better acquainted, anyway."

Rebecca hadn't expected it to hit her so hard.

Stepping through Samuel's doorway was like stepping back in time. All her previous patients had been elderly folks or new mothers. Not since her husband's death had she taken care of a grown man in the prime of his life. Memories flooded her mind pulling her spirit low. Day after day, she had watched Walter grow weaker and less interested in what went on around him and more dependent on her. She willingly became his crutch, not realizing the damage she caused until it was too late.

Rebecca struggled to hide her dismay at the sight of Samuel. She had forgotten how much he resembled Walter. They were of the same height. They had the same broad shoulders and straight golden brown hair cut in the familiar Amish bowl hairstyle. Could she do this? Could she be a better nurse to Samuel than she had been to her dear Walter?

God had placed this challenge in her path. It was a test of her strength and her faith. She would not waver but stand firm and do her best. Even if the patient didn't like what she had to do.

She made shooing motions with her hands to get Anna moving. She knew she was being hard on Samuel and his mother, but after listening to Isaac on the buggy ride here, she already understood some of the family's problems. Samuel's mother was smothering him with kindness.

While Rebecca felt sorry for Samuel, more sympathy wouldn't do him any good. Isaac had expressed his concerns about Samuel's state of mind. Samuel wasn't getting up. He wasn't trying to do things for himself. It was so unlike Samuel that no one knew what to do. Luke and Noah both felt guilty about the accident. They blamed themselves for not taking better care of the equipment. They were trying their best to make it up to Samuel.

His mother had taken to treating him like a child instead of a grown man. The more she did for Samuel, the less he did for himself.

Rebecca's husband had been a strong man suddenly struck down with a heart attack at the age of thirty-five. It left him weak, unable to work his land and feeling useless. It took a long time for her to understand what was wrong with him, why he wouldn't try to get better. He had simply given up and eventually his damaged heart failed him.

That wasn't going to happen to Samuel, no matter what outcome he faced. With God's help, she was going to make a difference this time. Samuel needed to be shocked out of his complacency and self-pity. Thankfully, Isaac had had the good sense to hire her.

She was embarrassed to admit how fast she had jumped at his offer. Isaac hadn't even had a chance to mention her salary before she told him she could start. He had agreed to her usual wage without comment, clearly relieved she was willing to take on the job.

The same could not be said for her mother.

Rebecca put that conversation out of her mind and sincerely hoped her mother and John were having a pleasant visit at her home. No doubt, she would be the primary topic of their conversation, but she was here in this house for a reason. Anna Bowman wasn't going to release the reins of her son's care easily. Rebecca braced herself for the coming battle.

"It's a beautiful day outside. Why don't you go sit on the front porch and enjoy it. This nice fall weather won't last long."

"I'm fine where I am."

"You may be fine, but trust me when I tell you these sheets need to be laundered."

"They're fine. Go away."

"I'm not going anywhere. Your father hired me to do a job."

"What job? Annoying me?"

"If that's what it takes to get you better, I will do it gladly. Come on, up you go." She flipped the covers back. He wore blue-striped pajamas. He curled his bare toes and crossed his burned arms gingerly. "I'm not going anywhere."

"All right. I guess I shall have to wash these sheets with you in them." She picked up the glass of water beside the bed and poured some on his feet.

"Are you crazy?" Samuel jerked his foot away from the cold liquid. Had she just poured water on his bedding? The woman was off in the head.

"Now the sheets are wet so you'll have to get up."

"I can't believe you would do such a thing to a sick man. Where is my father? If he hired you, he can fire you."

"You are injured—you aren't sick. There's nothing wrong with your feet and legs. I do understand that even simple tasks are now a challenge, but hiding in bed is not the answer. Swing your legs over the side and sit up for a few minutes. Don't stand too quickly, and you won't get dizzy."

"What choice do I have?" He rubbed his foot on his pajama leg to dry it.

"Several. You can stay in your damp bed."

He didn't respond.

"Not to your liking? All right. You could yell for

your brothers or father to come and escort me home. I'm sure your brothers won't think less of you for letting a woman get the upper hand and having to rescue you from my clutches. Shall I go get one of them for you?"

He would never hear the end of it. "Leave them be. They have work to do."

"*Goot*. I'm glad to hear you say that. So do I. I'm going to move your legs to the side of the bed."

"I can do it." He didn't wait for her help. He swung his feet off the bed and used his elbows to push himself into a sitting position. He kept his hands raised so he wouldn't bump them.

She touched his shoulder. "Are you dizzy?"

"A little." He hated to admit it.

"Take some deep breaths."

He did and the wooziness passed.

"Now, I'm going to keep hold of your elbow while you stand."

"What if I fall?"

"I'll try not to trip over you while I'm making your bed."

He wasn't amused. "Very funny."

"I thought so."

"I'm serious. I could fall and hurt you."

"You could, but you won't. If you start feeling weak, I'll have a chair right behind you."

He heard her drag the ladder-back chair that sat at his desk closer. "Are you ready?"

"Will you pour water on my head if I say I'm not?"

"*Nee*, I would not want to get your bandages wet. However, I notice you don't have any dressings on your back."

His father was going to have to get rid of this woman.

"What kind of nurse would pour cold water down her patient's back?"

"One who is tired of waiting for her patient to get out of bed!"

He rose to his feet, fully expecting to pitch forward on his face the way he had the first time he'd tried to stand by himself. It had been agony getting up and back into bed without help. He never wanted to feel so helpless and alone again.

"Very good. Take two paces forward and then turn left. The doorway will be directly in front of you."

With her firm grip on his elbow to guide him, he managed half a dozen steps, but his hands were starting to throb and his legs were growing weaker. He held his hands higher. The thought of descending the stairs without being able to see made his legs shake. Fear sent cold shivers crawling down his spine.

"That's enough for now," she said. "Go ahead and sit down. The chair is right behind you."

He had to trust her. His knees gave way. He sat abruptly, but the chair was in the right spot. At least he wasn't lying facedown on the floor.

"Raise your hands a little higher. I'm going to pile some pillows on your lap so you can rest your arms on them."

He braced for the ordeal, but she handled his burned hands with gentleness, arranging the pillows at the perfect height for his comfort. "You did very well, Samuel."

Was that praise from her? *"Danki."*

"Will you be all right here for a few minutes?"

Her tone was definitely kinder. She had a pleasant voice when she wasn't ordering him around or poking fun at him. "I'll be fine. Close the window. I don't like the draft."

She began humming as she closed the window. It was an old hymn, one he liked. He heard her pulling the sheets off the bed and bundling them together. She was still humming as she carried them out of the room. The sounds of her light footsteps on the stairs faded and he was alone.

He shifted in the chair. He was comfortable enough. It was better than lying down. Not that he would admit as much to Rebecca Miller. He wiggled his toes and then lifted his legs, first one then the other. How had they become so weak so quickly? He kept working them until he heard her coming up the stairs.

"I'm back."

"I can hear you."

"It won't take me a minute to remake the bed if you're tired."

"The mattress is wet. You can't expect me to sleep in a soggy bed."

"I barely got the linens damp. The mattress is fine, but I'll flip it over if it makes you feel better."

"There's no need if it isn't wet."

"Okay." She continued humming. The flap of the sheets told him she was making his bed. He heard the slight sound of her hands smoothing the fabric into place. The flowery scent was stronger now.

"What is that smell?"

"Lavender. I sprinkle lavender water on the sheets before I iron them. It keeps them fresh-smelling a lot longer. Is it bothering you?"

He took a deep breath. "*Nee*, it smells good."

"I grow lavender in my garden and I make it into

soaps, oils and sachets. It's a very beneficial plant and it has so many uses. It's soothing on the sheets and the scent can help some people sleep better."

She stopped talking. He sensed that she was standing beside him. He tipped his head away from her. "Do you have a glass of water in your hand?"

"Why? Are you thirsty?" She was trying to keep her voice even, but he heard the humor lurking underneath. She was laughing at him.

"I was afraid you'd think I need a bath."

"You do."

He hadn't had one since before the accident. Maybe it was past time. He'd have Timothy help him with that this evening. He was the only one of Samuel's brothers with enough patience and the ability to work in silence. Samuel quickly changed the subject. "Do you sell your homemade soaps?"

"*Nee*, I give them away to family and friends."

"You should consider selling some in our store. The *Englisch* love Amish-made stuff and they pay well for things like my mother's jams and jellies."

"I'll think about it. I could certainly use some extra income. Are you ready to get back in bed?"

Was he? Not really. It wasn't bad being up as long as he wasn't alone. "I might sit here awhile longer."

Rebecca allowed her smile of triumph to widen. She knew he would feel better once he was up. "All right. I'm going downstairs and start supper."

"You're leaving?" The touch of panic in his voice surprised her.

"I'm only going downstairs. I will hear you if you call. What would you like for supper?"

"Some of *Mamm's* chicken broth will be okay. I'm not fond of the beef broth."

Her mouth dropped open. "Is that all you've been eating? Broth?"

He shifted uneasily in his chair. "My face hurts. I can't use my hands. *Mamm* figured out that something I can sip through a straw works best."

"No wonder you're so weak. I need to get some real food into you."

"I'm not going to have someone spoon-feed me. Especially you."

"That sounds like pride. Our faith teaches us to put aside all pride and be humble before God. Are you a prideful man, Samuel?"

She waited, but he didn't answer. "I didn't hear what you said," she prompted.

"I'm not prideful," he answered softly, but with an edge of irritation.

"Of course not. I'm sorry I misunderstood. Please forgive me. If you're okay in the chair, I'm going to get the wash started and then supper. Which one of your family members shall I ask to help you with your meal and your bath?"

"Timothy. But I'm not coming downstairs to eat."

"That's fine. Just call if you need me."

She crossed the room to the door, but didn't leave. Instead, she waited and watched.

He turned his head to the side as if listening for her. After a long minute, he muttered, "Fat chance I'll ask her for help."

She smiled. He wasn't sure she had gone. He was testing to see if she was still about. He kept his head cocked with one ear toward the door. She silently slipped out, taking care to avoid the squeaking stair treads she had noted on the way up.

Rebecca was used to finding her way around strange kitchens. A quick check of the refrigerator and the pantry gave her the fixing for a hearty chicken and noodle casserole. That would be easy for Samuel to eat and filling for the rest of the family. After putting the chicken on to boil, she started the laundry in the propane-powered washer in the basement, swept the kitchen and washed the kitchen floor. While she worked, she kept an ear out for any sounds from Samuel's room. She was prepared for his call, but not for the loud thud that shook the ceiling above her.

She dashed up the stairs and found him sitting on the floor at the foot of the bed. There was blood on the bandage covering his left hand. She rushed to his side. "Samuel Bowman, what have you done to yourself?"

Samuel gritted his teeth against the unbearable pain in his hands. He couldn't breathe let alone answer her.

"Are you hurt anywhere else?" Her voice penetrated the fog in his brain.

"Why? Isn't this bad enough? Maybe I can break a leg. Would that make you happy?"

"I'm sorry you're hurting, but that's not an excuse to be rude."

The pain receded, but his humiliation grew by leaps and bounds. This was exactly what he had been afraid would happen. Hitting the floor hurt every bit as much as he knew it would.

This was her fault. "Why didn't you come back? You said you only be gone for a little bit. I was stuck in that chair for ages."

"I'm sorry about that. Forgive me. I thought you would call for me when you were ready to go back to bed. Let me help you up. Do you think you can stand, or should I fetch your father or one of your brothers?"

"I can do it. Get out of my way."

"Very well."

He heard her move aside. He gathered his legs under him and lurched to his feet. He would've fallen again if she hadn't stepped in front of him and placed her hands on his chest.

"I've got you. Relax. Take a deep breath. Get your bearings."

He tried, but it was hard to do with a woman holding him up. The flowery fragrance was from her hair. The top of her head came to his chin. Was her hair blond or pale brown? He couldn't recall. He remembered her pale face streaked with tears at her husband's funeral and the flash of gratitude in her eyes when she noticed the cedar panels in Walter's coffin, but Samuel wasn't sure if her eyes were blue or gray.

"Are you steady now?" She stepped back but kept a firm grip on his arms.

He was dizzy, but he wasn't about to admit it to her. His hands still smarted. "I'm fine."

"You could've fooled me."

"This is funny to you, isn't it?"

There was a slight pause, then she said, "Maybe just a little. The bed is four steps to your left."

Determined not to give her anything else to laugh at, he shuffled in the direction of the bed until he felt the mattress against his leg. He sat down with a sigh. Gingerly lowering himself onto his side, he raised his feet. She was there helping lift them and slipping them under the covers.

"I hope you have learned your lesson," she said sternly.

Was she really going to lecture him? "What lesson would that be?"

"It is less painful to ask for help."

"It would've been less painful if I had stayed in bed in the first place."

"I can see you are a glass half-empty kind of fellow. We will work on that."

"I'm not sure I will survive any more of your lessons."

"Why didn't you call for me?"

"Why didn't you return?"

"I didn't realize how stubborn you are. I won't make that mistake again."

"Not with me you won't. As soon as my father comes in, he will take you home."

"Something you don't realize is how stubborn I can be, too. I'm not going anywhere. Your mother needs help. Whether you believe that or not. I am here to help her by looking after you. We got off to a bad start, Samuel. Let's try to get along."

"A bad start? You poured water on my sheets."

"Only because you wouldn't do as I asked. In the future, we will both have a better understanding of our limits."

"Don't get comfortable here. You'll be leaving."

"Oh, ye of little faith. It's time for your pain pill. According to your father, the doctor wants you taking them every four to six hours. I'm sure you must need one now."

He did, but he hated to admit it so he kept silent. She returned a few moments later and said, "Open wide."

He did need something for the pain. Reluctantly, he opened his mouth and swallowed the pill with a long drink of water from the straw she held for him. *"Danki."*

"I'm going to mark on your bandage with an ink pen. I promise to be careful."

"Why?"

"I need to make sure the bleeding has stopped."

"I'm bleeding?"

"Only a small amount through the bandages on your left hand. If I mark the edge of the bloodstain, then I can check in a little while and make sure it isn't getting bigger."

He braced himself for the task, but she completed it without hurting him. She straightened the bed and turned his pillow. The fresh coolness against his neck helped ease his tension.

"I'm going downstairs now. If you need anything, you can call for me, or you can make a loud thump on the floor again, whichever you prefer."

"Nice to know you enjoyed seeing me fall on my face."

"Actually, I didn't get to see it. Give me some warning next time so I don't miss it again."

"Are you deliberately trying to make me angry?"

"Are you deliberately trying to make me out to be a cruel shrew?"

"I didn't say you were cruel."

"Oh, just a shrew."

"You're twisting my words!"

He heard her approach the bed. "Samuel, you will be

fine in a very short time. I know it doesn't feel like it now, but you will. This road to recovery is painful and frustrating, but it has an end. Your mother needs help and I need the job. Let's not fight. If we carry on like this in public people will think we're married."

"We wouldn't want people to think that."

"Exactly."

He hadn't considered that she needed work. She was a widow and dependent on others for her livelihood. His conscience smote him. The Lord compelled men of faith to care for widows and orphans. "I can be civil if you can."

"*Goot.* We'll get along fine, Sammy, as long as you do what I say."

Just when he thought she was being sensible. "It's Samuel. We'll get along fine, *Becky*, if you listen to what I think before you decide what's best for me."

"Very well, we have a deal. You won't regret it."

Had he just agreed to her staying?

Chapter Three

Rebecca almost laughed when Samuel opened his mouth to protest but snapped it shut again. He wasn't used to losing arguments. He was a man used to getting his own way.

Goot. He needed to find that inner strength again. If irritation with her brought it to life that was fine. He would most likely speak with his father later, but for now, she had the upper hand. But the upper hand wasn't what she was here for. She was here to help him get better and to cope with his injuries.

Maybe she should try seeing things from his perspective. Taking care of Emil Troyer had taught her a lot about the ways blind people coped. She closed her eyes, turned around once and tried to cross the room without losing her sense of balance. She quickly became disoriented. No wonder Samuel was insecure and fearful. Without the use of his hands to feel his way around, he was twice as blind. His fall had reinforced his belief that he needed to stay in bed. It was a setback to be sure, but she wasn't willing to let him.

She had an idea. "How are your elbows?"

"What kind of question is that?"

"Are your elbows burned like your hands? Are they bandaged? I can't tell under your pajama sleeves."

"My elbows are fine. So are my knees. Would you like to see me crawl on them?"

"Maybe later." She crossed to the wall and tried using her elbows to help keep her balance and find her way. As she suspected, keeping one elbow or her shoulder in contact with the wall made moving easier.

"You are nuts," Samuel muttered.

She ignored his comment and returned to his bedside. "I'm going to suggest that you keep one elbow against the wall when you move around the room. It will help you maintain your balance and give you something to lean on if you feel dizzy. It won't help you cross an open room, but it will allow you to get up and move around without someone with you."

"I'm not going to be moving around my room."

"Of course you will be. Several times a day, in fact, but you've done enough for today. I'll bring your supper up after your brother has helped you bathe."

"You are not going to spoon-feed me," he muttered.

Her resolve weakened in the face of his embarrassment. It had to be hard to depend on others for every aspect of his care. It must be doubly humiliating to have a strange woman telling him what to do. Still, she was here to do a job and that job was to get Samuel well. Coddling wouldn't help him.

"Would you rather lick it off the plate like a dog? I guess that will work, but it might get the bandages on your face dirty not to mention my clean sheets. If that's the plan, I'll have your brother wait until after supper to bathe you."

"Go away. You're making me crazy."

That was better. There was more life in his voice. "I'm going. All you have to do is ask. Verna Yoder was right for a change. You are a cranky patient."

"I haven't spoken a word to Verna Yoder. Why would she say I'm cranky? And why are you gossiping about me? Who else is gossiping about me?"

"Samuel, you know full well if Verna Yoder is talking about you, *everyone* has heard what she has to say. The woman would gossip with a tree stump."

"She would be cranky, too, if she'd been through what I've been through."

"On that we can agree. She isn't one to suffer in silence. But, we shouldn't speak disparagingly of her. She is a member of our church and we must accept her, flaws and all, as a child of God. I'm sorry for my unkind thoughts, as I'm sure you are, too."

"I'll keep my thoughts to myself so you can't share them with Verna and who knows who else."

She laughed outright. "Smart man."

A grunt was his only reply.

She softened her tone. "Do not fear. I will spread the word that you are a *wunderbarr* patient, Samuel. Easy to care for and sweet natured. Everyone will know you as kind and good-natured with never a cross word to be said about anyone."

A twitch at the corner of his mouth could have been a smile. "Then you'll be guilty of lying."

"I think not. Is there anything you need before I go finish the laundry?"

"My eyesight restored."

She heard the fear underlying his words even as he

tried to make a joke out of it. "If God wills it, Samuel, it shall happen. Many people are praying for you."

"We both know prayers aren't always answered."

A stab of familiar pain took her breath away. Her prayers for Walter's recovery had gone unanswered, but in the last days of his illness, she finally understood that she had been praying for the wrong thing. "Our prayers are answered if we ask to humbly accept God's will, Samuel."

"I'm not sure I can do that. Not until I understand why this happened to me."

She understood his despair and confusion. He felt betrayed. She had, too. "Why did He call my husband home so soon? I have no answer for that or for your injury. We must not question His will. We must accept that His plan is greater than we can see."

"Since I can't see at all, that won't be hard."

He was determined to look on the gloomy side of things. She would tolerate that for a while, but not for long. "God was merciful to you, Samuel. I'm surprised you don't see that. Your clothes didn't catch fire. You could have been burned everywhere."

"I had a large leather apron on over my clothes and wide leather cuffs over my sleeves to keep them from getting caught in the lathe. They protected my arms and body. I don't know that God was looking out for me."

"How can you say that? Who prompted you to put on your apron and cuffs that morning? I am sorry this happened to you, Samuel. I can't begin to imagine what it must be like. I'm sure the pain is hard to bear, but not knowing if you will see again must be deeply frightening."

* * *

Samuel pressed his lips tightly together. He didn't want to talk about fear or the future. Changing the subject, he said, "I'm sorry you lost your husband."

Rebecca was quiet for a long moment. Then she said, *"Danki."*

Samuel heard the tightness in her voice. So it was still hard for her to speak about Walter. She must have loved him very much. Samuel didn't want to feel sorry for her, but he did.

"I never thanked you for adding the cedar panels to Walter's coffin. It was a kind touch. How did you know he liked the smell of cedarwood?"

"I once saw him admiring a cedar trinket box at our shop. He kept opening it and inhaling with a funny little smile on his face."

"I love the smell of cedar, too. It had a special meaning for us. Did he buy the box?"

"He didn't, but he told me he might be back for it. Later that same day, a tourist stopped in and purchased it. Walter came back the next day and I had to tell him it was gone. I made another one but he never came back to the shop. I learned later that he had taken sick. I should have brought it by the house, but I didn't."

Had Walter been planning to buy it for her? Samuel wanted to ask what special meaning the scent held for them, but decided against it. It was much too personal a question. He didn't want to start liking this bossy tyrant. He didn't want to hear about her feelings for her husband, or how she survived his loss. He just wanted to be left alone with his own misery. "I'm tired now."

"I understand. Do you need anything before I go?"

As soon as she spoke, he realized he didn't want her

to leave. He wanted her company for a while longer. Her voice was pleasant when she wasn't ordering him around or poking fun at him. Companionship wasn't something he'd needed before. He worked best alone. He preferred it to having to watch others who couldn't do a task as well or as quickly as he could. People frustrated him. His brothers frustrated him. Rebecca frustrated him. He didn't like that he wanted her around.

"I'm fine. Peace and quiet, that's all I ask," he snapped.

"I'll be downstairs if you need me, Samuel," she said gently. It was an unspoken rebuke for his churlish attitude. And deserved.

"I know. Call or fall on the floor to get your attention, whichever I prefer."

She laughed. "Something along those lines."

After she left his room, the sound of her laughter stayed in his mind. She had a pretty laugh. Not horsey or simpering. Rebecca Miller laughed like someone who enjoyed life. His grudging smile pulled at the bandages on his face and made him wince.

His grin faded. Rebecca had faced great sorrow. How did she find the strength to be happy? He shared the same Amish faith she did. Was her faith stronger than his was? Or was she a stronger person? Was it true that she didn't question God's plan for her life? He had a hard time believing that. How could she not? No husband, no children. Her future must look bleak at times. As did his when he found the courage to think about it.

Samuel listened for her throughout the next hour or so. He had no way of telling time. The days and nights tended to crawl by with nothing to do but feel pain. Rebecca kept humming or singing softly so he knew where she was. When he heard the washing machine running in the basement, he sat up gingerly on the side of his bed. His mother had an ancient wringer washer that his father had adapted to run off propane. Samuel knew Rebecca would be down there feeding the clothes through the wringer for a while. Standing slowly, he moved up the bed until his elbow touched the wall by his headboard.

Although he was still unsure of his balance, he discovered he wasn't afraid of falling on his face as long as he had the wall to lean on. He made one slow circuit of the room. He remembered the chest beneath the window in time to avoid stubbing his toe on it, but knocked his shin against the leg of his desk. It was a minor discomfort compared to his previous fall. How much damage had he inflicted on his burned hands?

Rebecca had marked the bloodstains. Were they getting worse? Should he call her to check? He made his way back to bed first. He didn't want her to know he had taken her suggestion for getting around.

He lay down with a sigh of relief just as he heard her coming up the stairs. She came quietly to his side. After several minutes of silence, he couldn't stand it anymore. "Has the bleeding stopped?"

"It has. I'm sorry if I woke you."

"I wasn't asleep."

"There isn't any way for me to know that unless you speak, Samuel."

"I did speak."

"After I stood here in awkward silence for ages. Are you worn out after your stroll?"

He almost denied that he had been up, but thought better of it. "How did you know?"

"I noticed the papers on your desk had been disturbed and one was on the floor. The window isn't open, so I knew they couldn't have blown around."

"I bumped into it."

"I thought so."

He grudgingly gave her credit for her good idea. "Leaning against the wall makes it easier."

"I'm glad my suggestion was helpful."

He heard the front door open. "Samuel, I'm back. I'm sorry I was gone for so long. How are you?"

His mother came charging up the stairs, breathless by the time she reached his bedside.

"I'm fine, *Mamm*."

"So many people have stopped by to ask about you. I must've told the same story about your injury ten times already today. I thought I would never get free."

"Samuel and I have gotten along fabulously. I changed his sheets. He was up in the chair and even took a short walk. I'm very pleased with him."

His mother laid her hand on his cheek. "You haven't overdone it, have you, Samuel? The doctor warned against that. I would feel dreadful if you suffered a setback. Is the pain worse? I don't know why she thought you needed to be up."

He'd forgotten the pain in his hands and his face for a short time while he was talking with Rebecca. They came roaring back to life now although the pain pill was taking the edge off. "I might have overdone it."

"Is that blood on your bandages?"

"It's nothing to worry about. He bumped it, but the bleeding has stopped," Rebecca said calmly.

"You shouldn't have let him get up."

"Maybe we should let him rest for a while and discuss this downstairs," Rebecca suggested.

"An excellent idea. You and I need to have a talk."

Samuel knew that tone. His mother wasn't happy. He felt a stab of pity for Rebecca, but quickly smothered it. She would be on her way home shortly.

He was glad about that, wasn't he?

Anna Bowman was upset.

Rebecca followed her to the kitchen and prepared to receive a scolding. She didn't have long to wait.

Anna spun to face her with her arms clasped across her chest. "I'm grateful you came to help, Rebecca, but my husband made a mistake in bringing you here. You have overtired Samuel, and I won't have that."

"He is tired, but he can do more than you think. He needs to do more."

"I know how to take care of my own son better than anyone. If you had children, you would realize the truth of that."

Rebecca kept her face carefully blank, but she cringed inwardly. She would never have children of her own unless she married again, and she couldn't see herself with anyone other than Walter. She stiffened her spine, determined not to let Anna drive her away. "Your son isn't a child. He shouldn't be treated like one."

"I know you mean well, but I won't be dictated to by you. Now, I've got to get supper started. The men will be in soon."

Before Rebecca could reply, the outside door opened. Isaac Bowman and his three sons filed in. They all nodded toward her and bid her welcome.

"Smells *goot*!" Noah said with a broad grin. The youngest of the Bowman siblings, Noah was nineteen and still in his *rumspringa*—the years when Amish youth were allowed to sample things normally forbidden to baptized Amish members. He wore blue jeans and a red plaid shirt. His curly brown hair was cut short beneath a black ball cap. He whipped it off at his mother's frown and hung it on the pegs by the door where his father and brothers had placed their identical straw hats.

Anna glanced with surprise at the stove where Rebecca's chicken and noodles were simmering. Apparently she had been so intent on returning to Samuel that she hadn't noticed the enticing smell.

Isaac looked around in satisfaction. "The house looks *wunderbarr.* The floor is spotless. The counters are clean and neat. It's *goot* to have my industrious wife back. I knew bringing Rebecca to look after Samuel was exactly what you needed. You have always kept our home as neat as a pin until Samuel's accident."

Anna glanced around the room. "Well, I try."

Rebecca took pity on the woman. "I wasn't able to get the biscuits started, Anna. Would you like me to do that, or would you like me to sit with Samuel?"

"Well, I don't know." Anna chewed the corner of her lip as she gathered her apron into a wad.

"Let her sit with Samuel," Isaac said. "No one makes biscuits as good as yours."

Anna looked as if she wanted to argue, but instead she nodded. "Tell Samuel that I will be up to feed him as soon as the family is finished with supper."

"Anna, I brought Rebecca here to lighten your load. Let her do her job."

Anna folded her arms over her chest. "She made supper and picked up the house. It was a kindness and I thank her, but I can take care of my own family."

Rebecca caught Isaac's eye. "Samuel asked that Timothy help him this evening."

Isaac arched one eyebrow but didn't comment. Rebecca hoped he understood Samuel's reluctance to be seen as an invalid by others, even by her. She turned to the young men washing up at the sink. "Do you mind, Timothy?"

"I don't mind a bit." Timothy dried his hands on a towel and tossed it over Noah's head. Noah snatched it off and gave his brother a good-natured grin. "You make a fine nursemaid, Timmy. I'm not surprised he asked for you."

"Better to be the nursemaid than the baby." Timothy laughed at Noah's quick scowl and then went upstairs.

Anna smoothed her apron. "May I speak to you privately, Isaac?"

"Of course." He followed her into another room.

Rebecca sighed deeply. She had been too forceful, too pushy, too sure that she knew what was best. She had allowed her experience with her husband's illness to cloud her judgment. Samuel wasn't Walter. Anna would see that she was sent home. It was a shame, because Anna really did need help even if she wouldn't admit it.

"How is he?" Luke asked. He had a wary look about him. Standing apart from the others near the front door, he looked ready to make a quick escape. She had the feeling he was as much an outsider in the home as she was.

Rebecca smiled to put him at ease. "Samuel is healing, but these things take time."

Luke shoved his hands in his pockets. "He's been like a bull with a sore head. Nothing pleases him."

Noah hung his towel on the rod at the end of the

counter. "*Mamm* says we must be patient with him and do everything we can for him."

Luke moved to take his turn at the sink. "That's what we've been doing, and his mood hasn't improved."

"Sometimes doing everything for a person does more harm than good." Rebecca moved to the stove, lifted the lid off the pot and stirred the contents. Fragrant steam rose in a cloud.

"What do you mean?" Noah asked.

She decided the noodles needed a few more minutes and replaced the lid. "Just that if you don't encourage your brother to try harder, he will only grow weaker."

Luke rinsed his hands and turned off the water. "Samuel has never been the weak one."

"That's why this is so hard for him." Rebecca glanced toward the doorway where Anna and Isaac stood. She couldn't tell what decision had been reached, if any.

Isaac hooked his thumbs through his suspenders. "Let's get out of the way until supper is ready. Noah, you owe me a chance to beat you at checkers."

The men left the kitchen. Anna began mixing the biscuit dough. "Rebecca, will you set the table? The dishes are in the cabinet on the left side of the sink."

"Of course." At least she wasn't being sent home before supper. She knew that Isaac was on her side, but how much sway did his wife's wishes hold?

Supper was a quiet meal. After a silent blessing, the food was passed around with a minimum of fuss. Amish meals were not a time for small talk. Isaac laid out the work they would need to do the following day. Other than a few brief questions from his sons, their attention was given to the food. When the meal was over, Isaac took a tray upstairs to Samuel. Timothy offered to do it, but his father brushed aside the offer.

Samuel struggled into a sitting position on the side of his bed when he heard footsteps enter his room. He was feeling more human after Timothy had helped him bathe, and his appetite had been whetted by the wonderful smells from the kitchen. "It's about time."

"If you are impatient for your meal, you should come down to the table."

Tensing at the sound of his father's voice, Samuel quickly apologized. "I'm sorry, Father, I thought you were Timothy. He said he was bringing up my supper."

"I wanted to talk to you, and I thought this was a good time to do it."

"What did you want to talk about?" Samuel heard the sound of the tray being placed on his bedside table and the scrape of the chair legs as his father pulled up a seat beside the bed.

"Your mother is unhappy that I brought Rebecca here."

"I don't blame her. The woman is touched in the head. She actually poured water on my sheets to get me out of bed."

To Samuel's chagrin, his father began chuckling. "I never would've thought of that. Did it work?"

"That is hardly the point."

"Isn't it? Open your mouth. I have a spoonful of chicken and noodles for you."

"Mother said I was to stick with broth."

"Doesn't sound like much of a meal to me. Open."

Samuel did as his father bid. The first bite had his stomach rumbling for more. The noodles were firm, not mushy. The chicken was tender and the chunks of vegetables were done to perfection.

"She's a good cook, I think," his father said, giving him several more bites.

"Not bad, but I'm still glad she isn't staying." Samuel opened his mouth for another spoonful. Although he was embarrassed to be fed by his father, he was hungry enough to accept the help.

After a few more bites, his father spoke again. "How are you feeling, *sohn*? Really. Don't tell me *fine*. I know that isn't true."

"I have a lot of pain. My eyes burn like the fire is still in them. My hands are useless. I hate being helpless."

"I'm sorry God has placed this burden on you. I would take your place if I could."

"I know that. I'm sorry my carelessness placed such a burden on you. I know you need my help in the fields."

"Our neighbors have been lending a hand."

"That's nice to hear. My brothers can't do it all, not without Joshua, but I reckon they'll have to try. It was a bad time for Joshua to marry. They should have waited until the fall like most Amish people do."

"Your brothers are doing fine. Joshua followed his heart and I can't fault him for that. You will be back in the fields in no time."

Samuel's appetite fled. "What if I'm not? What if I'm blind forever as the doctor fears?"

"That is a bridge you can't cross until you reach it. You must have faith that God will provide all you need."

Faith. Did he still possess it?

"Would you like some more supper?" his father asked.

"*Nee*, I'm done."

"Very well. Your mother will be up shortly."

"She's good company." She didn't make him do things he'd rather not.

"She fusses over you."

"I can stand it. She understands that I can't do things for myself."

"All right. *Guten nacht.*"

"Good night." Samuel realized his father hadn't said what he intended to do about Rebecca. "*Daed*, wait."

"What is it, Samuel?"

"You are sending Rebecca home, aren't you?"

Chapter Four

Rebecca had just finished washing the last supper dish when Isaac came downstairs. He handed the bowl and spoon to her before facing his wife. "Samuel would like you to come up now."

Anna turned her back on him and began wiping down the table. "Only if you think I should."

"Of course you should go up. There is no substitute for a mother's love and comfort. Have you any chores that Rebecca can help you with this evening?"

Anna turned around with her arms folded tightly across her chest. "Nothing I can't take care of myself."

"Anna," he chided gently.

"Oh, very well. The gift shop needs dusting. It wouldn't hurt to be swept out, too."

Rebecca washed and rinsed the bowl then dried her hands on a towel. "I will be happy to do that for you. Is there a broom in the building?"

Anna nodded. "There is a broom closet near the back. You'll find what you need in there."

Isaac smiled and nodded at her. She managed a small

smile in return and went upstairs. Rebecca waited for Isaac to speak. Did she have a job or not?

He hooked his thumbs under his suspenders and ran them up and down the bands slowly. "I have spoken with my wife and with Samuel about you staying here."

She laid the towel on the counter. "I assumed you would. They were against it, weren't they? That's okay. The last thing I want is to bring tension into your family."

"Did you really pour water on Samuel to get him out of bed?"

She stared at the towel. "I did, but only a little on his feet. His sheets needed to be laundered, and he refused to get up."

"I would have paid good money to see that."

The laughter lurking in Isaac's voice caused her to jerk her head up. He was grinning. She smiled in relief. "Samuel was quite upset."

"But he got out of bed."

She had to tell the whole truth. "He did, but he fell later when he tried to get back on his own. I don't think he did serious damage to his hands, but I know it hurt him a great deal."

"To try and fail is better than not trying. He and his mother both have trouble asking for help."

"It's a fault many of us share."

"True. I have told them both you are staying. You must be prepared for some resistance."

She drew a deep breath of relief. "*Danki*. I am prepared. Hopefully, I can convince them it's for the best."

"I'm sure you will. My sons need to start cutting corn. They will be in the fields all day tomorrow and I have a table that needs to be delivered to Anna's niece.

I have insisted that Anna come with me. Her niece has a new baby that we have not seen. Samuel has an appointment with his doctor in town. Would you be able to drive him?"

"Of course."

"*Goot.* In spite of what my wife thinks, I believe you will be a great help to this family."

"I hope so. I should go and clean the gift shop before it gets dark. Thank you for keeping me on."

"Anna will show you to your room when she comes back. It is at the back of the house below Samuel's room."

"*Goot.* I should be able to hear if he falls or has trouble at night."

"I wish I could make this easier for you."

She fisted her hands on her hips. "Don't worry about me. I'm a big girl. I can take care of myself."

He chuckled and nodded. "I believe you can."

Rebecca left the house and walked up the lane toward the nearby gift shop with eager steps. She was staying. She didn't have to go home and face her mother's constant pressure to wed John. Her mother meant well, but Rebecca wasn't ready to wed again. She might never be. Her life's mission now was to care for others, for the sick and those in need of help. Her mother refused to accept that.

The sun hung low on the horizon, but she had a good hour of daylight left. Behind the white board fence to her left, the family's horses grazed in the pasture. Six big gray draft horses dwarfed a pair of cream-colored ponies munching beside them while four brown buggy horses stood nose to tail drowsing in the evening air. It was a good farm. A neat farm. The outbuildings and the fences had recently been painted. The animals looked well cared for. The corn in the field across from the horses was tall and turning brown as autumn approached. Orange pumpkins peeked through thick green leaves in a patch behind the gift shop.

She reached the small shop and went in. The door wasn't locked. She hadn't expected it to be. The Amish believed in the goodness of all men and rarely locked their homes or businesses. What did surprise her was that she wasn't alone. Luke was setting up a display of birdhouse gourds just inside the door. He had more in a large box on the floor beside him. They were gaily painted in hues of red, blue and yellow.

She gestured toward them. "Those are pretty. Did you make them?"

"I may not have Samuel's skill with wood, but I'm not without my own talent."

His sour tone shocked her. She folded her hands in front of her. "I never thought otherwise, Luke."

He glanced her way. "You didn't? Aren't you one of those who believe the drugs scrambled my brains?"

"For all I know, your brains were scrambled long before you took drugs. Where is the broom closet?"

A slow smile crept across his face. "You might be the right one to take care of Samuel, after all."

"And why do you say that?"

He rearranged his collection to his satisfaction before turning to her. "You've got a quick wit and a sharp tongue. I don't think you'll take much guff from him."

She saw a door behind the counter and opened it. "I don't imagine he'll give me much guff."

"Oh, he will."

She withdrew a broom and several dusting rags. "Are you worried about him?"

Luke crossed his arms and leaned his hip against the counter to watch her work as she pulled the supplies out of the closet. "Samuel is indestructible."

"No man is indestructible."

"He only cares about what is best for the family. He sees the vine, but he doesn't see the branches. No, I take that back. He sees the branches that need to be pruned away so the vine will prosper."

"Meaning you?" She handed him a dust rag and then began sweeping.

Luke stared at the cloth in his hand for a moment, and then got to work on the shelves filled with jars of apple butter and jams. "Samuel would like it if I left."

"I would be very surprised if that was true."

"You'll see. I've been the thorn in his side since the day I was born."

"Why is that?"

"Because I don't like to do things his way."

"I see. What if his way is the right way? He can't be wrong all the time, can he?"

"Then I do it my way just to annoy him."

She chuckled. "That sounds like my *brudders*. They fight like cats and dogs, but they love each other. Do you think Samuel's accident has changed him?"

"I don't know."

"Your father is worried that it has."

"Maybe Samuel will develop more patience with the rest of us now that he knows what it's like to suffer."

She stopped sweeping and leaned on the broom. "You have suffered, haven't you?"

Luke stopped dusting. "Prison is no picnic. Neither is kicking a drug habit."

"As one who has suffered greatly, do you now have more patience with Samuel?"

Luke gave her a wry smile. "You like to turn people's words back on them, don't you?"

"I like to see all sides of things, even people."

She picked one of his gourds out of the box. "If all I could see was the inside of this house, I might think it was a dark and ugly thing. But I can see the outside is bright and pretty as a flower. Bright outside to delight the eye and attract a nesting pair of birds. Dark inside so the baby birds can sleep. Two sides. Inside, outside. Same birdhouse."

"Samuel is hardly a gourd."

"And neither are you. You are capable of seeing more than one side, too. Samuel is in a very dark place now. He can't see how bright and pretty life is outside of his pain."

She handed the gourd to Luke. "I think you understand how that feels. Samuel is going to need your understanding and your strength to help push him out of his dark nest."

"He won't like it."

"*Nee*, he won't. We'll have to give him a target for his ire."

"You?"

"Why not? I'm not part of the family. I'll leave when he gets well or when he can convince his father to fire me. What do you say? Will you help me help him?"

"Sure. He's going to be mad at me, anyway. He always is."

She resumed sweeping. "*Goot.* What does he like to do?"

"Work. He's always working, and he expects everyone else to work as hard as he does. The woodworking shop was his life. He had high hopes for it. He was sure he could turn it into a prosperous business. Now it's a pile of ashes and twisted metal."

"I heard that members of the church will rebuild it in a few weeks. Once the harvest is done." Rebecca swept the pile of dirt into the dustpan.

"It will be the cost of replacing the machinery that will keep us from reopening anytime soon. And Samuel's injuries. He is a genius with wood. He carves beautiful pieces. It's a God-given gift."

"The Lord gives, and the Lord takes away. We'll have to find a way to include him in the family business even with his limited abilities."

"How?" Luke asked.

She opened the door, tossed out the dirt and then leaned on her broom. "I'm not sure, but the Lord will show us the way if we trust in Him."

Luke looked around the small store. "If Father would consider adding everyday hardware items to this place, we would get more business and Samuel wouldn't have to worry so much about expanding the furniture end of it."

"What kind of things would you add?"

"Battery-operated lanterns. Solar-powered battery chargers. Brooms and mops. Things that won't take up much space, but that people need all the time. Nails, screws, bolts. It's nice to attract the tourists, but the farmers and businessmen in the community have money to spend, too."

"It's an interesting idea. What does your father think of it?"

"I don't know."

"You haven't mentioned it to him?"

"I ran it past Samuel. He said it would be too much work for mother. The gift shop was her idea, and we should leave it alone. Samuel thinks his furniture would bring in more money. He's probably right. Samuel is always right."

"Interesting. You've given me a lot to think about, Luke. I'd also like to buy one of your birdhouses. May I have the red one? You might want to answer your phone."

"What phone?" He tried to look innocent.

"The cell phone set on vibrate in your boot."

His expression fell. "Look, don't tell anyone. Okay?

Rebecca shook her head and walked out the door.

Samuel couldn't believe his own father had turned against him.

He was still fuming the following morning as he lay in bed listening for Rebecca's footsteps. He didn't hear her voice. She wasn't humming or singing today. Where was she? Wasn't she supposed to be making sure he was comfortable? No one had been up to his room since Timothy brought him breakfast. That had been hours ago.

He shifted restlessly on the mattress. Timothy had dressed him in pants and a shirt instead of his pajamas because he had a doctor's appointment in the late morning. It should be almost time to leave. He sat up and swung his feet over the side of the bed. He had his socks on, but he needed his shoes. It was hot, even with his sleeves rolled up past his elbows. He wanted his window opened. Where was that woman? "Rebecca!"

"What is it, Samuel."

He jumped when her soft reply came from nearby. "How long have you been in here?"

"I came up when Timothy was feeding you breakfast this morning."

"You've been standing in my room this whole time?"

"*Nee*, I've been sitting at your desk mending socks and shirts for your mother. What do you need?"

"I need you not to be creeping into my room."

"I didn't creep. I walked."

"Announce yourself next time. I don't like being spied on."

"I can see how it would feel that way. I'm sorry. I was trying not to disturb you per your mother's instructions."

"Sing or hum like you did yesterday so I know where you are."

"Okay. Are you ready to head to the doctor?"

"Who is going to help me get downstairs?"

"I am."

"By yourself? You're not strong enough."

"I'm not going to carry you, Samuel. I'm going to walk down with you and lead you to the buggy."

"What if I fall?"

"You won't. I forbid it. Your shoes are right here. Pick up your left foot."

He lifted his right one.

She sighed. "Luke isn't the only one in this family who seeks to annoy others. You should be ashamed of yourself."

"At least I don't pour water on people in their sick-beds."

She slipped his shoe on and tied the laces. "Didn't I apologize for that?"

"I don't think so."

"Then I'm sorry. Please forgive me."

He held up his other foot. She didn't touch him. After another minute, his patience grew thin. "What are you waiting for?"

"Forgiveness."

"I forgive you."

"Is that true forgiveness?"

"What?"

"You can say you forgive someone without really meaning it. Am I truly forgiven?"

"*Ja*, Rebecca Miller, I have truly forgiven you for pouring water on me as long as you never do it again."

"I'm not sure true forgiveness can be conditional, but it will do. *Danki*. And I have forgiven you, too."

Forgiven him? "For what?"

"For trying to get me fired."

"We both know how that turned out. Can I have my other shoe, please?"

"I have it right here." She slipped it on and tied it. "There, now you are ready. The horse is hitched, and the buggy is waiting outside."

He wasn't ready. The thought of going down the stairs let alone riding in a buggy without being able to see was terrifying.

It shouldn't be. They were things he'd done his entire life. Simple, ordinary things.

Like putting gasoline in the generator. He'd done that a thousand times, too.

"There is an old Amish proverb that says courage is only fear that has said its prayers. I will be with you every step of the way." Rebecca's soft voice sent a flush of embarrassment through him. He didn't want her feeling sorry for him.

"Fine. Let's get it over with." He shot to his feet and wobbled slightly. She grasped his elbow to steady him and steered him toward the door. He struggled not to show his discomfort.

"The stairwell is directly in front of us. I'll go down first, but I'll only be a step below you. Keep your elbow or shoulder against the wall to help maintain your balance. Take it very slowly. If you feel weak or dizzy, just sit down on the step behind you."

"If we wind up in a heap at the bottom, I'm going to say I told you so."

She laughed softly. For some reason it helped steady his nerves. "The first step is right in front of you."

It wasn't as hard as he had imagined, but that didn't make it any less frightening. Thankfully, they reached the bottom of the steps without incident. He took a steadying breath. "Lead on."

"You're doing fine." She had his elbow again.

"I know." He wasn't, but as long as she thought he was, that was good.

"I've got something for you to drink before we get started. It's warm ginger tea. It should be cool enough to sip through a straw. Open."

He pulled his head back. "Why?"

"It will settle your stomach."

"There's nothing wrong with my stomach."

"Please, it will keep you from getting sick on the ride."

"I won't get sick, and I don't want your tea."

"Oh, very well. Here is your hat." She slapped it on his head.

He tried to adjust it, but his bandaged hands were too clumsy. "It's not straight."

She pushed up, pulled down and twisted it back and forth. "Now is it straight?"

"I doubt it, but I reckon it will have to do." He couldn't accomplish the simplest task by himself. Depending on her was galling.

She led the way outside. A fresh breeze was blowing. He could smell the scent of newly cut corn and hear the sounds of the grain binder in the distance. His brothers must be working in the cornfield along the river. He should be there to oversee the work. Luke didn't care how things got done, and Noah spent as much time trying to get out of work as he did working. Timothy could do the job, but he was slow and methodical. "What's the forecast for the next three days?"

"The newspaper said sunny and warm today with a chance of rain in the late afternoon."

"How much of the field do they have cut already?"

"I can't be sure. It looks like about a quarter of it."

"They'd better step it up or they won't get finished before it rains."

"I'm sure they know that. Here is the buggy. Do you want to drive or shall I?"

Did she have to make a joke of everything? "Very funny. You're always laughing at me."

"*Nee*, Samuel. I'm simply trying to lighten your mood."

"There's nothing wrong with my mood."

"From where I'm standing, there is."

"Feel free to go home."

"That's a good idea. I'm sure your father won't mind if I borrow his buggy. Have a nice day, Samuel. The house is behind you. I'm sure you can find your way back."

"You won't leave me here alone without anyone to look after me." Sweat broke out on his brow at the thought.

"Wouldn't I? It wouldn't be any harder than pouring water on your sheets."

She was a heartless woman. "All right."

"All right, what?"

"I believe you. You're just nuts enough to do it. Lead me to the buggy."

"You should stop insulting me. I'm here to help. You should be thanking me for taking you to the doctor."

Samuel pressed his lips tightly together. When she didn't lead him forward, he knew what she was waiting for. He loosened his lips enough to mutter, "I'm grateful for your help, Rebecca."

"There, that wasn't so bad, was it?" Her chipper tone rubbed him the wrong way, but he refrained from commenting. At this rate, they would never reach the doctor's office.

And maybe that wasn't a bad thing. Would the doctor tell him today he would be permanently blind? If he didn't go, he could hold on to the slender hope that he might see again one day. If the doctor told him there was no hope, what would he do? Pray for a miracle? Accept his fate as God's will?

No matter what he was told, he knew the dressing changes would be unbearably painful. He had experienced them three times a day when he was in the hospital and each time was as painful as the last. Knowing he would only have to endure them twice a week was the best part of getting out of the hospital.

"The buggy is in front of you. Raise your foot and feel for the floorboard." Rebecca took his arm. In spite of the way she irritated him, there was something comforting in her touch. Her hands were small and soft. A tingle of awareness lingered on his skin where her fingers gripped him. He tried to ignore the sensation as he climbed in, being careful not to jar his hands. When he was settled, she produced a pillow for him to rest them on.

He felt the dip of the buggy as she climbed in. "Are you okay?"

"Peachy."

She clicked her tongue to get the horse moving. "If you start to feel ill, let me know and I will stop."

"I'll be fine. Just get me there."

The heavy odor of charred wood hung in the air, and he knew they passed the wood shop on their way to the end of the lane. The burned remains of his father's business were one thing he was glad he couldn't see.

If only he hadn't been in such a rush that day. If only he'd taken the time to let the machine cool down. If only he hadn't convinced his father to invest the last of the family's savings in the venture. They were on the brink of ruin and all because of him. When the harvest was done, his brothers would have to look for work elsewhere.

All Samuel had ever wanted in life was to keep the family together. Instead, he would be responsible for sending them away.

Rebecca turned out onto the highway and before long

he could tell they had entered the covered bridge over the river. The sounds of the horse's hooves echoed inside the massive timbered structure that had been built at the turn of the century. It was two lanes wide and spanned the river above the place where his ancestors had run a ferry service that had given the community the name of Bowmans Crossing. A covered pedestrian walkway had been added to the west side of the bridge when he was a child after a car struck and killed two of his classmates on their way to school. It was one of the few covered bridges with a walkway for those on foot, and his father had been instrumental in getting the community to add it.

Someone called a cheerful greeting, and Rebecca answered.

"Who was that?" he asked.

"The bishop's wife. How are you doing?"

"I said I'll be fine. Stop fussing."

"As you wish." Her smug tone made him determined to enjoy the trip.

Within ten minutes, he realized he wasn't going to be fine. The trip to the physician's office would take a little over an hour depending on which horse was in harness. If it was Noah's high-stepping Standardbred mare, they could make the trip in forty minutes. If it was his father's slow and steady horse, it could take well over an hour. To him, it seemed as if they were crawling along. Rebecca was good enough to warn him when the occasional car approached. The sound of them rushing past was less unnerving if he knew they were coming.

The carriage rocked and swayed as they traveled along the highway. Unable to see, he had nothing to distract him as a queasy sensation began to build in his midsection. He started taking deep breaths.

Rebecca pulled the buggy to a stop. "Would you like some of that tea now?"

He nodded. "I think I would."

She produced it in an amazingly short amount of time. He took a sip from the straw she held, and his stomach immediately felt better. He finished the drink. "I should have listened to you."

"Did I just hear you right?" The undercurrent of laughter in her voice drew a smile from him.

"When I'm wrong, I admit it."

"As we all should. I have a few gingersnap cookies if you would like them."

"I think I'll be fine, now. Save them for the trip home. How much longer?"

"A few more miles. Are you up to it? We can wait as long as you need."

"I'm ready.

He heard the slap of the reins against the horse's rump and the buggy jerked forward. He tried to concentrate on anything other than his stomach. "Which horse are you driving?"

"A brown fellow with a white star on his forehead. No one told me his name."

"Father's horse, Gunther. He's not very fast, but he's got stamina."

"Noah offered to let me use his horse, but she looked like a handful."

"She is. My little brother likes the flashy spirited ones."

"Most boys his age do. Is he courting someone?"

"I don't think so. Why?"

"I saw him talking to a young woman this morning out by the road."

"A redhead?"

"She had auburn hair."

"That's just Fannie Erb. She's the daughter of a neighbor. She and Noah have been friends for years. They're both nuts for horses. Her father raises them."

"Is that what Noah wants to do? Raise horses?"

Samuel's queasiness continued to subside. "He wants to drive fast horses and make a fool of himself."

"He strikes me as a serious young fellow."

"Noah? Serious? You've mistaken him for someone else."

"You, perhaps. You're the serious one among the boys."

Was she able to gauge that from her limited contact with him or had she been talking to someone else about him. "I'm the one who sees that things get done."

"There's nothing wrong with that."

"Too bad not everyone feels that way."

"Who feels differently?"

"Luke for one." Samuel normally didn't care to discuss his differences with his brothers, but talking to Rebecca was better than concentrating on his unsettled stomach.

"Luke respects you."

"You're confusing him with someone else now. Luke doesn't respect anyone."

"You're his big brother. He looks up to you. Before you say anything, I can assure you I've seen the way he longs for your approval."

"My approval? You're mistaken."

"I'm not. A word of praise from you would go a long way in helping Luke deal with his troubles. When a person doesn't feel appreciated or respected by the family, they can lose their sense of belonging and start looking for other ways to fill that void."

Was she right? Maybe he hadn't given Luke enough credit for the difficulties he had overcome.

"Oh, no."

The dismay in her voice caught him by surprise. "What's wrong?"

"Nothing." Her quick reply didn't ring true. Why was she upset? She slowed the buggy and stopped. He heard the sound of another buggy pull alongside.

Chapter Five

"*Guder mariye*, Rebecca."

Samuel tried to place the jovial man's voice. Who was he?

"Good morning, John." Rebecca's reply was anything but lighthearted. It was more like long-suffering, but at least Samuel realized who the other person was. It was John Miller, her late husband's brother.

"Good day, Samuel Bowman!" John shouted.

Why was he yelling? "*Guder mariye*, John."

"I was sorry to hear about your injury!"

"I'm blind, not deaf, John. I can hear you just fine."

"Oh. Right. How are you?" John's embarrassed tone said he got the point.

"Fine. And you?"

"As right as rain. I'm glad I ran into you, Rebecca. Your mother and I miss seeing you."

"Nonsense. I haven't been gone that long. You can hardly miss someone who has only been gone a day."

Something in Rebecca's voice surprised Samuel. He leaned back slightly. Was she flustered by this chance meeting with her brother-in-law? It sure sounded that way. What did that mean? Had there been bad blood between the brothers? Samuel didn't recall anyone mentioning it. John was a widower. Could it be that he was courting Rebecca? If that was the case, why was she so reluctant to return to her own home? Was it because she truly wanted to help Samuel and his family or was there another reason?

"I don't think there's a restriction on missing someone whose company you enjoy." John sounded disappointed with her response.

"I agree," Samuel added. "I have known my *mamm* to say she sometimes misses my *daed* the moment he walks out the door."

"Your parents have been married a long time," she said with an edge in her tone. She wasn't happy with his interference.

Good. Let her be the one to be annoyed for a change. "I don't think it has to do with time. I think it has to do with how much they enjoy each other's company."

"That's exactly what I was saying. I enjoy your company, Rebecca," John added happily.

"And I'm sure she enjoys your company, John. Don't you, Rebecca?" Samuel said.

"Of course I do. My husband's brother is always welcome in my home. However, I have a job to do, and that job is to get you to your doctor on time, Samuel. Please, excuse us, John. We need to get going."

"Surely a minute or two won't make a difference. Besides, I was to pass on a message from your mother if I saw you."

John was determined to spend a few more minutes in her company. Samuel caught the edge of desperation in his voice and wondered at it.

"And what is the message?" Rebecca asked with reluctance.

Samuel grew more amused by the minute. The woman who had an answer for everything seemed to be struggling today. There was something simmering beneath the surface between John and Rebecca, but he couldn't figure out what it was.

John said, "Your mother wants to know if you are coming home on Sunday. She thought we could all go to the preaching together."

"I can't," Rebecca said quickly.

Too quickly. Samuel smothered a smile. "You don't need to stay with me. I'm sure my family can look after me for one day. You should go home on Sundays."

"Your father and I didn't agree to that." Her terse tone told him to mind his own business, but this was too much fun.

"John, I can assure you that my father will give Rebecca the time off."

"*Goot!* It's settled. I will pick you and your mother up at seven Sunday morning. Good day to you, Samuel. I pray God heals you quickly."

Samuel heard the sound of John's buggy moving away. "Nice fellow."

"*Ja.*" She slapped the reins against the horse and the buggy jolted ahead.

Her clipped tone implied she was done with the subject, but he wasn't. He sensed that John was somehow a raw nerve for Rebecca. He wished he could see her face. Unable to resist needling her, he pressed ahead, "He's been a widower for a while now, hasn't he?"

"*Ja.*"

"A man can get lonely after a time. Maybe he's looking to marry again."

"You would have to ask him about that."

"He was recently chosen to be a minister in the church. He could be a deacon or even a bishop one day."

"I reckon that's true. If God wills it."

"He's a farrier. That's a *goot* job with a steady income. He could support a family easy enough."

"You sound like you've been talking to my mother."

So the subject had come up at home. Samuel chuckled. "It's hard to be on the receiving end, isn't it?"

"I don't know what you mean," she answered primly.

"*Ja*, you do. I'm going to take a stab in the dark here and say that your mother thinks John would make a good husband for you."

"Poke fun all you like. You won't get a rise out of me."

"I'm not looking to get a rise out of you, but meeting John has put me in mind of some work he can do for us. Be sure to tell him that on Sunday. He's welcome to come by any day he is free."

"You don't have work for him."

"But we do. Timothy was saying just the other day that the ponies need new shoes. Noah normally does the shoeing, but we could have John do it since my brothers are all busy. I'll let *Daed* know. *Mamm* might ask John to supper afterward."

"Don't invite him on my account."

"Why not? Do you have something against the man?"

She was silent for so long that Samuel thought he'd pushed his teasing too far. Then she said, "I don't have anything against John. He's a fine man. He was a great help to my husband and me when Walter was sick. John has helped when I needed repairs to the house, and he does little things for my mother. I'm grateful for his kindness."

"But what?" He sensed there was more to her meaning than she was saying.

"But nothing. He's a fine man. We are almost to town. I can't remember if the doctor's office is right or left at the traffic light."

"Left." Samuel decided to let her drop the subject of her brother-in-law, but that didn't keep him from wondering about the relationship between them. He wished he could see her face. He had always considered himself good at reading people. If a man's words were jovial but his smile wasn't reflected in his eyes, Samuel knew the fellow was putting on a front.

He was handicapped in more ways than one when it came to understanding Rebecca. Was it shyness that caused the tension in her voice when she spoke to John? Did she dislike the man for some reason? Or was she playing it cool, hoping her feigned disinterest would capture John's attention?

Samuel had a hard time believing Rebecca could be coy, but no man understood the workings of a woman's mind. Besides, when the heart ruled, good sense often went out the window. He'd seen that often enough with his friends. He intended to avoid the pitfalls of romance himself. The family needed him to manage the woodworking business and expand it. He couldn't be distracted by marriage and a family. Not now. Not until he had the family business up and running again. If he couldn't see or if his hands didn't heal properly, that would never happen. He would become a burden on his family and that was the last thing he wanted.

He had to get better. He would promise God anything if only the Lord would heal him. Imagining a lifetime of darkness sent chills down his spine. He couldn't live that way.

"We're here."

He had been so engrossed in his fear that he hadn't realized the buggy had stopped. Now he was about to face that fear head-on. He dreaded hearing the doctor's words. He dreaded the pain. "Why don't you take me home, instead?"

Rebecca laid her hand on his forearm. "It's going to be okay, Samuel. No matter what troubles come into our lives, our Lord is always with us. With His love in our hearts we can bear all things."

Her gentle touch brought him a sense of comfort and something more. Her voice was soothing and yet stirring. Her palm lay warm against his skin. The scent of lavender enveloped him now that the buggy wasn't moving. A flush of heat traveled up his arms and pooled in his chest, making his heart beat faster.

"You smell nice."

He heard her quick indrawn breath. She pulled her hand away. "I was cutting up sprigs of lavender last evening to make another sachet. Some of them fell into the pocket of my apron. I meant to shake them out and I forgot."

She sounded flustered and a little breathless. The sensation of warmth faded from where she had touched him. He missed it and wanted the comfort of her touch again. He wished he knew what she was thinking.

"We should go in." She got out, and the breeze dispelled the faint fragrance along with the odd fog in his brain.

It wasn't possible that he was attracted to her, was it? *Nee.* Surely not. She was stubborn, willful and brash. She could be kind, but more often than not, she was poking fun at him. He wouldn't be attracted to her. He wasn't.

Besides, he had far more important things to consider.

Rebecca was thankful there wasn't anyone close enough to see her face. She knew by the heat in her cheeks that she was blushing. *You smell nice.* Three simple words were all it took to send her pulse skittering wildly.

Three simple words in his gravelly voice underlined by faint wonder. She shivered again just thinking of it. She would remember to shake out her pockets from now on. She had touched him to offer comfort. Instead, the feeling of his strong muscles and the sight of her pale hand against his dark tanned skin unleashed a surge of emotion she wasn't ready to face.

Samuel required her help. He required her compassionate care. To consider there was anything else between them was unacceptable.

She came around to his side of the buggy. He stepped down without her assistance before she reached him. She took his arm above his elbow making sure she touched only his sleeve and gently guided him into the doctor's office.

After checking Samuel in, Rebecca led him to one of the blue upholstered waiting room chairs that lined the walls. A television was playing in the corner of the room. Three *Englischers* were watching a news channel. Rebecca ignored the distraction and focused on

Samuel. Leaning closer, she spoke softly in Pennsylvania Dutch. "How is your stomach?"

"Better now that I'm not moving. I wish they would get this over with."

"Do you think your father should expand the gift shop to include hardware items?"

"Are you talking about Luke's harebrained scheme?"

"What is harebrained about it?"

"Tourists don't want to see nuts and bolts. They want to see Amish-made jams and jellies, Amish-made cookies and cakes. They want to buy Amish-made furniture and hand-stitched quilts."

"That is true, but having a handy place to buy essentials locally could bring in a fair amount of business. I know John has complained that he has to travel all the way to Berlin when he needs new hoof picks or rasps. A lot of farmers take care of their own horses. You said yourself that Noah normally shoes yours. Where does he get his tools when he needs new ones?"

"The hardware store in Berlin."

"It is something to think about. Luke makes very pretty birdhouses. Did you know that?"

"I knew he carved holes in a few dried gourds."

"Oh, it's much more than that. He has a talent for decorating them. I purchased two. I know several of my *Englisch* friends who would love to have them hanging in their yards and even give them as gifts. I see no reason why Luke couldn't sell dozens of them."

"You think so?"

"I do. It's a shame he doesn't have a way to advertise them."

The nurse came to the waiting room door and called

Samuel's name. Rebecca's heart went out to him when she saw how he tensed. He knew it was going to be painful.

Samuel allowed the nurse to lead him into the exam room. When he was settled on the padded table, she left the room. He braced himself for the coming torment. The last dressing change had been less painful than the ones he endured in the hospital, but it was still excruciating. The minutes ticked by as he sat by himself. Where was everyone? He hated being left alone.

He heard the door open. "How are you doing, Samuel?" Dr. Marksman asked.

"I've been better."

The young doctor had only recently opened a practice in their rural community. Samuel had never been to a doctor until his accident.

"I'm sure you have been better. How is the pain? Are you getting any sleep?"

"The pain is less, but I don't sleep much."

"All right, let's take a look." He felt the doctor begin to unwrap the bandages over his eyes. He had been told not to expect too much, but he prayed he would see a glimmer of light, if nothing else.

When the last wrap fell away, the doctor removed the pads covering Samuel's eyes. "Open your eyes slowly. I'll dim the lights if it is too bright in here for you."

Samuel let his lids flutter briefly, then opened his eyes fully. The room was pitch-dark. "I can't see anything. Turn up the lights."

He felt the doctor's fingers under his chin. He turned Samuel's face in one direction and back again. "The inflammation I first observed is better. The lights are on, Samuel."

"Then why can't I see?" Samuel's heart began hammering in his chest. His palms grew sweaty.

"Let me try something." The doctor stepped away and came back a few seconds later. "What about now?"

"Nothing. I'm still blind. Why can't I see?"

Still blind.

Blind for life. Forever.

The words tumbled over and over in Samuel's mind. He had trouble listening to the doctor. Dizziness made his head swim. He couldn't catch his breath.

Dr. Marksman laid a soothing hand on Samuel's shoulder. "It's going to take a little more time, that's all. I would still like you to see a specialist."

Samuel forced himself to slow his breathing. He shoved the fear to the back of his mind. This was what God had planned for him. He would accept it. "We can't afford to see a specialist. What would he do for me that you aren't doing?"

"That's a valid question. I'm treating your burns and letting your eyes rest and recover on their own, but I'm not familiar with this type of eye injury. A specialist might have other ideas about treatment. At least let me consult with one."

"There is no harm in that if it doesn't cost me anything."

The doctor applied ointment to Samuel's eyes and covered his face with new bandages. "Are your parents with you today?"

"*Nee*, my father is harvesting corn. Rebecca Miller brought me."

"Ah, I know Rebecca. She would have made an excellent nurse if she hadn't chosen the Amish way of life. She knows how to follow instructions and what to look for."

Samuel heard the door open. The doctor spoke to someone in the hallway outside. "Nurse, will you have Rebecca Miller step in, please."

Great. "Does she have to be in here?"

"No, but I definitely need to know someone understands how to take care of you. You aren't in a position to see what's going on. Will you allow me to discuss your condition with her present?"

"I reckon."

"Nurse, bring an information consent form, too. You and I will have to sign it as verbal witnesses to Mr. Bowman's wishes."

"Yes, Doctor."

A few minutes later, the door opened. Samuel caught a whiff of lavender and knew Rebecca had come in.

"Hello, Dr. Marksman. It's good to see you again."

"You, too, Rebecca. Mrs. Stulzman and her new baby are getting along fine. I thought you'd want to know."

"How nice."

"Samuel, you are blessed to have this woman looking after you."

He pressed his lips closed. Rebecca laughed softly. "I'm afraid Samuel doesn't see me as a blessing."

"Well, he should. I want you to take a close look at his injuries. You should put on a pair of gloves when changing his bandages just to keep things clean." The doctor began unwrapping Samuel's left hand.

When the air hit his tender skin, Samuel sucked in

a sharp breath. Rebecca did the same. "That looks so painful."

"It is," Samuel said through gritted teeth.

The doctor removed the last of the dressings. "Samuel had mostly second-degree burns, but some of them are very deep and may be third-degree. The blisters that are broken are second-degree burns for sure. Those that continue to fill and ooze are most likely third-degree. They will produce some scarring. The burn can go one of two ways. The blisters will dry up or break, then the outer layer of damaged skin will also dry and peel off. At this stage, a new outer layer of skin develops. Peeling usually starts several days after the blisters pop. Normally, it takes three to five days for the peeling to run its course. The sensation should shift from pain to itching within a few days after the blisters break, but it can take longer."

That was good news. Samuel was ready for something other than pain.

"The new skin will be very sensitive so even a mild bump will still cause discomfort."

"What are the signs of infection?" she asked.

"If the burn gets infected, the blisters won't dry up. Instead, they'll develop crusty, yellowish scabs that continue to cause pain. If that happens, the crust needs to be softened and removed by applying a washcloth soaked in warm soapy water. Just let it rest on the site until the stuff is soft enough to come away easily. Don't scrub. After the extremity dries, apply an antibiotic cream and cover with a nonstick gauze. If an infection is present and doesn't show signs of improvement within two or three days of using an antibiotic cream, get back here. I'll have to put him on a stronger oral antibiotic."

"I understand."

"I'll show you how to redress these. Make sure his fingers are well separated. We don't want them sticking together."

When they finished both hands twenty minutes later, Rebecca could see the ordeal had taken its toll on Samuel. His lips were pressed into a thin line with a pale ring around them. She took his arm as he stood and noticed he swayed slightly on his feet.

The young doctor handed Rebecca a slip of paper. "I want to see him again in a week. This is a prescription for more pain medication. Make sure he takes it before he comes in next time."

Rebecca frowned at Samuel. "Was he supposed to take some today?"

"Yes. The dressing changes can be very painful. You are doing well, Mr. Bowman. Make sure you drink plenty of liquids and get plenty of rest. Come in sooner if you experience a fever or signs of infection."

"What about his vision?" Rebecca asked.

"It's too soon to tell," Samuel muttered.

The doctor sighed. "I still feel that Mr. Bowman should see an eye specialist."

Samuel shook his head. "It's too far to travel, and it's too expensive. If God wishes my sight restored, it will be so."

"I respect your beliefs, Mr. Bowman, and I pray for your healing." Dr. Marksman smiled sadly at Rebecca and left the room.

"Get me home," Samuel said through gritted teeth.

Rebecca led him out to the buggy and got him settled. "You rest here. I'm going to have this prescription filled. It should only take a few minutes. The pharmacy is right next door."

"Rebecca, I don't need pain pills," he snapped.

"I may need them if you're going to bite my head off all the way home."

"Suit yourself. You always do what you want, anyway. You have no *demut*."

"You're right." It was useless to point out that he was lacking in humility, as well. He was clearly in pain and determined to endure it. Without another word, she walked away and left him to stew while she had his prescription filled. For the next ten minutes, she kept an eye on him through the drugstore window. When she had his medication in hand, she returned to the buggy.

Sitting on the seat beside him, she withdrew a jar of ginger tea from her bag. "I can't bear to see you in such misery, Samuel. Please take one of your pills and some tea. It will help. You do yourself no favor by suffering needlessly."

"All right. Anything. Just take me home."

Relief let her draw a deep breath. *"Danki."*

She gave him the medicine and when he was ready, she backed away from the hitching rail and headed the horse toward Bowmans Crossing.

Samuel was resting in bed when Luke came in with his supper later that evening. "Would you like something to eat?"

"I am a little hungry." Samuel sat up on the edge of the bed.

Luke pulled a small table over and sat in the chair beside him. "Are you in a lot of pain?"

"Some. It's better than it was earlier today. As much

as I dislike Rebecca bossing me around, she was right about the pain medicine. She's not in here, is she?"

"It's just you and me."

"*Goot*. She has a way of sneaking in that's unnerving." And yet he missed her when she wasn't around. She had avoided him all afternoon, leaving his mother to sit with him after they returned. He could hardly blame her. He hadn't been good company. At least the pain meds allowed him to nap briefly. He would have a hard time sleeping later.

"I like her." Luke fed him a bite of mashed potatoes and meat loaf.

Samuel swallowed his mouthful. "You would. She's not a normal Amish woman."

Luke chuckled. "That's for sure. She speaks her mind."

"It's strange, but I can't recall exactly what she looks like. I guess I never paid much attention to her before."

"No reason why you should. She was another man's wife. Our families weren't close. She and her husband lived almost ten miles from here. I don't know about you, but I'm always checking out the single girls, not the married ones."

Samuel ate in silence for the rest of the meal. When he was finished, Luke asked, "Would you like some coffee? I have some right here."

"Maybe half a cup. Is she pretty?"

Luke held the mug to Samuel's lips. "Is who pretty?"

"Rebecca. Who else have we been talking about?"

"Pretty enough, I guess. She has a trim figure, good teeth—she seems strong enough."

"You sound like you are describing a horse."

"Okay, her eyes are a deep violet-blue. Very pretty.

She has a direct stare that proves she is listening to you. Her hair is blond. She's very fair skinned. Her eyes sparkle when she smiles, and she smiles a lot."

"Even when she is browbeating me?"

Luke chuckled. "I think you can take it."

Samuel frowned. It almost sounded as if Luke was becoming infatuated with Rebecca. Was he?

Chapter Six

The idea that his brother might be falling for Rebecca didn't sit well with Samuel, but he wasn't sure why. "She tells me you have made some birdhouses out of the gourds from *Mamm's* garden."

"I've made a few. Rebecca liked them." Luke's tone turned cool.

"She thinks they'll sell well if we can find a way to advertise them. Any ideas?" Was he really going to give credence to her notion?

Even when she wasn't in the room, Rebecca was a hard woman to ignore. The things she said stuck in Samuel's mind as if she had nailed them there. For the past hour, he had been thinking about the sound of her voice and mulling over her praise of Luke's work. Was there something between the two of them? He shifted uncomfortably on the bed.

Samuel heard Luke walk away from the bed. "I haven't thought about ways to advertise. I guess I just hoped someone who stopped in for something else would buy one of my gourds."

"I've been doing some thinking. There's not much

else to do up here. You know that big tree on the north side of the road at the stop sign."

"Sure."

"If you were to hang a few of your birdhouses on that tree within easy reach for folks, you could bolt an honor payment box to the tree and sell them that way."

"That's not a bad idea, Samuel. I could even put out unpainted gourds for folks who would like to decorate their own."

"You could."

"We could add an arrow that points the way to our store in case folks wanted more Amish crafts."

Samuel listened in amazement to Luke's growing eagerness. "What do you think a fair price would be?"

The two men discussed costs and settled on a figure for painted and plain gourds. Samuel remembered Rebecca's comments that Luke needed and wanted his approval. He wasn't used to praising his brothers. It felt odd, but maybe she was right.

"Luke, I appreciate how much you have stepped up to help the family. I know you, Timothy and Noah are shouldering my share of the work along with your own."

"You would do the same. I don't know why you're surprised that I would," Luke said with a hint of resentment.

So much for Rebecca's idea. Even when Samuel tried to be nice, Luke's bad attitude reared its head.

Swallowing his resentment, Samuel tried again. "I'm not surprised that you stepped up. I just wanted to say I appreciate it and I know the rest of the family does, too. The birdhouses are a good idea. Rebecca seems to think they'll make money for us. We're going to need more ideas like it if I—if I can't carve again."

"You will."

"With hands that don't work and eyes that can't see. I'm more likely to become a burden on this family." The anger and sadness in his heart pulled him toward a dark place.

Luke was silent for so long that Samuel wondered if he had left the room. He leveraged himself back into bed. He just wanted to sleep. To forget everything that had happened.

Luke cleared his throat, proving he was still beside the bed. "I never did tell you how sorry I was that I didn't take care of the generator that morning. I should have put gas in it when you told me and not handed the chore off to Noah. I'm so, so sorry." The pain and sorrow in his voice were unmistakable.

Samuel's throat constricted as tears burned behind his bandages. "I don't blame you, Luke. We've disagreed on a number of things over the years, but I never once thought you wanted to hurt me. God chose this path for my feet to walk."

"I wish it had been me." He barely whispered the words as Samuel felt the weight of Luke's hand on his shoulder.

"I don't, *brudder*. Not even for a minute."

Rebecca was seated at the table when Luke came downstairs. She caught a glimpse of him wiping his eyes before he came into the room. She rose to take the tray and dishes from him. "How is Samuel feeling?"

"He's still in pain."

All the dishes on the tray were empty. "At least his appetite is improving."

Luke followed her as she carried the dishes to the sink. "I want to thank you."

She glanced at him over her shoulder. "For what?"

"For telling him about my birdhouses. We've come up with a way to advertise and sell them along the highway."

She smiled at him. "I'm glad."

"He doesn't blame me. I thought he did. I thought he believed it was my fault."

She turned around. "Why would you think that?"

"Because it *was* my fault. I was the one who didn't fill the gas tank that morning. I told Noah to do it, but he was walking away from me and never even heard me. I should have made sure that he was listening. No, I should have done it myself."

"We can't change one minute of the past, Luke. Regrets are useless. We can only change how we move forward."

"I guess you're right. That might take a little practice on my part."

"I have news for you. It isn't easy for anyone."

"What isn't easy?" Noah came in from the living room. He pulled open the refrigerator door and studied the contents.

Luke ruffled his younger brother's hair. "It's not easy keeping you fed."

Noah swatted his hand away and made a muscle with his arm. "I have to keep up my strength. We have more corn to stack tomorrow."

Rebecca dried her hands, opened the cupboard and pulled out a chocolate bundt cake. "I made this earlier."

"Perfect." Noah took the plate from her hands.

Luke snatched it away from him and held it behind

his back. "You can have a piece, but you have to take one up to Samuel. You know how much he likes chocolate cake."

"Did I hear chocolate cake?" Timothy strolled in with a book in his hand.

Rebecca took the plate away from Luke. "Before the three of you inhale it, you should see if your parents want some."

Timothy opened a drawer, pulled out some forks and handed them around. "*Mamm* and *Daed* have gone to bed."

"All the more for us." Noah grabbed a plate drying in the rack on the counter. Luke and Timothy did the same.

"All right." She cut the cake into generous slices and filled each plate the men pressed at her. When Luke held out a second plate, she smiled to herself. "Do I have to supervise or will you actually take it up to Samuel?"

Luke flushed. "We'll all take it up."

"That's a fine idea," Noah declared.

The men trooped up the stairs together. After a few minutes, the sound of quiet laughter drifted down. Smiling, she turned around to see Anna glaring at her.

Rebecca pasted a smile on her face. "Good evening, Anna. I'm sorry if we woke you. The boys wanted some cake."

"You have made yourself right at home with my family."

Rebecca couldn't tell if Anna was upset or not. "Your family has made it easy to feel welcome. You have been blessed in your children. Would you like a piece of cake?"

"I think I would." Anna went to the cupboard and

got her own plate down. She held it out as Rebecca placed a slice on it.

Anna carried her plate to the table and sat down. "Won't you join me?"

Was this an olive branch? "I was about to make some chamomile tea. Would you like some, too?"

"That sounds nice."

Rebecca fixed two cups of tea, cut a small piece of cake for herself and carried it all to the table. She sat down across from Anna and decided to let the older woman lead the conversation. They ate in silence for a few minutes.

"Tomorrow I must go and help my sister-in-law get ready for church services at her home. Edna always waits until the last minute to clean."

"What can I do to help?"

"If you could make the men a light lunch and take it out to the fields tomorrow that would be a blessing."

"Consider it done."

"My husband was right," Anna said without looking up from her plate.

"About what?" Rebecca didn't want to assume anything.

Anna glanced up. "He was right that I needed an extra pair of hands to help with Samuel."

"If I have lightened your burden in any way, then I'm happy I came."

"Samuel spoke about you a lot this afternoon."

"Did he? It wasn't all good, I'm sure."

"He said he noticed John Miller seems quite taken with you."

Rebecca's cheeks flamed red. How did she explain?

"My brother-in-law has been very kind to me since Walter died."

"You don't think it's more than that?"

"Perhaps it is. Our families have been pushing for a match between us."

"It's understandable. John is a widower. There are far more bachelors in Bowmans Crossing than there are single women. You inherited your husband's lands. I'm sure his parents would like to see that land come back to the family."

"I have heard all the arguments about why it would be a beneficial match."

"But?"

"I'm not in love with John. I'm not sure I will ever love anyone the way I loved Walter."

"A good marriage is not always about wide-eyed, heart-thumping love. It should be about respect and common goals. It should be about raising children and teaching them to fear the Lord. Isaac is my second husband. Did you know that?"

Rebecca looked at Anna in surprise "I didn't."

"I came from a small town in Pennsylvania. I had married my childhood sweetheart but he died in a hunting accident a few months later. I didn't believe I could ever love again."

Rebecca understood that sorrow. "I'm sorry for your loss."

"*Danki.* I met Isaac at my cousin's wedding. We courted briefly. When he asked me to marry him, I wasn't in love with him the way I had loved my husband, but I wanted a family and a home of my own, so I said yes."

Rebecca crossed her arms on the table and leaned

toward Anna. "Was it the right decision? Would you do it again?"

Anna stirred her tea slowly. "It was the right decision for me. Over the years, I have come to care deeply for Isaac. He has given me five strong sons and provided for us all. I could not ask for more."

"But, do you love him?"

Anna smiled softly. "There are all kinds of love, child. The love a mother has for her children. The love a man has for his wife. The love God has for all of us. All different, but all love nonetheless. *Ja*, I love him."

Leaning back, Rebecca pushed the last bite of cake around on her plate. Maybe she was wrong to reject John's advances. Maybe mutual respect and common goals would be enough. Maybe.

"Samuel, what are you doing?"

He stopped pacing at the sound of Rebecca's tired, irritated voice. "I'm sorry if I woke you."

"What's wrong?"

Having her near lessened his pain. "Nothing. Go back to bed."

"Something is wrong. Let me help."

Too tired to fight alone, he sighed. "I can't sleep. My hands hurt. My face hurts. The dressing changes always do this."

"I'll get you a pain pill."

"*Nee*. They make me so groggy." He turned and took the five steps he knew would bring him to the open window. The breeze was slight, but it carried a hint of coolness and the smell of the river. He braced his fore-arms on the window jamb and leaned forward until his forehead rested on the cool glass.

"It's two-thirty in the morning, Samuel. Groggy would not be a bad thing about now." The hint of humor in her voice made him smile.

"They make me hot, and it's already too warm to sleep. I just need to take my mind off of it. I wish I could go outside where it's cool."

"I agree that it's a warm night."

"Really, I'm fine. Go back to bed. I'll stop pacing."

"I'm not sure I can get back to sleep. I'll take you out on the porch for a while."

"I'd rather go down to the river."

"In the dark?" Her voice rose in surprise.

"It's always dark for me. Go back to bed." He tried to keep the bitterness out of his tone and failed.

He heard her bare feet padding across the wooden floor. He wasn't surprised when she laid a hand on his arm. "I'm sorry."

"Don't be. I'll have to get used to comments like that."

"You don't know what God has planned for you. I will take you outside if that is what you want."

"It is. *Danki.*"

She had a long robe on over her nightgown, but she should have put on her shoes.

The grass was cool and damp, but Rebecca discovered a number of small stones with her bare feet as she led Samuel out the back door and toward the water. She used a small flashlight to help her pick a path. The farmhouse was situated on a small knoll that overlooked the river below. The lawn had a gentle slope to it. She was happy to see Samuel had no trouble keeping his balance as they walked slowly along.

"What are the stars like tonight?"

She paused and looked up. "They are hidden behind the clouds. I see only a few peeking through."

"Is the moon up? It should be full tonight."

She studied the heavens and detected a spot of unusual brightness behind the layer of clouds to the east. "It is, but it's behind the clouds. Did you have someplace in mind to go?"

"There is a low stone wall below the bridge. I like to sit there."

She swung her light in that direction. "I see it."

Keeping a firm grip on his elbow, she led him forward until they reached the wall. He sat down with a contented sigh. A fresh breezed rustled the leaves of the trees and shrubs along the bank. The water made faint gurgling sounds as it flowed around the bridge piling. A bullfrog croaked nearby. She turned the light in that direction. She didn't see him, but a loud splash proved he had been hiding in the reeds.

"I love to sit and listen to the river at night."

"Do you?" She swung the flashlight in a wide arc when a rustling in the nearby bushes startled her. A pair of eyes blinked once and vanished. She had no idea who or what they belonged to. Slipping closer to Samuel, she kept her light trained on the shrubbery, but nothing else appeared.

"Being blind isn't so bad at night. I can smell the scent of mud and decay. I can hear the water tug at the branches of the plants lining the edge of the waterway. I know exactly how the river looks when the moon rises and casts its sparkling light on the ripples. It's peaceful, don't you think?"

She jerked the light toward the bridge when she heard the sudden flap of wings. "What's that?"

"An owl who lives in the rafters of the covered bridge. He's going out to hunt. It's so much better out here than being cooped up inside. Don't you agree?"

"It's nice." As long as the eyes didn't show up again and the owl didn't swoop in her direction. It wasn't long before the bugs found her light and began to flutter in front of her. She batted them away and finally snapped it off.

"Close your eyes."

"They are closed." She blinked then checked the bushes again. Nothing showed itself. She didn't like the dark.

"Tell me what you hear?"

"Insects and frogs."

He raised his face to the sky. "I hear the earth slumbering."

Samuel had a fanciful side? She never would have guessed that. "What a beautiful thing to say."

He lowered his face. "It's silly, I know."

"I don't think it's silly at all. God created many wonders. Some we see in the light of day, some are only revealed at night. Have you always liked the night, or is this because of your injury?"

"I've always loved to sit out here after the household is asleep. I like the night sounds. The wind is softer. The air is cooler. The trees sway and dip. Small animals rustle through the leaves and underbrush. Bats and owls glide by with barely a sound."

"Bats?" Something buzzed by her ear, and she swatted at it. What other sort of creepy-crawlies were out here? She scooted a hair closer to Samuel.

"Are you afraid of bats?"

She heard another sound and switched on the light again. "Of course not. What kinds of animals crawl through the leaves?"

"Rebecca Miller, are you afraid of the dark?"

The humor in his tone made her spine stiffen. "Why would you think that?"

"I keep hearing the flashlight click on and off."

"So?" She shut it off and put it in the pocket of her robe.

"We aren't walking. You don't need to see your way, so why are you swinging it around unless it is to make sure something isn't sneaking up on us. Leave the light off, and your eyes will adjust to the darkness."

"It's off, okay?" She slipped another inch closer to him. Without the light, she heard even more sounds.

He chuckled.

"What's so funny, Samuel?"

"If you move any closer, you'll be sitting in my lap. Do you really think a blind man could protect you?"

She wiggled a few inches away. "Maybe. Maybe not. But I could push you down and let the bear eat you while I run away."

"There are no bears around here."

"There are wild dogs. Coyotes. Other things."

"What other things?" She could tell he was struggling to contain his mirth, but she didn't care if he did think it was funny.

"When I was little, my brothers used to tell me that the coyotes and foxes would eat me if I went out of the house at night."

"And you believed them?"

"Maybe." She'd never heard of anyone being attacked, so she was pretty sure they had only said it to frighten her. It worked.

"A coyote is much more afraid of you than you are of him."

"Don't be too sure about that." She closed her hand over the solid cylinder of the flashlight in her pocket. It would make a decent club if need be.

A loud splash made her jump back into Samuel. His arms went around her. She struggled to pull the light out, but Samuel blocked her arm with his elbow. "Wait. You'll see what it is in a minute," he whispered in her ear. His breath sent a shiver across her skin. She was pressed against the length of him. His chest rose and fell with each breath. Her fear of the night faded rapidly.

"That was something big jumping in the water." She used the same low whisper although she wasn't sure why.

"I know."

She strained her eyes, staring at the inky blackness below the bridge. Finally, she made out a shape crossing the river. The clouds broke apart, and the light of the moon silhouetted a huge buck swimming across the river. The moonlight sparkled like diamonds on the V-shaped ripples behind him and the droplets of water on his antlers.

"It's a deer," she whispered, awestruck by the beauty of the scene.

"I thought so. They often cross near here."

"Why don't they use the bridge?"

He laughed. The buck changed course and began swimming downstream until it was out of sight behind some bushes. "They don't use the bridge because they are wild things. To them, it must look safer to swim the river rather than chance entering a man-made cave if they think about it at all."

"I suppose." She stepped away from him and missed the warmth of his contact.

"Are you ready to go?" he asked softly.

Rebecca glanced at the man beside her. He wasn't the invalid she had first come to know. There was much more to Samuel Bowman than met the eye, and she liked what she was learning about him. "Not yet. Are you?"

"*Nee.* I could sit out here for hours. Maybe that's why God took my sight, because I have always liked the night."

"His ways are hard to comprehend."

"I never wanted anything except to take care of this family. Instead, I've become a burden to them. I have lost my father's entire savings along with his business."

"The building can be replaced. Our church will help."

"With the building, but what about the machinery? It will take years of scrimping for my family to replace it. My brothers will have to move away to get jobs when the harvest is over instead of working here. My mother will be heartbroken to lose them. I dread to think how she will feel if Joshua and his new wife can't settle here and raise their children within her sight."

"No one sees you as a burden, Samuel. Your family loves you."

"I don't doubt that now, but what about in the future? What about when they see all that my foolishness has taken away. My save-the-family scheme was a failure. I dread the reproach in their eyes more than I dread the pity I know they have for me now."

She laid a hand on his shoulder. "It will all turn out as He wills. God takes care of our future. We must live for today and leave the rest up to Him."

The simple feel of her hand and her softly spoken words gave him more hope than he'd found in days. What she said was true, but he knew he had to do more. "A man must trust God to give him a good harvest, but he still has to hoe the weeds from the garden."

"Is that what you did out here at night before the accident, hoe weeds?" She pulled her hand away and he missed the comfort of her touch.

"Mostly, I gave thanks out here. It's a fitting place to seek the Lord's guidance and listen to His wisdom."

"You surprise me, Samuel Bowman."

"Why? You don't think of me as a spiritual man?"

"It isn't that. I guess I thought you were the kind of man who gives the Lord thanks at the table and at church services and then doesn't think about Him the rest of the time."

"I reckon I deserve that opinion. I haven't been the best patient."

"You have been stubborn and bullheaded, but you haven't been a bad patient. I once took care of an elderly woman who spit at me every chance she got. I became very quick on my feet."

"I must say you have surprised me, too."

"Because you found out I'm scared of the dark? It is creepy out here, but at least the moon is out now and I can see my hand in front of my face. But who knows what is watching us from the shadows."

"It's surprising that you are afraid of anything. You seem so sure of yourself."

"I have a reason for my discomfort in the dark. Some people thought it was funny to frighten me."

"Your brothers?"

"They started it, but it was my husband who took it up a notch. He would hide and then jump out and scare me when I least expected it. I used to get so mad at him for that."

Her voice, tinged with sad yearning, made Samuel long to comfort her. "You miss him, don't you?"

"Of course I do. It's only natural. But I know he is with God in Heaven."

"What do you miss about him the most?"

"The most? So many things. I think I miss the sound of his voice the most. We would lie awake until all hours of the night just talking about our dreams and our plans. About what went right that day and about what was wrong. I miss him scolding me and telling me to hurry or we would be late to church. We never were. After every meal I made he'd pat his stomach and tell me it was real fine cooking. And jokes! That man was forever telling me jokes. Silly ones, knee-slappers. He loved a good joke."

"Will you marry again?"

She was silent a long time. Had he gone too far? Her personal life was a private matter. He had no business prying into it.

Chapter Seven

Rebecca wasn't sure how to answer Samuel's question. Would she marry again? It seemed that everyone had an opinion about whether she should or not, but how did she truly feel about it?

He waited patiently for her answer. Somehow, it was easier to express her feelings under the cover of darkness. She didn't have to school her features into blankness and pretend that she was content with the way life was. It was easy to confide in Samuel. Maybe it was because he couldn't see her face.

"I don't believe I will marry. I find great satisfaction caring for the sick among us. I can be useful, and I like that."

"A wife and mother does the same. There are many good men in our community."

"I find it hard to imagine someone who could make me laugh the way Walter did. It's harder still to imagine going through life with someone who doesn't make me laugh. I don't think I could abide that."

"That's understandable."

"Is it?"

"You've played some good pranks yourself."

She giggled. "I'm a bully. Say it like it is."

"Okay, I agree with that. Anyone who would pour a glass of water on a blind man."

"Sprinkled, not poured. I sprinkled water on your feet. Give me any more grief about it, and I'll leave you alone out here."

"If I had one good hand I'd take your flashlight away and leave *you* alone out here. I think it would bother you more than it would me. Don't forget, these bandages will come off one day. I may yet have my revenge for that *sprinkle*."

She enjoyed his teasing. Maybe too much. This Samuel was easy to like. "I've been warned. Are you ready to go back to the house?"

"I think so." He stood. "Wait! Do you hear that?"

"You can't trick me so easily."

"Something is coming this way."

Laughing, she jumped to her feet. "I have been assured there are no bears around here, so you can't frighten me."

He held up one hand and tipped his head to the side. "Hush a minute."

He sounded so serious. She bit her lip as she glanced at the bushes nearby. Was it the wind making them move or something else? "Do you really hear something?"

"I do." He turned his head slightly as if trying to locate the sound.

"What is it?" She fumbled for her light and snapped it on as she took a step closer to him.

"I hear… Rebecca Miller quaking in her boots." He sat down and started laughing.

"That is just mean." She punched his shoulder.

"Ouch. I'm an injured man. You can't hit me."

"You should be thankful I don't have a glass of water handy."

Chuckling, he rose to his feet. "I think I can sleep now."

Rebecca's smile faded as she took his arm and led him toward the house. He was doing better, growing more confident, and she was glad. Soon, he wouldn't need her anymore.

With sudden clarity, she realized that she needed to be needed. Without someone to care for, she had been little more than an empty shell waiting for life to be over. She didn't want to go back to that. She wanted to love life again.

Timothy drove her home Saturday evening, and on Sunday morning, as promised, John arrived in his buggy to take her and her mother to church. Rebecca wore her best dark maroon dress with its matching cape and apron. She tied her black traveling bonnet over her *kapp* and pulled on a cloak. Picking up a basket filled with food for the noon meal, she mentally braced herself before joining John and her mother in the buggy.

"Guder mariye," John called out.

"Good morning, John. Good morning, *Mamm.*" Rebecca opened the door to the backseat and deposited her basket on the floor beside her mother's identical one.

John smiled at her as he got down. She had no choice but to climb in beside her mother. John got back in. It was a tight squeeze with all three of them in the front. She was pressed shoulder to hip against him. "It's a fine morning for a buggy ride," he said.

His voice sounded strained although his smile was bright. Too bright. As if he were forcing it.

"Any day we gather to praise God is a fine day," her mother added cheerfully when Rebecca didn't respond.

She didn't doubt they had been talking about her on the way over. Although it wasn't a comfortable trip for Rebecca, it was a pretty one. The hillsides and fields had exploded with fall colors in the past week. The air was crisp but not cold. Her mother kept up a steady flow of chatter that only required an occasional comment. John remained silent as his horse trotted along at a steady pace, and they soon reached the covered bridge over the river.

The weathered red wooden structure blended into the red-and-gold autumn leaves on the trees that grew along the roadway. Wide enough for two lanes of traffic, the opening loomed like a cave. As the horse entered the dark interior, Rebecca stared through the slatted sides at the Bowman house on the hillside across the river. She could see all of them standing in the front yard. It was easy to pick Samuel out among the men wearing identical dark suits and black felt hats. His white bandages stood out in stark contrast to the somber colors.

She lost sight of the family when John's buggy came out the other side of the bridge. A quarter mile farther along, they reached the stop sign on the main road between Berlin and Winesburg.

Rebecca's mother leaned to see around her. "Look at all the birdhouse gourds. Aren't they pretty."

Smiling, Rebecca murmured her agreement. "Very pretty."

A car had pulled off the road and was stopped beneath the spreading branches of the old oak tree. An

Englisch family was looking at the gourds. As John sent his horse across the highway, Rebecca saw the woman select two yellow ones while the man with her placed money in the box Luke had nailed to the tree.

John noticed her looking back. "I wonder who is selling them?"

"Luke Bowman makes them." Rebecca faced forward again.

"You know I did notice a few of them in Anna's shop. It's a very clever idea to display them that way," her mother said.

"Samuel thought of it."

John glanced at her. "I haven't asked. How is the poor man doing?"

"He's getting better every day."

Her mother's eyes filled with sympathy. "Burns can be so painful. Is he suffering a great deal?"

"When the doctor changes his bandages he endures a lot of pain, but he doesn't complain."

John shook his head. "It's a shame his work was destroyed in the fire. I know the family had high hopes for his business."

"Anna told me they had a furniture buyer coming from Cincinnati just to look at Samuel's work. Of course, they had to tell him not to come because of the fire. Samuel made my china cabinet. It's a beautiful piece. Your father bought it for me the year before he died," her mother said.

"I know you cherish it."

John slowed his horse behind several buggies ahead of him. At the front of the line, Rebecca saw an elderly Amish couple moving at a sedate pace along the road. No one passed them. It would be impolite and pretentious to do so on a Sunday. No one wanted to show such a lack of humility on the Lord's Day.

A buggy drew in behind them. Rebecca glanced back and saw the Bowman family had caught up with them. Noah leaned out the side window and waved. His mother spoke sharply to him, and he pulled his head in. Rebecca ducked her head to keep from laughing.

They all arrived together at the home of Roy Bowman a little before eight. Roy was Isaac's eldest brother. Each family in Rebecca's congregation hosted services in their home at least once a year. Since the prayer meetings were held every other Sunday, a family rarely had to host it twice. The long gray bench wagon sat beside the house. Men were unloading the benches that traveled to the designated houses twice a month. The men carried them inside and set them in rows while the women greeted each other, laid out the food and looked after the children running to and fro.

Almost half of the congregation was made up of extended Bowman families. Isaac had four brothers and each of them had numerous sons and daughters. When a church group became too large to fit into a single home or barn, a new congregation would be formed, mostly of the younger married couples. The current group was made up of some twenty families and only about one hundred and twenty-five people. It would be a few years yet before they would need to split up.

John positioned his buggy among the others lined up across the hillside. He got out and unhitched his horse. While he led the mare to the corral where a dozen other buggy horses were already lined up and munching hay, Rebecca and her mother carried their baskets to the house. As she passed Samuel standing beside his father, she stopped and spoke quietly. "I saw someone buying birdhouses this morning. They took two."

"I'll tell Luke. He'll have to get busy and make more."

"Using the tree to display them was a good idea."

"I'm glad you think so."

Her mother frowned at her and motioned for her to come along. Rebecca ignored her. "How are your hands today? Are they still hurting you?"

"Not as much. Only when I bump them. Which happens a lot. They itch more now."

"The doctor said that meant they are healing. I see the bishop heading in. I'd better get this food inside."

"Will you be back at our place tomorrow?"

"I will."

The corner of his lip turned up in a little smile. *"Goot."*

It surprised her just how hard it was to walk away from him.

Although he had been reluctant to come, Samuel was glad he did. He enjoyed the three-hour-long service. It was familiar and comforting. He knew the drawn-out hymns by heart and didn't need to read the words from the *Ausbund*, their Amish hymnal, but he missed the weight of the large black book in his hands. Jonas Beachy, the bishop, was a good preacher. He and his two deacons spoke eloquently on the gathering in of the harvest and giving thanks for the bounty of the land.

Yet all the time Samuel sat on the hard backless bench or knelt on the floor, his mind constantly slipped back to when he sat beside Rebecca in the coolness of the night. It seemed that she was always on his mind these days. He listened for her voice among the singers and picked it out easily. It was the sweet alto that he had come to know while she was working in the house. She sang or hummed to let him know where she was ever since he had asked her to. She was kind that way, always being available without being intrusive now that he was up and out of bed.

When the prayer meeting finally ended, he allowed Timothy to lead him outside. That was when the hard part started. He was soon surrounded by the men of the community. He had to retell the story of the explosion to his friends and cousins and answer their questions about his sight. He had to listen to their words of sympathy and nod when he just wanted to crawl into the buggy and go home. They all meant well, but he quickly grew tired of being the center of attention.

Noah stood at his side. "We can go in and eat now. Do you want to come in or would you rather wait out here?"

He wasn't about to have everyone watch him be fed like an infant. "I'll wait out here. Just put me in the shade somewhere."

Noah led him to a set of steps at the side of the house and then went to get his meal. Thankful to be left alone, he relaxed for a few minutes. The sounds of a Sunday gathering poured through the air around him. The clatter of plates, tableware and conversation came from inside the house behind him. He must be near an open window. He listened to the voices and could pick out his *Onkel* Roy and his father discussing the corn harvest and the weather. From across the lawn, he heard the shrieks and laughter of the youngest children playing tag. Soon, his father and his cronies would get up a game of quoits once the midday meal was finished. His mother would be among the women cleaning up inside. When they were done, they would gather in rockers and lawn chairs in the shade and catch up on all the news.

A few of the young people would slip off to the barn, where they would stand in awkward groups with the boys in one pack and the maidens in the other until someone brought them together with a game of volleyball or baseball. A few would be missing. Those would be making dates for later that evening. Many a young man came to church in his open buggy with the hopes of convincing one special girl to ride home with him after the singing that evening.

Unlike his brothers, Samuel had never been among that group. His focus had always been on making sure the family business became successful. He knew he had earned a reputation of being stuck up among his peers, but he knew a family of his own would have to wait.

Had he waited too long? If he had chosen a wife, he would have had someone to look after him now instead of burdening his parents. Someone like Rebecca.

Before long, he heard footsteps approaching. He assumed it was Noah coming back. "I'm not hungry so don't worry about a plate for me."

"I thought you might not want to eat in front of others so I brought you a milk shake," Rebecca said as she sat down beside him. "It's chocolate. It will tide you over until you get home. You should be able to hold the glass yourself. It's plastic so it won't break it if it slips away, and it has a lid with a straw so you can't spill it."

"You think of everything."

"I try."

She pressed the glass between his bandaged hands

and he was able to hold it. He located the straw and drew a deep sip of the creamy cold drink. "It's *goot*."

"I like strawberry better myself. Do you need anything else before I go?"

For you to stay awhile. He didn't say it out loud.

"Noah is coming. I'll see you in the morning." She rose and he heard her move away.

His brother plopped down by his feet. "I brought you a plate. Do you want me to feed you or should I get mother?"

"Rebecca brought me a milk shake. You can have my plate, too."

"*Wunderbarr. Aenti* Edna gave me the last slice of her *snitz* and made me promise to give it to you. Are you sure you don't want it?"

Their aunt's dried apple pie was one of Noah's favorite treats. Samuel smiled. "You can have it."

"*Danki.* What were you and Rebecca talking about?"

"Nothing special. She just stopped by to give this milk shake."

"That was kind of her. I'm glad the two of you are getting along so well."

"What do you mean by that?"

"Just that you didn't seem to like her when she first came, and now you do."

He did like her. More than he wanted to. "She's bossy. I don't care for bossy women. They should be humble and quiet-spoken."

Noah chuckled. "Like *Mamm*?"

"Point taken. *Mamm* might be opinionated at home, but she is always demure in public."

"So is Rebecca."

"I guess I never noticed."

The sound of running feet approached and thudded to a stop in front of them. "We're getting up a game of volleyball, Noah. Want to join us? I picked you for my team already." The breathless female voice belonged to their neighbor's daughter Fanny.

"I can't today."

Samuel took a sip of his drink to keep from laughing. Noah couldn't have sounded more disappointed if he tried.

"Oh. Okay. I'll see you later. Are you staying for the singing tonight?"

"I don't know if I can. It all depends."

"Sarah Hochstetler is going to be there tonight. She turned sixteen last week and this will be her first one. She has her eye on you, but some fella might steal her away if you don't make a move soon," Fanny teased.

"She does?"

"She's on my volleyball team. You could make a good impression if you came and played with us."

"It doesn't matter. I have to stay here."

"All right. It was good to see you, Samuel. I hope you get better soon."

"*Danki*, Fanny." Samuel heard the sound of her running away. Fanny seldom moved at half speed.

Noah sighed, and Samuel took pity on his brother. "You don't need to babysit me. Go have fun with your friends."

"Are you sure? *Mamm* said I was to stay here and watch out for you."

"I'm sure. Go on. Impress Sarah Hochstetler with your skill and charm." Was his baby brother old enough to be chasing after a young *maedel*? It didn't seem possible.

"You're the best." Noah took off as if he was afraid Samuel would change his mind. Or maybe he was afraid their mother would catch wind of his desertion.

Samuel sat back and waited for Rebecca. Was she watching?

Rebecca couldn't believe it when she saw Noah take off after Fanny Erb, leaving Samuel all alone. She waited a full minute until she realized Noah had joined the volleyball game getting underway. He had no intention of keeping an eye on Samuel. She turned to her mother. "Excuse me. I must see if Samuel needs anything."

"Dear, you aren't working today. Let his family look after him."

"I'm not doing it because it's my job. I'm doing it out of Christian charity." She knew her mother couldn't argue against that.

She crossed the strip of lawn just as a pair of rowdy boys chasing each other around the house barreled into Samuel.

The two young boys apologized profusely and then took off. Samuel had one bandaged hand pressed to the side of his face. She rushed forward. "Samuel, are you hurt?"

"I don't think so. I wasn't expecting to be blindsided. Who were they?"

She sat down beside him in relief. "Fanny Erb's two youngest brothers."

"The whole family runs faster than the horses they raise."

She chuckled. "I think the horses have more sense. Are you sure you aren't hurt?"

"Is there any blood?"

She examined him closely. *"Nee."*

"Then I'm fine except for a few new bruises."

She heard the door of the house open and saw his father come out followed by the bishop. "Your father and the bishop are coming this way."

"Samuel, it is good to see you are well enough to attend the services," the bishop said. Rebecca rose and stepped a few feet away, making room for the men to sit down beside Samuel on the steps.

"God was merciful to me. My eyes are closed, but he left my ears open so that I might hear your good preaching."

Did she detect a note of sarcasm? Was he still angry at God? None of the others seemed to notice.

Isaac wrapped his hands around his knee. "The bishop and I have decided on a day for the workshop raising. Everyone should be done with the harvest by next church day. We will hold it the following Thursday."

"That should give everyone enough time to finish their own work," the bishop said. "Is that agreeable to you?"

"If it is okay with my father, it's fine with me." Samuel's lips flattened as a muscle twitched in his jaw.

"Goot. We will have your wood shop open again in no time." The bishop patted Samuel's knee and rose to his feet. "Isaac, will you join me for a game of quoits?"

"I was thinking you might want to play someone who doesn't beat you so badly," Isaac said with a twinkle in his eye.

The bishop straightened and fisted his hands on his

hips. "There's a challenge I can't refuse. Get ready to eat those words."

The two men walked away, and Rebecca sat down beside Samuel again. "You must have faith that you'll be able to return to the work you love. All things are possible with God."

"That's the day the dealer from Cincinnati was to come and look at my work. All he would find now is a pile of ashes."

"When your eyes and hands have healed you will show him your best work."

"If I worked for six months, I wouldn't be able to build all the furniture that was lost in the fire. Without money to buy new lumber and new machinery, I couldn't do it, anyway. Besides, when Timothy spoke to Mr. Clark on the phone after the fire, the man mentioned he had other woodworkers he intended to visit that week. He will place his contracts elsewhere. He has a business to run."

"Then you will find another dealer who will buy your furniture at a fair price, and you will not need Mr. Clark's money. When God closes a door, He opens a window."

"And sometimes He's telling us we can't have what we want," he said bitterly.

"Sometimes, He asks us to pay attention to His plan and not our own," she added softly.

"If His plan is to scatter my brothers by sending them elsewhere to find work, then I don't think much of it. I have to accept that my risk resulted in failure. Would you get Luke or Timothy for me? I'd like to go home now."

He stood and moved back to lean against the house

with his arms folded protectively across his chest. She had little choice but to do as he asked. She found his brothers by the barn talking with a group of young men their age. A few of them had short beards indicating they were recently married. Most, like the Bowman brothers were clean-shaven. She paused beside them. "Samuel would like to go home now. Could one of you arrange to take him?"

A young man beside Luke spoke up. "I brought my open buggy today. I can take him."

"I'll go with you," Luke said. "He can't be left alone for long."

"Danki." Rebecca smiled at the group. As they left to hitch up the buggy, she started back toward the house.

Timothy followed her. "Is Samuel feeling poorly?"

She stopped walking. "Your father and the bishop chose the day for the wood shop raising. It will be on the same day Samuel had planned for Mr. Clark to visit."

"And it reminded him he has nothing left to show for all his months of hard work." Timothy's eyes filled with understanding as he gazed toward Samuel standing alone.

"It was your work that went up in smoke, too." She didn't sense any bitterness in Timothy. Was it only Samuel who struggled to come to grips with the loss?

"My brother believes he's the only one who can hold the family together. He doesn't realize each of us must make that decision for ourselves."

"Would his plan have worked if not for the fire?"

"Probably. Samuel is a fine craftsman, but he can't run a big business alone. Until he accepts that, he's going to drive us away even if there is work to keep us here."

She thought of her beautiful table at home and the lovely Bible cabinet where her great-great-grandfather's Bible was displayed. There were examples of the Bowman's fine craftsmanship all across the county. It was a shame the Cincinnati dealer couldn't see them.

A sudden thought occurred to her. Why couldn't he see them? "Timothy, would you stay if the workshop reopened?"

"If I could earn enough to support a family, *ja*."

She looked over the community gathered in groups, chatting and enjoying their day of rest amid the stunning fall colors of the hills around them. She smiled and rubbed her chin. "Timothy, I have an idea."

"Okay, do I get to hear it?"

Luke was leading Samuel toward his friend's waiting buggy. "Let's share it with Samuel and Luke. It will take everyone's cooperation."

She reached Samuel's side just as he climbed in and sat down. She grabbed the door before Luke could close it. "Samuel, I have an idea how we can show your furniture dealer the kind of work you can do."

"Rebecca, stop. That dream is over. It's gone. I don't want to talk about it anymore. Luke, get me home."

She touched his arm. "But you haven't heard what I have to say."

He pulled away. "Don't you know when to stop talking? It's over. What are you waiting for, Luke? Take me home!"

Defeated, she stepped back and allowed the carriage to roll away. He wouldn't even listen to her.

Chapter Eight

Samuel regretted his rudeness to Rebecca before he had gone half a mile. His failure was no fault of hers. She deserved to be treated with respect.

The following morning, his brothers and his father had all gone out to the fields before she arrived. He was seated at the kitchen table listening with half an ear as his mother read the morning paper to him.

"Good morning, Anna. Samuel." The flat way she said his name was his first clue that he was still in trouble.

His mother turned the page of the newspaper. "Hello, Rebecca. Would you finish reading to Samuel while I start my laundry?"

"I'll do the laundry. You keep reading, Anna." He heard the door to the basement bang shut. Was she avoiding him?

After his mother finished the paper, Samuel fumbled his way to the washroom downstairs. "Rebecca, may I talk to you?"

"I'm busy." She brushed past him and dashed up the stairs.

He found out it was easy for her to play hide-and-seek with a blind man. After following her several places only to be left standing alone, he gave in.

"I'll be going to my room now," he announced in the kitchen. He wasn't sure anyone heard him until his mother replied.

"That's fine."

He left the room feeling like a fool. How hard was it to apologize to one woman? And why was he trying so hard?

He settled in upstairs, but couldn't find a comfortable spot in bed. He wasn't tired. He was bored and he was getting angry. Rebecca had been hired to take care of him, not avoid him.

Time dragged by. Being idle chafed. His entire life had been taken up with work, with doing more and doing it better so that the family could reap the benefits of his labors. It felt as if it had all been for nothing.

Rising, he paced the small confines of his room for a while, and then fell back into bed with his arm over his face.

Sometime later, Rebecca spoke from his doorway. "Your mother has asked that I take the lunches out to the men. I thought you might like to walk along with me. It's a crisp morning."

So she was finally speaking to him. "Why not? There's certainly nothing to do in here."

She led the way outdoors. She waited until he made it down the porch steps. "Your mother told me they were cutting corn by the old railroad. I'm not familiar with where that is."

Her cool tone said more than her words. She was still upset. Their merry chase had erased his desire to apologize. He could be cool, too. "The old section of railroad tracks runs along the river behind the barn. I can hear the corn binder from here."

"Then your hearing is better than mine. Will you be comfortable walking with your hand on my shoulder? I'm afraid I need both my hands to carry these lunch pails."

He couldn't maintain this indifference if he was touching her. "Maybe I should stay here."

"Now that you've made an effort to get outside, I think you should enjoy a little of this glorious weather." Her softened tone held a hint of an overture.

He really didn't want to go back in the house.

"I know it's frightening to think of walking so far. I promise to go slow so you won't trip over anything, but I would like to deliver these meals before they get cold."

The corner of his mouth ticked up. "I'm not frightened. I trust you."

He did. Implicitly.

She placed his hand on her shoulder. "I'd be scared if I were in your shoes. Then again, if I were in your shoes I would be tripping over everything because they would be miles too big for me."

"Do you make a joke out of everything?"

"Not everything. It's just better to laugh than it is to cry."

They walked in silence for a while. He had to adjust his stride to her short steps, but they soon reached the cornfield where his family was working. He didn't need his eyes to tell him what was going on. It was a task he had helped with since he was a child.

His father would be driving the corn binder. A small gasoline-powered engine mounted on the side of the cutter operated the blades while a team of horses pulled the machine along as it sliced the cornstalks off at the base. A special belt lifted bundles of stalks up to a second flatbed wagon. One of his brothers would be driving a team alongside the cutter while the other brother had the dirty job of gathering the cornstalks and piling them at the back of the wagon. Many an argument had been started about who got to drive and whose turn it was to catch.

When the catch wagon was overflowing with cornstalks, the driver would turn the team away and head for the silo. A second wagon would move up and take its place. Only one person was needed to drive the loaded wagon back to the silo, so one of the brothers would hop off and race to jump on the new wagon. Once there, he took over the reins or began catching. The process would be repeated flawlessly each time the wagon was full. The corn cutter never had to stop as long as the wagons were emptied and returned in a timely fashion.

Rebecca came to a halt. "I think the corn stubble is too rough for you to walk through. I'll have you stay here."

"Not a problem." He squatted on his heels to wait for her return. At least they were speaking to each other again.

"Will your father stop for me?"

Samuel nodded. "He'll stop the corn binder for a brief lunch as long as the weather looks favorable. If there is a threat of rain, my *daed* will eat standing up and driving the team until he gets his crop in or it's too dark to see."

"My father used to say rain is the friend of the plants and the enemy of the harvest."

"It's true. If the corn stored in the silos is too damp, it will mold and rot. The moisture content of the plants has to be just right to maximize the nutrition the cows will get from their feed over the long cold winter months."

"He's waving for me to come out. I'll be back as quick as I can."

"Rebecca, I'm sorry I was abrupt with you yesterday." He waited tensely for her reply.

"You are forgiven, Samuel. I can be pushy sometimes."

"I appreciate that you want to help, but I know what needs to be done. I'll take care of it as soon as I'm healed."

"I know you will."

Her voice carried more confidence in him than he felt. She believed in him. Somehow, he would find a way to make things right.

Rebecca was pleased with Samuel's steady improvement over the next few days. He rarely spent time in his room, preferring instead to be out of doors. Although the tasks he could perform were limited, he did manage to help his mother by waiting on customers at the gift shop. He even devised a way to sweep the floor by having Rebecca tie towels to his shoes so he could slide his feet across the wide planks while she dusted the shelves. He still refused to eat with the family. Timothy and his father were the only ones he allowed to help him with that since he still had to be fed.

On Wednesday evening, she went home to do her own housekeeping. Bright and early the next morning, she returned to the Bowman farm. As her horse trotted through the covered bridge, a growing sense of joy enveloped her. She was happy to be a part of this family, even for a short time. Being with Samuel was the reason her spirits soared higher each day.

Anna was busy in the kitchen washing glass canning jars and barely glanced Rebecca's way when she came in. Samuel normally sat at the kitchen table this time of day while his mother read the morning paper to him, but he wasn't around.

"*Guder mariye*, Anna. Where is Samuel?"

"He hasn't come down."

That was odd. "What can I do to help this morning?"

"I have a bucket of fresh dug potatoes on the back porch. If you would wash them and leave them to dry, that would be great. I'll pack them into paper bags later and take them down to the store when I go."

Glancing around, Rebecca noticed a large pail of apples on the table. "Would you like me to take these apples down to the store for you, too?"

"*Nee*, I've already taken down the good ones I plan to sell today. These are for applesauce. I have to start canning soon. The fruit will be falling on the ground before long."

Rebecca nodded in sympathy. The early days of autumn were the busiest time of the year for Amish housewives. Gathering in the harvest meant a steady stream of vegetables and fruit to preserve on top of the daily chores, cooking for harvest crews and working beside the men in the fields when needed. Spare minutes were few and far between.

After washing and arranging the potatoes on racks to dry, Rebecca went back inside. Samuel still wasn't up. Today was the day she needed to change his dressing, so perhaps he was reluctant to make an appearance. "I'm going to check on Samuel."

"Okay." Anna didn't look up from her task of coring apples.

Samuel was sitting at the desk by the window. He tensed when she knocked. "*Guder mariye*, Samuel. How are you this morning?"

"I've been dreading your appearance."

"You certainly know how to flatter a woman." She saw the tiniest hint of a smile before it fled.

"You know what I meant."

"This time it won't be so painful."

"And how can you know that?" His derisive tone signaled his disbelief.

"You said your hands have been itching. That means healing."

He extended them palms up on the table. "We might as well get it over with."

"Did you take your pain medication?"

"I did."

"I'm amazed."

"I learned my lesson at the doctor's office."

Rebecca left to collect her supplies and returned five minutes later with a box of bandages, a large basin of warm water, liquid soap and the latex gloves the doctor had given her. She set them all on the desk along with a towel and pulled on the gloves. Using a pair of sewing scissors, she began cutting away the old dressings on his right hand. When she was down to the last layer, she guided his hand to the basin. "Soak it for a few minutes. Have I hurt you yet?"

"Not enough to mention."

"I'm thankful for that."

"So am I."

After a few minutes, she unfolded a towel and spread it out. "Lift your hand out of the water. How is it?"

"Stinging."

Gently she removed the last layer of bandages to reveal his reddened skin and peeling blisters. Some areas of his palm were bright red while others were a ruddy brown indicating old skin that had yet to slough. She began lightly wiping the entire palm, trying not to scrub.

"How does it look?"

"Not bad."

"You don't lie very well."

"It looks painful, but I don't think there is as much swelling." She applied some soap and began massaging his hand in slow circles trying to loosen the dead skin.

She had never noticed how long and supple his fingers were. They weren't soft or weak. Even injured, she could feel the underlying strength in his wrist and arm. He had hands made to craft delicate designs into hard wood and smooth the rough edges until the oak or cherry felt like satin to the touch. He had skilled craftsman's hands and she liked the feel of them. The simple task of washing his injuries took on a whole new meaning. This was the way a wife might touch her husband.

He inhaled sharply and her gaze flew to his face. "What's wrong?"

He'd never had a woman hold his hand and caress it with such tenderness. The sensation, aside from the mild pain, was a disturbing one. Her hands were small and delicate, and yet they were strong, too. The fragrance of her lavender soap filled his senses, and he knew the scent would forever remind him of this moment.

"I'm sorry if I'm hurting you," she said softly. There was a breathless quality to her voice that sent his pulse soaring.

If only he knew for certain that his vision would return. Then he might have the right to speak about the affection growing in his heart. Until then, it was best to remain silent and pretend her touch was like any other.

"You're doing okay, but can we speed it up?" He didn't know how much longer he could keep a lid on his emotions.

"Of course." She rinsed and dried his hand and applied the antibiotic cream the doctor had prescribed. Samuel pulled away from her and propped his elbow on the table while she repeated the procedure on his other hand.

In his mind, he worked out the dimensions of a new shop and the placement of the equipment he hoped to purchase one day down to the smallest detail. It kept him from thinking about how much he wished he could see her face. Was she being the dutiful nurse or did she feel this connection, too, this pull toward each other?

Finally, she was done. "There. That wasn't so bad, was it?"

"It all depends on your definition of *bad.*"

"Are you ready to have me do your face, or would you rather take a break?"

Her hands on his face? No, he wasn't going to endure that. "I'll let Timothy do it this evening."

"Oh. Are you sure? I don't mind." She sounded disappointed.

"Wrap my hands and then go help my mother. I'm sure she has something for you to do."

"Samuel, I was hired to take care of you."

"And you have. I'm getting up and around without much trouble. I feel stronger now that I'm eating solid food. You have helped immensely. Once these dressings come off my eyes, I won't need you at all."

"That is the day I pray for," she said softly.

"As do I."

She wrapped his hands and taped the ends of the bandages. "I haven't used as much gauze because the drainage is much less. Can you move your fingers?"

He tried and was able to press his first two fingers against his thumbs without undue pain. "That's better. I'll be able to hold my own spoon and fork now. Timothy will be overjoyed."

"You can join the family for supper tonight."

"I'd rather have one evening of practice up here before I risk pouring soup down my chin in front of everyone."

She giggled. "I'll be sure and send up extra towels with your tray."

Her laughter was a balm to his spirit. If only he could judge her interest in him. Was there a shadow of hope that she held him in affection? He had heard that the eyes were windows into the soul. He wanted to gaze into her eyes and see if she smiled from within when she looked at him. "*Danki*, Rebecca. You were right. It was much less painful."

"I could read the paper to you before I go and help your mother."

He didn't want her to go. Any excuse to keep her close was one he liked. The sound of her voice would soothe him and make the long hours of the morning bearable. "That would be nice."

"Wunderbarr. Let me put away these supplies and I'll be right back with the paper."

Her footsteps hurried away and he had a chance to draw a full breath. It didn't help. The scent of lavender still lingered in the air. He stood and took a turn around the room. What was he doing? Why was he thinking romantic thoughts about Rebecca Miller? She was a widow who still mourned her husband.

Although he'd known her for years, Samuel couldn't recall her face clearly. What had triggered this sudden interest in her? Nothing she had said or done. Pouring water on a sick man's feet wasn't romantic in the least.

She was bossy and opinionated. She wasn't the kind of woman he imagined would interest him. The sound of her hurrying up the stairs reached him and he sat down.

She breezed into the room. "I found the paper."

He heard her chair scrape back and he knew she had taken a seat across from him. What would she look like with the morning sunlight pouring across her fair skin? "Samuel, you're flushed all of the sudden. Do you feel all right?"

Before he could form a reply, her hand cupped his cheek and neck below his ear where he wasn't burned or bandaged. Her fingers were damp and cool. He froze, not wanting her to see how much she affected him. "I feel fine."

"You aren't feverish, but your voice sounds raspy. Maybe the paper can wait until you've had a rest. I'll come back later." She withdrew her hand.

He leaned away and folded his arms over his chest. "Don't go. I want to hear what's going on. Read."

"Very well."

In her low musical voice, the first thing he had liked about her, she read the front page news about traffic improvements the county was hoping to make. After that, she went on to weather reports and the hog and corn market news. It was amazing anyone could make the hog market reports sound interesting and soothing, but she did. By the end of half an hour, she had covered the entire paper from the local ball games and highlights to the specials at the grocery store in Berlin.

The paper rustled as she closed it. "That's all for now."

The appetizing smell of simmering apples had overpowered the scent of lavender in the room. "*Mamm* must be making applesauce. Maybe I'll sneak a few apple slices when she isn't looking."

"Would you like me to distract her for you?"

"I think I can manage on my own."

"I'll slip you one or two if you can't."

"It's a deal." He chuckled as they made their way downstairs.

"I was wondering if you two were ever coming down. I was about to come up and check on you." His mother's words held a hint of reproach.

"Rebecca read the paper to me. She said you were busy." He found the table and sat down.

"That was kind of you, Rebecca. I can't get away from this applesauce for another hour or two. Would you mind opening the store for me? If anyone comes in just write down what they buy. There is a cash box under the counter. It has enough money in it to make change."

"I'm sure I can manage."

"Do you want me to keep you company?" he offered.

"*Nee*, keep your mother company. I'll be fine by myself. I'll take those potatoes with me," Rebecca said quickly. Too, quickly.

He had the feeling he had missed something. When she was gone, his mother didn't beat around the bush. "Samuel, you are a grown fellow, and I should not have to have this conversation with you."

He sat up straighter. "What conversation?"

"Rebecca is a single woman. You risk her reputation by treating her with such ease in your company. You are much improved. It is unseemly now for her to spend time in your room."

"We have done nothing wrong. She changed my dressings and read the paper. What harm is there in that?"

"None, but such familiarity can lead to temptations."

Hadn't he already discovered that for himself? "I would not harm Rebecca's reputation for anything. She has been kindness itself to me."

"I like her, too. Very much. If you should decide to ask her out I would approve."

He squirmed in his seat. "I didn't say I wanted to go out with her."

"Silly boy, you don't have to say those things. A mother has eyes and ears. Not much goes on in this house that I don't know about. Remember that."

Later that week, Rebecca once again took Samuel to the doctor's office. He tolerated the long trip much better the second time and remembered to take his pain medication before they arrived. At the office, she remained in the waiting room while Samuel was taken back to an exam room.

"How are you doing, Samuel?" the doctor asked when he was finished with his initial examination.

"Better every day." Physically it was true, but the worry about his family's future never left him.

"Any problems? Any signs of infection?"

Samuel shook his head. "Rebecca Miller and my brother Timothy are taking good care of me."

"I thought you must be doing well. Rebecca would have let me know if there was a problem. Let me get these dressings off and have a look for myself."

Samuel waited as the doctor unwrapped his hands. He made only a few noncommittal noises. "They feel better. There is less pain."

"I'm impressed and pleased with your progress. There seems to be very little scarring considering the extent of the burns. You can leave the wraps off soon. There are a few places that still look raw, but letting them dry out may be best. Now, let's take a look at your face. I'm going to dim the lights. Let me know if they're still too bright."

Samuel tensed as he waited for the doctor to remove the bandages from his eyes. If his hands were healing, his eyes were healing, too. They had to be.

"This looks good. Your eyebrows and your eyelashes will grow back. Your eyelids are still raw looking, but that's to be expected. All right, open your eyes slowly. Stop if it hurts."

Samuel let his eyes flutter open. His heart began to hammer in his chest. "I can't see anything."

"Can you distinguish between light and dark?"

Samuel's throat tightened. "It's all dark. I don't see any light at all. Turn on the lights. Face me toward the window." His breath came in short, harsh gasps.

"I'm going to put some drops in your eyes and some light gauze pads over them. You won't need the heavy bandages anymore."

"Why can't I see? My burns were healing. Why can't I see?"

"There may be several reasons. In the event your vision hadn't improved today, I made an appointment for you to see the ophthalmologist I've been consulting with. He's a friend of mine. There won't be any cost for his examination and he can see you now. Would you like Rebecca to go with us?"

Samuel shook his head. This was something he needed to face alone. "Will it take long?"

"His office is fifteen minutes from here, and he has cleared his schedule to see you. If you don't feel up to doing this now, we can make it another time."

"I need to know what's wrong. Have someone tell Rebecca that I'll be back shortly."

The doctor wrapped a new bandage around Samuel's eyes. "Hopefully, Dr. Westbrook can give us some answers."

The doctor led Samuel outside and was helping him into his car when Samuel heard Rebecca's voice. "Wait up. I'm coming, too."

Samuel paused. "It's not necessary, Rebecca."

She opened the door to the backseat. "Your father is paying me to take care of you. He would not like it if I let you go alone. And we both know that your mother would have a fit. Please drive on, Doctor."

Although he would not have admitted it, Samuel was glad she was there.

At the ophthalmology clinic, Samuel endured a lengthy exam. The doctor put drops in his eyes. It made them burn, and Samuel had to resist the urge to rub them. His face was positioned in a holder. He was told to look right and look left and to stare straight ahead. Rebecca stood close beside him through it all. He was never more grateful for her stubborn streak.

While the doctors finished conferring, Samuel waited anxiously for their verdict. Finally, Dr. Westbrook sat down at Samuel's side. "I'm going to send you home with some special dark glasses. You don't have to keep the bandages on anymore."

"Will I be blind forever?" Samuel choked out the question.

"I'm afraid I can't tell you that."

"What can you tell us?" Rebecca asked.

"In a flash burn such as the one Samuel endured, the blink reflex is so quick that the eyes are almost always protected. His eyelids sustained burns, but the corneas of his eyes did not. There is no scarring or clouding. The muscles of the pupils respond appropriately to light and dark. The pressures in the eyes are normal and the retinas are both intact."

Samuel rubbed his itching palms on his pant legs. "What are you saying?"

Chapter Nine

"They're wrong! I don't wish to be blind. Why would they think such a thing?"

Rebecca glanced at Samuel's angry face as she drove him home from the doctor's office. It was the first time he'd spoken since they had been told his blindness wasn't caused by his injury. "They are men of science. They believe what they have told you. It's possible."

"*Nee*, I'm not *naerfich*."

"They didn't say you were crazy." She didn't want to believe it, either. Samuel was a strong, determined man, but he had suffered a great blow. Perhaps this was God's way of teaching him humility. She reached the Bowman driveway and turned in.

"I don't want my family to know this," he said quickly.

"Samuel, it can't be hidden. The doctor has asked for a meeting with your family so that he can explain this to them."

"He couldn't explain it to me."

"You weren't willing to listen." She hated seeing him so tormented.

"You think I'm crazy, too."

"Far from it. I think you are upset and angry. When you are calm, you can hear what Dr. Marksman was trying to tell you. This was not your choice. This was your mind's reaction to a horrible trauma." She pulled the buggy to a stop beside the barn. She got out and went round to help him down.

He brushed past her and took a few steps away until he came up against the corral fence. He raised his fists to the sky. "Why do you allow this, God? I have prayed every day and every night that You will restore my sight. Why won't You let me see?"

Rebecca laid a hand on his shoulder. "I think you are asking the wrong question, Samuel."

"I don't know what you mean." Frustrated to the point of screaming, Samuel held on to his last ounce of sanity. She didn't understand. How could she?

"Maybe the question you should be asking yourself is what does God *want* you to see?"

He gripped the fence rail in front of him making his tender hands throb with pain. "I can't see anything!"

"Maybe that's because you aren't looking in the right direction. We must use faith, not our eyes to see what God asks of us. Try looking inward, Samuel."

"You're babbling."

"I'm going to visit my mother for a few hours. Tell Anna I won't be here for supper."

He bowed his head on his hands and heard her climb in the buggy and drive away. He listened a while longer. She wouldn't leave him out here alone, would she?

"Rebecca?"

Silence answered him. He was alone. Alone and afraid on his own farm. He had been brought low. Lower than he ever imagined he could feel. The hope-

lessness was like a bottomless pit yawning at his feet.
One step and he could drop into it forever.

"Is this what you want me to see, Lord? That I'm
not a strong man? That I'm nothing more than a frightened child?"

He leaned his forehead against the wooden fence.
The board was solid and smooth and still held the
warmth of the late-afternoon sun. Would the sunset be
a pretty one tonight? When was the last time he paid attention to the color of the clouds at dusk? Years, maybe.
How could he have known he'd never see another one.

"I will never ignore another of Your wonders if
You'll let me see them again. What do I have to offer
You, Lord? What is worthy of such a gift?"

Nothing. He had nothing to offer. He could promise
anything. He could promise to use his gifts to aid others, to be kinder to his brothers, to devote his life to
praising God, but they were all things he believed he
was already doing. What more did God want from him?

Was this how Luke felt when he lost his way? Did
he see an abyss of despair and reach for drugs to keep
from falling into it?

Samuel had always seen Luke's addiction as a weak-
ness. Was this something they shared, like the color of
their eyes?

He couldn't accept that. He wouldn't.

Rebecca said he was asking the wrong questions.
*Okay, Lord, I won't ask why me. What do You want
from me? Show me. I may not see, but I can listen to
You. I'm listening, Lord. I'm listening.*

"Did your little nurse leave you out here all alone?"

Samuel straightened at the sound of Luke's voice.
The clip-clop of horse's hooves told him his brother

was returning with a team from the field. "It appears she did."

"That's not like her. Do you…do you need some help?" His brother's tentative offer made Samuel realize how often he had rejected Luke's help in the past.

"*Danki*, but I can figure out where the house is."

"Nice shades, by the way. How is your vision? Can you see now?"

Samuel touched the dark glasses that wrapped around his face. "Not yet."

"Give it some time. Your hands look awful. Do they hurt?"

Pushing away from the fence, Samuel flexed his fingers. His hands were still stiff and tender, but he was ready to do some work with them. "Which team do you have?"

"Oscar and Dutch."

"Would you like some help rubbing them down?"

"Sure. If you think you can."

"I can brush a horse in my sleep. We all can. I reckon I can do it without looking." Samuel reached out until his fingers came in contact with the mane of the nearest horse. He held on tight. "Lead the way."

He walked beside his brother and waited outside the stall as Luke unharnessed the pair. Samuel felt along the bench by the wall until he located the currycomb and brush they kept on pegs.

"Do you want Oscar, or do you want Dutch?" Luke asked.

"Either."

"This is Oscar." Luke guided Samuel to the horse's side.

Once he started the task he had done since he was a small boy, Samuel forgot for a few minutes that he couldn't see. He didn't need his eyes to let his hand glide the brush over the big draft horse's shiny dappled-gray coat. He drew a deep breath and let the familiar barn smells of horses, hay and old timbers fill his lungs.

"What did you say to Rebecca to make her run off and leave you?" Luke asked.

"Why do you assume it was something I said?" Samuel worked his way along one side of the horse.

"Call it an educated guess."

Samuel chuckled. "It usually is me doing the scolding."

"That's what I meant. So?"

"I was bemoaning my plight. Railing against God for taking my sight."

"I can see why you would. I'm sorry this happened to you, Samuel."

"Rebecca has less sympathy." He walked around the horse's rump and began brushing his other side.

"She's a very wise woman."

Samuel heard the respect in his brother's voice and wondered if Luke's feelings for Rebecca were deeper than friendship. "She is wise and single. Is she someone you might consider courting?"

He held his breath waiting for Luke's answer. As much as he cared for Rebecca himself, he wouldn't stand in the way of someone else, especially Luke, if he had similar feelings.

Luke laughed heartily. Samuel frowned. "I don't see what you think is funny."

"Are you offering to step aside if I'm interested?"

"I don't need to step aside. Rebecca was hired to help with my care until the harvest was over. It's nearly done. I'm just curious if you like her in that way?" He brushed harder as he reached Oscar's shoulder.

"I like her fine, but she only has eyes for you."

"What?" He paused and cocked his head. Had he heard Luke right? Oscar swung his head around to nip as he sometimes did, but Samuel blocked him with an elbow to the nose.

"Samuel, what did you just do?"

"Oscar was going to bite me and I elbowed him. What do you mean Rebecca only has eyes for me?"

"You saw Oscar swinging his head around?"

"*Nee*, I can't see anything. I just knew he was going to do it. I'm not foolish enough to think Rebecca would be interested in a blind man. You're wrong about that." Samuel finished brushing the horse and felt his way out of the stall. He tossed the brush and comb onto the bench.

Luke came to his side and laid a hand on his shoulder. "She cares for you a lot, Samuel. A man doesn't need eyes to hear the softness in her voice when she speaks to you or to notice that she is always at your side when you need something. She teases a smile from you when you are down. She makes you do more than you think you can."

"She's a fine nurse. That's all."

"I'm not blind. When I see Rebecca gazing at you, I see a woman who just might be falling for you. What you do with that information is up to you."

Rebecca sat at her mother's table in her bright and airy kitchen. A long row of windows let the late-afternoon light pour in. Pulling a pan of roast chicken with vegetables from the oven, her mother placed it on the stovetop. "I thought about inviting John to join us. What do you think?"

Rebecca frowned. "I don't want to invite John to supper. I'm not sure I want to stay for supper if I'm going to be lectured through the entire meal about what a catch he is."

"Rebecca May, do not speak to your mother in such a tone!"

Reining in her resentment, Rebecca sighed. "I'm sorry, *Mamm*. I'm tired tonight. It's been a long week. It is your home, and you may invite John if you wish."

"What has you so upset, daughter?" She checked the vegetables and chicken for doneness with a fork.

Rebecca decided there was no point in denying it. "Samuel Bowman."

Her mother spun to face her. "Why? What has he done?"

"It's not what he has done. It's what he won't do."

"This sounds like it may require a pot of tea to solve. Shall I put some on? This chicken needs another twenty minutes."

"I'll get it. You finish what you're doing." Rebecca busied herself getting the tea ready. When it was done, she carried the mugs to the table where her mother was already seated.

Her mother picked up her mug with both hands and took a sip. The steam rose and fogged her glasses until she moved the cup away. "So, tell me what Samuel won't do."

"He won't let go of his anger at God for his injury."

"God has broad shoulders. He can bear our anger for He is the one who gave us our emotions. Samuel is a good man. He will realize the error of his thinking in time and turn to God for forgiveness."

"I pray that you are right."

"I am. This is a hard thing to bear for a strong young man. What does the doctor say about his eyes?"

"That his blindness isn't due to his injury. It is his mind that won't allow him to see. The doctor is hopeful Samuel will recover, but I'm afraid he will give up and stop trying."

"As Walter stopped trying to get better?" her mother asked quietly.

Rebecca's throat closed and she could only nod.

"You have come to care for Samuel a great deal, haven't you?"

"I shouldn't, I know. I'm trying to control my feelings."

"Any why shouldn't you care for him?"

"I loved my husband. I don't want to love another man."

"Well, then, it is best that you don't."

"*Mamm*, why do you say that? You are forever pushing John at me."

Her mother stirred her tea. "That was when I thought you might fall in love again. If you are determined to stop trying, then I'm wasting my time."

"Is that what I'm doing?" If she refused to accept that she could love another, then love would never come her way.

"I think you can answer that question better than I can. Our negative thoughts can become self-fulfilling prophecies."

Tears sprang to Rebecca's eyes and rolled down her

cheeks. How could she profess to believe in God's plan when she was so angry herself?

"I'm no better than Samuel. He doesn't want to see. I don't want to love. The truth is I'm as mad at God for taking Walter away as Samuel is at his loss of sight. We are a sad pair."

Her mother came and wrapped her arms around Rebecca's shoulders. "A sad pair, perhaps, but neither of you is beyond hope. God heals all wounds in time. Here on earth or in the hereafter."

"I don't know why I'm so upset. I like Samuel and I want to see him get well. That's all. I want all my patients to get well. I'm grateful God has given me this calling. Caring for others is fulfilling work. I believe it is the path God has chosen for me. I'm content with that."

Her mother tipped her head to the side and regarded her with pity. "Rebecca, who are you trying to convince?"

Rebecca woke suddenly in the middle of the night. She lay still in the darkness listening for Samuel's footsteps overhead. She had learned when she returned from visiting her mother that Samuel had retreated to his room, refused supper and wouldn't speak to anyone.

Rebecca had fallen asleep listening to the sounds of him pacing overhead. Now it was quiet. Was he finally sleeping? Something told her that wasn't the case. Rising, she went to her window that overlooked the back of the house. She saw him sitting on the stone wall. Somehow, he'd found his way to his favorite spot.

Should she leave him alone?

She wouldn't be able to sleep, knowing he was out

there without anyone to guide him back. He could stumble into the river and drown. She dressed quickly and silently let herself out of the house. The moon was half-full and slipping down in the west, but it gave enough light so that she could make her way to his side.

"Go back to the house, Rebecca. I'm fine. Leave me in peace."

She wasn't sure how he knew she was there, but she wasn't going to be intimidated by his rejection.

"I happen to like watching the river at night." She sat down on the wall.

"I don't need a babysitter. I found my way here, and I can find my way back."

"Fine. Go back to the house and leave me in peace. Do you think you are the only one who is troubled in the small hours the night? You want to see again. I want to hear my husband's voice one more time. I want him to whisper to me that everything will be okay. I want to see him come strolling through the door with a big grin on his face. It isn't fair that he is gone and I am left alone. I know what sorrow is, Samuel Bowman. Explain to me why your loss is so much greater than mine."

"It isn't."

"Each of us must bear the sorrows of this world according to His plan. You have this—I have mine. Sitting here wallowing in pity will not bring my husband back. It will not restore your sight. So we are wasting our time sitting on this cold stone wall when we have comfortable beds. I'm going back to mine. *Guten nacht.*" She stood and started to move away.

"Rebecca?"

She paused. "Yes, Samuel."

"I appreciate all you have done for me."

"I was glad to do it." All she wanted was to comfort him.

"I'm not wallowing in pity out here. I'm searching for a new purpose. I'm listening to His will and trying to learn what He wants me to do."

"I'm sorry I assumed the worst."

"Don't be. I've been wallowing in pity for quite some time."

She sat back down on the wall. "Have you found what you were seeking?"

"Not yet. I feel as if the answer is right in front of me, but I can't make it out."

"I know the feeling."

"Really? You seem like a woman filled with purpose."

"I'm not. I'm struggling, too. I say all the right things, but deep in my heart I'm angry with God and I'm frightened by that anger."

"We are two wounded souls, are we not?"

She smiled, remembering her mother's words. "We are a sad pair, but not beyond hope."

"Will you be going home now? I can feed myself and dress myself. My hands are tender and sore, but I can use them. I don't need a nursemaid."

"I'd like to stay and help through the rest of harvest. Your mother has a heavy workload."

"That would be a kindness. You should go back to bed."

"If you don't mind, I'd like to stay a while longer."

"I don't mind at all."

She remained beside him in contented silence until the moon set, then together they went in.

* * *

Rebecca took a chair in the corner of Dr. Marksman's office. Luke leaned against the wall beside her. She wasn't sure why she was being included in this family meeting with Samuel's physician, but she was eager to hear what he had to say. Not only because Samuel was her patient and her friend, but because she cared deeply about him. Samuel chose to remain in the waiting room.

Dr. Marksman took a seat behind his desk and leaned his elbows on the cluttered surface. The rest of the family sat in a semicircle around him. The doctor folded his hands. "I'm sorry to interrupt your work. I know the timing of harvest is critical. I won't keep you long, but I felt strongly that I needed to have this conversation with Samuel's entire family."

"Have you bad news for us? Is his blindness permanent?" Isaac's tense tone echoed Rebecca's feelings.

Dr. Marksman sat back and drummed the fingers of one hand on his desk. "Samuel's burns are healing well, but I have another concern that I wanted to discuss with you. The damage to Samuel's eyes was minimal."

"Blindness is not a minimal thing," Anna said with a huff.

Dr. Marksman gave her a sympathetic smile. "I don't mean to trivialize his condition, but the physical damage to his eyes isn't severe enough to cause the ongoing problem with his sight."

Isaac tipped his head to one side. "I don't understand what you're saying."

Luke crossed his arms over his chest. "He's telling you that Samuel can see."

Everyone turned to glare at Luke. His mother shook

her head. "Samuel would not pretend such a thing if it were not true. You are calling your brother a liar."

Luke shrugged. "I was with him in the barn yesterday. Oscar reached out to bite, as we all know he can. Samuel blocked him with his elbow. I saw him do it."

Rebecca glanced from face to face. No one believed Luke. She wasn't sure that she believed him, either. "It could have been a coincidence," she offered.

"It looked like a deliberate move to me. That's all I'm saying. A few minutes later he would've fallen over a bucket in front of him if I hadn't guided him around it, but I'm sure he saw the horse was going to bite and he checked him."

Noah sprang to his feet, outrage shining in his eyes. "What reason would Samuel have for pretending to be blind?"

"I don't believe he is pretending," Dr. Marksman said, pulling everyone's attention back to him.

Noah sank onto his chair again. The doctor reached for a book and opened it. "Samuel is suffering from something that used to be called hysterical blindness. Medical professionals now call it a 'conversion disorder,' a condition that causes the patient to show psychological or mental stress in a physical manner. To be honest, I've never treated anyone with this disorder. There is a long list of causes, but most of them point to a type of anxiety or psychological trauma that triggers temporary blindness. Samuel's eyes can see, but emotional turmoil has caused him to block off visual impulses from his eyes to his brain. He isn't doing this on purpose. He is truly blind, but the reason isn't physical."

"Is he aware of this?" Timothy asked.

"I have offered him the same information that I have

given you. He doesn't accept it, and that isn't surprising. He insisted he could see if he wanted to, and he wants to see. A conversion disorder is something a patient can't control."

Isaac scratched his chin whiskers. "Is there a medicine that will help him?"

"There are some treatment options available. Counseling, stress relief, but medicine, no. Since the cause of this disorder is psychological and not medical, I suggested he seek the care of a psychiatrist or psychologist. He refused."

Anna leaned forward. "My son is not crazy. He is blind. You are a poor doctor if you must accuse the patient of not wanting to be well."

"Anna, that is enough." Isaac laid a hand on her arm and she fell silent. He looked at Dr. Marksman. "Will our son recover?"

"There is a good chance his vision will return in time. How much time…that I can't say. I'm hopeful. He has a strong faith and a strong family to help him get through this. Telling him to get over it won't help. Telling him it's all in his head can make it worse. Right now, he has little to dwell on except the horror of what happened. It's still fresh in his memory. As that fades, I believe his vision will return. Slowly or all at once, but there is a slim chance he will never recover his sight. That is up to God."

Rebecca was darning socks for Anna on the porch when Isaac came out of the house the following evening after supper. He took a seat beside her on the small bench. "How is Samuel?"

"Subdued. He's taking a walk along the pasture fence. He uses a long stick to feel his way."

"What do you make of what the doctor told us?"

"I'm not sure what to think. I was happy when he said he believes Samuel will recover in time, but when he admitted he had never seen a case like Samuel's, I did wonder if he knew what he was talking about."

"The thought crossed my mind, as well."

"Samuel is a strong man, but I know he is deeply worried."

"Worried about what?"

Rebecca laid her bowl aside and half turned to face Isaac. "He's worried about the family breaking apart. When I asked him what he meant, he said it was his responsibility to keep his brothers together and he has failed."

Isaac leaned back and stretched his long legs out in front of him crossing them at the ankles. "He has always felt that it is up to him to keep his brothers close even when I tell him young men must go their own way. When Luke left, in some ways it was harder on Samuel than all the rest of us."

"Why do you say that?"

"Samuel was about ten years old when his mother became deathly ill. Anna thought she was dying. I did, too. I had to rush her to the doctor. It was winter. I chose my fastest horse and the small sleigh in order to get Anna to the doctor as quickly as I could. There wasn't room for all the children so I left Samuel in charge. Anna told him he was responsible for all his brothers until I returned. She was barely conscious when I carried her out to the sleigh, but she took Samuel's hand and made him promise to look after the others. I could see in his face how scared he was. I was scared, too."

"We all look after our brothers and sisters. I was always given the task of keeping track of my siblings."

"As was I, but the snow was deep that year, and a big storm moved in. I got my wife to the doctor. An ambulance took us to the hospital, but the roads were soon closed and I couldn't get back. I was worried half out of my mind about Anna and about the boys. During the next three days, Samuel took care of everyone. He did the chores, fed the stock, brought in firewood—he did a man's work and he kept his brothers safe and sound. It couldn't have been easy. Noah was only two. Luke told me later that Noah cried for his mother all the time and Samuel had to carry him around to comfort him. Ever since that time, Samuel has had a profound sense of responsibility toward his brothers."

"Why does he feel he has let them down now?"

"Our farm is a small one. It was enough for Anna and me when the boys were small. But they are grown now and will soon have wives and children. Noah is the youngest, and his family will take over the farm. My other sons will have to find work. Samuel was sure that our woodworking business could be expanded enough to provide a living for everyone. He had the talent and he had the drive to make it work. His mother and I invested all we had to expand. The explosion set fire to the shop and destroyed everything. It was God's will. I don't blame Samuel, but I know he blames himself."

She looked at Isaac. No one knew Samuel better than his father did. "Do you think he will get well?"

Chapter Ten

A dark blue car turned in at the end of the lane and drove toward the house. Rebecca noticed that Isaac hadn't answered her question. He rose to his feet and stepped to the door. "Anna, they're here."

Rebecca tipped her head to look up at him. "Are we expecting someone?"

"Joshua. I had Luke call him yesterday evening. They made good time."

Anna came bustling out of the house drying her hands on her apron. The blue car stopped just beyond the steps. The back door opened. Joshua got out and waved at his mother. She waved back and raced down the steps. Joshua's stepdaughter, five-year-old Hannah, climbed out of the car and ran to meet her. "*Mammi* Anna, I'm so happy to see you again. Do you have some of those cookies I like?"

Anna lifted Hannah into her arms for a hug. "You've grown an inch. The cookies aren't ready. I thought we could bake them together. What do you think of that idea?"

"It sounds *wunderbarr*. I love baking. *Mamm* lets me help her all the time."

Isaac walked down to clasp his son's hand. "Welcome home. We are glad you are back."

"I should have come sooner. Where is he?" Joshua looked around.

"Taking a walk. Come in. Get settled. There will be time to visit after that. Mary, welcome to our home." He smiled at the young Amish woman who got out and stood beside Joshua.

"It's good to be back, although I wish the circumstances were different." The pretty young bride smiled at Rebecca.

The rest of the Bowman brothers came outside and Joshua was soon the center of backslapping and good-natured teasing.

Anna put Hannah down and turned to Rebecca. "You remember Joshua's bride, Mary, and this bundle of energy is Hannah, the granddaughter I have always wanted. Mary, this is Rebecca Miller. She has been helping me take care of Samuel. Come inside, girls. We have a lot of catching up to do. How are my sisters?"

"They are well and send their love. You can expect a letter telling you all about our visit shortly. Tell me, how is Samuel doing?" Mary asked, looking to Rebecca.

"He has had a rough time of it, but he's doing better. His bandages are off."

"But his vision hasn't returned?"

Rebecca shook her head.

Joshua finished paying the driver of the car after they unloaded the bags. "I see Samuel coming this way. I think I'll go out to meet him."

"I'll come with you," Luke said.

"Me, too," Timothy and Noah said together. All the brothers walked toward the pasture in a subdued group.

Isaac smiled after them. "I reckon I'll take the bags in. Tell me again why I had sons?"

Samuel stumbled when he stepped in a hole. He used the pole he carried to catch himself. Simply walking unaided was a challenge, but he was determined to relearn his way around the farm. He leaned his head on his hands to catch his breath. He might have chosen to walk too far on his first time out, but he wasn't going to sit in the house and learn to knit.

"What's new, *brudder*?"

Samuel jerked his head up. "Joshua? Is that you?" He held out his hand and his brother gripped it. Samuel winced.

"*Brudder*, you are a sorry sight. Leftover pizza that's been walked on looks better than you do."

Samuel grinned as he touched his face. He had been told it was red and raw-looking with scabbed-over areas and shiny red blotches mixed among patches of peeling skin, but Rebecca never mentioned pizza. "You say the sweetest things, Joshua. What are you doing home? I thought you'd be gone another month at least."

"*Daed* asked me to come back and help out. I shouldn't have left before harvest. We could have waited a few more months to get married. I would have been here to help and things might not have gone so wrong."

"You're here now and that's what counts," Timothy said.

"I'm glad you came home. Now I can stop being the only one catching those itchy, prickly corn bundles. It's your turn," Noah said with glee.

"Married men don't catch," Joshua said. Was he able to keep a straight face?

"They don't? Is that true?" Noah demanded. Everyone laughed.

The brothers fell into step together. Samuel realized he was in the middle. Surrounded, guided and protected by the brothers he thought of as his responsibility. It was a big change.

"What are your plans, Samuel? Do you have any?" Joshua asked.

"I don't. I'm still trying to figure out what I can do. Woodworking is out, that's for sure."

"Why?" Noah asked.

Samuel shook his head. "Because I can't see."

"You don't need to see to sand a cabinet panel or a tabletop. We do that by feel," Timothy said.

"I hadn't thought of that." Those were tasks he could do. His hands were still tender, but with a pair of gloves on, he could hold a sanding block or a sheet of sandpaper.

Luke chuckled but didn't say anything. "What?" Samuel demanded.

"You can still stand around and yell at us to get a move on. I know you have eyes in the back of your head that you've used for that."

All of the boys laughed and Samuel joined in.

"We are going to rebuild the workshop, aren't we?" Joshua asked.

Everyone grew silent. Samuel sighed. "The church is building us a new one next week. It won't be as large and it won't have all the equipment we need, but it will be a start."

"All we need is a place to start," Timothy said with

conviction. "God willing, we'll be doing a booming business in a few years and everyone can come back to work here."

"A few years sounds like a long time without you fellas." Noah's voice trembled slightly. "You might find work close by."

"The hardware store in Dover is hiring," Luke said quietly. "So is the place that makes siding in Beach City."

"Beach City? That's more than two day's buggy ride from here," Noah said in disbelief.

"Most decent-paying jobs are more than two days away," Luke snapped.

"No one has to go anywhere." Noah sounded desperate.

"I have a wife and child to support. We could scrape by living here, but what about the next one of us to marry and the one after that?" Joshua fell silent.

"We've always made do." Noah's tone conveyed how much he wanted to believe it was still possible.

Samuel said, "What about the years when the harvest is lean and we don't have enough food to feed all of us? The sad truth is there isn't enough farmland available to support all the Amish in this church district. We need cottage industries. We need to attract customers. We are five miles off a major road. Few people find us unless they are looking for us."

"We'll get by. God will show us what needs to be done." Noah's conviction struck a chord with Samuel. He wanted to believe that, too.

"We trust God to give us a good harvest, but we still have to hoe the weeds from the garden," Timothy said quietly.

Samuel tried for a lighter tone. "I have to find a way to distinguish between a weed and a radish without being able to see them. Any suggestions?"

"Looks like we have more company," Luke said.

"Who is it?" Samuel asked.

"If I'm not mistaken, it's John Miller. I wonder what he's doing here?"

"He's here to put new shoes on *Mamm's* pony." Had he also come to see Rebecca?

Rebecca was visiting with Mary and being entertained by the antics of Hannah and Samuel's mother as they giggled and chatted while they spooned cookie dough onto baking sheets. The aroma of snickerdoodles and gingersnaps filled the kitchen. Isaac was sitting by the window watching, as well. He turned and looked outside. "We have another visitor."

"Who is it?" Anna asked.

"John Miller. Wonder what he wants?"

Anna slipped a full sheet into the oven. "Samuel had me write and ask him to shoe our pony. He said Noah was too busy to do it."

Rebecca moaned inwardly. She hoped John would shoe the horse and leave without asking for her.

"That's a funny face."

Rebecca opened her eyes to find Hannah watching her. "Did I make a face? It must be because I don't like snickerdoodles."

Hannah's eyes widened. "You don't? That's just weird. Did you know my town got blowed away by a tornado?"

Nodding, Rebecca said, "I heard that. It must have been awful."

"It's getting fixed, but it sure is a mess. Lily's *onkel* said one man's troubles are another man's blessings. He has lots of work now for his horses cause they pull logs to the sawmill. There's busted trees all over the place. Lily is my best friend. We're going to go to school together."

Rebecca would have preferred to continue her conversation with Hannah, but John made an appearance in the doorway. "*Guten owed*, everyone."

Anna wiped the sweat from her brow with the back of her hand. "Good evening to you, too. Won't you come in? We're getting ready to enjoy a few hot-from-the-oven cookies."

"That sounds mighty fine. I may take you up on your offer later. First, I'd like to speak to Rebecca. Her mother sent me with a message."

Rebecca tried not to make that face again. She managed a smile and rose to go outside with John. He led the way to a small swing at the end of the porch and sat down. Rebecca reluctantly did, too.

"Is something wrong with *Mamm*?" she asked quickly.

"Ease your mind. It's nothing like that. I happened to mention I was coming this way and she wanted me to tell you that Katie Chupp stopped in to see if you could help out with the children when her baby is born."

"I'll have to find out when she is due. I'm not sure when I'll be finished here."

"Has the family here been treating you well? I've heard Samuel isn't the best patient. He has a reputation for being a hard taskmaster."

"I've been treated very well." She saw the brothers returning from their walk. She realized Joshua would be a welcome addition to the harvest crew. That meant Mary would be able to help Anna. Would Rebecca have a reason to stay on? Samuel no longer needed her care. His brothers or his mother could do all that she was doing. His dressing changes were minimal. He was out and about. If he needed to see the doctor again, Mary or Anna could drive him. Rebecca wasn't needed anymore.

John stared at her with an odd expression. "What's the matter?"

She shook off a feeling of sadness. "Nothing. I was lost in thought."

"Will you be coming home soon?"

"That's exactly what I was thinking about. I'm not sure how long I'll stay, but I'll come home again on Sunday to see *Mamm*." Rebecca would have her old life back soon. Another family wanted her to help with a new baby. Soon her time with Samuel would become another memory. The thought saddened her.

"Your mother will be happy to hear it. May I drive the two of you to Sunday services again?"

His eyes were so hopeful. She smiled at him. "That would be nice. I'll see you on Sunday."

He nodded, but he didn't look as pleased as she thought he would. "Reckon I should get that pony's new shoes on. I'll see you later, and I'll give your mother your message."

"*Danki*, John. I never told you how much I appreciated all the things you did for me after Walter died. You've been very kind to me."

"It's what the family expects of me. That's all."

She found the statement puzzling, but she smiled, anyway. "Don't forget to get some cookies before you go."

"I won't." He walked down the steps as Samuel and

his brothers reached the house. They called a greeting, and Noah went with John to help with the shoeing.

The rest of his brothers went inside, but Samuel stayed by Rebecca. "Did John bring you news from home?"

"Just that my mother misses me, and I have another job offer."

He frowned. "You can't take it. You are still working for me."

"You don't require much care anymore. You said so yourself."

"My fingers are sore and stiff. They may be infected. What do you think?" He held them out.

Taking each one in turn, she examined them carefully. A few of the peeling areas had small cracks in the new skin underneath. She didn't see any serious redness or weeping. "I have some salve in my bag that will help. Wait here and I'll get it."

She wove her way through the crowd in the kitchen, sampling the cookies and teasing Hannah, and returned with a small jar of burn salve. She stepped out onto the porch and saw Samuel was sitting in the swing. Her heart started thudding heavily when she sat down beside him. Being close to John hadn't produced this effect. She schooled her voice into a casual tone. "Let me see them."

He held his hands toward her. She uncapped the salve jar and began smoothing the cream over his palms. "You can use this several times a day. On your face, too. It will help protect the new skin."

"It tingles."

"That means it's working."

"What's in it?"

"It's my own concoction. Aloe vera gel and a few other things. You should wear soft cotton gloves for a while to keep the dirt out. At night, it will be okay to leave them open to the air."

"You like taking care of people, don't you?"

"I have a talent for it the way you have a talent for carving. God gives each of us unique gifts to use for His glory."

"I *had* a talent for carving."

"You still do. How are your eyes today? Any change?"

"The world is still dark. It's strange, but at night, I think I see glimmers of light, almost like stars, but in the light of day, nothing."

"The doctor said this kind of blindness is almost always temporary. You have to have patience."

"It's hard, but I'm trying. Who has offered you another job?"

"Katie Chupp will need a mother's helper when her baby comes. She has five little girls and two boys already."

"Do you like taking care of *kinder*?"

"I love taking care of children. My adult patients are the hard ones to deal with."

"Have I been hard to deal with?"

She crossed her arms. "Do you really want me to answer that?"

"Maybe not."

"You must be glad to have Joshua home."

"It will make things easier for my parents. I'm grateful for that. I could tell he was upset by the scars on my face. Does it look bad?"

"Most of them will fade. In a year, you won't know you were ever in a fire."

"I'm worried about Joshua's daughter. Will I frighten her?"

So that was why he hadn't gone in with the others. "I'm sure Joshua and Mary have prepared her for how you will look. Just remember that children can say hurtful things without meaning to."

"My brother said I looked like a stepped-on slice of pizza. I'm pretty sure his daughter can't do worse than that."

She chuckled. "Aren't brothers wonderful?"

"Yeah, they are."

She heard the pain in his voice and knew he was still thinking that he had failed them. "Might as well get it over with. Your reward will be a warm snickerdoodle."

"How can I say no to that?"

Rebecca guided him into the kitchen and to a seat at the table. His mother brought him a glass of milk. Hannah was standing by her mother at the stove. She frowned when she saw Samuel and glanced up at Mary.

Mary gave her an encouraging smile. "You remember your father's brother Samuel."

Samuel straightened and turned his head toward them. "We met before the wedding, Hannah. You helped me make a trinket box for your mother. Do you remember that?"

Hannah nodded. Mary leaned to whisper in her daughter's ear. "I remember," Hannah said loudly.

Mary gave her a plate of cookies and a little push in Samuel's direction. Hannah approached him cautiously. She set the plate on the table. "Would you like a cookie?"

"Only if they are snickerdoodles. That's my favorite."

"Mine, too. Rebecca doesn't like them. She makes faces."

Rebecca waited for him to comment, but he didn't.

Samuel groped for the plate. Hannah pushed it under his hand. "How come you can't see?"

"My eyes were injured in an explosion." He bit into a cookie.

"Did it hurt?" Hannah asked in a loud whisper.

"A lot, but it doesn't hurt now. These are good. Did you make them?"

"I helped *Mammi* Anna."

"She's about the best cookie maker in the state."

"My *Mammi* Ada is the best."

He chuckled. "Is that your other grandmother?"

"One of them. Are you going to help us pick apples tomorrow?"

"I reckon I could. You'll have to help me. I won't be able to see them."

"I'll show you where they are. He's not scary, *Onkel* Luke."

Luke, leaning against the wall, slapped a hand over his mouth. Timothy punched his shoulder. "You're so busted."

"It wouldn't be the first time," Samuel said. There was a second of stunned silence, then all the brothers laughed.

Noah slapped his knee. "He's got you there. You've been busted by the police and a *kinder*."

Isaac rose from his seat by the window. "Time for bed. We have a silo to finish filling tomorrow, soybeans to start harvesting and hay to cut. The paper says we can expect a chance of rain all next week."

The gathering broke up. The men left and the women

finished cleaning the kitchen. Rebecca was wiping down the table and counters when Anna said, "You have done him a world of good. I'm sorry I doubted you."

"I'm glad I could help."

"It's good to have my family home again. I consider you part of this family now."

Anna went off to bed leaving Rebecca alone in the dark kitchen. She did feel as if she were a part of this family. More so than any other family she had worked with. It was going to be hard to leave. Much harder than she had ever expected.

Instead of going to bed, she slipped out the back door and walked down to the stone wall. Sitting there, she watched the river flowing by. The currents and eddies were marked by ripples, but the true power of the river lay beneath the surface. Like the waters in front of her, her emotions seemed quiet and sedate, but there was turmoil underneath and Samuel was the reason. Her growing attraction to him frightened her. She knew what it was to love and to lose that love, and she never wanted to be in that position again, but Samuel was pulling her toward that very cliff.

Was it possible to turn her feelings back to those of friendship? She had to try.

"A penny for your thoughts."

To her surprise, Luke came out of the shadows beneath the covered bridge. "I'm afraid they're not worth a penny."

"Does that mean you will give them away for free?"

"I was thinking about how hard it will be to leave here."

"That's funny. I'm always thinking about how easy it would be."

She crossed her arms. "You do not like living Amish?"

"I don't have anything against it, just doesn't seem to suit me." He picked up a pebble from the shore and tossed it into the water. The ripple was quickly swept downstream and disappeared under the bridge.

"What does suit you?"

He continued to gaze out at the water. "A fast car. A loud radio. Video games. They suit me."

Tipping her head slightly, she studied his back. "I thought you had more substance than that. They seem like trivial things, not something that could pull a man away from God and from his family."

He glanced at her over his shoulder. "Have you ever ridden in a really fast car?"

"Would it surprise you to know that I have driven a fast car?"

"Don't tell me that pious Rebecca Miller had a wild *rumspringa*?"

"Not as wild as yours from what I've heard, but I left for a while."

He walked to within a few feet of her. "I get what brings kids back. But what keeps them here?"

"First tell me what brings them back?"

"Loneliness. They find they can't fit in. They are square pegs in round holes. The only place where they feel normal is the place they most wanted to leave."

"You didn't mention love."

He shoved his hands in his pockets and walked to the water's edge. "You're right. Love does bring them back because they can't stand being alone."

"So you have answered your own question. Those of us who return and stay, do so because we feel loved.

Loved by God, loved by our families and loved by ourselves. For if you do not love yourself, the world is a very dark place."

He threw another rock in the water. "Yes, it is."

"*Guten nacht*, Luke."

"You're good for him. I hope he sees that."

Rebecca had no reply for him. She simply walked back to the house.

After a long minute, Luke spoke. "Do you see it, *brudder*? Or are you really that blind?"

Samuel came out from beneath the bridge using a long stick to feel his way across the grass to the wall. When he reached it, he sat down. "You should mind your own business."

Luke gave a bark of laughter. "I might make a play for her if you don't. I think she could hold a man's interest for a lifetime."

For once, Samuel knew Luke was right. A lifetime with Rebecca by his side was an image that had cemented itself in his mind and wouldn't fade. Would it be possible or was he only torturing himself?

Luke came to Samuel's side. "Do you think you can make it back to the house?"

"The headache is gone. I'm not dizzy. There's nothing left in my stomach. I think I can. Thanks for your help."

"I don't understand why you didn't have your nurse take care of you."

Samuel rose to his feet, glad to find the dizziness didn't return. "I didn't want to frighten her. If it happens again, I will tell her. Tonight, I'm glad you were the one who stumbled over me. Do you think you can take me back to the house now?"

"Sure, but you should tell Rebecca this happened."

The flash of light Samuel saw when he looked out over the river tonight had produced a blinding headache. The pain dropped him to his knees. For a second, he thought he'd been struck by lightning only there wasn't any sound.

If Luke hadn't come along, Rebecca would've found Samuel sick and rolling on the ground in agony. He was glad she hadn't seen him in that condition.

When Luke said Rebecca was coming, Samuel begged him to stall her until he had a chance to recover. His brother managed to do that, but Samuel knew Luke didn't feel right about deceiving Rebecca.

Samuel didn't, either. He didn't know what the flash of light meant, but it didn't feel like a good thing.

Chapter Eleven

"Something isn't right with Samuel."

Rebecca couldn't put her finger on what was wrong, but he seemed different. Withdrawn somehow. It worried her.

"He looks fine to me," Mary said.

They were all walking toward the small apple orchard a few hundred yards from the house early the next morning.

Samuel held Hannah's hand and let the child lead him. Hannah was excited to pick apples and chatted happily with her grandmother and him. Rebecca walked a few paces behind with Mary.

"Hannah seems quite taken with Samuel," Mary observed.

"He was worried that he would frighten her."

"Joshua and I spent quite a bit of time making sure she understood what had happened to him."

"She's handling it very well."

Mary smiled. "She's strong and she has a wonderful kind heart. How much longer will you be staying? Joshua mentioned that his father hired you to take care of Samuel after his injury. He doesn't appear to need a nurse anymore."

They reached the orchard and Rebecca watched Hannah help Samuel fill his basket with fruit by telling him to reach higher or lower. At one point, he lifted her to his shoulders and let her pick the high ones and hand them down.

Rebecca began filling her basket with the red ripe fruit. "I expected to be sent home when you arrived, but no one has mentioned that. I will have to leave soon or risk losing my next position."

"You have an unusual occupation for an Amish woman."

"I came into it naturally. My husband was ill for many months before he passed away. A friend asked me to be her mother's helper when her baby was born and it was such a joy to take care of a new life. After that, the Lord supplied me with a steady stream of people in need of care."

"My adoptive mother is a nurse. She says it is more than a profession—it is her calling."

"I feel the same way. There are times when I wish I had more education. I may speak to the bishop about that possibility. I know there are some Amish churches that have made exceptions to allow women to be trained as nurses' aides and LPNs." Rebecca finished filling one basket and started on another.

"It's funny that you should mention that. My mother is hoping to help train some of our young women to work at a new clinic being built in Hope Springs. It's a clinic for special needs children. We have a fair number of children with genetic disorders in our district. My mother was raised Amish but chose not to join the church. She speaks Pennsylvania Dutch and that makes it easy for worried Amish families to trust her. She knows how important it is for health care workers to understand and respect the Amish ways."

"That is so true. Our ways are different from the *Englisch*."

"If you can get permission and would be interested in training with her, I'd be happy to introduce you. We called and told them we were coming back before we left Illinois. She and my father will be coming for a visit soon. I'd like to think they want to see me, but I know it's Hannah that they miss."

"That is an intriguing offer. I will have to give it some thought." Formal training? It was something she had only dreamed about.

"*Mamm*, come see this apple. It's all flat on one side. Isn't it funny?" Hannah came running with her unusual find.

Mary and Rebecca admired it. Hannah took her mother's hand. "Help me find another one."

The two of them went around the next tree. Seeing that Samuel had been left alone, Rebecca moved up to join him. "You have been deserted for an odd-shaped apple."

He smiled slightly, but didn't comment as he gingerly searched the spreading branches of the tree for more fruit.

"Samuel, are you feeling okay?"

His hands stilled. "Why do you ask?"

"You seemed quieter than normal. Is everything all right?"

"I have a bit of a headache. Sorry if I'm putting a damper on the outing."

"You aren't. Hannah is having a good time picking apples, and Anna is having a good time watching her."

Hearing her name, his mother came over to join them. "That Hannah is the sweetest child. After all my sons, I finally have a little girl in the house. I will hate it when they leave."

Samuel scowled. "Who said anything about them leaving?"

"Joshua told us this morning that he is going back to work construction in Hope Springs after the harvest is finished. I know they will come to visit when they can, but I had hoped they would settle here."

"There's no work for him around here, *Mamm*. You know that."

"He must get work where he can, I understand. I just wanted my sons and grandchildren closer."

"I'm sorry I couldn't do that for you," he said quietly.

"It was *Gott's* will. I think we have enough apples for this morning. Let's take them back to the house and start cooking."

Anna called to Mary and Hannah, and the three of them made their way out of the orchard.

"You can't take the blame, Samuel. It was an accident. Accidents happen."

"I know that."

"But you still blame yourself."

"It gives me something to do in the evenings since I can't read a book." He pulled off his dark glasses and rubbed his forehead.

"Is your headache worse?"

"A little."

"Perhaps I should take you to see the doctor."

He settled his glasses back on. "I'm done with doctors for a while, but I am going to need your help getting out of this orchard."

"It will be my pleasure." Rebecca took his arm and led him back to the house, but she couldn't shake the feeling that something was wrong. He was hiding something.

Samuel was sitting on the swing when he heard his mother laugh. He glanced toward the kitchen window and the white curtains fluttering in the breeze. Pain shot through his skull and sweat broke out on his body as he doubled over. Grasping his head with both hands, he held on, enduring the agony until it vanished as rapidly as it came on. At least this time he hadn't been sick. He leaned back in the porch swing and drew a deep breath.

"Another one?" Luke asked. Samuel hadn't heard him approach.

"Yeah."

"You should tell Rebecca."

"This one wasn't as bad."

"It looked bad to me. I thought you were going to fall out of the swing. I'm going to call your doctor."

"Don't."

"Pretend for a minute that it was Noah bending over and grabbing his head. Imagine he's white as a sheet only a few weeks after he went flying through the side of a building following an explosion."

"I flew out an open door, not through the side of the building."

"Good point and that may have saved your life. Back to my story. I say, Noah, I'm going to call your doctor. This head pain isn't right. Now you say?"

"If it was Noah, I'd tell you to call the doctor. I don't need one."

"Because your head is harder than his is or because you think you are less valuable to this family?"

"Fine. Call the doctor, but don't tell Rebecca. I don't want her to worry."

"Good old Luke is the only one who gets to worry. Thanks for that."

"Aren't you supposed to be working somewhere? What do you want?"

"Rebecca asked me to bring these up here and give them to you." He set a box on the swing beside Samuel.

"What is it?"

"A box Rebecca found in the gift shop. They're toys that Timothy cut out before the fire but didn't have time to finish."

Samuel frowned. "What does she want me to do with them?"

Luke took Samuel's hand and laid a sanding block in it. "I think she wants you to finish them. I'm on my way to bale hay with Timothy. I'll call the doctor from the community phone booth."

Leaning back, Samuel folded his arms over his chest. "Why don't you use the cell phone you keep tucked in your boot?"

"Rebecca squealed on me? I don't believe it."

"I heard the low battery alarm beeping while you were washing up last night."

"Oh. I only use it for emergencies."

"I don't care. You aren't a baptized member of our church so you aren't breaking any rules, but don't let *Mamm* find out. Where is Rebecca?" He hadn't seen her all morning. The day seemed incomplete until she was giving him grief about something.

"She's coming this way. I'd better get going."

"Bless you for carrying that box up here, Luke. Samuel, Hannah would like to see how we make our wooden toys. I told her you could show her how it's done. I put a pair of gloves in the box for you to use. The sandpaper will be too rough on your skin. I must get back to the orchard and fetch Anna another half bushel of Red Delicious. Have fun."

He heard her footsteps fade away, and then he heard a tiny sigh from beside him. He hid a grin. "Did you really want to know how these are made or is Rebecca just trying to entertain me?"

He felt Hannah crawl onto the swing beside him. "She's trying to keep you busy so you don't mope."

"She said I mope?"

"Yup."

"She's bossy."

"Yup."

"Which toy do you want to make?"

"Do you have a dog? I miss mine. Her name is Bella, and she lives with *Mammi* Ada."

"You'll have to look and see if there is a dog shape in the box."

"I found one. Now what?"

"We use our sandpaper to rub away the rough wooden edges and make the wood smooth so it looks more like the animal it needs to be."

He heard her start working and before long, he was engrossed in the task of improving a wooden horse and showing Hannah how to do the same with her dog.

* * *

Rebecca glanced out the open window to check on Samuel and Hannah a half hour later. They were both working away. She heard them talking but she couldn't make out what they were saying. Occasionally, she heard Samuel's deep laugh. She loved that sound.

"How are they getting along?" Mary asked as she mashed cooked apples through a strainer.

"Hannah is fine company for anyone."

"It was a good idea."

"I know he would rather be in the fields with the men, or in his workshop, but this is as close to wood-working as he can do at the moment."

"I understand the workshop is being rebuilt soon. Joshua is excited for me to meet all the neighbors and the family members. I know he wishes we could stay here, but I'm happy we are going back to Hope Springs. That reminds me, I finished the letter to my adoptive mother this morning and I told her about your interest in furthering your education. Hopefully, I will have an answer soon and I can tell you when she is coming to visit."

"What is this about more education?" Samuel stood in the doorway. Rebecca hadn't heard him come in. She bit her lower lip, unsure of how he would react. Amish children only went to school until the eighth grade. Additional education was forbidden. The only way a student could go on was to refrain from joining the church.

"Mary's adoptive mother is an *Englisch* nurse. She is looking for Amish women who want to become lay nurses at a clinic for special needs children. She has obtained permission from several of the bishops in the area to train the women. Isn't that a wonderful idea?"

He crossed to the refrigerator and opened it. Pulling out a soda, he popped the top and took a drink. "Is this something you want to do, Rebecca?"

"I'm certainly interested in learning more about it."

He nodded but didn't make another comment. Hannah came in with two wooden toys in her hand. One was clearly a trotting horse; the other, Rebecca wasn't sure what it was.

Hannah carried it to her mother. "See? It looks just like Bella?"

Mary held the toy up and struggled to keep a straight face. "It does look a lot like Bella. You did a great job. Are you finished?"

"Yup. Can I help you now?"

"You can. Bring a chair over here and stand beside me. I'll show you how to make applesauce. Do you want to make plain or cinnamon?"

"Cinnamon."

Samuel went to the broom closet and pulled out his mother's broom. When he went outside, Rebecca followed him. He brushed the sawdust and wood shavings off the swing and then began to sweep the floor. She watched him for a moment.

"Am I missing a lot?"

"*Nee*, you are doing a fine job. Are you upset to learn I wish to further my education?"

"Surprised, but not upset. I see that what you do is important and that you wish to do it well."

"Then why were you surprised?"

"I assumed that you would wish to marry rather than remain single."

"I had considered marrying again so that I might know the joy of my own children, but I don't know if it would be fair to bring *kinder* into a marriage not blessed with a deep love between the parents."

"I understand why you'd feel that way, but respect and friendship can grow into love over time. My mother tells me it's true."

"She told me the same thing. Is your headache better?"

He touched his forehead. "It is. Don't worry about me."

"Are you trying to tell me how to do my job?" She struggled unsuccessfully to keep from smiling.

He held up one hand. "*Nee, nee,* I would not dare. I never know if you have a glass of water handy or not."

"You grow wiser as well as stronger, Samuel. I'm pleased with your progress." She went back in the house with the sound of his laughter raising her spirits.

The next day, Rebecca and Samuel were left at home when all the rest of the family went out to gather hay. Even Hannah was allowed to go along and help. The forecast for pending rain forced Isaac to put everyone to work in the fields. The apples could wait.

Rebecca felt guilty about not helping, but she was still worried about Samuel. She often saw him rubbing his forehead or knuckling his eyes as if they burned. Anytime she asked, he denied having a problem. With everyone gone, she was looking forward to a quiet afternoon of reading to him.

That hope evaporated before she had time to enjoy it. The sound of a horse and buggy pulling up outside drew her to the window. Her heart fell.

"Who is it?" Samuel asked, laying aside his work. He was adding a carved mane and tail to another toy horse with a small penknife.

"It's John Miller."

"No one mentioned that we had more work for him. I wonder what he wants?" Samuel started to rise, but Rebecca forestalled him.

"I'll go see."

She went into the kitchen and opened the door. "Good afternoon, John. What brings you out this way?"

He pulled his hat from his head and bowed slightly. "I thought I would see how Samuel is getting along and perhaps have a private word with you."

That didn't sound good. "Do come in. Samuel is in the other room. I'm sure he will be glad of your company. Everyone else is working in the hay fields."

"A wise move. The paper says it will rain." He smiled tentatively, stepped inside and stood in front of her. He turned his hat around in his hand several times, and then seemed to realize what he was doing. Abruptly, he hung it on one of the pegs beside the door.

She led the way to the living room and he took a seat on the sofa. He looked so ill at ease that she worried he had bad news to share. He ran a finger around his collar. "It's a warm day for this time of year."

"Would you like to sit outside?" Samuel asked. "The breeze off the river is cooling."

John popped up. "That would be fine."

"Why don't you two go out on the back porch and I'll fix some refreshments for you."

John shot out the door like a startled rabbit. What was going on?

Samuel settled on a picnic table bench against the back wall of the house. There was a good breeze, and it was cooler coming off the river. John paced across the porch and back several times.

"Is something troubling you, John?"

"*Nee*, I'm fine. Why do you ask?" He sounded as nervous as a new preacher on his first Sunday.

"You seem restless today."

"I reckon there's no disguising it. I'm nervous as can be. This is a big step for me, but it's the right one I'm sure."

"What is this big step, and how does it involve me?"

"Not you. *Nee*. I've come to ask for Rebecca's hand in marriage. I know these things aren't usually spoken of, but since she is living here, I see no reason to keep it a secret. We are not teenagers sneaking around at night during our *rumspringa*. We've both been wed before."

John's announcement hit Samuel like a fist to the stomach. Was Rebecca interested in John? She had loved Walter. Who better to take his place than his own brother? There wouldn't be any objections from the church."

"I didn't know that you and Rebecca had been courting?"

"We've seen a lot of each other since my brother died. She is well aware of my feelings. I have been led to believe that she returns them."

"Then you are a blessed man. Rebecca is a wonderful woman." Wonderful and about to fall out of Samuel's reach forever. He cared for Rebecca, but until this moment, he hadn't examined those feelings close enough to realize that he was falling in love with her.

Should he have spoken? Would his blindness matter to her? It wouldn't—he knew that. Not if she loved him. But it mattered to him. John was a good, strong man.

He was the better choice for her, but Samuel couldn't imagine how he would feel if she wanted John.

She brought out coffee and cinnamon rolls and sat at the small table beside him, but he had no interest in the food. Fortunately, John had little interest in prolonging the visit. He rose and said, "It was nice talking to you, Samuel. I hope you continue to mend. I'll be back for the workshop raising next week. Rebecca, could you walk me out?"

"Of course."

She sounded puzzled, not like a woman who was eager to hear what the man had to say to her.

Standing, Samuel held out his hand, and John shook it before leaving. Would Rebecca refuse him? Samuel prayed she would, and then he prayed to be forgiven for such a thought.

A headache sprang full-blown behind his eyes. He pulled off his dark glasses and dropped them as he pressed the heels of his hands to his brow to stem the pain. It didn't work. He tipped his head back and opened his eyes. Blue sky and white clouds arched over him. A second later, intense pain dropped him to his knees and he fell forward.

Rebecca walked with John to his buggy. He didn't get in. Instead, he turned around and surprised her by taking her hand. She tried to pull away, but he held on. "Would you like to go for a buggy ride with me?" he asked with a stiff grin.

"That's very nice of you, but I must stay here with Samuel. No one else is at home." She pulled at her hand again. He finally released her.

"I reckon there's no need for that romantic stuff. I'll

say what I have to say, and you can give me your answer." He pulled off his hat and clapped it to his chest.

A sinking feeling settled in her midsection.

"Rebecca Miller, would you do me the honor of becoming my wife?"

She folded her hands below her chin and pressed them together tightly. "This is rather sudden, John."

"No point in beating around the bush. We rub along well together. You'll not want for anything as my wife. God willing, we will have many children to give us comfort in our old age."

With absolute clarity, she saw what her answer had to be. "I like you John, but not enough to marry you. You are fine man, and you deserve a woman who loves you for who you are."

He frowned. "You don't want to marry me?"

She hated hurting his feelings. "I'm sorry. I don't."

He sighed heavily, and then slowly smiled. "Well, that is a relief."

Growing more confused by the moment, she raised both eyebrows. "It is a relief that I won't marry you?"

"It is. My folks are all for it. They have been pushing me for close to six months to wed you. I said yes so they would leave me alone. To think what I put up with when all I had to do was get the right answer from you."

It wasn't very flattering, but she was relieved she'd given him the answer he wanted. "I hope we can still be friends."

"No problem with that. That's all I ever wanted to be. You were Walter's girl."

"And you are his brother. You will always be dear to me."

"I loved my Katie Ann, and I haven't met a woman

who could replace her in my heart. I know my folks wanted me and you to be happy together, but this sure wasn't the way."

"Apparently not."

He slapped his hat on his head. "Good day to you. Is it okay if I still take you and your mother to church on Sundays?"

"Of course." How was her mother going to take this news?

"Much obliged. It doesn't feel right traveling to church alone. I'll pick you up at seven sharp tomorrow. The meeting is at Verna Yoder's place."

"You're welcome to stay for supper afterward, too. Anytime."

"*Danki*. That's real nice. I'm glad we had this talk."

He drove away, and it was as if a heavy blanket had been lifted off Rebecca. Shaking her head at the oddity of the whole conversation, she walked through the house headed for the back porch. She pushed open the door. Samuel lay crumpled in a heap beside the table.

Chapter Twelve

Something cold and wet covered his face.

Samuel reached up to pull it down, but someone stopped him. "Leave it on for a few more minutes."

It was Rebecca trying to boss him around again. He was done with that. He yanked the cloth off and threw it aside. He kept his eyes closed tight. He didn't want a repeat of his earlier experience. "I don't need another few minutes."

Had he seen the sky or had he been dreaming? He was afraid to try again. "Where are my glasses?"

"Right here." She laid them on his chest. Fumbling, he managed to get them on and sit up.

"Samuel what happened?"

"I had a dizzy spell."

"Have they happened before?" She had that tone in her voice. The one she used when she was digging for medical information.

"A few times."

"I knew you were keeping something from me."

"How long was I out?"

"Not more than three minutes after I found you. Do you remember anything that might have triggered this?"

Like finding out another man wanted to marry her? "No. Can I get up off the floor now?"

"I don't know if you can, but you may."

"Don't be funny. It's not working at the moment."

"I'm sorry. You're right. Should I go get your mother or one of your brothers?"

He heaved himself to his feet, a little surprised to find he was quite steady. "I don't think they can do anything you haven't done."

"Samuel, I don't think you are being honest with me." He wasn't even being honest with himself. The concern in her voice was genuine. He had no right to worry her.

"This is the third time it's happened, but it's the first time I blacked out."

"You are going to the doctor straightaway."

"Luke has already made an appointment for me. I see the doctor on Monday."

"I guess that will have to do. How are you feeling now?"

"Foolish."

"I don't know why. Very few people have control over their ability to faint."

What about their ability to fall head over heels for a bossy, caring, infuriating widow?

"You haven't been exactly honest with me, either."

"I don't know what you mean."

"John shared his reason for his visit today."

"He didn't."

"Are you going to keep me in suspense until the *banns* are read in church?"

She slapped the wet towel on the back of his neck. It felt good, actually. "I am not going to marry John or anyone else."

His heart gave a happy leap. "You aren't? You turned him down?"

"John and I will continue to be friends. Nothing more."

Relief made him dizzy all over again. He still had a chance. He might have seen blue sky. He might have imagined it. He needed to know for sure before he spoke about his feelings.

He reached out and she took his hand. "I'm sorry that John wasn't the one for you. You deserve to be happy."

She pulled her hand away. "I am happy, but thank you. We need to tell your family about what happened today."

"Really? You want everyone to know you refused John?"

"Don't be funny. It's not working at the moment."

He wanted to make her laugh. It didn't work, but he thought he detected a smile in her voice. He would settle for that. "I don't want to alarm my family."

"How much more alarmed will they be if they discover you in the same condition I did?"

She had a point. "All right, I agree they should know."

Rebecca remained in the background when Samuel shared a watered-down version of his episode that evening when his family came in from the fields. Only his parents appeared to be shocked. The looks shared between his brothers told her they had already discussed the previous episode Luke had witnessed.

It wasn't until she was home and in her own bed that night that the shock of what happened really hit her. The sight of him sprawled across the porch floor would stay with her for a long time. It had taken an eternity to reach his side and make sure he was still breathing. Images of Walter's illness and death swirled through her mind. She couldn't do it again. She couldn't face the possibility of losing someone she loved.

Of losing Samuel.

She had to admit she was already half in love with him. It wouldn't take much to push her over the edge. The question became what could she do about it.

Leaving her employment there was the first step, but she would still see him at every Sunday service, every picnic, every barn raising and school Christmas program.

Only one viable solution presented itself. She could travel to Hope Springs and begin training with Mary's mother. A clinic for special needs children would be the perfect place to follow her calling, and a good place to forget about Samuel Bowman.

She rose hollow-eyed and exhausted from a sleepless night and got ready for church. Her mother and John arrived promptly at seven. She could tell by the look on her mother's face that John had already spilled the beans.

As she climbed in the buggy, her mother squeezed her arm. "I'm so sorry for pressuring you to marry John. He explained that he felt pressured by his family, too. You made the right choice."

"Danki." The right choice yesterday, for what would her mother's reaction be when she told her about her

new intentions. Rebecca decided to save that conversation until they were alone.

During the service, Rebecca kept a watchful eye on Samuel, but he didn't have any problems. Afterward, she was serving the last half of the meal to the younger members when Timothy approached her.

"Could I have a word with you when you are finished here? I'll be out by the greenhouse."

Puzzled, she nodded and Timothy left. Twenty minutes later, she located him sitting on a bale of straw. "What's going on? Is Samuel worse?"

"He's the same. Two weeks ago, you tried to tell us about a plan you had for our business. Samuel wouldn't listen to you then. I'm listening now. What's your idea?"

"It's going to take more than your family to make my idea work. We are going to need the bishop and elders to support this and agree. Do you think you can arrange a meeting for tomorrow afternoon?"

"I can try, but Samuel has a doctor's appointment. Do you want to wait until he can be there?"

"I don't want it put to him until I'm sure the community is on board."

He took a step back. "What are you planning? The takeover of the *Englisch* government?"

"Honestly, that might be easier."

A meeting was hastily arranged, and Rebecca was able to present her idea to a large group in Isaac's living room. Initially, there wasn't overwhelming support, but eventually she made them see the benefit of what she had planned.

Rebecca finished speaking just as Joshua drove into the yard with Samuel in the buggy.

Anna spoke up quickly. "I don't want Samuel to know what we are doing. If what we have to show Mr. Clark isn't what he wants in his stores, then there's no harm done and Samuel never has to know."

Isaac gave a long thoughtful pause. "You mean well, Anna, but I'm not sure I agree with that. A man must learn to face both hope and disappointment in his life. What do you think, Rebecca?"

"Samuel is stronger than he knows. He can face this. He must. It is his dream that we are tampering with."

"She's right, Anna, and you know it." Isaac glanced around the room. "You raised five strong sons. They are not without their flaws, but they are good men in my eyes. Each and every one of them. Rebecca, step out and ask Samuel to come inside. We are anxious to hear what the doctor had to say."

Samuel had hold of Joshua's arm as they approached the steps. Rebecca couldn't keep silent any longer. "What did he say?"

"That there is nothing physically wrong with my eyes." Samuel's terse tone showed his frustration.

"Your parents have company. They would like to talk to you."

"Who is it?"

"The bishop, your uncles and their wives. Some of your mother's kin."

"A crowd. Did I forget someone's birthday? Is it *Mamm's*?"

"You didn't miss her birthday. They have something they wish to discuss with you. A business venture of sorts."

"Of sorts? What does that mean?"

"Come in and see."

* * *

What was Rebecca up to now?

Samuel paused in the doorway to the kitchen. He could feel the crush of bodies in the room. This was more than a few visitors. "What's going on?"

"Come here, Samuel," his father said. Rebecca took his arm and led him to a seat in the living room.

"Who is here?" Samuel asked, staring straight ahead.

One by one, the visitors announced their names. The bishop spoke last. "We have come with a favor to ask of you."

"Of me? I'm not sure what help I can be to anyone."

"Rebecca has presented an idea and we want your opinion of it," the bishop said.

"Rebecca has?" Samuel turned unerringly toward her. He always seemed to know where she was in a room.

"It was my idea, but I don't know if it has merit," she admitted.

"I'm listening."

His father cleared his throat. Whatever it was, he seemed unsure of how to proceed. He drew a deep breath. "We have talked about rebuilding our workshop for our family, but it seems that we have many more people interested in this venture."

Samuel cocked his head slightly. "I don't understand."

"You had hoped to employ your brothers in the workshop making furniture for an *Englisch* firm, is that so?" It was the bishop.

"I did."

"I have some questions about this plan. Was your goal to make money? Or was it something else? If financial gain was the sole reason for the venture, that is not compatible with our beliefs. I cannot condone those efforts. But, I'm willing to listen to what you have to say."

Samuel struggled to put his fading dream into words. "It was never about making money so that we could grow wealthy. My only hope was to provide a living for my brothers so they would marry and raise families here. We all know there isn't enough farmland for our young people. I have seen Amish carpentry businesses that flourished near towns and employed dozens of workers, but not in a rural area such as ours. The *Englisch* can use their internet to show what we make here all around the world. They could take orders, we would build and ship what we make and the *Englisch* would rarely have to come to our place of business. It seemed like the perfect plan."

"I believe your motives are in the best interest of our church and I think the church elders are in agreement with me. We are hoping you can employ more than just your brothers. We have seven young men who will have to leave this area soon to find work elsewhere. None of us wants to see that happen."

Samuel shook his head. "Bishop, even after we rebuild the shop, it won't be big enough to need so many workers."

"But it could be made larger," Rebecca said.

"With better equipment," Timothy added.

"It could," Samuel admitted. "Any building can be made larger. But what is the point if we don't have a place to sell what we make?"

"You already have a man willing to buy what you make. Mr. Clark," Rebecca said quietly.

Samuel threw up his hands. "*Nee*, I do not. He was

willing to come and look over our inventory. We have none."

"That is not true." His mother spoke for the first time. "I have the wooden bench you made for my birthday last year and the china cabinet in the living room. My niece has the table and chairs you finished for her wedding gift. It was on the wagon and not harmed in the fire."

"I have the Bible stand you made for Walter. It's a remarkable piece. The carving is done in deep relief and the lines of it are beautiful." Rebecca spoke softly.

They all wanted so much to help. How could he make them understand how pointless it was? "I can't very well ask this man to travel to every home in our church district to look at a scattering of furniture."

"You won't have to."

He turned toward Rebecca's voice. There was an undercurrent of excitement in her tone. "What do you mean?"

"On Thursday, every household in this church district and many from the neighboring districts will be here to help with the workshop raising. They'll come in wagons with tools and supplies and they can bring their furniture with them. All we will have to do is assemble it where Mr. Clark can look it over."

She made it sound almost logical. A curl of optimism began to form in his chest. "What if it rains?"

"We'll bring the tents and awnings we use at the farmer's market," someone said from the back of the room. A murmur of assent followed his words.

How could he get their hopes up? What if his work wasn't up to the standards of this unknown man? "What if he decides he doesn't want to purchase furniture from us?"

Someone laid a hand on his shoulder. "Then we shall have a fine new workshop thanks to the generous spirit of our friends and neighbors and we'll have a *goot* time raising it," his father said. "What more could we ask? If this is *Gott's* will, it shall be so."

Samuel wasn't convinced. "Mr. Clark might not even come. He knows what happened here."

"I'll convince him," Timothy said. "I can be very persuasive when I put my mind to it."

Samuel couldn't believe what was happening. He was being given a second chance at fulfilling his dream. Not just for his family, but for other young men in his community who didn't want to leave. If his sight didn't return, he would have to depend on others to carry on the bulk of the work. It was no longer about his skill, but about the skill of those around him.

"All right, but I won't be making furniture for a while, if ever. I want people to bring Father's work and Timothy's work, too, so we can showcase it. I want the table and chairs you made for that *Englisch* family over by Berlin."

"The Rock family?"

"That's the one. It was good work. Your best. See if you can get it here. Luke, you made a chest for the doctor's office. Ask if you can borrow it for a day."

"It wasn't a typical Amish piece," Luke said. He had been sitting quietly at Samuel's side. "All the drawers are different sizes and shapes.

"I know, but it is well crafted and eye-catching. You've all made a number of pieces. Track them down and get them here. It can't be about my work. It has to be about *our* work." Excitement began to build inside Samuel. Where was his mother? "*Mamm*?"

"What, *sohn*?"

She was across the table from him. He reached out his hand and she took it. "This whole thing is going to rest on your shoulders," he said as seriously as he could manage.

"On mine? How?"

"If Mr. Clark comes, you will have to soften him up with your *wunderbarr* cooking. Once he is in a state of lemon meringue bliss, he won't be able to say no to our proposal."

A round of laughter followed his teasing. A flurry of discussion and details followed. It was growing late by the time everyone went home. At last, there was only Luke in the kitchen with him. "Do you know where Rebecca went?" Samuel asked.

"I saw her go out the back door a little while ago. Do you want me to find her?"

"*Nee*, I think I know where she is. I want to thank you, Luke."

"For what?"

"For believing in me even after I failed to believe in you."

"Who said I believe this harebrained scheme will work?"

"You did."

"When?"

"When you sat shoulder to shoulder with me and listened to all my doubts without agreeing with any of them."

"Maybe I was waiting until we were alone."

"We're alone now. Do you think it can be done?"

"Building a workshop? Sure."

"I meant keeping this family together. I meant keeping you here with us."

"You know I'm not fond of living in the dark ages. I like the city lights. Having a business that will support a number of families will keep Timothy and Joshua here. Noah, I'm not so sure about him. I know he's the one who will eventually inherit the place, but he has a bit of wanderlust in his heart."

"As long as there are horses on this farm, Noah will stick around. I'm not worried about him. If you have to go, Luke, I'll understand this time and I won't hold it against you."

"I'll stay until I see how this harebrained scheme plays out. Longer than that? Who knows?"

Samuel reached out to find his brother's shoulder. "God does."

Seated on the low stone wall beside the river, Rebecca watched the sunset behind the covered bridge. The last faint rays of light came through the wooden slats in bands of brightness filled with spiraling dust motes.

"Rebecca?"

She heard his low query behind her. Tempted to remain silent and let him go away, she closed her eyes.

"I know you are here. Please answer me."

"How do you know?" she asked without opening her eyes. She was aware of him, too, even when she couldn't see him.

"I hoped you were." He felt his way along the wall and took a seat beside her. "What does the river look like tonight?"

"It's gray and muddy."

"*Nee*, it isn't."

"If you know, why did you ask?"

"Because I want to know what you see when you look out from here."

She sighed. It was going to be so hard to leave, but going away was for the best. Every time she crossed the bridge in the future, she would think about sitting here and watching the sun go down or seeing the moon cast rippling silver light all the way to the water's edge.

"Take pity on me and tell me what you see."

"I don't pity you, Samuel. In some ways, you are more blessed than most."

"I am blessed, but I miss my old friend the river. How is he?"

"The sun is setting behind the bridge. There is a stream of golden light running toward us from beneath the timbers. Spears of light are shining through the sides of the bridge now. It looks as if the sun is inside it."

"It must make the colors of the trees glow like fire. The reds are redder and the yellow leaves are bright golden in the light. There are dozens of them floating along in the water, turning this way and that."

She glanced at him sharply, wishing he wasn't wearing dark glasses and that she could see his eyes. "Can you see them?"

"*Nee*, but I know what the river looks like this time of year. I remember. Was it truly your idea to gather up my work to show Mr. Clark?"

She pulled on the ribbons of her *kapp*. "I had the idea, but your father and Timothy worked out most of the details."

"I'm afraid what we have to offer won't be what he wants."

"He won't be able to take any of it back with him. Will that make a difference?"

"The time I spoke with him he mentioned that his plan was to photograph the work and build an online and print catalog where people could order similar items but customize them."

"That makes me feel better."

"I wish I could say the same."

She took his hand in hers and held it to her cheek. "Have faith, Samuel. I have faith in you and the gift God has placed in you."

He pulled his hand away. "I no longer have the gift He gave me."

"You do. You just have to find a new way to use it that will glorify God."

The urge to take her in his arms and kiss her was almost more than Samuel could bear. He rose to his feet and took a step away. She was kind and sweet and full of life. Being near her made him think about a future that couldn't be. Not unless he regained his sight. She had already lost one husband. She deserved a whole man. Not John, but someone she could love as she had Walter. He wouldn't ask her to settle for less.

He moved another step away. "I appreciate your confidence, but I'm not sure it's well-placed."

"Tomorrow will be my last day here, Samuel."

He knew it was coming. "You'll be missed."

Did she have any idea what she did to him? He couldn't think clearly when she was so near.

"I've enjoyed my time here. I proved Verna Yoder wrong. You weren't a bad patient."

He smiled because he knew she wanted him to. He blinked back the sting of tears and squeezed his eyes shut.

When he opened them, her face swam into focus. There were tears on her cheeks.

His breath froze in his chest. There wasn't any pain this time. He took in her delicate beauty, her white-blond hair beneath her *kapp*, the small white scar on her chin. He wanted to shout for joy.

He blinked again, and she was gone. Nothing but blackness surrounded him.

For a second, the despair nearly overwhelmed him, but he hung on to one ray of hope. The stars, the blue sky, her face, they were real. His vision was recovering.

Should he tell her?

What if it was a fluke? What if that glimpse was all he ever had of her face?

He would wait to be sure before he mentioned it, but he had hope for the first time in weeks.

The morning of the workshop raising dawned clear and bright. The chance of storms never materialized. Before the sun rose, wagon after wagon began arriving loaded with lumber, ladders, well-wrapped pieces of furniture and entire families from grandparents to new babies. *Englisch* as well as Amish families came to share in the work.

Mary darted forward in excitement when she saw a white SUV turn in. Hannah clapped her hands. "That's Papa Nick and *Mammi* Miriam. I hope they brought Bella." She ran after her mother, and Rebecca watched a happy reunion take place between the child and a big yellow dog.

Buggies and carts continued to come and soon a long line of them bordered the driveway. The corrals were crowded with horses and the lawn was overrun with children, while the men set up long trestle tables and tents and the women brought out mountains of food.

The foundation of the building had been poured the week before and the concrete slab was dry. The ring of hammers filled the air as the walls were assembled. When the first one was ready, Noah brought out a team and hitched them to a rope attached to the top of the wall. At a word from Isaac, he put the team in motion. The animals leaned into the collars as they pulled the wooden structure upright aided by a dozen men leveraging long poles. The poles were then braced into the ground to hold the wall steady until it could be secured. The adjoining wall went up the same way, and by noon, the skeleton of a building was standing where only empty ground had been the week before.

At Samuel's suggestion, the building site had been moved closer to the highway to make deliveries of lumber easier. A gravel parking lot would be added for cars and trucks when the building was complete.

Rebecca stared at the building being finished before her eyes by an army of men swarming over it. Soon the siding would go on and the young boys would be recruited to start painting. Where was their furniture buyer?

Mary came to Rebecca with a tall *Englisch* woman at her side and introduced her as her adoptive mother, Miriam Bradley. Rebecca shook her hand. "I'm pleased to meet you."

"Mary tells me you are interested in working with us in Hope Springs. We'd love to have you."

"Truly?"

"Mary tells me you've done a lot of lay nursing already. I can't guarantee you a job, but I can promise you an interview with our doctors. Just show up."

Glancing toward Samuel handing boards to others from the back of a wagon, Rebecca hesitated. She cared so much for him. The longer she stayed the more her love would grow. She turned to Miriam. "I'll be there as soon as I can get a bus ticket."

"Wonderful."

Rebecca worked beside Anna as they got ready to serve lunch to nearly one hundred people. She tried to keep her mind on her tasks, but she couldn't keep her gaze away from the highway. Where was Mr. Clark? Why wasn't he here yet? Had he found another carpenter to supply his needs?

An *Englisch* fellow with a gourd birdhouse under his arm strolled up to Anna. He was wearing faded jeans and a green plaid shirt with the sleeves rolled up. He had a tool belt on and wore a pair of worn work boots. "Are you the woman I see about buying one of these? I took it off the tree out by the highway, but it didn't feel right to leave the money there. Aren't you afraid someone will steal it?"

Anna smiled at him. "If they do, then they need the money much worse than I do. All the birdhouses have been paid for, and all the money has been there each morning when I check. If you treat people honestly, they will behave honestly."

He handed over several bills. "That is an interesting

philosophy. I'm not sure it's one my stockbroker could live by, but I think you're right."

"Bless you for coming to help my family rebuild."

"It's been my pleasure. I've always wanted to attend an Amish barn raising. This was as close as I could get. It felt great to pound some nails. It's been a while. The craftsmanship going into that simple building is amazing. I think it will be standing long after I'm gone."

"God willing, sir. God willing. Let me fix you a plate of food. You must be hungry after all your work this morning."

"I am. Thank you."

Rebecca looked again toward the road. Samuel stood beside his father at the end of the driveway. Noah and Timothy were patting each other on the back and grinning.

Anna handed the workman a plate piled high with fried chicken, fresh corn on the cob and creamy mashed potatoes. He smiled broadly at the sight. "My cardiologist would have a heart attack just looking at this."

"Hard work deserved *goot* food. I'm Anna Bowman."

He nodded. "I'm James Clark, and you have some fabulous pieces of furniture assembled here, Mrs. Bowman."

Noah came charging through the crowd and skidded to a stop beside his mother. He whispered something in her ear. Anna's eyes brightened at his words. She slapped her hands to her face. "God be praised. Praise His holy name."

Chapter Thirteen

Samuel sat with his family at the kitchen table late that evening. He was bone tired but too excited and happy to head to bed. "Rebecca's plan was a success. Mr. Clark not only liked what he saw in furniture, he liked the layout of the workshop and made some excellent suggestions about tools and equipment that could be purchased at a later date."

"When the contracts are signed, we will have orders for twenty-five pieces worth hundreds of dollars and the promise of more work once the website and online catalog are updated." Timothy sounded happy enough to jump for joy.

"It was a long day, but a *goot* one," Anna said with a deep sigh.

Noah held up his left hand. "My thumb is sore."

Luke laughed. "You are supposed to hit the nail with the hammer, not your thumb."

"Ha, ha. Yours is black-and-blue, too."

"Because some fool stepped on it when I was climbing the ladder."

"Who are you calling a fool?" Timothy demanded.

"Was that you? I could've fallen to my death if I had lost my grip."

Samuel removed his dark glasses and rubbed his eyes. "You couldn't have fallen to your death. You were standing on the ground at the time, and you stuck your hand right where Timothy was coming down."

"How did you know I was standing on the ground?" Luke grumbled.

"Actually, I saw the whole thing."

His brothers chuckled at the joke. Samuel folded his glasses and tucked them in his pocket. "You have some mashed potatoes on your dress, Mother."

"Do I?" She brushed at her chest. "I always end up with something down the front of me."

Noah's eyes grew round. "Do you really see the potatoes, Samuel?"

"What?" Anna stopped cleaning the spot and gazed at her son. "Are you making a joke?"

"I can't see everything. It's like looking through the bottom of a canning jar, but I can see you."

Everyone began talking at once. Anna broke into tears. When the first rush of astonishment died down, Luke waved his hand in front of Samuel's eyes. "How many fingers do you see?"

"Five and they need to be washed."

"When did it come back?" Isaac asked.

"Last night. I was down by the river talking to Rebecca and I saw her face for a second before everything went dark again. Actually, I had seen flashes before, but they were so painful I didn't know what was happening. When I woke up this morning, I could see where the window was, but not much else. On and off throughout the day it would come and go. About seven o'clock, it stopped fading to gray and stayed bright. I've been waiting for it to go away again, but it hasn't. I didn't see the potatoes until just now, *Mamm*."

He wished Rebecca were here to share his joy.

"God is great, and God is good." Isaac declared. "Let us bow our heads and give thanks for the many blessings we have seen today."

Samuel voiced his deepest fear. "I don't know if I'll still be able to see when I wake up tomorrow."

"That bridge cannot be crossed until you reach it, Samuel." Isaac bowed his head and the entire family followed his lead.

The next morning, Samuel reluctantly opened his eyes and focused on the ceiling above him.

"Well?"

He turned his head to the side and saw all four of his brothers seated beside his bed. "Your faces are the scariest things I've ever seen."

They all grinned.

"What's on the agenda for today?" Noah asked. "Harvest is over. The workshop is built but we don't have enough lumber to start anything. I say we go fishing down at the river."

"Seconded." Joshua raised his hand.

Samuel sat up and stretched. He couldn't remember the last time he'd slept so well or felt so strong in the morning. "You guys will have to go without me. I've got something I have to do first."

"He's got to go see Re-bec-ca. I smell a romance." Timothy winked.

Joshua's grin faded. "I'm not sure Rebecca is still here."

Samuel let his arms fall to his sides. "What do you mean?"

"Mary said Rebecca was leaving on the bus today. She's joining Mary's mother at the special needs clinic in Hope Springs."

"She wouldn't go without saying goodbye." Samuel glared at his brothers. "Get out of here. I've got to get dressed."

Packing took less time than her breakfast, and that had only been a cup of coffee.

Rebecca folded her last pair of socks and put them in the suitcase. She owned four work dresses and two good ones. The deep blue one she was wearing at the moment was her Sunday best. She would wear it on the bus. *Kapps*, aprons and assorted articles of clothing went in next.

With each addition to the pile, she grew less and less certain that she was doing the right thing.

How was Samuel today? Was he happy with the success he had achieved? Were his eyes bothering him? Had he had any more spells? Was he taking care of himself or was he ignoring her advice to wear gloves?

Did he miss her the way she missed him?

That was a foolish question.

They were all foolish questions. Samuel wasn't her patient anymore. He was a friend. They would wave when they saw each other on the road. He might speak to her when she served his meal after church, but their lives would drift apart. The closeness they shared would fade. It had to. Unless it did, she was going to be miserable for many, many years.

"Rebecca, do you want me to pack any of your books?" her mother called from downstairs.

Her mother was helping close up the house until they found someone to rent it. She hoped it would be a young couple with children. A home should have children to make it feel loved.

She heard her mother coming up the stairs. Rebecca wiped the tears from her eyes and started folding her handkerchiefs.

"What are you doing?" Samuel's voice froze her in place. Why hadn't her mother warned her he was coming up?

Rebecca couldn't face him. She fought to hold back her tears and keep her voice steady. "I have a new job in Hope Springs. I'm moving there. I'm so excited."

"You don't sound excited."

She cleared her throat. "I am. What are you doing here?"

"I came by to tell you the good news."

"I heard Mr. Clark say he was going to place his orders with you. That's wonderful."

"My vision has come back, Rebecca."

She closed her eyes and pressed her hands to her mouth. "I couldn't be happier for you. That's wonderful. God is good. I told you to have faith."

There was a moment of awkward silence. She almost turned around, but she didn't.

"Do you want to leave?" he asked quietly.

"I'm following my heart's desire."

"What about us?"

She sniffed and pressed the clothes flat in the case. "You're well. You don't need me anymore."

"I reckon it's true enough that I'm well. I can see

almost as good as I used to. My hands are still tender, but I can work if I'm careful."

She began packing her jars of herbs into her satchel. "They will get better, too. Don't forget to rub my salve on them. It will help."

"What potion do you have for my heart, Rebecca?"

She paused but still couldn't turn around. She heard him step closer. The nerves in her skin sprang to life. He was so close that if she leaned back she could rest against his chest as she had done that night by the covered bridge.

"There's nothing wrong with your heart, Samuel."

"But there is, and you are the cause."

"I never meant to hurt you."

"You're hurting me now. I want to spend my life proving how much I care for you. Tell them you've changed your mind. Stay here. Please, don't go.

Oh, how she longed to remain in Bowmans Crossing and be near him. Only it couldn't be. He deserved a woman who could love him without fear. Without dread holding her back as it held Rebecca back now.

She fixed a smile on her face and turned around. "I can't stay. I want to take this job."

He looked stunned. Her fingers itched to caress his face, to ease his pain, but she curled them into a tight ball. His voice wavered when he spoke. "I know I can't replace Walter, and I don't want you to forget him. Do you care for me at all?"

"I'll always hold our friendship dear, but my husband still holds my heart." It wasn't true anymore, but she couldn't admit it.

"I'm sorry I bothered you." Samuel turned away, but

paused with his hand on the doorknob. "I bid you farewell, Rebecca Miller."

"Goodbye, Samuel."

When he closed the door behind him, Rebecca spun around and threw herself onto her bed. The tears she had struggled to hold back broke free, and she sobbed as if her heart were breaking. She was still sobbing when her mother came in a short time later.

"There, there. Don't cry, child." *Mamm* gathered her close and held her until her tears finally ran dry. Rebecca's sobs tapered into occasional hiccups.

Mamm put a hand under Rebecca's chin and lifted her face. "You refused Samuel, didn't you?"

Rebecca sniffed and nodded. "Did he say something?"

"Nothing needed to be said. I could tell from the way the light had left his eyes that you turned him down. I hoped and prayed that you had found love again, Rebecca. I'm rarely mistaken about these things. Do you love Samuel, or has John claimed your heart?"

"I don't love John. I'm sure of that. I'm not sure that I love Samuel, but I think I do."

"Then why send him away?"

"When Walter died I almost died, too. I wanted to lie down on his grave and never get up. I wanted the snow to cover me and numb all my heartbreak. Living alone is better than risking such pain again."

"Nonsense!" Her mother scowled at her.

"What if I accepted Samuel's offer of marriage and I found I didn't love him as I should? How unfair would that be if Walter were always between us? Samuel would grow to hate that. I had a wonderful husband, but he is gone. My calling now is to care for others."

"I understand fear, child. I understand that it is hard to trust that God knows best. Yes, you have suffered a great loss, Rebecca. No one can deny that, but to believe God wants you to spend your life without love is folly. Surely you believe in God's boundless love."

"Of course I do."

"He loves us beyond all understanding."

"What do you want me to say?"

"I hear you saying the right things, but do you truly believe them?"

Did she? Why was it so hard to believe God would bring love back into her life and not whisk it from her?

"Rebecca you have to make a choice. Will you let love or fear rule your heart? You can give your fear over to God, or live a shadow of the life He has planned for you."

"I rejected Samuel. There's nothing more to say."

"Tell me one thing. In all the days you were with Samuel, taking care of him, working to make his business dream a reality, spending time alone with him, how many of those moments did you feel Walter standing between you?"

"Never."

"I thought so. You are the only person standing in the way of your happiness. Stop blaming Walter. Stop hiding behind your fear of loss.

Rebecca closed her eyes. She had made such a mess of things. "What do I do?"

"Find Samuel and tell him what's in your heart. That's all you can do. And pray."

She didn't love him.

Samuel took refuge from his family's prying eyes

on the banks of the river below the covered bridge. He realized as he stared into the water sweeping past that it wasn't the best choice of hideouts. There were too many memories associated with this place.

He remembered the nights when he and Rebecca sat in companionable silence on the stone wall or teased each other with glee. He could almost hear the sound of her laughter in the gurgling water. He could feel the peace she brought him in the warmth of the sun overhead. It was impossible to imagine life without her.

What could he have done differently? What could he have said that would've convinced her of his love? He knew the answers. Rebecca had made her choice and nothing he said or did would change that. He prayed for her happiness even as he knew it would be a long time before he felt joy again.

He stared at the reflection of the bridge in the water. It was like the future he had dreamed of with Rebecca. It was pretty to look at, but a man couldn't cross the river through it.

Movement in the reflection caught his eye. Someone was walking on the bridge. He saw glimpses of a blue dress moving between the slatted sides. It took a second for him to realize the woman had stopped moving. She was staring over the railing at the water below. The current kept her face from coming into focus. It was easy to imagine it was Rebecca looking down at him, because that was what he wanted with his whole heart and soul.

He picked up a stone and threw it in. The ripples distorted everything. When the water settled, the woman was gone. Maybe his eyes were playing tricks on him again.

No, she wasn't gone. He looked closer and then looked up. Rebecca stood staring at him over the railing. His heart thudded so hard that he feared it couldn't keep beating. She was here. She hadn't left.

Why was she here?

"Samuel, I need to speak with you. I'm so sorry. I was afraid, and I hurt you. Can you forgive me?"

He sprang to his feet. "What are you saying? Never mind, I'm coming up."

"No, stay there. I'm coming down." She vanished from his sight and for a moment, he wondered if she had been a hallucination.

He bolted up the bank toward the road just as she started down. He wasn't dreaming. She was real.

The footing on the hillside was treacherous. In her haste, she lost her balance and tumbled forward, straight into him. The impact knocked him backward. He staggered but managed to stay upright.

She was in his arms at last. He had dreamed of this moment. He didn't want to breathe. She gazed up at him with wide startled eyes. The desire to press his lips to hers overrode his better judgment, and he kissed her.

After the briefest hesitation, her lips softened and yielded to his and she was kissing him back. His heart soared and he didn't care if it was beating or not. He could have died from happiness. He never wanted to let her go. The glorious kiss went on until his body demanded air.

He drew back and the rush of passion settled enough for him to make sense of what was happening. "I love you, Rebecca, but I thought you were leaving."

"I couldn't go without telling you that I love you,

too. I'm sorry I turned you away. I won't turn you away again. Ever."

He cupped her cheeks in his hands. "I can't believe that I'm holding you."

"I can't believe that I almost let you slip away."

"You said that you were afraid. Of what? I would never hurt you."

"I was afraid to reach for happiness again. I was afraid it would be taken away and I would be left alone. Then I realized that if I didn't reach for it, for you, I was still going to be alone. I want to share every minute of my life with you for however long God grants us."

He kissed her again and then enfolded her in his embrace and held her tight. Nothing had ever felt as right as this moment. "Thank you for being brave, my love. Thank God for bringing you into my life and giving me the chance to see how wonderful you really are." He kissed the top of her bonnet.

"You are the one who gave me the strength to try." She raised her face to his in a silent invitation and he gladly complied.

Rebecca couldn't believe the joy swelling her heart. He loved her and she loved him, too. She knew Walter was watching from Heaven and smiling on her.

"*Onkel* Luke, look! *Onkel* Samuel is kissing Rebecca!"

She and Samuel looked up to see Hannah leaning over the bridge railing staring at them with startled eyes. A second later, Luke appeared.

He propped his elbows on the wooden rail. "It's about time. I thought I was going to have to hog-tie the two of you together."

Heat rushed to Rebecca's face, and she hid it against Samuel's chest. How embarrassing.

Samuel waved him off. "Go away. I'm busy, as you can see."

Luke didn't move. "Don't mind me. Just pretend I'm not even here."

Rebecca chuckled and glanced up. "Don't you have work to do?"

"Nope. Hannah, do you have work to do?"

The child shook her head. "I don't have a job, *Onkel* Luke. I'm too little. Should we tell *Mamm* and *Daed* about this?"

He took her hand. "We should definitely tell. Come on. Let's go find them."

They vanished from sight and Rebecca pressed her face to Samuel's neck again. He was so strong, and he smelled wonderful. She knew she would never tire of being held by him. "How much time do you think we have?"

"Sixty years or so. Why?" He slipped a finger under her chin and lifted her face.

"I meant until your brothers show up."

"Two or three minutes."

"Then you had better kiss me again, Samuel Bowman, before we are interrupted."

"Have I mentioned that you're bossy?"

She giggled at the memories of their early times together. "A time or two."

"Have I told you how much I love you?"

His voice, so deep with emotion, sent a thrill of joy pouring over her. "Not nearly enough."

"I love you, Rebecca Miller. God has blessed me

beyond my wildest dreams. I think I'm going to have to marry you."

"You come up with the best ideas." She cupped his cheek with her hand. His scars were fading, but he would always carry a reminder of the events that brought them together.

"Will you?" he asked.

"Will I what?"

"Don't tease me. Will you marry me?"

"Is that the only way I'll get another kiss?"

"If you say yes, you'll get a lifetime of kisses thrown in for free."

"Then how can I refuse such a deal?"

His eyes grew serious and he pulled back a little. "Are you sure? I don't want you to regret this decision. My sight may fail again. Our business may not prosper as I hope. I want you to be happy. I don't want to tie you to a failure."

"Are you trying to talk me out of it now?"

"Maybe. Holding you feels too good to be true."

"Shall I toss some water on you to prove I'm really here?"

"You would, wouldn't you? What was I thinking to propose beside a river?"

She smiled as she placed both hands on his cheeks. "I know you are afraid of losing your sight. I'm afraid of losing you. How can we honor God in our lives if we live in fear of what may happen to us? I love you. God brought me love when I thought I could never feel it again. If today is the only day I'm given to show you how much I love you, then it will be enough."

He kissed her forehead and then her eyes, and she rejoiced in the tender touch of his lips against her skin.

He pulled her tight against his chest and whispered, "I will never tire of your wisdom, Rebecca."

"And I will never tire of being in your arms. I'm going to trust God to make our lives joyful. I'm going to trust that he will give us children to love and years to work together side by side. I know He is going to give us obstacles to overcome and trials to endure, but I will do my best to make you a good wife if you will have me."

"I can't ask for more."

"Then we have a deal?"

"We do." He kissed her soundly to seal the bargain. Wrapped up in each other's arms, they didn't notice two more witnesses standing on the back porch of the house.

Isaac, a twinkle in his eye, pulled his wife close and gave her a peck on the cheek. "Two sons matched and only three more to go. The Bowman bachelors are falling fast."

Epilogue

The last Thursday in November

"So you're really going to go through with this?"

Samuel chose to ignore Luke's question and raised his chin. "Button this stubborn button for me and then button your lip."

Luke chuckled. "I'm not the fellow with shaky hands. All I'm saying is that I have a fast horse and buggy outside if you need one."

Run away from a life with Rebecca as his wife?

Never.

As quickly as they had come on, Samuel's unexpected jitters fled. He drew a deep breath and flicked Luke's wide-rimmed black hat off his head. "The only need I have for a fast horse is to carry me to my wedding that much quicker."

Luke caught his hat before it hit the floor and settled it on again. "Then I'm at your service, *brudder*. Let's hope the bride feels the same."

Samuel pulled his new black coat on over his white

shirt and quickly tied his black bow tie. "She does. I've no cause to doubt her. God chose us to love and care for each other."

He picked up a small packet from his bedside table and tucked it inside his vest, then he led the way downstairs and out onto the porch where Timothy, Noah and Joshua waiting. They were all dressed alike in dark trousers, white shirts, dark coats and wide-rimmed black hats. They all sported the same foolish grin Samuel knew he was wearing.

Joshua stepped forward to brush a speck of dust from Samuel's shoulder. "Did Luke give you his 'I've got a fast horse' speech?"

"He did."

Luke shook his head as he walked past and paused at the top of the steps with his thumbs hooked under his suspenders. "He gave me the same answer you did, Joshua. I don't get it. I can't imagine a woman who would make me want to settle down and live my entire life in Bowmans Crossing."

Samuel shared a smile with his married younger brother. "I pray I live to see the day he does find her."

Noah pushed Luke off the step. "I pray for the poor woman who thinks she wants a lazy good-for-nothing like you."

Luke whirled around with his hands clenched into fists, but there wasn't any malice in his eyes, only a good-natured invitation to start some fun. The entire family had been up since four-thirty getting ready for the wedding day. The cows had been milked, the stock had been fed and the buggy had been washed. The men were all dressed in their Sunday best. Samuel's parents had left hours ago to help with the wedding feast preparations at Rebecca's home, where the wedding would take place. It was almost seven-thirty and time to be on their way.

Samuel stepped between his brothers and put a hand on each one's chest. "Get me to my wedding before you get into a wrestling match. Please."

Timothy had already climbed in the waiting buggy and held the reins. "If Rebecca wants to marry into this family, she's one brave woman."

His heart pounding with happiness, Samuel hopped in beside Timothy, leaving the others to jostle for position in the back. "*Ja*, Rebecca is that and so much more than I deserve. God has truly blessed me."

"I'm such a coward." Rebecca rubbed her hands together to warm her freezing fingers. She cast imploring glances at her four *newehockers*—her side-sitters, the women who would be her attendants and sit at her side during the ceremony and afterward at the wedding feast. They were all dressed as Rebecca was in identical pale blue dresses with white capes and aprons. Only Rebecca, as the bride, wore a black *kapp*. She would trade it for a white one later in the day.

Mary, Joshua's wife, stepped forward and took Rebecca's hands in hers. "You are not a coward. Every bride has an attack of nerves. It's only natural. Do you love Samuel?"

"Of course I love him, but what if I'm not the best wife for him? I wasn't always the best wife to Walter. I should have been a better helpmate. I should have seen what was wrong sooner. I don't want to make a mess of Samuel's life. He has struggled so much already."

Rebecca's dear cousin Emma Swartzentruber sat primly on the edge of Rebecca's bed. A smile twitched at the corner of her mouth. "My brother has a fast horse and buggy outside if you don't want to go through with this."

Everyone turned shocked gazes toward her. Rebecca pulled her hands from Mary's grip and fisted them on her hips. "Run away from Samuel on our wedding day? That would break his heart."

"I'm just offering." Emma rose from the bed and crossed to the window. "I think it's too late, anyway. The groom is here."

"He is?" Rebecca's heart leaped with joy as she hurried to her cousin's side. She scrubbed at the frost coating the inside of the glass and made a hole large enough to see out. Samuel, looking as handsome as ever, was gazing up at her from beside his buggy. He gave a jaunty wave and hurried inside the house.

"He doesn't look ready to run," Emma said as she elbowed Rebecca in the side.

"He looks very handsome today." Every time she saw Samuel, Rebecca was struck by how differently their lives might have turned out if not for God's intervention in the form of one terrible accident. Samuel's burns were completely healed, but he still bore patches of reddened skin on his cheeks and forehead. They didn't detract from his looks. Not in her eyes.

"Luke looks handsome, too," Emma said with a hint of sadness, then turned away from the window. Emma and Luke had gone out for a time before he left the

Amish and got into trouble with the law. At the time, Emma had been heartbroken, but he wouldn't have been the right man for her. Everyone knew it.

Rebecca caught her lower lip between her teeth. Was she doing Samuel a disservice? Was there someone who would be better suited to be his wife? She had to be sure she was doing the right thing for him and not just because she wanted to be his wife. Downstairs, the strains of the first hymn rose in reverent recognition of the solemn occasion. Marriage was forever.

"Time to go." Mary took Rebecca's hand and led her toward the door and the crowd of family and friends waiting below.

Outside her door, Bishop Beachy stood waiting for her with Samuel at his side. Her heart skipped a beat, and then thudded into a wild gallop at the sight of her beloved's tender smile.

"If you two will follow me, I have a few words I share with all the couples I marry." The bishop turned and walked down the hall toward a smaller bedroom that had been prepared for the counseling by adding a little table and three chairs.

Rebecca started to follow him, but Samuel stopped her with a hand on her arm. "I haven't given you my engagement present yet."

Amish brides typically received small gifts from their intendeds when they agreed to wed. "A gift is not necessary, Samuel."

"I know, but I wanted you to have this." He pulled a packet from inside his vest and handed it to her.

Rebecca pulled away the paper to reveal a tiny cedar box. The hinges were smaller than any she had seen.

The top was carved with the scene of a single raindrop striking the surface of the water, spreading ripples in all directions. The details were amazing. "Samuel, it's beautiful."

"Like you," he said softly.

She touched the delicate carving with her fingertips. "I adore it. *Danki*."

He lifted her chin with his hand so she had to look at him. "I chose cedar because I know it will always remind you of the man you loved before me. I know he holds a special place in your heart. The water drop is because you have quenched the thirst in my soul I didn't know existed until I met you, and because you threw water on a sick man."

"Sprinkled, Samuel. I sprinkled water on you. You're never going to let that go, are you?" He could make her laugh even when she was nervous, and she loved that about him.

"Never. The rings in the water are the goodness that radiates from you toward everyone you touch. God willing, those ripples will spread to our children and grandchildren and for future generations untold. I'm so very blessed that you agreed to marry me. I will be the best husband and father that I can be. I promise you that."

Smiling at him, every reservation floated away from her heart and mind. They were meant for each other. Who was she to doubt the goodness of the Lord? She glanced down the hall to make sure the bishop wasn't looking, then she rose on tiptoe and planted a kiss on Samuel's lips.

"Save that until after the wedding, children," the

bishop said from the end of the hall. His voice held only mild disapproval, but his face was set in stern lines.

Rebecca smothered a grin and saw Samuel do the same. He winked and said, "Let's get this over with. I have a lifetime of free kisses I'm holding for you."

She walked down the hall ahead of Samuel, confident that she was the woman God had chosen for him. She would never doubt it again.

* * * * *

WE HOPE YOU ENJOYED THESE TWO

LOVE INSPIRED®
BOOKS.

If you were **inspired** by these **uplifting**, **heartwarming** romances, be sure to look for all six Love Inspired® books every month.

Love Inspired®

Save $1.00
on the purchase of any
Love Inspired®,
Love Inspired® Suspense or
Love Inspired® Historical book.

Available wherever books are sold,
including most bookstores, supermarkets,
drugstores and discount stores.

- ✂

Save $1.00
on the purchase of any Love Inspired®, Love Inspired® Suspense or Love Inspired® Historical book.

Coupon valid until April 30, 2018. Redeemable at participating retail outlets in the
U.S. and Canada only. Limit one coupon per customer.

52615519

Canadian Retailers: Harlequin Enterprises Limited will pay the face value of
this coupon plus 10.25¢ if submitted by customer for this product only. Any
other use constitutes fraud. Coupon is nonassignable. Void if taxed, prohibited
or restricted by law. Consumer must pay any government taxes. Void if copied.
Inmar Promotional Services ("IPS") customers submit coupons and proof of sales
to Harlequin Enterprises Limited, P.O. Box 31000, Scarborough, ON M1R 0E7,
Canada. Non-IPS retailer—for reimbursement submit coupons and proof of
sales directly to Harlequin Enterprises Limited, Retail Marketing Department,
225 Duncan Mill Rd., Don Mills, ON M3B 3K9, Canada.

U.S. Retailers: Harlequin Enterprises
Limited will pay the face value of
this coupon plus 8¢ if submitted by
customer for this product only. Any
other use constitutes fraud. Coupon is
nonassignable. Void if taxed, prohibited
or restricted by law. Consumer must pay
any government taxes. Void if copied.
For reimbursement submit coupons
and proof of sales directly to Harlequin
Enterprises, Ltd 482, NCH Marketing
Services, P.O. Box 880001, El Paso,
TX 88588-0001, U.S.A. Cash value
1/100 cents.

5 65373 00076 2   (8100)0 12342

® and ™ are trademarks owned and used by the trademark owner and/or its licensee.

© 2018 Harlequin Enterprises Limited

LIINC1COUP0118

Leaving the cellar door open, Luke came down the stairs
and settled on one of the lower steps. "I suppose Sara is
trying to match us up. It is what she does for a living. And
from what I hear, she knows what she's doing."

Honor pursed her lips, but the look in her eyes didn't
appear to be disapproving.

Luke took it as a positive sign and forged ahead. "I
already know we'd be a good fit. Perfect, in fact, if it
wasn't for what happened last time you agreed to marry
me. We have to talk about it someday," he insisted.

"Maybe, maybe not." She shrugged. "But definitely
not today. I'm having a wonderful time, and I don't want
anything to ruin it."

"Sit with me? Unless you think you'd better go up and
check on the children."

Honor regarded him for a long moment, then lowered
herself onto the step beside him. "*Ne*, I don't want to
check on the children. There are enough pairs of eyes to
watch them and, truthfully, I'm enjoying having someone

else do it." She glanced away and he noticed a slight rosy tint on her cheeks. "Now I've said it," she murmured. "You'll think me a terrible mother."

"I think you're a wonderful mother," he said. "An amazing person who never deserved what I did to you."

Her eyes narrowed. "Didn't we agree we weren't going to discuss this?"

"Not really. You said we weren't. I never agreed. Thinking back, I wonder if we'd just—"

The door at the top of the cellar steps abruptly slammed shut. Then they heard the latch slide into place and the sound of a child's laughter.

Luke got to his feet. "What's going on?" He reached the top of the steps and tried the door. "Locked." He glanced down at Honor. "Sorry."

"Not your fault." She pressed her lips together. "Unless I miss my guess, one of my little troublemakers is at it again."

He chuckled. "When you think about it, it is pretty funny."

She flashed him a smile so full of life and hope that it nearly brought tears to his eyes, a smile he'd been praying for all these years.

Looking for inspiration in tales
of hope, faith and heartfelt romance?

Check out **Love Inspired®** and
Love Inspired® Suspense books!

New books available every month!

CONNECT WITH US AT:

Harlequin.com/Community

Facebook.com/HarlequinBooks

Twitter.com/HarlequinBooks

Instagram.com/HarlequinBooks

Pinterest.com/HarlequinBooks

ReaderService.com

Love Inspired®